DAUGHTERS
OF ICARUS

DAUGHTERS OF ICARUS

new feminist science fiction and fantasy

EDITED BY JOSIE BROWN

PINK
NARCISSUS
PRESS

DAUGHTERS OF ICARUS
© 2013 Pink Narcissus Press

Stories in this book have first appeared in the following:

"Girl of Prey" by Tina Starr first appeared in *Dark Valentine Magazine* (2010). Reprinted by permission of the author.
"MAP REF. -4.296° N 239.193° E" by Zachary Jernigan first appeared in *M-Brane SF #13* (2010). Reprinted by permission of the author.
"The Night Before the Mission" by Margaret Karmazin first appeared in *Mobius* (2007). Reprinted by permission of the author.
"Plantlife" by Eric Bosse first appeared in *Magnificent Mistakes* (Ravenna Press Books, 2011). Reprinted by permission of the author.
"Pretty Maids All in a Row" first appeared in *M-Brane SF #12* (2009). Reprinted by permission of the author.

Cover design by Rose Mambert
Cover photograph: Jordan Tao Mambert

Published by Pink Narcissus Press
P.O. Box 303
Auburn, MA 01501
pinknarc.com

Library of Congress Control Number: 2012920627
ISBN: 978-1-939056-00-9
First trade paperback edition: March 2013

DEDICATION

To my mother and my sister,
who create a better world,
and to BG,
who spends his days in the sky.

Daughters of Icarus is further dedicated
to the memory of Janett L. Grady,
who remembered that the future
will remain human at its core.

contents

INTRODUCTION

Most feminists have come up against a charge of man-hating in the course of their discussions with others, be it a personal stab or presented as a piece of the tired "how feminists are" narrative that often involves such dead giveaways as ugliness, an enthusiasm for flannel and rampant bralessness. While these charges are infuriating, feminists must—and I believe generally do—understand that these shallow stereotypes are warm blankets to those who endorse them. These narratives are built to cope with a changing world, and while it does not behoove feminism to take them lying down, it is essential to understand that they have assumed the worst of a positive change: the advance of women, socially, politically and culturally, can be terrifying for those uneasy with adaptation. Men and women both have often been presented with the image of a benevolent patriarchy, where men "took care" of the supposedly weaker sex, so why would women reject this construct if not because they hate men?

As all women know, however, a desire for personal autonomy has little to nothing to do with any kind of love or hate for men. One need not hate men to want to shake off the bonds of patriarchy and add their talents to the world's collective progress. When feminists envision new worlds of gender equality, there is a great variation in ideas. It may surprise some of those who believe that feminists hate men to discover that feminist worlds are not necessarily variations on Dante's *Inferno*, with men suffering for their past crimes, but rather places where women can explore their desires freely, limited only by their own personal abilities and never by social convention.

Science fiction allows us to create new worlds in text. While the term often conjures up images of spaceships and aliens, the genre, rightly understood, involves so much more. In this book, we asked our authors to create feminist worlds. What would the new world look like? The responses were wonderful and varied widely from slick modern worlds of robotics and spaceships to post-apocalyptic wastelands ruled by women after the fall of man. One quality was consistent: the women in these pieces did not have *time* to hate men. Nor, in many cases, did the society portrayed. This, to me is the most exciting part of a feminist worldview. Rather than spending our lives mired in gender politics, these stories envision societies that leave men and women free to pursue their own lives, and re-frame the events in them as being independently directed.

It is important to note that these stories do not uniformly cast off tradition or social concepts. Many pull deeply from traditions that inform our societies today, and enrich them. One need not demolish history or abandon tradition to desire or construct a better world, in which women are allowed more latitude to make their mark on the spaces, people and societies that they love. In this we can understand one thing clearly: it is the love that women have for this world that drives them to demand a better place in it. While some social constructs may need to be torn down or set aside, the erasure of history or the enslavement of those responsible for the past's crimes is not the goal of feminism. Rather, it is a move toward a society in which women are able to make mistakes and achieve success without limitation. It is not, as these stories show, a promise that women will create a perfect world, but that they will create a fuller one.

This book should stand as a challenge to women and men alike: how will you shape the world? If the apocalypse arrives or if another boring Tuesday rolls around, what would you have it look like? Where would you direct the world in which you live? This is not an easy project, but there are few more worthy. Each election, each purchase, each conversation, each thought is a small decision about how we want the world to look; whether you do so intentionally or not, you weigh in on the kind of environment you want daily. Science fiction is little more than a dare to imagine our world dramatically anew, and while these authors have weighed in, we all await your answer as well. Once you have an idea, get started on making it real, will you?

—*Josie Brown, Editrix*

THE MESOMORPHIC WOMAN

DAVID NORTH-MARTINO

Irena Kira knew nothing could stop the events from unfolding. Her destiny looked grim, marred with visions of a prison cell or a cold grave vault in New Boston East.

She had the tools to pave her future in blood. The 9mm, strapped to the inside of her muscular thigh and hidden under her chemise, was a prized weapon, a wonderful antique, given to her twenty-two years ago by Charlie Reed, an ex-mob boss, now the Arch Governor of the Pleiades Sphere.

Irena walked briskly down a street façade that mirrored old New York. The gray and glass illusion was so overwhelming it was easy to forget she was orbiting Venus in the Audallis Sphere.

Irena stopped by a railing that kept pedestrians from wandering into the Free-Fall Zone, and looked across the great expanse of zero-gravity highway to York City West.

The commercial city lay awash in mundane shadows, but it would soon be beautiful as the artificial sunlight dimmed and the energy switched to the buildings. The bubble-cabs and transport tubes danced through free-fall in hypnotic fluidity like drunken fireflies swimming in slow motion.

Irena shook her head to regain her senses. There

was no time for a breather, even though her muscles ached and her ribs throbbed. The pod station, like an ancient bus stop, still loomed in the distance.

Irena rushed past four pods and half a dozen people, cursing Jack under her breath for his habitual punctuality and refusal to wait. She watched Jack sigh behind the clear dome of the two-seater bubble-cab and look at his watch. She wasn't pleased to see him, especially since he openly carried a Slack Deck. She knew he did it to taunt her.

"Hey, doll, where's your hand?"

Irena ignored him and buckled herself into the burgundy foam seat. Jack silently pressed one of a dozen flashing blue buttons, cueing the pod to retro into freefall. The engine shut down and a great hiss of steam propelled them vertically from York City East to New Boston East.

"Jack, the 1920s do nothing for you." Irena gave him a once over. His retro-pinstripe suit, all the rage on the Audallis, accentuated his gut.

"It's the cat's meow, doll," Jack said as he held the breasts of his suit, with mock pride. "Let's not be harsh, I'm on your side—remember?"

"Jack, you're not on my side," Irena said then looked away. "My sweaty wad of cash is the only friend you'll ever have. 'Sides the Slack Girls."

"Touchy, touchy." Jack tapped the Slack Deck that synchronized with his cortex implant, providing him with what Irena thought of as cyber streetwalkers. "Don't burn any bridges here with Jacky-Boy. The Sphere is becoming rather unfriendly for women like yourself. You're the majority now..."

"I'm gonna keep it that way. We're almost to the stop," Irena said, holding out her remaining hand as a sign of impatience. "The information, then the envelope."

The silence hung thick and Jack's face seemed to soften as if the harsh years they had both faced were only a nightmare. Jack had to clear his throat before he could speak.

"The word is Alder's comin' out tonight."

"Tonight!" Irena said unable to hide her exasperation or the adrenaline that spoke in her veins. "He's been in seclusion for five years. Why tonight, Jack?"

The events were unfolding.

"It seems our friend just acquired a not-so-easy-to-get permit to go hunting."

"Don't tell me 'tonight,' Jack. My daughter's on her way from San Francisco, and I was just jumped by one of his cronies on the way here."

"Guess the crony got the worst of it. Lucky he only took your prosthetic."

"Yeah, lucky me. I'm out a thousand and I'll be out another tonight."

"I'd like to think you're out a couple of C-notes, too."

Jack smiled and ended the conversation, turning to the clear plastic, pretending to be occupied with the Jump-Police who passed by the pod on their bikes. When the ride was through, Irena stuffed a wad of bills into his shirt pocket. He in turn gave her a small manila envelope. She knew what was inside. Contraband of all contraband—ammunition.

O-O

Submissive women gave her strange looks on Washington Street. These were the new women of the sphere.

Irena looked into their eyes and saw free souls imprisoned by the flesh of the emerging society.

She wondered how many of these women were real and which were clones. It was hard to tell, easier to notice the perfect curves of the It-girls and wannabes who also received the eye from the respectable demure ladies.

Washington turned into China Town, then became Zalman Street with its speakeasies, brothels, and slack arcades. She didn't like this section of town, but there were also pawnshops and back-alley crust-surgeons, and if she were going to pull off the job tonight she needed both.

Irena picked a pawnshop at random. The Z-Shop

stood on the corner of Zalman and Tremont Street. The blacked-out windows made seeing the merchandise or the occupants impossible. Below the lit Z-Shop sign was another flickering neon that stated:

If It Don't Rust We Sell It for Crust.

Inside, the smell of spray lubricant clung to the stagnant air. Irena walked up to a fingerprint-stained glass counter and watched the shopkeeper fussing with the display of used crust gadgets. A stringy-haired female shopkeeper finally looked up and not so subtly gave Irena a once-over.

"What can I do you for?" The question drawled out apathetically.

"Hand," Irena held up her arm and the shiny metal stump that once acted as a conduit between her flesh and the prosthetic.

"You lookin' for touch?" The shopkeeper flashed a wicked smile, exposing a lifetime lack of oral hygiene.

"I need at least approximate sensation."

"That will cost ya." The stringy haired lady laughed beneath her reddish strands. "Thousand. You got that type of cash on ya?"

The question made Irena uneasy. She hadn't paid much attention to the room. Now she glanced around but only noticed how chaotically the wares were placed. As far as she knew, she and the shopkeeper were alone.

"I can do that."

"I need five in my hand before I can shows it to ya—insurance."

Irena gave her a wad. The shopkeeper enjoyed the damp bills, pawing at them as she counted.

"Very nice. Very nice... Mez." Irena caught the last word harsh and stinging, the derogatory slang bit into her mind and filled her soul. "Now you die!"

Seeing the katana gleam from its hiding place, Irena instinctively shifted her weight to her rear leg and rocked back.

The blade, thirsty for her blood, thrust just inches

from her face as she subtly positioned herself on the outside of the shopkeeper's attacking arm.

Irena connected with a left thrusting punch, sending her fist into the shopkeeper's throat.

The stringy-haired lady coughed and sputtered, dropping the archaic weapon as she gasped for breath.

The blur of Irena's peripheral vision caught a man bursting from a dark back room, rushing toward her.

Irena stopped herself from drawing the 9mm, ammo was precious, and instead awkwardly grasped the red silk-wrapped handle of the sword.

Again, without thought, Irena moved diagonally, dropped to her right knee, and extended the Japanese weapon toward his armpit.

The young man found empty space where she had been and was impaled by steel. Irena whipped the blade from his wound and he fell backward, hitting shelves of pawned items and knocking them to the grit below, as his body made a B-line for the floor.

The shopkeeper looked at the young man with cold indifference. Instead of a weapon, she now held the prosthetic hand. Although it was a late model, long out of production, it still looked new.

Irena tried to slow her heart, breathe like she had on Togakure Mountain, with her teacher Chuni in virtual. The breathing did not help and she could not focus. The adrenal rush of combat was becoming too much or perhaps she had endured it too many times.

"I'll take the hand and what's left in the register," Irena said, her voice wavy. "I also need a Vlox and a cranial kit."

"You wants to go lookin' for your brains?" The stringy-haired woman paused as if to laugh, then nervously threw the small metal case on the counter.

O─O

The night air felt synthetic cool outside the shop. Irena slung a faded olive-drab backpack filled with crust over her left shoulder so she could hold it with her remaining hand. She took a deep breath of the conditioned air and looked about. All around her the zone bustled with life.

The prickle on the back of her neck told her the night had become too dangerous for walking.

O—O

In the back seat of a Checkered Cab electric taxi Irena removed a prox-phone from her backpack.

The phone was an old model that used suction cup conduits to stimulate the user's frontal lobes. The other crust phones at the shop had been bore-hole models requiring cranial surgery for use.

She licked the conduit cups and stuck them to her forehead. Irena gave a glance toward the driver, a cockney-looking fellow with a plaid derby hat. His eyes stayed on the road, that was good, but she worried more about his ears. It wasn't a rare event to mumble and slur while conversing mind to mind.

Irena dialed up the connection. The faux leather interior and smell of the cab flickered behind her eyes, replaced by the feeling of weightlessness and a distorted image of a star field. White noise burned inside her head and she adjusted the reception with her thoughts.

An image of the Blue Star Shuttle made a slow approach. The connection completed and Irena gritted her teeth.

"Mother, are you there?" Irena's daughter's voice shimmered above the static.

"Yes, my phone must be defective." Irena's mind strained to project her voice through the interference. "Listen, Caz, I have a job to do tonight. I—I'll need your help."

"What do you need me to do?" Cazlene answered without hesitation.

"Meet me at the Charlemont stop in New Boston East. I'll have something for you."

O—O

"Now ain't that a relic." Alexis Shardonnay M.D. Bio-A smiled as she examined Irena's newly acquired crust hand. The harsh lighting in the hidden examining room of the Hack Shop Computer Emporium, a front for Alexis' unlicensed medical practice, revealed the unnatural color of the prosthetic.

"It's not pretty but I don't have the kinda cash to grow a real one." Irena and Alexis smiled at the shared joke. Cash or no cash, biotechnology couldn't be found here for the common person.

"I'm just glad the economy is so bad up here that there's a need for crust-surgeons." Alexis laughed. "If we were back on Earth, I'd be the relic and unemployed."

"If I counterfeit any more cash my old float-buddies from the Arch Governor's Secret Guard are gonna come a-calling." Irena laughed nervously and shifted on the examining table. The sterile room and smell of rubbing alcohol always made her feel uneasy. "I have some inform-ation that you might find as good as payment."

"Let's hear it." Alexis seemed eager for this new bit of intelligence. Irena had always been secretive about her involvement in the resistance movement.

"Alder has a new secret technology A.A.P., Artificial Aging and Programming." Irena's expression hardened. "He's using it on the clones."

"I don't get it," Alexis said as she pulled a white coat over her gray jumpsuit. "What's he so secretive about?"

Alder had always been open about his dislike for the Audallis vision of an Amazon colony. He did everything in his power to get his company, Generation Genetics, into the sphere so he could legally grow male clones to fill the sphere's supportable limits. Everyone knew that his plan was to take over as he worked in the loopholes of the laws.

"He's replacing people."

"Replacing?" Alexis' eyebrows crinkled in puzzle-ment.

"Look around you. Alder hasn't been able to gain complete control of the sphere. This isn't the glorious patriarchy of his dreams. Instead, his efforts changed the sphere into the crime-ridden slum I tried to escape when I was running with the subway gangs on Earth.

"A.A.P. allows him to clone and then artificially age and program an undetectable replacement for those who are in power. Alder may not get his glory that way, but he will get control."

There was a long pause, a physical silence almost too strong to bridge.

"Let's have a look at that hand."

O—O

Irena was sure the Jump-Police were looking for her and about a dozen of her public enemy contemporaries.

Public transit was out of the question.

She had taken the Vlox from Z-shop to access the inaccessible, and she fingered the rubber control stick as she floated to the top of the sphere toward Adrian Forest. Controlled blasts of steam stabilized and propelled her through the concrete darkness.

Bubble-cabs and public transport tubes glided past her in both directions. Alexis' borrowed jumpsuit, a size too small, accentuated Irena's developed musculature and rendered her a speck of gray in the shadows.

Her mind calm, focused and quiet, no one could feel her intentions and she passed unnoticed.

A strange feeling of calmness eased through Irena's body as she adjusted to the gravity of the forest. The life energy of the flora and fauna caressed her spirit and she felt connected, whole and homesick for Earth. In the woods the night did not seem contrived.

The oxygen from the living plants, mixed with their wet scent, belied the world of concrete and Plexiglas that defined the sphere. Once she found the safe spot in the forest, so close to Alder that he and his men could be observed but far enough away to optimize her chances of avoiding detection, she shut down the GPS implant.

Irena tested the fine motor skills of the prosthetic, ensuring that they were fluid. She paid special attention to her trigger finger.

Drawing her weapon, she felt the weight of the pistol in her hand again. The sensation wasn't real but it comforted her.

The low bass of the .22-caliber rifles popped in the distance. Alder and his men were going archaic, sniffing out their game without the aid of any technology.

Irena covered the distance between them silently, watching these four men in the glow of the pregnant real-time projection of Earth's moon.

She rolled her feet from heel to toe, keeping her knees bent and her head on a single plane.

Irena stopped twenty feet behind the group to quiet her mind and slow her heart. She could not risk detection. Her fingers interlocked in Kuji-In hand postures, an ancient technology of mind-setting techniques that could not become dated. Her breathing slowed, heart rate decreased. Irena's mind was deadly focused.

"You see that?" A tall man dressed in black BDU's called out, pointing at the gliding shapes in the branches of nearby trees. "You see them against the moon?"

"Yeah, reload." Alder's voice was a distinct authoritative bravado. He took a swig from a silver flask, placing it into a pocket of his Lindbergh Jacket before hoisting his rifle for the shoot.

The two others, a bald stocky framed man dressed in black corduroy, and one shorter, who wore his hair unfashionably long, raised their weapons for the slaughter.

Beyond the four hunters Irena caught a glimpse of what she thought at first must be large bats. These creatures sailed from tree to tree in a high low pattern that was more glide than actual flight. She realized that these men were hunting flying squirrels for sport.

Irena tasted the anticipation of the kill, an electric flavor that pulsed and made her body shiver. Her newly attached hand, fingers incapable of shaking, held the weight of the nine steady and ready.

O–O

Irena felt the kick, tasted the sulfur vibration, and the bald man dropped to his knees. He stared in amazement at the smear of blood on his palm as he removed it from his chest.

The long-haired man turned as if moving through water, and dropped to his knees as he met the violence of her weapon.

The tall man and Alder were quickly disappearing into the darkness of the forest. Irena watched the tall man reach into his jacket and brandish a pistol. The slug from her weapon met with the flesh of his upper arm. The tall man dropped to his knees, clutching the damaged appendage while Alder ran.

Alder was faster than she'd thought. He was twenty years her senior but making good time. He may have been enhanced genetically but most likely he had been installed with crust.

She didn't dare shoot him. Irena needed to make sure her information was correct before she made holes in his body.

As they reached the clearing, she looked past Alder to the farmland across the zero-G gorge. The sensation gave her vertigo and she had to look away.

Then she heard a crackle of thunder. A bullet wound appeared in Alder's back. A numbing sensation engulfed her upper right quadrant. They'd both been hit with the same shot.

Still running, Irena pointed the weapon behind her and emptied the clip. The tall man dropped.

Alder swooned—mortally wounded she thought—but to accomplish her task, death was not enough.

They reached the protective railing. Irena grabbed Alder by the waist and muscled him over.

When she had dragged him far enough that her stride turned into leaps, she hit the Vlox and broke the gravity barrier. She fingered the stick and the Vlox thrust them toward New Boston East.

Irena concentrated on getting the cranial kit out of

her jumpsuit. The tool she needed, a specially forged metal rod-key, fit perfectly into the nub on Alder's skull. Now she knew her information had been right.

The cranial door held firm.

Irena wrapped her legs around Alder's waist. She grabbed the tool awkwardly, her large hands jerking and prying at the compartment.

Her hands away from the Vlox controls, she and Alder spun violently off course, toward the floating sea of transport pods.

Each tug sent them closer to their deaths. Irena flexed her enormous muscles and tore the cranial door out of Alder's skull.

She felt the pods behind her.

Eyes tight, bracing for impact, Irena found the Vlox control and pulled it back to full throttle.

The mesomorph and the old man punched beyond the zero-G envelope, gravity took hold and they met the hard reality of Charlemont Street.

A crowd gathered and, as usual, the media were on scene before the police.

Irena, still conscious, felt the world floating away from her. She saw Caz pushing her way through the crowd.

"That's my mother! Let me through!" Cazlene was a beautiful sight, the same sculptured face and the beginning ripples of fine muscular definition. Irena knew Caz had truly become her own woman. And in Cazlene's DNA, Irena would live again, was now living twice.

Irena looked at her clone and wondered if it would have been easier not to raise her, to have let her develop like most do in a tube, waiting to be a conduit for her consciousness.

Would she live again in Cazlene or would Cazlene live for herself in her mother's image and continue with the same blood, the same bone, but a different mind? It didn't seem to matter now that death was robbing her of all her strength. The powerful muscles of her body seemed to belie the weakness that had washed over her soul.

Irena reached into Alder's mind and found the blob of clear pulsating mass that held all the secrets of his madness, a madness that had infected Audallis for thirty years.

As she held it up into the air, the mass hardened and she handed it to Caz.

Irena smiled, unable to speak, her mouth dry with death, hoping her daughter would understand what she needed to do.

Irena reached behind her left ear and removed a once invisible implant. The COR-X device was a reminder of Earth—it held all of her memories up and until this moment. Cazlene wept, her eyes sparkling as the tears sought escape.

"Irena. Mother," Caz whispered through her sobs.

Irena heard her name, soft and wet from her daughter's lips, but knew it was also the dark whisper of death. And she spoke her daughter's name softly, hoarsely, willing it up from the depths of her being, holding her daughter's palm, feeling the approximation of that sensation and slipped her the COR-X device.

"Cazlene," Irena said. And she knew her daughter's name meant life.

UNIVERSAL UNDEGROUND

SUMMER HANFORD

Polly sighed as she looked down at the pile of mail on her desk. She had to open, skim, and liquefy every piece. It was just junk mail. Anything important went straight to her boss, Mr. Bryant's, desk, but it wasn't like she had anything else to do. Concentrating on getting the workday over with, she cut open the top one and fished out its content.

"What do you have there, Polly?" Mr. Bryant asked from behind her, causing her to jump. She didn't hear him come out of the conference room, but she did hear the anger in his voice.

"I don't know, sir," she said, glancing over her shoulder to see if he looked as mad as he sounded. He did. Returning her gaze to the room in front of them, she could see people looking up from their cubicles. She blushed at being reprimanded in front of every-one. "It's a list of names the mail guy left on my desk."

"That's for Mr. Polly," Mr. Bryant said, pulling the list from her hand. "See me in my office."

Polly sank in her chair, waiting while he turned and reentered the conference room which further separated his office from the rest of them. How could she have missed that the envelope on her desk said Mr. Polly? It seemed like a small mistake, but she knew it was a big one.

Mr. Polly was Mr. Bryant's personal assistant, as was she, but Mr. Polly took care of things no one liked to talk about. Polly didn't know what those things were. In the four months she had worked there, no one had ever said a word about what Mr. Polly did. They got all nervous and twitchy when she asked. She could sympathize, because when he came to see Mr. Bryant, Mr. Polly made her feel twitchy and nervous too. He made her skin crawl, although he was always polite and never looked down her blouse. His mail went straight to Mr. Bryant's desk.

An easy enough mistake by the mail carrier because every one called her by her first name. Polly had no idea why the letter would be important enough for her to be called into Mr. Bryant's office, or why it was anything Mr. Polly would want to see. She had seen only the first page, but it looked like it was just a list of people, from personnel.

She got up and went through the conference room to Mr. Bryant's office, hoping she wasn't in too much trouble. At her knock, he told her to come in and take a seat in the stiff wooden chair across from his desk.

"Why did you open Mr. Polly's mail?" her boss asked as she sat down.

"I didn't mean to, sir. I was opening a whole pile of mail. I didn't realize it wasn't for me."

"You've done a very bad thing, Polly." Mr. Bryant held the papers she'd been reading in his hand.

"I'm not sure I understand," she said. She toyed with the hem of her skirt nervously, wincing when the plastic snapped as it came unstuck from the chair. *Someday, I'm going to be able to afford clothes made of something other than recycled plastic,* she promised herself.

"There's not really any reason for you to understand, my dear," her boss said. "Just tell me what you read." Mr. Bryant leaned back in his massive leather chair, scrutinizing her across the desk.

"It was just a list of names from personnel." She tried to keep her voice from shaking. She couldn't lose her job at Universal Foods. She couldn't afford to move to another dome, and Universal owned pretty much everything in this one. "I don't have any idea what they were for. I only read a few. I didn't mean to make you mad at me." She took a deep breath. *Don't babble. You don't want him to think you're a complete idiot, or he'll fire you for that anyhow.*

"Quite right." He nodded, still staring at her like she was a criminal. "It has nothing to do with you, and it should never have ended up on your desk to begin with." There was a long silence. He didn't believe her. He thought she was opening other people's mail on purpose. She was going to lose her job. "You just forget all about it."

She let out a slow breath, resisting the urge to cry. "Thank you, sir. It won't happen again. I'll be more careful. I'll read the envelopes."

"No, it won't happen again." He smacked the papers crisply on his desk. "That will be all, Polly." The massive chair swung around, showing her the formidable vastness of its back, with the top of his gray head peeking over.

"Yes, Mr. Bryant." She stood and let herself out, walking quickly across the meeting room and to her desk. Sitting down in her plastic standard issue officer chair, Polly let out a sigh of relief.

"Polly." Mr. Bryant's voice came over the intercom, causing her to gasp in surprise, all her relief at not getting fired scattering. "That boy who does the mail on this floor, make out a section transfer form for him. I think he would be better suited to our UG project."

Polly's eyes went wide. UG? That was the highest paid section of the company! That was like a reward. She thought for sure the mail guy, Doug, would get fired for putting the wrong mail on her desk, not promoted.

"And Polly," his voice turned to sugar, "would you like to work in UG?"

She bit her lip. "Oh no, sir! I really like it here with

you." She did her best to sound flirtatious, as if she preferred to sleep her way to the top rather than earn it. In
fact, she'd wanted UG until that very moment. She'd
applied for the job of his secretary because it had a very
high transfer rate to UG, and everyone knew working in
UG brought you incredible pay. She just couldn't think of
any reason why she would be promoted right now. That,
and something in his voice, caused her to decline the offer.

"All right, then. You may stay for now." She couldn't
read his emotion through the intercom. She thought he
sounded subdued.

"Thank you, sir," she said, but with the impression
that he was already not paying attention anymore.

As she dug out the appropriate form, it occurred to
her that several of the names on that list were of people
she'd recently transferred to UG for him. Could that be
what it was? A list of new UG people? That would make
sense, because although all of the jobs at Universal Foods
required some sort of security clearance, UG jobs required
a stricter one. Maybe Mr. Polly was feared simply because
he was the one who looked through your life for 'bad'
spots.

Polly relaxed, feeling foolish now for letting
unknown worries stop her from accepting the transfer.
She considered pressing the intercom and asking if she
could change her mind, but that would make her seem so
dumb, he would probably say no and never offer again,
and she really did want to get into the UG program someday.

o–o

Polly sighed as the door to her apartment slid only
partially open, removing her hand from the scanner to tug
at it. Just what she didn't need after her bad day at work.
The door wouldn't budge. The beauty of the doors was
that they were nearly impossible to open by force, after all,
and her one-hundred and twenty-five pounds was not
cutting it. She turned sideways and wiggled inside. As her
second foot hit the interior floor, the door slid shut. Polly

yanked her arm away. Supposedly there were sensors to keep it from closing on any part of her, but the building dated practically back to the twenty-first century, and last week someone's little dog had learned firsthand how well-maintained the sensors were.

She rolled her shoulders and let her head flop back on her neck, staring at recycled plastic ceiling tiles. There were two-hundred and twenty-five. Not that she had counted them, but she knew each one was one square foot, and she knew the size of her private living space.

She took the two steps needed to enter the mister. Inside, she unzipped her top and skirt, hanging them on the racks to make sure both sides got clean while she did. Warm mist poured out of little holes in the walls, ceiling and floor at her command, enveloping her.

I wonder if the mail guy and his family are celebrating right now, she thought idly, but then recalled a conversation with him in the break room once about how he didn't want to start a family until he made something of himself. *I bet he lives alone, like me.*

That woman I filled out the forms for last month said she had no family too. Polly frowned, looking down at her toes through the mist. A timer went off, warning her that she was moving into double-charged water in thirty seconds. *I wonder if rich people have the timers too,* she thought, not for the first time.

She stepped out of the mister and moved her chair away from the table that stuck out of the wall. She wanted to eat in bed. Turning the plastic tabletop over, she revealed the other side, her bed. Her recycled foam blanket clung to a mattress of the same material. She peeled it back and got inside.

The good thing about a small living space is you can reach the food dispenser right from your bed, she mused, smiling to herself as she reached for a shake and turned on the wall screen. No more thinking about work until tomorrow!

O—O

The next day, she wore her pink top with her black skirt. Polly owned a pink skirt and top, a black skirt and top, and a white skirt and top, so it wasn't a long decision-making process. She would have to wash the ones from yesterday again today, because she forgot to pat them dry before bed and now they were covered with water spots. The white skirt and top were good because they wouldn't do that, but she liked to save white for special occasions. White recycled items were always more expensive. She patted down her blond hair, wishing she could afford enough water to keep it long. She tried once, but none of the products you could buy were any real substitute for being able to wash it.

Not that is really matters how I look, she thought as she sat down at her desk and clipped her ear piece on. *Everyone here has seen me before, and mostly I just answer phones.* She toyed with the zipper on the front of her blouse, waiting for something to do.

"It looks better lower." The slightly-accented voice caught her off guard, and she almost blushed. She raised an eyebrow at the dark-haired man as he proceeded to sit on the corner of her desk. She favored him with a long, cold look before speaking.

"May I help you?" Her ear piece beeped. Instead of leaving it on hold, she took the call, holding up one finger to indicate he should be silent. By the time she was done talking, he got the hint and moved to stand across from her.

"I'm looking for my little brother," he said. She folded her hands on the desk. "When I asked, they said you transferred him yesterday, so I thought you might be able to tell me where he is now. Please?" he added as an obvious afterthought.

"The mail guy?" she asked, surprised. Here she thought he had no family.

"Douglas," he said, nodding. "I haven't seen him in over five years. I finally tracked him down and he's just moved on."

"I'll have to ask Mr. Bryant. He assigns actual sections. One moment, please." She got up and walked to the conference room door, instead of using the pager. Once alone, she stopped. She had the strangest feeling it was a bad idea to ask Mr. Bryant the man's question. She'd just wait, then go back and tell him it was classified and she was truly sorry she couldn't help. She was about to go back when Mr. Bryant's door opened. He and Mr. Polly came out. They must have been there since before she arrived that morning.

"Polly." Mr. Bryant noticed her standing on the other end of the dimly lit room. "Did you want some-thing?" He and Mr. Polly seemed in good spirits.

Mr. Polly turned up one corner of his mouth in something that might have been a smile. She kept her face pleasantly vacant.

"There's a man out there looking for the mail guy we transferred yesterday, sir," she said. "I was coming to ask you what to tell him, because you fill in the actual section numbers and all, so I don't know where in UG he was sent." The two men exchanged glances. Mr. Bryant frowned, but if anything, Mr. Polly seemed happier than a moment ago.

"I daresay that is my department." Mr. Polly always spoke so softly, she wanted to lean forward to hear better, but she never did because she didn't want to get any closer to him. "I will take him out to lunch, I think," he added in dulcet tones, sounding inordinately pleased.

"Yes, I suppose you will have to," Mr. Bryant said.

"On the company's tab," Mr. Polly said, his mouth twitching with secret amusement.

"Yes, on the company's tab." Mr. Bryant sounded slightly annoyed. "You may go back to your desk, Polly. Mr. Polly will take care of this."

She stepped aside as they walked across the room, letting them leave first. Out in the brighter light of her office, she saw Mr. Polly take the man by the arm, escorting him toward the exit. She swallowed, shook her head, and went back to her desk.

○─○

Lunch break that day found her at the computer of one of the personnel workers, scanning the files of people she recalled from the list. She knew it was a bad idea, but she wanted to know what was so important about a list of names that it almost got her fired. She wasn't learning anything, though. It really seemed to be just a list of people transferred to UG. The only similarity she noticed about any of them, aside from their promotion, was that they were all people who had no one listed for 'closest of kin,' or 'who to call in case of an emergency.' She pulled up her own file. She hadn't filled out those sections either.

"Can I help you?" came an annoyed voice from the cubicle entrance. Polly jumped, clicking the application closed. "I assume since you are at my desk you're looking for me, after all," the woman said sarcastically.

Polly didn't know her. She didn't spend much time in the employee lounge, and she knew rumor was that, as Mr. Bryant's personal assistant, she thought she was too good for the rest of them. The real reason was she couldn't afford coffee or cakes or any other amenities, and so had no reason to go there.

"I'm sorry," she said, doing her best to look contrite. Why was the woman back so early? Didn't she have anything better to do with her lunch hour? Why couldn't this have been a man's cubicle? "I was just checking my email. I ducked in here because Mr. Bryant makes me keep working over lunch if he sees me at my desk." That wasn't true, but she thought it sounded good, and maybe it would get her some sympathy.

"Poor you. How about you get out of my chair before I file a complaint?"

Polly winced. So much for sympathy. She jumped up, squeaking her clothes across the wall as she squeezed by the woman, who didn't seem inclined to move.

Later that day, she caught a glimpse of Mr. Polly coming out of the woman's cubicle. She stared hard at her own screen, holding her breath until she saw his shoes walk past her desk without stopping. When Polly looked up, the woman was standing outside her cubicle, staring at her. When she saw Polly, she smiled and went back to her desk.

Polly bit her lip, but couldn't think of anything she'd done that was really wrong. She hadn't taken anyone's personal information or anything. Just glanced at it. Could they tell she looked at more than just her own file? Polly wasn't very good with computers. She sighed. There was nothing she could do to fix it now.

o–o

That night, she didn't go home. Polly didn't have any friends or relatives. Her application hadn't lied about that, so when she was feeling restless and out of sorts, she went for a ride. She took the ring line O-cars around the city. All of them, starting at ground level. She started with ground level, because although the O was usually safe, even it got a little dangerous late at night on the lower levels. By morning, she was completing the last circle, the highest one, where all the fanciest parts of the buildings stuck up near the top of the dome, and there were no wisps of pollution around it inside or out, and the rising sun sparkled off everything. She sighed, tired, but more at peace.

I better hurry home to change, she realized, and when the ring car teed in at the correct place, she got into the horizontal and went back down. It was still dark down where she lived. The sun would only shine there around midday.

I hope no more puppies got crushed by doors, she thought idly as the moving walkway carried her past a peacekeeping vehicle hovering out front of her building. She was so tired, it wasn't until she got within a few paces of her door that she realized a peacekeeping woman was standing outside it, interviewing her neighbor.

"There she is," the young man said. Polly walked forward, bemused. Who would have thought the guy would even recognize her? She realized the peacekeeper was talking.

"...been out all night?" the uniformed woman was asking.

"Yes, I couldn't sleep," Polly said. Not entirely true, as she hadn't tried to sleep, but close enough.

"Can you often not sleep?" The peacewoman didn't bother to look up. She was jotting down notes, plastic pen tapping rapidly on her screen.

"Usually when I mess up at work, I can't," Polly said. She looked at her door. Well, at least it's open all the way, she observed. "Um, what happened?"

"Someone forced your door and the alarms went off," the woman said, looking up at last. "By the time we got here, they were gone. They had a good look around. Who knows what they were hoping to find in there," she observed dryly.

Polly had to agree. All she owned were her clothes and her sheets. She didn't even have a plant in there or a pet. People stole those and resold them. She'd better check they hadn't used up all her food credits. She didn't keep her dispenser password protected.

"Maybe they thought she had a cat or something," the young man put in helpfully.

"You sure you didn't hear anything?" asked the peacekeeper, obviously not for the first time. The guy from across the hall shook his head adamantly. "It would take something high tech to get in there without making a racket."

"But you just said the alarm went off," Polly said, not liking where that line of reasoning could take her. Why would anyone use expensive contraband to break into her place?

"Only once they left. If they had by-passers hooked up, as it looks like they did, alarms wouldn't go off till they were removed and the building cycled through its security checks again. Could have been open with them gone for a good thirty minutes." Polly just stared at her, not really sure what to say. "Will you tell me everywhere you were last night?" the woman asked.

"Uh, sure, but I have to get changed for work." Polly made as if to step inside. The woman didn't stop her, but followed her in and closed the door. Polly called out answers to the woman's questions from inside the steamer. She quickly dried herself and the pink outfit. The plastic stuck to her, not wanting to pull straight on her damp skin. She rubbed at her hair so it would dry sticking up. She always thought that was cute.

"Well, I guess we're done here," the woman said as Polly reemerged, looking exactly the same as when she entered the steamer, except now she was all in pink instead of just on top. "Let us know if you find anything missing. Touch here for identification." The peacekeeper held out her pad. Polly pressed her fingers onto the designated squares. They left her living space and the door closed behind them. Polly noticed that it seemed to be opening all the way now.

o—o

She thought she was going to work, but instead she found herself taking the O to the UG building. There were old pictures around the office, but she wanted to see this coveted building Doug got to work in, where she could be too, if she had just told her boss yes yesterday. Not wanting to inhale the pollution at ground level, she got off the O at the building across the street, going down past floors of private offices until she found a café with windows she could look out. Fortunately, it was fully automated because she didn't feel like talking to anyone. All she needed to do was touch her fingers to the spot that showed a cup of coffee and one appeared behind a sliding panel for her. Sitting by the wall-sized window, she looked down at the UG facility.

If you do stuff like buy coffee, you'll never be able to save up enough credits to pay for classes, and without more certifications, you'll never get promoted, she reminded herself, but she couldn't stay in the café without a cup at her table, and she hadn't had coffee in the almost two years since she came to the Universal dome.

It was a strange building, the UG. Mostly because it was only three stories tall. All around loomed buildings that soared into the air thousands of stories, but the UG had three. Rumor had it that was because the UG had all of its stories underground, but no one really knew for sure. She could hardly see it from her perch seventy-five stories up, but there were no cafés on any lower floors. The UG building lurked in the heavy churning air debris that blanketed the first ten stories of the dome, before the air cleared to smoggy up where she was. It was the brownish-grey color recycled plastic has when you don't bother to bleach or dye it. There was one small door on the front side, and no windows. She knew from pictures that above the door was a small plaque reading 'Universal Food Under Ground Facility.'

Universal Food was one of the three sustenance companies, and the top human food company. Great Northern Foods controlled about fifteen percent of the human market, but eighty percent of pet care. FeedFeed made the bulk of its wealth off the growing market, controlling ninety-nine percent of that and only cornering five percent of the human market. FeedFeed was constantly striving to go more human, because the growth market was all pre-consumer, selling to Great Northern and Universal, and didn't have as nice of a markup. The government saw to that, saying most foods had to be kept cheap.

That little bit of the growing market FeedFeed didn't carry was where Universal made its fortune. Years ago, FeedFeed and Great Northern had split the market between them, growing and feeding, until the discovery of percos mushrooms. More rare than truffles, more desirable than caviar, they grew in only one place in the entire world. Under the UG building. That was the source of Universal's rise in power, and now they were the leading human sustainer, working their way into the pet market, and sitting on a goldmine of gourmet mushrooms.

"Shouldn't you be busy at work, turning people over to that monster?"

The man who slid into the other chair at her table wore a hood pulled up over his head and kept his face down, but she recognized the slightly accented voice immediately.

"Doug's brother?" she asked, leaning forward to get a better look at him.

"Surprised to see me still alive?" His voice held a sinister anger and she froze, wondering if she should scream.

"Why wouldn't you be alive?" she asked instead. She reached for her hot coffee, ready to throw it at him if he tried anything.

"You set that thug on me," he snapped.

"I did what? I just asked them for the section number your brother was sent to. If they got mad at you, it must be something you did."

"You're his assistant." He said it like it was an accusation.

"Yeah," she said. "That's why I was sitting behind his assistant's desk."

He leaned back, scrutinizing her from under his hood. "You really don't have a clue, do you?"

"Look." She stood. "If you made Mr. Polly mad at you some way, I don't want anything to do with it. I need my job. I can't even afford to live in an apartment people don't break into. I have to get to work."

She was aware he followed her out, and into the O. When she got to the vertical she needed, he grabbed her arm, keeping her from joining the mass of passengers squeezing in. She turned to glare at him. If they'd been alone, or if it was late, she might have worried, but the station was crowded and security prevalent.

"What do you want from me?" Polly asked, exasperated. "I don't know where Doug is."

"Do you mean your apartment was broken into?"

"Yeah, last night."

"Who was it?" His eyes burrowed into hers, looking for what, she didn't know.

"I wasn't home last night, and they didn't leave their business cards." She was getting annoyed. She was already crazy late for work. She'd never been late before. It would probably get her demoted.

"Why weren't you home?"

"I couldn't sleep. What's it to you? I have to get to work."

"You can't go there." He pulled on her arm, trying to lead her back to the O, away from the vertical that would take her to the Universal building she worked in.

"I have to go there." She lowered her voice, hissing, "If you don't let me go, I'll scream."

He stopped pulling, facing her again. She could see his dark hair trying to curl up around the edge of his gray plastic hood. Behind him, a peacekeeper was watching them, probably trying to ascertain if he should interrupt.

"I don't know how you managed to keep away from them." His voice was so low, she had to lean in to hear. "But if they came to your apartment, they came to take you. You can't go back there, or to work."

"You aren't Doug's brother," she realized. Douglas hadn't put any next of kin. He didn't have an accent. He was much younger than this man, and they looked nothing alike. "Who are you?"

"I'm Federal. I'm here to investigate certain accusations against Universal."

She stared at him, not sure if she believed him. To most people, the Federal Government was something of a myth. Only the very wealthy and big corporations could afford to travel between domes, so each dome was almost autonomous. It took Polly all the money she could scrape together, working from age fifteen to twenty, to buy a spot in cargo to get herself to this dome, home of Universal's headquarters, so she could try and make something of herself. The dome she was born in was old, leaky and agricultural. If hard work didn't kill you, the pollution seeping in would, and people had low priority for the cleaner areas, compared to food.

"How do I know you aren't just here to steal the secret of the mushrooms?" she asked.

"I'm not here to steal it." He seemed unfazed by the accusation. "I'm here to shut it down."

"The UG plant?" she gasped. People looked their way. He lowered his face, keeping it hidden.

"Yell that a little louder next time," he muttered.

"Did you even know Doug?"

"He was my contact. He agreed to help us. Then he disappeared."

"I transferred him to UG," she stammered.

"Yeah, well, I don't think anyone enjoys the transfer."

"What happened to him?" She wasn't sure she wanted to know. Doug was a sweet guy. About her own age. One of the few in the office to ever chat with her. She'd even toyed with the idea of dating him, but she knew neither of them could afford the money or the time.

"They killed him."

She swallowed a gasp, her eyes darting around the platform. None of the peacekeepers seemed to be watching them anymore. "I don't believe you," she whispered, her voice cracking, but her mind was picturing Doug's file. The other UG transfer files. No next of kin. No one to contact. No one to know.

"Yes, you do."

They were near a bench. She walked over and sat on it. He sat down beside her, staring at his feet.

"But why would they?" she asked. "I don't understand. UG is a promotion. He just delivered some mail wrong."

"I don't know," was his subdued reply. "All we know is no one ever comes back from the UG building. Only Mr. Polly. He takes people in, machines bring percos out."

"They're working in there."

"Working in there and never coming back out?"

"Never?"

"Never."

"What are you going to do?" she asked finally. Another car sped down the vertical. She was so late for work now, there was no point in ever going back, even if she wanted to.

"We're going in there."

"We?" She glanced at him sharply. "Why do you need me?"

"I need to get that door open. I need you to go stand by it and wait for Mr. Polly to show up to take you in."

"You just said no one comes back out of there."

"Look." Narrow eyes scrutinized her from under the hood. "Only one man can open that door and you're going to get him to do it. I won't let him take you in."

"What happened at lunch yesterday?" she asked.

"We didn't go to lunch," he said. "Polly tried to force me into a transport. I escaped."

"So they're searching for you," she said, realizing that was the reason behind the hood, the down-turned face. "How did you find me?"

"I wasn't looking for you," he said. "I was in that café for the same reason you were. Because you want to know what's going on in that building."

"I've invested my whole life into working at Universal."

"You can't go back there anyway. Trust me."

She sighed, looking at her feet in her pink recycled shoes. She did trust him. More than that, she trusted herself. She trusted that instinct that told her yesterday she didn't want to be transferred to UG. She trusted her dislike of her boss, and of Mr. Polly.

"I'm Polly," she said.

"That's coincidental."

"No." She shrugged. "I think that's why he picked my name off the employee list. If I were Susan, I wouldn't be in this mess."

"So you're going to help me?"

"I don't have anything better to do today." She

shivered, feeling her stomach lurch as the agreement left her mouth. This was dangerous. She could tell. She clenched her teeth. If they were going to do this thing, they better do it fast before she broke down into a useless puddle of tears. This wasn't what she wanted when she came to the Universal Dome. "I just wanted enough money to afford a dog and a door that won't crush him."

"I'll see what I can do about your door later."

He stood, leading them to a vertical headed down. When they reached their stop, Polly realized she hadn't walked on ground level since leaving her home dome three years ago. Only the lowest of low were ever forced to walk on ground level amid the heavy pollutants, even in an agricultural dome like she came from. Back there, her family was so poor, they lived under one of the giant rotating trays that grew the food goods. Both her parents had died of the pollution, never able to save up enough to get out.

Polly could just see the outline of the UG building through the smog when he put a hand on her arm to halt her.

"Just go stand at the door." He was blinking rapidly. Her eyes were watering as well. Airborne debris swirled around them.

"Just stand there? For how long? Where will you be?" She was shaking now. So much that she could see it as well as feel it. She felt like she might vomit up her coffee, although it was probably as much from the pollution as her nerves.

"I won't let him take you in, Polly." His eyes were filled with sincerity.

She swallowed. "How long do I have to stand there?"

"It won't take long. I'm sure he'll know the moment someone gets near that door."

She set off alone across the empty street in front of the UG building. The air was so thick with anonymous dust particles that she couldn't read the Universal Food plaque until she was at the door. She stared up at it. Just two days ago, that name represented every hope she had for a decent life. What did it mean now?

"Polly, isn't it?" Mr. Polly materialized out of a swirl of dust. She looked around, but didn't see any sort of transport nearby. Only the wealthy could afford personal transportation, but she knew Mr. Polly had some. "What are you doing here?"

"I was looking for Doug." Mr. Polly showed no recognition of the name. "I transferred him yesterday."

"The young man from the mail room?" A smile spread across Mr. Polly's broad face. "Oh, he's inside, alright. I brought him over myself. Did you know him?"

"Well, he asked me out before. And now he got transferred, well—" She let her voice trail off. Let him fill in the idea that she was a gold digger.

"We wanted to transfer you too, Polly, but you didn't come to work today." His face still smiled, but his eyes were lit with an evil-looking fire from within. "Where have you been, Polly?"

"I couldn't sleep last night," she stammered. She took a step back as he moved closer to her, corralling her toward the door. "I was out. I got home too late to go to work. I knew I'd get demoted. I knew I'd need someone to help me out till I could work my way back up to assistant again." She realized she was babbling. Her voice was getting higher and louder. He kept moving closer and she kept backing away. "I came to find Doug!"

"I'll help you find him."

Mr. Polly's face was inches from hers. His breath was more stagnant than the smog around them. She was pinned against the door. He reached one arm to the right of her, placing his hand on the panel. It was the sophisticated kind. The kind you couldn't fool. It could tell exactly who touched it, and if they were alive or not, even awake or not, and who knew what else.

The door slid open and she fell in, landing hard. She had just enough time to realize the whole three-story building was open and to gag on the stench that washed over her before she screamed, rolling out of the way as Mr. Polly's body was flung after her, the dark-haired agent on top of it.

Fortunately, the struggling men rolled away from her, smashing into the plastic legs of a table. She wasn't supposed to be in here. The agent had said he wouldn't let her go in. He'd said no one who went in came back out. She needed to get outside, but the door slid shut before she could reach freedom.

She pulled herself up against the door, pounding on it. She was dizzy from falling, from smog, and from the sweet, harsh odor filling the building. She knew she didn't want to turn around. She knew she didn't want to see, but she could hear the agent and Mr. Polly fighting behind her, and if the agent lost, Polly was sure she was never leaving the UG building again.

Behind her, a man cried out in pain, and she whirled. Across the massive open space, the two men grappled. Above her were bright white lights, radiating heat. The men were surrounded by tables. The building was full of them. Rows and rows of tables. She inched forward.

Each table had something on it. Her mind wouldn't wrap itself around what. It was a shape. Long, shrouded. At one end grew a massive smooth percos mushroom. The one nearest her was worth enough to support her current lifestyle for five years. It had an almost metallic glint. A tangy smell hung in the air. The mushroom's broad base grew from a gaping human mouth.

Polly screamed, stumbling away from the table, falling into another. The two men still struggled, a flotsam of dislodged corpses and smashed mushrooms detailing their path across the room. She shut her eyes, but that didn't block out the smell. She opened them again. Shaking, panting. Her eyes fixed on the movement of the other two living bodies, the rational part of her brain urging her once again to influence the fight. She stumbled forward, trying to see a weapon without seeing the bodies around her.

There was a booming sound and the agent fell. Polly dropped to the floor as the noise pierced her skull, bouncing off the walls. She scrambled under one of the tables, hugging her knees to her. Shaking, tears coated her face. An arm had come loose and hung down in front of her. She stared at it, trying to breathe.

"Polly." Mr. Polly's voice was oddly soft, almost soothing. "Come on, sweetheart. Come out where I can see you."

She closed her eyes, squeezing her arms round her drawn-up legs, trying to keep her shaking from making enough noise to give her away. He started walking, retracing his steps to the door.

"It doesn't have to be so bad, Polly," he called again in that calming voice. "It will all be over before you finish standing. I'm a very good shot."

He was moving closer. She started to crawl, for once thankful she couldn't afford longer skirts. Her skin could slide smoothly over the hard floors, but plastic would have stuck. She didn't know which way she was going. She didn't have a plan. Just be quiet and keep moving away from those footsteps.

Above her, the giant lights buzzed. Around the room, filters whirled, bringing in air. Noises she hadn't noticed before, they were loud now. They filled her world as her ears strained for those footsteps, as she cringed at the slight sound of her skin skidding on the floor.

"It will only be worse for you if you keep this up, little one," he said in his pleasant voice.

She realized she was in a different sort of space now. Above were tables, but she'd reached cabinets, a counter, plumbing. An outer wall. Her first inclination was to go back. She didn't want to be cornered, but the cabinets weren't locked, and his voice, his droning, soothing monologue, was far across the room. She cracked a cabinet open, her ears straining for any sound it made. She hoped desperately for a dark, empty hole into which she could crawl, even as the logical part of her brain cried, *Don't get trapped.*

"I'll make a deal with you." His voice was smooth, warm. "I won't kill you. I like you too much. We'll be friends."

The cabinet was full of drawers. Too full to hide in. She started to ease it shut when she noticed one of the drawers had a picture of a syringe on it. She slid it open. She was shaking again, risking rattling the plastic. She was more exposed by the cabinets. She could hear his footsteps, his droning voice. He was talking about taking her out for drinks. She pulled a wrapped syringe out of the drawer. It was full of something. A scientific name. She couldn't focus on the letters. She slid the drawer shut, the cabinet closed, herself back under the tables.

A low groan broke into Mr. Polly's monologue and she swallowed a scream, the effort of holding it in filling her vision with black specks. She forced herself to suck air through her nose, the rotting smell assailing her anew.

"What's this?" Mr. Polly's voice floated across the room. "Not dead?"

Polly squeezed her eyes shut, her body onto itself, expecting the sound of another gunshot. Instead, she heard movement, a grunt of exertion. The footsteps resumed, accompanied by a sliding sound. They drew closer.

"Don't feel neglected, sweetheart." Mr. Polly's voice was near now. A spasm ran through her body. She twitched, unable to commit to hiding or fleeing. "I'm still going to find you. I can see the door from here. I just need to start this one before he checks out. Waste of money not to. Somehow, the mush-room always knows if it doesn't get a live one."

She could see him now. He was dragging the agent. She shrank back under the table. The air around her seemed to compress as he stopped before it, heaving the agent onto the surface. Mr. Polly turned to the sink, running water. She thought he was washing his hands. She peeled the plastic wrapping off the syringe, the sound filling her head until she was afraid she'd go blind from the pressure. He didn't seem to hear. He was still talking, projecting his voice across the room.

"Yes, you have to start with a live one. Not that it lasts long. Mushrooms love that last sweet breath out when someone dies. Without it, they just don't grow."

He was back at the table now. She clenched the syringe so hard, the plastic indented. With an inarticulate screech, she jammed the needle into the side of his leg. It went in almost all the way before jarring off bone. With her other hand, she hammered the plastic plunger home, sobbing.

Mr. Polly bellowed, pain and rage billowing from him. She could see his hand fumble for the gun at his waist. She lunged at him, a wild force flying from under the table, hitting him in the chest and knocking him backward. His head slammed down on the edge of the counter. Her fists beat at him as he slid to the floor. Her scrambling hands found his gun, wrenched it out of the holster. Her body was hurtled backward into the table as she shot him in the chest.

She stood, panting, crying. Her shaking arms lowered inch by inch as she tried to convince herself he was dead. Blood coated the edge of the counter, streaked down the cabinet face. A pool of it formed around him, from the back of his head, from the hole in his chest. His face was angry, but his eyes were rolled back, fixed on the ceiling. The needle still stuck out of his leg.

She raised the gun and shot him again, bracing herself against the table this time. His body bounced against the cabinet at the impact, but he didn't come back to life. Satisfied, she turned to the table behind her. There was a hole in the agent's shoulder, and his nose was bleeding. One eye was turning black. She set the gun down next to his head, placing a shaky hand on his neck to see if she could find a pulse. With her free hand, she found her own, an erratic staccato against her shaking fingertips, to locate the right spot. She adjusted the hand on him, feeling a faint flicker.

"What do I do now?" she asked, her voice cracking.

He didn't stir. Ignoring Mr. Polly's body, she rummaged around the cabinets until she found something to tie around the agent's arm. She didn't know how to tell if the bullet was in there. It was oozing blood, and she knew that couldn't be good. The blood should be stopped.

While she was bandaging him, she found his phone. Fortunately, it wasn't as high tech as the door. His living thumbprint was enough to open it. It only had one contact, and no other numbers saved. She pressed call.

"Hello?" a pleasant female voice answered immediately.

"Hi."

"This is not your phone." The voice went a bit cold.

"No." Polly's voice came out as a squeak. "It's this guy's phone. He got shot. I need help."

"Is he conscious?"

"No."

"Do you know him?"

"Not really." She didn't even know his name.

"Where are you?" The voice was very official-sounding now.

"We're in Universal's UG building."

There was a long silence. Polly bit her lip. Someone would come help her, wouldn't they? She didn't want to leave the agent. She couldn't move him. She didn't want to have to walk back across that room, that sea of rotting people, let alone try and drag a full-grown man across with her. She started looking around, her eyes avoiding the tabletops with their putrid blooms. Something here must have wheels. She looked only at legs.

"Hold please," the voice finally ordered, causing Polly to start. She'd almost forgotten about the person on the other end of the phone. She kept herself busy looking for wheels, not wanting to see or think anything else.

"Hello." It was a warm male voice now. "To whom

am I speaking?"

"I'm Polly. Look, can anyone come get your agent? Can you help me? I can't stay here!" She started choking, trying not to cry. The voice on the phone was murmuring, but she couldn't focus on it. She set the phone down and shut her eyes. Three deep breaths.

"I'm sorry," she told the man in the phone, picking it back up.

"Polly?"

"Yes?"

"We want to help you. We need you to stay calm. I just need to know one thing."

"Yes?" she repeated, feeling a lurch of hope.

"Can you tell me if you see enough evidence of a crime there to justify Federal action?"

Polly felt her eyes go wide. Her gaze flickered over the room. She held up the phone and took a picture. "I'm sending it," she tried to tell the phone, but she was hyper-ventilating again. She sent the picture.

Now that she looked at the tabletops again, they were all she could see. Rotten faces horribly split open by the giant mushroom stalks. On some of the biggest ones, she couldn't even tell if it was a man or a woman anymore. The features were sunken down as the mushroom ate the content of the skull, their nose and eyes smushed into thin lines by the giant stems growing from where their mouths used to be.

I'd still be able to recognize Doug. Her brain forced the thought on her. She tried to keep it from the next logical step. *I transferred him to UG.*

She willed it not to, but her gaze slid across the room anyhow, picking out a distant area where the bodies under the sheets still looked like people, where the mushrooms coming out of the mouths were so small, the mouths could have been eating them, instead of the other way around. She could see a gray-bearded face, a woman's body with dyed orange hair, a thin young man. All people she'd transferred to UG. She didn't need to get close enough to see their features to guess which one was Doug.

She dropped the phone with a clatter. She realized they were probably still talking, but she never put it back to her ear. Wrenching her eyes from the tabletop victims, she turned, sliding limply to the floor, her legs splayed out in front of her. Across from her, Mr. Polly had become a dull gray color. She let her head hang down, shutting her eyes. She concentrated on the sound of the agent's breathing, waiting for someone to come.

○─○

"Will you be all right?"

They were sitting in a café in the Federal dome. The agent sat across from her, his arm in a sling. His name was Tom. He was actually quite nice. Polly leaned back in her chair, a slight smile on her face as she reminded herself that when she leaned forward, her new cloth shirt wouldn't stick to the back.

"I guess it depends on what you consider all right," she said. If he meant would she ever stop having nightmares about the UG building, probably not. If he meant would she be happy in the new life they'd set her up with as an assistant at the agency, the huge bonus they'd given her for her part in bringing down Universal's percos operations, and her three-room apartment in the Federal dome with her very own dog, probably. It was everything she'd always wanted. A bedroom, non-plastic clothes, a dog, and a front door that wouldn't crush him, but she'd be happier if she'd earned it all with long years of work and never saw what was inside that building.

"You did a good thing. You have a good life now. You deserve it."

"Yeah." She sighed. "You guys have been great. Please don't get me wrong. I just wish I could have taken a different road here. Any different road."

"You'll be fine," he said, leaning back in his chair. He lifted his coffee with his good hand, taking a sip.

"I will be," she agreed, squaring her shoulders. "I'll be fine."

He smiled in approval. They both sipped their coffee, letting their minds wander.

PRACTICE BABY

HEATHER FOWLER

Practice Baby needed to be watered before it was born, soaked in a warm saline solution like womb fluid, and then nursed to life with a literal teat in its mouth. If no teat were available, say for single fathers or women reticent about milk hormones and use of their own breasts, a false one was provided in the box that easily attached to a standard issue bottle you could remove and replace. Use of formula was most common.

Practice Baby took in this "milk" and converted it to urine, which then created messy diapers, but the child was required to at least mimic the idea of sucking with its silicon lips and toothless mouth, at the same rate as an organic child, more so in the beginning. It had a chart, week by week, and grew cognitively, as a real child would. In fact, Practice Baby had to be fed meticulously, according to its daily schedule provided in the shipping crate, or it would die.

To avoid this happening, though some practice parents of early models had complained about this very thing, the newest model helped you keep it alive by issuing horrifying and escalating screams, just like a real infant. Laura had listened and listened to these before ordering—to see if she could take it.

She'd heard the other sounds too. Practice Baby farted audibly after just one week, even smiled as real babies did when passing gas, though new parents were told not to regard this as a budding sense of humor yet, and Laura had been amply warned: Practice Baby's death would turn the small plastic baby blue, the color of baby blue baby blankets, similar to those funny little dolls that changed color when dropped in bathwater. If dropped in bathwater face down, Practice Baby would also turn blue. Cranially sensitive to facial immersion, it would "drown."

The goal, Laura knew, was no blue baby. Pink baby: good. Blue baby: bad. Color-coded like pregnancy tests. She had watched the infomercial a hundred times, knew all its ins and outs. With her own Practice Baby waiting for her on her table, no name provided as yet, she reviewed its still body with fear as she powered up the set and listened again to the happy mothering sounds of the recorded infomercial mommy, cooing at her own commercial Practice Baby. Laura watched the following text scroll across the screen: "Practice Baby is made to mimic all real parenting situations a couple will confront with an infant—making them fully competent before a live arrival!"

Onscreen commercial daddy then entered and tickled Practice Baby's belly and toes. Practice mommy and daddy smiled. The ad continued, this time in a deep announcer's voice: "Not sure if you want to breed? Try Practice Baby first, for a fraction of the cost of a real child. Will not develop beyond six months. Breast-milk formula or hormones not provided. See your practitioner. Manufacturer's warning: If you 'kill' your Practice Baby with maltreatment that would truncate life for a live-birth child, the parent company Bazacker will not provide a free replacement. Additional limbs are available on the website. Visit www.practicebaby.com."

"When I first got my Practice Baby," Ad Mommy said just after the company warnings, "I thought for sure I was going crazy! The thing screams night and day, but feeding it was precious. You can even let it suckle your real breast to get the feel for nursing. Whether your milk's come in or not! Don't forget to give it milk afterward, though, if you don't have any. Your Practice Baby can be cranky when it's hungry. Having this Practice Baby with Don—it's the best thing we've ever done with each other. Now we know we are ready to be good parents. We had to be, to raise our Practice Baby." Ad Mommy fairly glowed as she said this, a squat brunette woman with visible facial acne. Laura liked her imperfection.

She hesitated opening her own Practice Baby box for one main reason: Pregnant already, jacked up on estrogen, everything in the infomercial since Practice Baby had been delivered seemed to have a nefarious double meaning.

She worried about the fact that, once turned on, there was no off switch because the technicians chose this. Programmed with cries recorded from real infants and made with authentic human hair ejected from the scalp at legitimate growth rates, it was an expensive doll, resembling a real child. You could even customize its skin tone and eye color, to inspire the love, and when it arrived, you would be astounded, if not a bit freaked out, about how much like your own photos it resembled you as a child, if you'd sent in several pictures along with payment. But it would all be quite benign at first, that was until you—godlike you, practice mama or papa—brought the thing to life. "It's like being a robo-God," Laura told her husband Cary.

"It's like flicking a light switch," he replied. "On an expensive chandelier that happens to look like you and cry."

Laura agreed that the thing looked creepily like them, for she'd sent both their baby pictures for a fusion; she even deliberated sending it back after a week of her own observation of, and yet refusal to open, the clear box in which it arrived.

The bill on her credit card would cripple them. "If we don't open it," she said, "we can send it back."

"Why not just have our Real Baby and see how we do?" Cary asked, looking tired. "I can't keep taking it off the dining room table so we can eat and putting it back up there for you to consider."

"We are not ready for the Real Baby," Laura said. "I want to be meticulous about this whole parenting thing! With Practice Baby, we could get ready for good parenthood before parenthood."

He looked at her stomach, recently ballooned outward in a round ball. "Three to four months to go," he said. "Won't that be exhausting. Two babies at the same time, Laura? You up for that?" He put his hand on her stomach, asked, "Is the real one kicking much?"

She did not reply. She went to the table and stared at the machine.

"Well, if you're going to use that thing, you'd better open it now," he said. "Get the box opener."

"I don't want to open it," she insisted.

"If you don't open it, I'm sending it back. I've decided I would like a small sports car when we get rid of it. If we can afford this, we can afford that."

"Cut Practice Baby out of that box," Laura replied. "Don't slice its face. As you already know, it's a boy! For you, Cary! A boy! Get the tub ready. Let's start its soak. Don't put the face down. I think we can recycle him later if we don't like him."

Cary looked at her wryly. When he said, "How do you recycle a baby?" she replied, almost instantly, with irritation, "Oh, look, babe, he has your penis."

Pregnant, moody, and increasingly violent in her responses, she feared all kinds of things the infomercial addressed, including that she hoped not a have a stronger bond with a mechanized human than her own flesh and blood. But, she reminded herself, Practice Baby maxed on development at six months: The thing wouldn't even talk much when it stopped "growing." Excessive bonding was not possible.

Cary lifted it from its plastic wrapping and put it in the solution, back down. "This is it," he said. "We can't return it now. Don't kill it."

They smiled at each other. It was kind of like their

first date. The baby in her stomach gave a series of turns and kicks. "Okay," Laura said. "Tomorrow we'll turn it on."

○–○

After the first few weeks, she got the hang of it. At feeding times, she did not let the baby latch onto her breast as the commercial suggested, regardless of milk there or not there, but used the bottle with the faux teat. It's not that she hadn't tried the "breast-feeding" once or twice, but with her nipples as sore and swollen as they were, stimulation felt horrid. Lactation hormones were out of the question, in case they damaged her Real Baby. Practice Baby also didn't have adjustment dials for nursing, which she messaged the website about, its suck hard and irregular during her early brief intervals of attempted breast-bonding. With no reply to her email, she'd even called and asked a live representative what to do.

"Oh, well, a lot of ladies like that suck," the teenager on the other end said. "Some of them even like the suckling at the four month mark where they felt some teething. Your Practice Baby is programmed to evolve. Teeth leave the gums."

"I'm pregnant," Laura said. "I don't like the sensation without teeth."

"Okay, be like a guy then, who won't BF," the teen said. "Like gay guy couples who get one. Some 'mommies' don't nurse, just use the fake teat. Or you could, like, um, use the manual thing from the box, look at the pictures there, and just try out the different holds for breastfeeding. For practice, right?"

"Thanks," Laura said. "But I'm pregnant, like I said. That's getting harder."

"Well, you wanted to be like a mommy, right?" the girl replied, as if telephone advising had told her everything about it, like she was a bona fide shrink. "But you're about to be a real mommy. If the Practice Baby's too much trouble then, you could just throw it in the closet. Or against the wall. He won't cry forever. But wait six months so you don't go Bad Mommy on our site list."

"Have you worked here long?" Laura asked, regarding Practice Baby, who appeared to be asleep. "I don't think you should be saying that stuff to people. It might influence them later." The Practice Baby lightly squirmed in its blanket. At times like this, it seemed very sweet. Laura smiled down. She'd been holding it a lot, like the book said. She kind of loved it. "How old are you, anyway?"

The girl seemed ticked. "Look, lady, I went off book for you. I'm just trying to help."

Laura pictured the girl she spoke to like an ill-fed troll with thin hair, twirling the company pencils on her fingers and bouncing a round bangle on her thigh. "All right. Another topic. What can you tell me about a Practice Baby that needs to be fed every three hours after a whole month? I thought the infomercial said some babies would sleep through the night after two months—and the three hour windows would gradually lengthen from the time you wake it up."

Teenage Phone Girl sighed. "Oh, the program's random—I mean, some people get a Practice Baby who does follow that. Others will get a staggered schedule that lasts much longer before full-night sleeping. Almost everybody gets off the hook after four months, though. You only have to go through this once with Practice Baby. Then it's like six months old for forever! And eats. Then you'll see stool!"

Laura rubbed her back with her hands, thought: *Stool? Joy!* Practice Baby awoke and began to wail. When Practice Baby cried, the Real Baby in her abdomen, as if sensing trauma, balled in her stomach and sat on her bladder. Holding the phone, Laura grabbed Practice Baby and tried to grab for the bottle. First feed Practice Baby and then hit the restroom, she decided, while Teenage Phone Girl told her more about superior parenting, but where was it, the bottle? Phone up to her ear, surveying the rooms, she finally saw the last bottle—empty with dirty teat—on the kitchen counter, and realized that she'd have to make one. But first she'd have to wash the teat. The wailing seemed to grow. "Do you sell extra teats? How fast can I get some?"

Without hearing her, the girl went on, "...because that's like really cool. Then you can give it to a neighbor! But don't..."

Meanwhile, Practice Baby cranked it up a notch. Escalating whimpers became light screams.

"Shhhhh, shhhhh," Laura said, but when Real Baby sat harder on her bladder, Laura ran with the phone in one hand and Practice Baby in the other, her arm wrapped around Practice Baby like a football gripped to run with, until she reached the hall restroom. She then promptly told phone girl, "I've got to go," hung up and dropped the phone, put Practice Baby on the ground beside her, and unzipped her pants. She could think only of urination, like how you only think of eating when you're starving. The screaming, though. It was bad. It rose and rose in volume. This was when, mid-stream, she remembered that any suckling would cause a temporary quiet.

Desperate, she picked up Practice Baby and brought it again to her breast, offering her nipple to be chomped as the liberating flood continued to exit her body and relief coursed through her.

Cary entered via the front door. "Babe," she shouted. "A bottle, please. Stat!" She put Practice Baby on the ground again and finished wiping, reiterating, "Quickly, please."

When he brought the bottle, she said, "I need a drink. I am going out to a bar to get one. Watch Practice Baby."

He was smart enough to say nothing. Laura wouldn't be going for a drink, of course, she realized as she exited the house. She'd be going for ice-cream. No bartender would want to serve her a drink with a belly that large in this part of town. She found, though, that she didn't want to go home after the fiasco with the phone girl, no, not for hours. Cary could feed the next few bottles. "I want you to bond with Practice Baby," she texted him. "I'll be home late."

He texted back, "Hate Practice Baby. Have fun."

She replied. "He looks just like you. What if you hate Real Baby?"

"Not possible," he replied.

"Should we kill it now?" she asked, tapping the letters into her phone. "Practice Baby? It would be a lot less hassle. I've been doing this a month. That's probably enough." But when she closed her eyes, she pictured Practice Baby's soft fuzz on his head, the way he nuzzled her face and seemed warm in her arms. "No. Let's not kill him," she said. "He's a good baby. He'll teach me how to treat the real one."

"He's okay," Cary replied.

"Besides, he was so expensive," Laura texted. "All that money for one month of crying. He's supposed to get better. Squirt his head with that love juice perfume they sent us, the one that smells like biscuits."

Cary typed " sigh " and "I miss you. Come home. See you soon."

o—o

In another month, due to her enormous belly and a rise of acid reflux, Laura could not sleep flat. "I'm glad," she told Cary as he shifted beside her, the alarm clock reading three a.m., "that Practice Baby sleeps more now. Five hours at a go. Should we name it yet, Practice Baby?"

Their own child would be called Devon. Both had agreed. "Aren't we going to give the fake one away when the real one comes?" Cary asked. "Maybe better not to name it."

"We have to keep it for six months," Laura said. "You saw we get named on the website if Practice Baby doesn't 'live' six months."

"So you think whoever we give it away to will just kill it?"

"They won't be as invested."

"We could sell it to them, at a discount."

"I don't think someone we gave it to would kill it; I'm just saying, if they did," Laura said. "It would be our names listed as the murderers. Our money, our names. That's in the contract unless you purchase as a gift. I don't want to take the blame for someone else."

Cary thought about it, his breathing slow as he rested beside her. "Does it really matter if our names are up on that site?" he asked. "Like we care what other people think. Who checks that site but other Practice Baby owners? "

"You could Google it," she said. "Future employers could know."

"Consider this, Laura," Cary said. "Let's be realistic. When you go to the hospital, who will care for Practice Baby then? Do we plan to pay caretakers?"

"My mother will care for Practice Baby," Laura said. "She already agreed."

"Your mother will care for Practice Baby? Yeah, for all of ten minutes or a day," Cary said. "And then she'll throw it on the couch or in her pool, aware it's not a real child, tired of the crying."

Laura pulled away. "No, she won't. She promised me."

Cary made a sound suspiciously like a snort.

"I want a hot bath now," Laura said. "And a half gallon of vodka."

Cary snorted again. She laughed. "I love you," he said.

"Put your hand on my belly," she told him. "Feel that? Real Baby is kicking."

He fell asleep that way, his hand on her stomach. Luckily, for the first time, Practice Baby slept through the night. The next day, as Laura played with Practice Baby, she realized he seemed more sensitized and observed new things, like complicated designs and colors and shapes. He also followed voices.

Towards the end of the month, he started to stretch more and push off with his legs. She got so excited, she called Cary. "Practice Baby is doing new things!" she said. "He's learning! He needs a name!"

"That's good," Cary replied.

"Should we name him now?"

"I'm still iffy. Do you love him?"

"Love is rather a strong term for what I feel," she said.

"So, if I put him in a cabinet, would that make you upset?" Cary asked.

"Yes, that's my baby!"

"Would the idea of a baby in a cabinet upset you in general?" Cary replied, fonder and fonder of these philosophical questions that made her blood boil. "Or do you think you'd care more that this was our Practice Baby, and you think you feel something for that thing?"

Laura refused to answer. That afternoon, she cleaned. She gave Practice Baby his bottles. When her mother called, she was eager for some understanding, but her mother just said, "Why don't you name it Devon if you're not sure how you feel about it? It's a Practice Baby to prepare for your Real Baby, after all—and that way you'd feel something. Tell Cary tonight that you'll both start using the name Devon. Because that will make the situation more real."

Laura agreed. Days later, she admitted her mother was right. Something special happened as she began to call Practice Baby Devon. It seemed more her baby. The baby in her stomach then almost seemed an alien disease. Only when she went for sonograms did she have a sense that Real Baby and Practice Baby were two different creatures.

But even Practice Baby had a heartbeat you could hear, with your ear close to its chest.

Cary, for his part, rejected calling Practice Baby Devon. It became her solitary practice. "You seem to have bonded with The Thing now," he observed, when she got close to the forty week mark.

"I have," she said. "I love Devon."

"So I bet you can't wait for our Real Baby?" he said,

like it was a question.

She nuzzled Practice Baby's face and replied, "Why not? The more babies the merrier."

o—o

Her labor was hard and long. The whole time exerting herself, she thought of Practice Baby: Was her mother giving Devon his bottles? What was he doing? Was he sleeping? Was he being read to, tickled just so? Between extreme pain and pushing and the insertion of a tool to turn her Real Baby and the time when Real Baby came out with one final heave, she had thought about Practice Baby Devon hundreds of times. In fact, when the doctor finally handed her Real Baby, saying, "Here is Devon!"—having already been told their selected name—she urgently fought the desire to say, "That is not Devon! Take it back."

Real Baby was a boy, too. Real Baby screamed and woke often, too. It was like going back to the beginning of the game. "Practice Baby Devon is already beyond this," she thought. And Real Baby is more messy. Real Baby did not stop crying just because a bottle or her breast was presented full. Yes, she had learned how to burp Practice Baby, but Real Baby took more variations, more work, even in the hospital where the nurses cycled in and out.

So did Cary. He loved Real Baby and stayed each evening when he got off work.

"Look how cute he is," Cary said, talking to the infant in a special coddling voice she'd heard only recently. "He is so cute!"

"How is Devon?" Laura asked.

"He's fine! Look right here! Look at our wittle baby do that cute wubby thing with his mouth—wait a minute! Did you mean Practice Baby?"

"Yes."

Cary's features took a grim aspect. "I don't know. I suppose fine."

"You don't know? You haven't asked my mother?"

"It's a machine. And listen, Laura. I think we need a different name for Practice Baby. This is Devon. We chose the name for our baby. I'm saying that thing—it's just a thing."

Laura sobbed. "I hate Real Baby. I miss that thing," she said. "This thing is much too complicated."

He held her in the hospital bed and came more frequently. By the time they left for home, Laura had at least begun to get excited about dressing Real Baby with the clothes they had always been saving for Real Baby.

"I bought you something else," Cary said. "A bright set of blankets for floor play and a mobile to put on the crib. It's stars, for our baby. You love stars."

This touched her, and when they got to their home, she saw he had even made a different bed for Practice Baby, out of a doll's cradle he picked up somewhere. "We can get it back now," he said. "The other baby."

"Oh, good, call my mother," Laura replied. She thought about the infomercial segment on having a Practice Baby in a house with other children, the clip with an older mother who had teenage children running through her mind incessantly, especially the part where the teens in the commercial said, "We love mom's new baby. She always wanted another, but this one won't rob our college funds."

The Practice Baby in that segment was a full six months old—like hers was about to turn. The kids brought it a toy and it smiled. They held commercial Practice Baby. "It is kind of adorable," one said. "Like something young's always here."

Then the mother came back on and took the Practice Baby away, coddling it lovingly until the end of the shot. Meanwhile, scrolling across the screen, the following text appeared: *Practice Baby has programming built in to help it adapt and play with other children. Following the developmental trends of real children, it can 'be' a sibling to those you have! Share the love with Practice Baby; it loves more than JUST you. Kids and pets too.*

Cary was pissed about the name issue.

"Hey, Cary," Laura said when he got off the line.

"I've been thinking we should call Real Baby Cary Jr. What do you think?"

"Yes. When can we have sex again?" he whispered.

"At least a month," she said.

"Oh well. I liked the fake one better for that part."

○─○

When Practice Baby returned, it seemed almost somber. Had her mother, Laura wondered, held it enough? At first, when she called to it, it seemed to have angry eyes, as if it felt it had been abandoned. "Devon," Laura said. "I'm so glad to see you!"

It cried more than it had before she left. Also, and Laura wondered if she was imagining things, it didn't seem to like its new crib. She consulted the manual for mood shifts, but between sleep loss from Real Baby and renewed skewed sleep from Practice Baby, she was exhausted.

Calling to and caring for both babies on some days, one real and one false, made her feel all the more delusional. Even trying to hold them both enough was difficult. Cary, of course, now paid nearly no attention to Practice Baby. "It's mean, babe," she said, "how you neglect one. Can you at least try to nurture both?"

"No," Cary said. "Look, Laura, I know you've bonded with that baby, but I didn't bond. It's just a thing to me. You're going to rob our real baby to give balanced care to a machine?"

Over the weeks that followed, his criticism bothered her. He was right. Practice Baby was six months now, wouldn't grow. Cary Jr. was the real thing. She could extinguish Devon easily by throwing it in the bathtub. They wouldn't even list her on that website—or she could resell him if anyone wanted to experience a six month old. As babysitter practice.

But all of these things struck her as cruel. When Cary Jr. was sleeping, she went and held Devon for a long time and then tried putting him in the armoire, just to test how she'd feel.

They've trained me to love this thing, she thought. *I can't just put it away now. When its cries will break my heart. Neither can I stand the thought of selling it.* Practice Baby cried immediately when she shut the wardrobe door. She pulled it out instantly and sat with Devon on the floor, saying she was sorry repeatedly as tears streamed from her eyes.

"Maybe," she told Cary that night. "We should just keep both."

"We'll do what you want," he said. "It's your Practice Baby. We paid for it. Just don't give any real breast milk to the thing, okay? Keep things separate for Cary Jr., at least that far." In their household, Laura saw the division of his affection clearly. Cary loved his baby, but more and more, Practice Baby was relegated to an unfortunate part of his routine.

Still, as Cary Jr. began to progress, it was exciting how real and energized Cary's reactions were; whereas before he had listened to humor her about her doings with Devon, he had huge ears for anything about Cary Jr., so much so that Laura felt, perversely, like telling him nothing.

They began to bicker. She found she made hurtful remarks when he ignored Practice Baby. Cary put a stop to this one day when he said, "I understand and accept your care for the other baby, okay? I told you that. But Laura, we made this one! With sex—egg and sperm. Our love. Can't you understand? This one will grow beyond six months, take care of us when we get old... This one actually looks like me. Of course I love it more."

"I wish you were home during the day to help me," she said in reply. "Sometimes taking care of two babies is very confusing."

The next day, she found herself vacuuming during a brief window where both babies were asleep on the living room floor. She stopped by Cary Jr., thinking of Cary, and kissed his forehead. "Of course I love you more, too," she admitted. "He's right. Of course."

As both babies slept, she regarded their small faces, one to the other and back again, for differences. There was simply something different about human skin and musculature. Cary Jr. struck her as more real every time. When she went to get the laundry from the garage, she came back in to hear screaming. "Which baby is it?" she said, running toward them down the hall, as if either baby were capable of answering. Devon had done his new trick of rolling, she saw as she entered, and had rolled right up beside Cary Jr.

She learned almost immediately that it was Cary Jr. who'd been crying, but not just crying, thrashing about bawling with as red a face as she'd ever seen.

Devon took to wailing in response. "Who did what?" she shouted to both babies, unable to figure out what had happened. Because he was smallest, she first picked up Cary Jr. and put him on her shoulder, patting his back and trying to bounce him to soothe him, but then she noticed Devon's open mouth, blood on his teeth. Looking down, she saw then a small bit of red on her sleeve, where Cary Jr.'s hand rested and moved.

"Did you bite my baby?" she asked Devon, as if he could answer. "Did you bite the baby?"

Devon wailed louder. Cary Jr. wailed louder. She didn't know whether it was the sight of Cary Jr.'s small injured hand when she pulled it up to examine it—the crushed way it appeared—or the sight and the scent of the blood, but she thought of Cary Sr.'s horrified reaction to the violence while having her own horrified reaction. "Shut up you little shit," she yelled mindlessly at Devon. "Just shut up right now! You have to stop crying!"

He did not.

Cary Jr., too, continued to wail, holding out his crumpled hand now as if it had gotten worse. Laura realized an ambulance may need to be called, especially after, all of the sudden Cary Jr. fell, as if thoroughly exhausted, into a lull of whimpers and then slept again, while Devon continued to wail.

Practice Baby will exhibit the behaviors of real chil- dren, Laura thought. *Jealousy. Rage.* She put Cary Jr. down on the floor and picked up Devon. She did not offer him her breast.

She held him first and tried to rock him calmer, but still she saw Cary Jr.'s blood on his teeth, and when he did not cease his crying right away, and it seemed Cary Jr. might wake for more crying of his own, she suddenly saw Practice Baby as a horrible little monster creature—a soul- sucking, attention-stealing device built to waste her atten- tion in the wrong places and destroy her own child!

She threw Devon into the wall.

His arm broke off, some wires poked free, sparking. He continued to wail. Bound to make him quiet, terrified by his robotic parts, she picked him up again to bash his face against the wall. She did this four times until he turned first yellow and then blue before she calmed. When she returned her gaze to her Real Baby, Cary Jr. was silent, watching her.

She took Practice Baby and hid his parts in her dresser. An hour later, she retrieved them and put them on the dining room table, deciding she'd let Cary see what she had done. But another hour later, the sight of the Practice Baby, mangled, pale blue, and otherworldly on the table, was disturbing, and though he had never liked it, she then wondered if Cary, seeing the electronic carnage she'd cre- ated, might worry about the safety of their own child.

He might hate her. Oh God. Not that he ever thought of the other one as a real child, but he might doubt her sanity. *Who kills a fucking robot?* Not to men- tion that he'd know their own child had *watched* her *dis- patch* what appeared to his sibling, right in front of him, a feat she hoped Cary Jr. would never recall in later life: "What brother?" she practiced saying. "You never had a brother."

She took Practice Baby off the table then, for she could no longer call it Devon without feeling enormous guilt, and placed it in the outdoor dumpster, burying it deep below some rotting food in black plastic bags and a pink bicycle from someone else's child.

When Cary came home, she told him she'd given Practice Baby away. "To whom?" he asked. "Did we know someone who wanted one? That's great!"

"Oh, I put him in this place," she said. "Where anybody could get him. Lots of people put stuff there, or look for stuff they want... It's a good regular place." It could have been the look she then gave, but he asked no more questions.

"Cary Jr.'s hand got injured today," she told her husband over dinner, dishing up his plate with ham and salad. "But I checked it again this afternoon and it should be just a bruise. He seems to move his digits okay. He can still hold my finger." From his bedroom, Cary Jr. then began to wail again, as, turning to Cary Sr., she finished by saying, "You want to go get Cary Jr. now? Look at his hand? It was a bite mark. A machine bite. Do you think that still means we should get him checked or get a tetanus shot?"

But, later that night, she realized she'd left the severed arm on their bed by accident. At the sight of Cary's dawning horror, him having viewed it before she could hide her failure, she quickly grabbed it and threw it under their bed while pleading with him, "You were right all along, Cary. It wasn't a baby. It was a machine. A machine that hurt our baby! I had to do something," and she kept speaking, trying to say these kinds of things he seemed to agree with before, things about its non-status as a live baby, about her foolishness in wanting to bond with it, until finally letting out all the details of her rage and zeal to protect their own infant, their blood-child, until Cary came and put his arms around her, patting her back like she was the new infant.

He breathed in deeply, like he did before sleep, and held her gently as he finally said, "So, it's done then, Laura. Devon is gone. Stop worrying about it."

But she knew everything had bothered him, especially the sight of that tiny arm on the bed with its open hand, out and up, so helpless—wires from the appendage still hanging to the shoulder blade—because this was the first time the tone of Cary's voice had bothered to sound even a little sympathetic for the Practice Baby, but, also, he had used its given name.

saturnina

ELIZaBeTH aLDRICH

Eris' skin is sticky with midnight-shift dancer sweat. Her scent is burning sugar, a little salty. On stage the lights make her and the other dancers look unreal and labyrinthine, like nocturnal creatures that don't need sunlight. If you could cut through their skin, they'd drip bioluminescent ooze; if they had veins, they'd be the metal wire advertisements of liquor stores.

Eris' platinum blonde wig is colored a shade of neon lavender from the kaleidoscope of lights. Blue LED ropes make her hair look shiny; red spotlights make her skin look flawless. Green and peach string lights line the wall-to-wall mirrors. Warm, white halos stay stranded on the ceiling. Eris knows each twist of her torso and reach of her legs as second nature now; she is a professional tease.

There is no acidspit hiss from the jukebox; the sound is smooth, wave-like. Slow, electric purrs of the song's bass hums through each dancing body, each chair, each drink, each custie.

Custies—the nickname for the peepshow's customers—go into narrow booths, slide cash in a narrow slit, and witness a window rising up to reveal a room where all that exists are femmed-up, naked girls dancing all day.

On the dancer's side, the windows look like mirrors, and when the window rises up, a pane of glass the size of a computer screen is revealed. Usually it's an older man in the middle of the black-painted booth, looking something like a phantom. Sometimes they smile. Sometimes they avoid eye contact. Sometimes all they want is eye contact. Sometimes they come in already furiously jacking off. Sometimes it's a group of drunken, giggling girls; other times, it's a couple dropping in to fuck for an exhibitionist thrill.

When dancing for hours, it's easy to make up different scenarios: the dancers are in a spaceship, the dancers are in a magic elevator, the stage is Limbo and the dancers decide whether each custie goes to heaven or hell.

It's even easier to develop a crush. Seeing someone you have a disastrously strong attraction to, naked for hours at a time, can either go in the direction of torture or fantasy. But fantasy doesn't pass the time nearly as well as masochistic desire.

Astrid has Marilyn Monroe's hairstyle—bubblegum instead of blonde—and is very, very shy. Eris feels like an outspoken rhinoceros in comparison, but in heels, naked, and earning $10.24 an hour to aid patrons in orgasm.

Late night shifts are a blur: a hazy occurrence smelling of pussy and alcohol-soaked paper towels, feet and peppermint tea, weed and hairspray.

When it's 3 a.m. Eris saunters off stage. She slips off her heels in the narrow hallway, punches her time card, and walks down to the dressing room with her ass coaster (a blanket so her ass and pussy don't touch the stage) wrapped around her. She pulls off her wig in front of the mirror that takes up the upper half of a dressing room wall.

Her yellow Mohawk stays flat from hours of wearing her wig cap, which is just black pantyhose with the legs cut off. She pulls on her sweats and a purple hoodie, and by the time she's walked to the bus stop to go home, she's finished smoking her ceremonial post-work cigarette, filled mostly with Valerian root.

Being a naked girl is convenient for the cash, but passing for a boy makes the walk home easier.

o–o

Eris had snagged a custie into the VIP room. Despite the fancy name, it's a room just as dark as the single booths. The only differences are having a bit more room and touching is allowed.

There was a video screen playing porn in the room as well. Porn star moans filled the room: the sounds of fucking, grunts.

The man hesitated for a moment. "It's different without the glass."

"Yes. It's more private this way as well." Eris sauntered toward him and lightly slid her right leg between his dark jeans. He moaned.

She grabbed his hands from either side of him and guided them up and down her body. Her waist moved in insouciant circles above his lap. She turned around so her boobs were in his face, her hands on his shoulders. She turned around again and palmed his cock through his pants.

And, as she had done so many times before, she shoved a hand in his pocket and grabbed whatever was in it. In the same swift move, she stuck the items in a small hole in the black wall.

The man was oblivious and in sensory overload: the loud music, the girl on his lap, the porn screen in front of him. Two songs had played. "Thanks so much," she purred.

"It was worth every penny," he said, grinning.

"I'm just gonna clean up," she said gingerly, waiting to see what she had scored from his pocket.

He got up slowly and left the booth.

Eris looked through the hole in the wall. No cash: she never went for their wallets. She reached in and her hand returned with a glass vial; she held it carefully and illuminated it with the light from the porn screen.

The liquid inside the vial was colored a deep violet. It was small enough to clasp her fist around it on the way to the dressing room where she slipped it into her purse.

O─O

Done with work, she zipped up her gray hoodie and hopped into her baggy jeans. Washed her make-up off in the sink and replaced the heels with orange Converse.

Eris needed to make a stop in the city. Usually she suavely commandeered baggies of coke from custies' coat pockets to sell to glitter queens, gutter punks, yuppies, and other populations of dopaminergic dopesters. If nothing else, she knew she could sell it as a party favor at a college house.

But what the fuck was this purple shit? Eris couldn't get the answer downtown—she had learned that lesson, having once paid $60 for what ended up being over-the-counter Tylenol from a wrinkled man in a Chinatown alley.

She couldn't look online either. People would say it was just ink or bath salts or something stupid like that.

She opened up the vial and put it under her nose. She sniffed a little more. It wasn't a popper. Casually she looked around and took a tiny sip. If she died then at least the bus driver would notice. Eventually.

It tasted like nothing.

O─O

As a general rule, Eris always had a bruise some-where on her body.

Bruises the dark, rich color of blueberries bloomed up and down Eris' thighs. Not from falling on her heels—she never did that—but from skirting away from a bicyclist. Speeding down nameless streets on her scooter was one of Eris' favorite ways to pass midnight.

This morning, however, her skin was unmarked and flawless.

She hadn't slept. She had spent the night reading one of the many books thrown on her bed.

She tried to eat a bowl of brown sugar and maple syrup instant oatmeal. But she didn't have the saliva to even dissolve it. It didn't taste terrible, it was just a horrible texture. Slowly she tried to move it around her mouth until she just gave up and wiped it off her tongue into a trash can.

O–O

At 3 p.m., she walked on stage, legs shaking. A few custie windows were open and the three other girls were dancing for them. Eris tried to pace herself, just wiggling around and rubbing her hands up and down her waist, vaguely in tune with the music.

Then a window popped up for her. It was one of those guys that don't walk in, they're jogging. Already have their dick out. He looked angry. Eris looked him in the eye. She knew how to deal with aggressive types: simply own your sexuality. She channeled her inner sex kitten, slowly moved her body, tracing invisible lines on her skin. He was looking at her pussy, but as soon as he looked up into her eyes he came, and before Eris could roll her eyes and say, "Thank you, come again!" she felt a wave of energy come into her. It wasn't the anger he felt; it was pure energy.

With each new custie that came to her windows, it happened again. And again. Each custie gave her more energy. Each time a custie had an orgasm, it was as if she absorbed the energy he had just released. Soon enough, she had more energy than the other girls that were slowly getting tired from the shift. And her oatmeal was left untouched.

Eris caught on by the end of the shift that this wasn't a joke. The energy was able to be absorbed in her body now.

Even the square of glass made a perfect funnel for energy.

O–O

It wasn't long before the other girls caught on and wanted in. Eris still had the vial, and decided to get the most done in one night as she possibly could.

O–O

The room was dark velvet but the bathroom had only red lights, like the after hours of a butcher shop. Girls lined up in the bathroom and sat up on the counter. Legs draped over another. Each girl had another girl to find a vein, shoot it up, lick the tiny drop of blood, and kiss it back, metallic into her mouth.

○─○

This is when Eris kissed and fucked Astrid between the beds, side by side.

Or, when she could have. This is what desire feels like: black adrenaline slicked through a straw of molasses, corkscrews spinning into each inch of skin. It takes a lot and you still only get a little, but it's because what you wanted was to want more. No one craves satisfaction, that's far too scary to actually experience. Because when you get it, what's left? Nothing was fun until it ran through the full road of excess; nothing was fun until it wasn't fun anymore.

○─○

The girls who still had reflections had long gone to work at other clubs. The main stage, which was formally a wall-to-wall mirrored room, was remodeled. The mirrors were turned into video screens, giant and colored to give the girls a lighter, less dead appearance. The girls fixed the lighting so they looked utterly ethereal. Lights illuminated them from all angles like their skin was wrapped in Swarovski crystals. The girls ended up glowing a brilliant neon, as if the light was shining from them, not through them, which it actually was. They danced in black fishnets and tulle skirts. They had completely adapted.

○─○

Eris spun around, feeling weightless. Naked except for the small lavender undies with the crotch cut out for a makeshift skirt, a silver Saturn necklace, and black seven-and-a-half inch heels. She danced and the box cutter in her hand slid across the pale inner skin of her arm. A foamy line of liquid silver sizzled up, then faded onto her skin within seconds. She looked at herself, alone on stage, dancing on the faded red carpet.

Eris knew how she looked from every angle. She knew the places she could sit and look distorted in another mirror cubed to fit within the panels. From behind, the side, the front—even lying down she'd look up and see herself mixed in with the lights, distorted. She danced, spun around in the dizzying mindfuck of each of her selves dancing and spinning along with her, and not one of them was bleeding.

"What could hurt me?" she wondered.

She fell down, collapsing, arms between her legs, ass on the floor. She looked up into the lights on the ceiling, blinded by neon, and laughed.

O–O

Eris had since developed more rewarding hobbies and learned more exciting ways to waste time than masochistically fantasizing about Astrid. In one of the mirrors Eris saw a distorted view of Astrid. But it didn't hurt to look at her anymore.

Isn't that the best thing about being a vampire—to only need one thing? Obsession didn't hurt anymore: only hunger did.

Veins as electric as the neon city constellations surrounded Eris' flesh, lighting up the city streets when no cars with red and white lights sped through for hours.

Eris now mostly lived on blood. It wasn't too hard to find. But she still liked to feed off the custies' energy once in a while. It had been weeks since she had done so, and she was craving the seamless wave of power.

O–O

He walked in especially for Eris. The mirror rose up and the window was revealed.

She bent down on her elbows and knees, her ass in the air and her eyes right in front of his cock. "Come on my face," she purred, licking her fingers in her mouth, wide open and still shaking her ass.

He came when she smiled. A thunderbolt-for-spine kind of blackout orgasm. She didn't smile to show joy, but to show off her teeth. Cum dripped down on the glass. Eris was still looking at it when the man fainted: falling forward, sliding his face against the glass, wiping up some of his semen along the way down. She heard a thud.

The window stayed up for a few more precious minutes from the dollars he'd put in before.

When the next custie walked in, looking for an open booth, the passed-out pile of limp flesh was all he saw— that, and a group of giggling girls dressed all in lace, propped up on seven-and-a-half inch heels, magnificently illuminated.

WHY DOES THE
MANATEE SING?

AO-HUI LIN

The starlight fell through the water like pearls, disappearing into the murk a few handspans beneath the surface. Selene swam towards the light, flipping her tail to send out playful ripples behind her. The flash of iridescent scales, her gleaming breasts peeking through the waves, the hair floating behind her like lustrous seaweed, all were meant to draw the eye of the sailor, mesmerize him despite the frigid water surrounding him and the trembling in his arms as he tried to eke out another hour or two of life before the water took him.

Selene twisted, rolling like a dolphin, her gently rounded belly glistening as it broke the surface. Eyes closed, she hummed to herself, slicing through the water in ever tighter circles until the sailor could almost brush her skin with his water-withered fingers, if he were willing to let go of the plank to which he clung and reach out in a final suicidal lunge. Her humming rose in pitch, became a song that picked up in tempo and volume until he cried, "Stop!" and his hands left the wood which had kept him afloat. The water slipped into his mouth and the next word was a gurgle, and the one after was swallowed up completely by the sea.

Without opening her eyes, Selene sensed the movement of his downward fall and changed direction, swimming round and round his sinking body until the last of the bubbles trailed from his lips. She dove at his unconscious form and gathered him in her arms, kissing him hard enough to press his lips open and grind her teeth against his. As her tongue, impossibly long, slipped past his tonsils and down his throat, his arms and then his legs began to twitch in an epileptic dance.

His eyes flew open and his head jerked back, but her hands on either side of his face held his mouth to hers, preventing his escape. From deep in her belly she felt the baby stir, felt the egg sac as it shifted upward. The pressure of the fetus, which had weighed her down for months, pushing her internal organs aside to make room for itself, lifted from her abdomen and moved higher to press on her heart. For an instant she gasped as the pain came perilously close to breaking her; the baby had been too long inside and had gotten big, perhaps too big.

No, the pressure moved on, though it left a curious ache in her chest, and her throat opened wide to let her daughter-to-be pass into the sailor's mouth. Her tongue, that prehensile organ, kept the man's mouth from clamping down as the fetus slipped past his jaws and along his esophagus to lodge midway and burrow through flesh and cartilage into the spongy lungs beyond.

He remained locked in Selene's embrace through the night and into the day as her daughter-to-be made a home in her new father's body and taught it the way of living in the sea. And as the babe remade the father's body, she also remade his heart and his mind, binding them to her for the rest of his years. When at last the mermaid withdrew her tongue from inside him and let him go, his pulse beat with a sonorous rhythm, and his lungs, reduced in size but tripled in efficiency, separated oxygen from salt water with the same ease as any other denizen of the deep.

Most of her kind would have left him then to fend for himself, to find the company of other mermen who would teach him how to avoid the many ways that death could find him in his new world. And if one of those ways should find him before the mermen did, ah well, that was the way of the sea, wasn't it? There would always be more sailors and more whelplings, and that was the way of the sea as well.

But unlike her sisters, Selene fretted. She'd carried her daughter for so long—too long; she couldn't bear the thought that some random shark might rend the baby's new vessel to pieces, or that the once-a-man would chase the light upwards and blunder into the shallows where his lungs would burst.

When she tugged at him, he recoiled. Years with her own father had taught her the way to communicate with a once-a-man, the gestures and the mouthing of words that can't be heard, but her daughter's father seemed too distraught to decipher her meaning. The slap she gave him knocked his head to the side, and for a moment she worried that she'd damaged him, but he shook it off, his hair drifting across his face in tendrils, red as dulse leaf.

Pointing upward toward the murky glow of the sun on the surface, she watched him, waited for the hope to blossom on his face, waited for his inevitable attempt to swim toward the light as if it held some kind of salvation. When it came, she clamped her hands down on his shoulders and opened her mouth wide, showing him the barracuda teeth that could rend him into leavings for the pilot fish. Though she knew he couldn't understand it, she screamed in his face that sunlight would be death for him now. To him it must have seemed as if a sea monster had lurched at him; he cowered backward and urinated in terror. Selene reconsidered her approach.

Again she pointed upwards, and again his gaze followed her finger, and his lips moved in what she recognized to be the same litany her father had used many a time when she'd gotten into trouble. To her father it had been a call for courage, a wish for rescue, and an expression of paternal dismay. This time she used another gesture from so many years ago—the index finger pointed up, waggling back and forth in that way that her father had taught her meant "no."

It might have been relief at seeing the monster reduced once more to the maid, or the unexpected familiarity of the wagging finger, but the merman's eyes opened wide in astonishment and he gave out a bubble of laughter, which must have been so oddly silent to him. His frown returned, and he looked up again, the longing for escape plain in his eyes.

Abandoning communication, she hooked him under the arms. At first she thought she might simply lead him to a nearby colony of mermen, but the inefficient kick of his legs and flapping of his hands gave him less direction than driftwood and made her want to rage with frustration. He fought against her pull, but his muscles were still weak at this depth and she brushed aside his struggles, dragging him behind her the way a killer whale might drag a hapless seal. She was heartily sick of him by the time they reached the nearest nursery.

The grotto that served as home to this particular tribe lay in warm waters, a blue-green network of caves and crevices made for hiding and exploring. Clown fish lurked in beds of sea anemones, and inky octopuses pulsed in and out of their hiding places in the sand, hoping to snatch at unwary fingers and tails. She had grown into adulthood in this very colony, first carried within her father when she was no bigger than a polliwog, then clasped to his back or trailing behind him after her birth. Later it was she who had led and her father who had trailed, chasing after her and her friends as they tested out their fins in wild escapades, the way young mermaids are wont to do. The colony had not changed much; she saw the bulge of a young merman's belly, still ripe with child, saw the birthing scar that cut across another merman's diaphragm, his daughter's arms wrapped around his neck, saw the flash of pale mermen's legs as they swam clumsily after their giggling charges.

Now as she towed her unwilling burden into the

midst of all this activity, she was aware of the curious looks. She recognized no one and hadn't expected to; her father was long dead, and her friends, like her, scattered upon the deaths of their own fathers, but the feeling of being other, unwanted and unneeded, still surprised her.

Once a mermaid left a nursery colony, almost always upon the death of her father (such delicate things they were), she never returned. What was there to keep her, when the vast oceans called to her with the promise of everlasting youth in their depths? It was not in a mermaid's nature, nor in her interest, to hang about domestic confines.

Selene let her charge go, shoving him away with a kick of her tail and swimming out through the twists and turns of the grotto that she had learned as a child. Her last view of her daughter's vessel was his red hair disappearing into the gathering of mermen who'd come to initiate one of their own.

That should have been the end of it.

Selene had gone further than most of her sisters would have, delivering her daughter into the safety of the nursery, and now it was time to leave the child behind in the care of her father-to-be until she was old enough to join the sisterhood of mermaids. It was the time to taste the salt of warm waters, where giant oysters gave up their pearls and jellyfish clustered as close as bubbles, the time to swim north and tease the polar bears or south to sing to the penguins, to dive deep into the crushing darkness and, as mermaids must, drink of warm sulfur springs.

There was nothing to do here for her. She needed to go. She was expected to go. It would be deviant to stay. The vast ocean called to her and Selene turned and swam away, ignoring the odd little pang in her chest that had plagued her ever since her daughter-to-be had passed by it on her way to her new womb.

She swam for days, weeks, forcing herself into ever-widening arcs away from the nursery. She fought an invisible tether, one she'd never been aware of or even considered possible. In moments of distraction, she would find herself following currents that brought her back to the nursery, her head too crowded with memories to concentrate on where she was going.

While she slept, it seemed to her that slumber returned her to the state of infancy, once again curled up below her own father's sternum, impossibly fragile even as her body exerted its inexorable influence on her host. In her nightmares she saw her daughter as a twin, equally small and isolated, the two of them tied together by an unbreakable umbilical cord, and every cry made by one was echoed by the other.

Upon waking she would have the compulsion to check on her daughter just to reassure herself that all was well. Lurking at the edges of the colony, she would surreptitiously search for the red-haired merman, her eyes lingering on the pairs of mermen and their daughters, perfect microcosms of familial love. Here was a merman with long blond locks, his sleeping daughter nestled against the crook of his shoulder. There was another playing hide and seek, his daughter's mouth wide with laughter as he pretended to be unable to find her, both of them secure in the knowledge that she was never truly out of his sight.

Her stomach unsettled, Selene would linger until the red-haired man wandered into view, his belly distended, a slow-moving walrus of a creature without grace or ease. It may have been in the way his hands would spread over his abdomen, protecting the precious cargo inside, or the way his head would bend toward it, as if crooning to his daughter as she waited to emerge, but somehow, despite his clumsy bulk, he managed to exude an aura of lightness, of joy. It aroused in Selene a deep jealousy as she remembered the same euphoria, made within her by her daughter's too long stay, and the pain, real and yet so bittersweet, when the fetus had passed so close to Selene's heart. The emotion would drive her away, but always she would return a few days later for the same dance.

The day her daughter was born, Selene had been ready. She'd seen the signs in the red-haired merman's body, the thinning of the skin over bones, the rash where it had begun to separate just above the diaphragm, the way his rib cage rose and fell in quick flutters as the pain overtook him. At dusk, a few other mermen gathered around him, ready to ease her daughter's passage into the sea. As the egg sac pushed its way to the surface, a suppurating boil that pulsed yellow-white through the rash, one of the attending mermen used the edge of a coral knife to slash open the sac, spilling its contents into the water in a cloud of milky fluid.

Her daughter burst forth from the gash, and even from Selene's distance, she could see that the mergirl was all perfect jade hair, perfect button nose, perfect ten fingers, perfect tail fin. Without thinking, Selene swam forward, eager to hold and behold this delicate wonder, to sing to her in the way that mermaids sing to each other.

Too late she remembered the other mermen and the coral birthing knife. Too late did she realize that her presence was unheard of, unwelcome. A second slash of the knife and this time the water clouded red with her blood, swirling from a cut on her arm. She gasped, pulled back, showed her teeth in a snarl, but her fierce demeanor was no match for the collective presence of the mermen and their condemning glares. Selene swam away to hide and nurse her wound, which hurt far less than the ache of leaving her daughter.

If she'd gone to the sulfur springs at the very bottom of the deepest, weightiest part of the ocean, the cut would have healed completely in the ice-cold, poisoned heat, part of the strange transformations there that kept her kind young and beautiful. But the trip would have taken months, and the risk of forgetting herself, as sometimes happened in that place, was too great. So she stayed, hardly noticing the ugly dark scar on her arm as she continued to spy on her daughter.

The red-haired merman named the mergirl

Adelaide, a name Selene despised. She couldn't understand why her daughter was not named after the stars or the moon, as Selene had been, or after some other beautiful, ethereal thing of the sea. Adelaide was nothing but a collection of ugly syllables, cobbled together from the once-a-man's remembered language, meaningless. The merman couldn't even make the noises, just mouth the sounds and trust the connection between him and his daughter to convey its essence.

That connection between father and daughter ate at Selene; she couldn't let it go any more than a fish could let go of a hook. She wanted to snatch her daughter from the merman's arms and take his place at the other end of that link. It didn't work that way, and she knew it, but her rage at being left out consumed her, destroyed her ability to think rationally. As she ignored the imperatives of her kind, body followed mind; her complexion lost its luster as her features drooped and softened, and her hair floated away like clumps of rotten sea vegetables.

Again and again she would swim up to the pair as if she could inject herself into their bond by physical force. Again and again, the mermen would turn her back, lashing out at her with sharp-edged weapons and leaving shallow cuts along her body, warnings rather than woundings. Eventually she learned to keep her distance, tried to satisfy her longing for her daughter vicariously. The baby grew into a girl, the girl into an adolescent, while Selene watched hungrily.

Rarely, one of her sister mermaids wandered into the vicinity and became alarmed at her freakish behavior. Their horror at her incipient metamorphosis would move them to act, and Selene acquired new scars as mermaid talons dug into her, trying to drag her away. Selene always resisted. As her body became heavier and the flesh sagged and darkened, thickening into brown hide crisscrossed with marks, her sisters stopped trying to persuade her to leave, too revolted by what she'd become.

When Adelaide turned sixteen, her father died.

Freed from the one thing that kept her tied to the colony, she would now make her way into the endless ocean. Selene swam to meet her, but her daughter was too fast. Adelaide shot past her mother with only a glance at the hulking sad-eyed monster that had lurked at the borders of her world for as long as she could remember.

○─○

The moon gleams over glassy water, so still and calm that the ship could be floating in a sea of liquid starlight. From across the water reverberates a lowing sound, not quite a song and not quite a cry, yet equal parts melody and mourning. The sailor on watch brings the spyglass to his eyes to scan the ocean before him.

"What is it do you think you're looking for, then?" says a gruff voice behind him.

"Sir!" The sailor jumps a little to have the captain so unexpectedly close. "I was looking for mermaids, sir."

The captain snorts. "Is that what you think made that noise?" He points to a glistening brown lump breaking the surface of the water. "There's your mermaid, boy. A sea cow."

The shape rolls in the water, exposing a cross-hatch of scars along its nose and belly. The captain stalks off, muttering to himself about green boys believing in fairy tales.

The sailor doesn't have the nerve to say that he's grown up around sea cows all his life and knows their moos and chirps and squeaks as well as his own mother's voice, and he's sure he's never heard a sea cow sing before.

Kapras of Many Voices

Thoraiya Dyer

It was something Mother had given him.

He was barely older than me, even if he was bigger. Why hadn't she given me one, too? I turned it over in my child's hands. It was made of clay, shaped like a bird's head, with a mother-of-pearl disc pushed into one side and a circle of metallic gold pushed into the other side. Sheppan had hidden it away, but I'd found it.

It looked very old. I scratched at the edge of the gold circle, trying to see if I could peel off the gleaming, beaten leaf.

The door to the Tumble House opened behind me and the wind rushed in, carrying sticks, dead leaves and Sheppan. He smelled of human waste and sweat, having spent the morning laying sewer pipes in ditches.

I jumped. The thing slipped from my hands and cracked in half on the slate floor. For an instant, we both stared at it, horrified. Then,

"I'm going to kill you," he shouted.

I ran.

My feet pounded up the stairs. Sheppan's footsteps were not far behind. I dashed down the corridor to the head tumblewatcher's sleeping room, throwing open the shutters on her window. Outside, a macadamia tree promised protection. Sheppan was getting too heavy to climb into the topmost branches.

He hauled me back from the window, throwing me onto the floor. His hands closed around my throat. Through my fear, I noticed the smell of his sweat was changed.

"You smell like a man," I gasped.

Sheppan's pupils were dilated, his dark cheeks purple with rage.

"You broke it. You broke the only thing Mother ever gave me."

"She gives you everything!"

"No, she gives you everything! Maybe you've got a prick and balls but everyone says you'll be a woman. Mother loves you more because you'll be a woman and stay with her. I'll be a man and never see her again and you broke the amulet my father gave to her."

My vision was beginning to dim. I felt my lips move thickly but all I could hear was the sound of blood pulsing in my ears.

"If you hurt me, Mother will send you away."

Sheppan leaned back. Reluctantly, he peeled his big hands away from my neck. I took deep breaths.

"Go on and tell her, then, Kapras," he said. "Tell everyone. You'd like that. The sooner they send me away, the happier you'll be."

He was wrong. Sheppan had been half-strangling me, pushing me and striking me for years, but I'd never told anyone.

"I won't. I don't want you to go."

But my neck was really hurting. He'd bruised me. I saw regret in his eyes.

"I'm going to the Bath House," he said. "You stay here."

When I heard the front door slam, I made my way gingerly down to the entry hall where the broken amulet still lay, cracked cleanly through the bird's golden eye. I picked up the two halves and went to the town's utility garden in the fading light.

The clay didn't hold together with fig sap glue. Maybe it could only be fixed with clay. Sheppan's father had been from the clay carrier pack, but Sheppan was tall, strong and fast. Yawo, the head tumblewatcher, said he had the makings of a fine thunderbird herder.

I didn't know who my father had been. My birth mother died six months after I was born. Sheppan's mother, Breen, nursed both of us. We slept in her bed until we were both six years old. Then, it was time to go to the tumblewatchers and be assigned such children's tasks as fetching, fishcleaning and herbfinding.

We'd both howled for her for days. I smiled at the memory.

I tried a bit more glue, mixed with soil.

"Kapras," called Yawo's voice from the other side of the garden. "Is it you? Children are called to the Mating House."

That explained why there was no-one else about. With the new moon, the man-packs came into Windless. At dusk they were admitted to the waiting hall, the children pestering the men with questions about life outside the Circle. Later the children assisted with the choosing.

I held the two halves of the amulet helplessly up to Yawo.

"I broke it, Yawo. I don't even know what it is."

"It's a very old Shield of the Lady," Yawo said kindly, squatting beside me. "The Rimu Tribe, whose lands now lie beyond the wall, believed that the Lady could take the shape of a giant bird, with an eye of silver and an eye of gold. They said that when the Lady looked on us with her golden eye, it was sunlight, and when she looked on us with her silver eye, it was moonlight."

"Sheppan's father was from the Rimu Tribe?"

"It is one hundred years since the wall was built, Kapras. Perhaps Sheppan's grandmother or grandfather was born in the ancient home of the Rimu Tribe."

She touched my neck. I flinched.

"What happened?" she asked.

"I fell out of a tree."

Yawo shook her head knowingly.

"Sheppan will leave Windless whether you lie for him or not," she said. "We can't keep our brothers forever."

o–o

Are my people happy?

A strange question. What is more important, more happiness or less misery? There are rules that some do not wish to follow. We are not incapable of changing them. Indeed, the Traveller's wisdom changed almost every rule we have, save one.

The strong must live apart from the weak. The war-like must live apart from the peaceful. Only that way can diversity be maintained in such a small area as this island. As the population grows, the barriers must still be maintained. The Settians have a saying. Coconut fibre makes excellent rope but poor fishhooks. It means that no single plant is useful for every purpose.

And we do not know what skills we will need, when your kin, the invaders, come.

o–o

The Mating House was by the lake, at the opposite end of the Circle.

The town was still roughly circular, given that buildings could not be raised on water. Once, Yawo told us, Windless was a summer camp, a circle of tents on grass. Now the stone-cobbled streets radiated out from the senseslogic tower and its encircling utility garden like the white petals of a flannel flower.

I thought I could still smell Sheppan on my skin, but it was only the wind from the south, where all the human waste from the town was carried in copper pipes to a series of aeration ponds. By the time the turds reached the last pond, they were broken up and did not smell so bad; the man-pack called the mess collectors took the dirty water in skin bags on long handles over their shoulders and fertilised the sunberries on Howling Plain.

Yawo said that it was kinder to send the dim-witted and deformed boy-children to a pack of their own than to leave them as babies out in the snow as the Culwinnans did. But when the mess collectors came to the Mating House, it was always the House of Sated Hunger that they went to and not the House of Swelled Bellies. No woman would wish to bear a child of stupid, clumsy men. If a boy was sent to the mess collectors, he knew he would never be an ancestor.

I remembered Sheppan's father and the broken amulet, and shame hit me all over again.

"Go to the waiting hall, Kapras," Yawo said.

I trotted, bare-footed, to one of the back doors of the enormous waiting hall. It was a stone tower with thick walls. It had been built with secret watch-rooms and port-cullises over the entrance tunnel where the men must enter, single-file and naked. There were glass-floored apartments above the vast chamber of the hall itself, so that women could spy on the packs while they waited and children could be sent to select the men for the House of Swelled Bellies.

Sheppan was not among the children in the hall. I guessed he would be scrubbed and clean, standing in the holding arena, clutching with pride the eagle-spears, trousers, boots and feathered headdress of a thunderbird herder, pretending that the things belonged to him. I hated it in there. Fires roared in the hearths to keep the naked men comfortable; to a boy standing beside one, it was like being a spitted carcass on a feast day.

With the men unclothed, it remained possible to guess their packs of origin from their body shape, their scars, or the way they clustered together or confidently roamed about the hall. Sapling benders lived and worked so far from Windless that their language was difficult to understand; their bearded faces were roughened by wind and salt water and they rarely spoke, even to one another. Bloodbeaters, because they trafficked with the thunder-bird herders and the women's Circles so often, were more social. Heavily muscled in arms and shoulders, they sought out men from other packs whom they had known as children, exchanging gossip, clasping forearms in greeting. Pelroot planters were short, slight and sun-blackened, the older ones with crooked backs from bending over in the fields for most of their lives.

Ashan, leader of the thunderbird herders, towered over everyone else in the hall, his cheeks sandpaper-leaf smooth and his flanks lean. He demonstrated to a group of children the best way to settle a hood over the head of the three-metre Greater Thunderbird Hen.

Mother had all but promised that I would be marked a woman, despite my male anatomy, so I didn't feel the desperate curiosity that the other boy-children felt. There was no man-pack that I was destined for; no future hierarchy for me to ingratiate my way into. So I joined the crowd around Ashan to listen, though I'd heard his stories before.

Ashan was Mother's current favourite. She'd taken him to the House of Swelled Bellies at the last new moon, but at the full moon she had bled. I knew she intended to try again, though it was almost time for her to drink the brew and go to the House of Sated Hunger for good. A pregnancy could be dangerous for her. But she was a dancer and she said that Ashan danced when he walked. She said their child would be so exquisite, nobody would be able to look away.

"Once the bird is hooded," Ashan exclaimed, "she stops running. We take her blood to give to the beaters and she's free for another month, to eat sunberries and lay the occasional egg. They're enormous eggs, but the Greater Thunderbird isn't a very good egg-layer, not like the Culwinnan Thunderbird. We keep a balance of all three types in the herd."

Mother admitted that I was not as naturally graceful as Ashan, but that I would make a capable dancer if I worked very hard. I longed desperately to make her proud.

"The Lady's Prayer Thunderbird is no good for bleeding, and no good for eggs, but she defends the rest of the herd with her sharp crest and the hooked claws on her big toes. She keeps away the venomous opaline and the little striped liver-eater. The only predator we men must watch for is the giant eagle, called the screaming sun-shadow."

The children shivered with delight as Ashan spread his arms like wings.

"Her nest is safe from us in the mountains beyond the wall. She can carry away a grown man in her talons, more easily than she can carry a Thunderbird. She falls on the herd from directly into the sun. When I was a boy, new to the pack—"

Before he could finish his story, a bell clanged.

Sighing children withdrew. It was time to go up the spiral stairs to the women's apartments.

I found my mother being berated by Fiyr, Speaker of the Windless Circle.

"How dare you suggest that a Speaker be removed from her Circle?"

Mother bowed her head.

"I did not say that Timorv should be removed. Merely that her will might be circumvented in this case."

Timorv. They were talking about the northern town of Gednay, then. Timorv was Speaker for the Gednay Circle. I knew Timorv had sent messages to the other Circles instructing them to keep away from the fire-ravaged Island of Abru, where disease-carrying animals had escaped their pocket of isolation and now roamed all parts of the island.

Yet Mother had discovered from one of the Gednay dancers that Timorv secretly planned to send an expedition to Abru to recover whatever knowledge might have been saved within the senseslogic towers.

"Timorv speaks for her Circle. The Circle's will can never be circumvented," Fiyr said coldly. She stood with her fur-lined cloak wrapped tightly around her despite the ample warmth. She was old and frail and did not normally visit the Mating House.

"Then it is the Circle that acts arrogantly and above its station. The Gednay Circle has no right to recklessly decide on behalf of the entire Nation," Mother said, her voice low and angry, and Fiyr's knuckles whitened on the cloak hem.

"It is not the Gednay Circle that acts arrogantly and above its station, Breen. Kapras, child," Fiyr snapped, "bring Ashan the Thunderbird herder to the House of Sated Hunger. I will be waiting."

Fiyr swept away toward the connecting women's passageway.

The blood drained from my face. I dared not look at my mother.

Instead, I went to summon Ashan to the House where only infertile women could go. He would be humiliated and insulted once he realised where I was leading him. The fleshkins and notetakers in the senseslogic towers worked hard to develop a contraceptive brew that was not permanent, but so far they had failed. Only women who had taken the sterilising brew were allowed in the House of Sated Hunger. Mother would not see Ashan this mating season. It was petty.

Scowling, I returned to the waiting hall. Ashan smiled when he saw me heading straight towards him and the other Thunderbird herders raised a cheer and stamped their feet in approval that their leader was first chosen.

"Ashan," I said, "you are summoned to the House."

He came with an eager spring in his step.

O–O

You wish to know how our laws are changed.

A Circle of fifteen women rules each township, and their judgement is absolute. The leaders of each man-pack and each trade society have a right to be heard. Information can also be brought by any falsefinder, notetaker, joyspeaker, comprehender or fleshkin. Ordinary people who have ideas or complaints approach the leader of their man-pack or trade society and the item is put before the Circle.

These conversations between you and I?

I am the Speaker of my Circle. I am Kapras of Many Voices. It is for the good of Gednay that you are here. You come from the land of the invader, and we must learn as much about your people as we can.

But you are now also a marked man of the thunderbird herder man-pack. There are things I may tell you, now, that I could not tell you, before.

How is a new Speaker chosen?

She is selected by the rest of the Circle, from amongst themselves or from the women of the township, when the old Speaker dies or is pronounced unfit to rule by a full hand of joyspeakers or fleshkins.

o—o

When Sheppan learned of the insult our mother had endured, he took a handful of his faeces and smeared the name of Fiyr-With-A-Dry-Vagina on the east-facing wall of the senseslogic tower.

In the morning, he was summoned to a meeting of the Circle.

I crept with a few of Sheppan's giggling friends to the cleaning supplies room, which we children had free access to, directly beneath the meeting room. Long ago, we'd bored a tiny hole in the wooden floor so that we could eavesdrop on the Circle when it was decided that one of the boys was now ready to be sent to one or another of the packs. Four of us climbed up onto the cupboard to be closer to the hole.

Three tumblewatchers would present their recommendations to the Circle. In the end, the Speaker would offer two alternatives to the boy in question. I knew that to Sheppan there was no alternative. He'd whispered fiercely to me before answering the summons that he would be a Thunderbird herder or die trying.

"Sheppan is an athletic child. He is well-developed for his age," Yawo, the first tumblewatcher, pronounced.

"He is suited to the Thunderbird herder pack."

"Sheppan is a tireless runner and keen of eye," the second tumblewatcher said. "He is able to cross great distances bearing heavy loads. He is suited to the enlightener pack. He is suited to the Thunderbird herder pack."

On top of the cupboard in the cleaning supplies room, we grinned at one another.

"Sheppan does not shrink from difficult tasks," the third tumblewatcher said. "Whether he is set to dig ditches or carry messages, he works quickly and without complaint. He is suited to the veinmaker pack. He is suited to the Thunderbird herder pack."

There was a shuffle of feet as the tumblewatchers withdrew. They would not be party to the decision made by the Circle. Only the Circle members and the false-finders, enforcers of the decisions made by the Circle, remained.

Mother was a member of the Circle. I heard her voice next, proud and clear.

"Sheppan shows the attributes of a Thunderbird herder. I say he shall go to Tribute Flat."

Fiyr cleared her throat.

"Sheppan shows an aptitude for handling shit," she said. "That is the attribute of a mess collector. I say he shall go to the Ponds."

On top of the cupboard, we gaped at each other, stricken.

The next member of the Circle spoke grimly.

"Sheppan shows the attributes of a mess collector. I say he shall go to the Ponds."

Like an unfolding nightmare, one after the other the members of the Circle pronounced that Sheppan would go to the Ponds. Only three of the fifteen members said otherwise.

"It is decided, then," Fiyr said. "You will go to the Ponds. You will learn to control your inner beast under the instruction of the mess collectors."

"You have to offer me a choice," Sheppan said,

enraged.

"This boy offers violence towards my person," Fiyr thundered. "Falsefinders, you will remove him at once. Take him to the Ponds."

When he was gone, the members of the Circle filed out after him.

Only Mother was left behind, weeping.

O—O

Corruption?

It happens. There are narcissistic individuals so insecure they require the whole Tribe to unquestioningly mirror their views. The trait is more common among men. That does not mean it is exclusive to them. We are all human. It is to be guarded against, where possible.

Have I ever extracted unreasonable personal vengeance?

No, I do not believe so. Not unreasonable.

But you would have to put that question to my enemies.

O—O

The honour of dancing the Life of Breen fell to me.

I was only fifteen and new to the ranks of dancers, but it was my mother who was dead and nobody sought to deny me. Solemnly, cloaked in the colour of the white moth, Wayhi, I walked along the path that spiraled up the Hill of the Dead. Aven and Paige, who were my juniors, as new and nervous as I was, walked beside me.

The graveyard overlooked Lake Tribute and was crowned with a stand of white-blossomed elixirleaf that encircled a stage of polished white stone.

When my bare feet touched it, it was implicit that I stood on the bones of my ancestors. I was bound to represent only truth. The cold, sleek surface was a shock; a promise; a warning.

The mourners were already assembled. They watched intently from their places between the trees. Fiyr's face was expressionless.

I left my cloak at the edge of the circle and began to dance. Wanting her to be proud, I danced as though Mother was watching. I danced her extraordinary beauty as a child and the love she bestowed on her two children.

My limbs ached and I struggled to remain composed. Though my racing heart demanded rest, I moved into the second part of the drama I had composed.

Aven, who was so very tall for a woman, danced the part of Ashan the Thunderbird herder. With spears and feathers an extension of her long, languid body, we entangled and disentangled our limbs, sliding skin over skin. Such was the passion of her performance that I felt my organ struggle to rise, though my hidden, unwomanly parts were strapped firmly to my thigh beneath the short wrap that I wore. I flushed. It was not proper, to be aroused by a funeral rite.

Then Aven was torn away from me by Paige, who, with lines drawn on her cheeks and chalk to whiten her hair, danced the part of the crone.

I did not look at Fiyr, though I sensed displeasure radiating from her as the crone circled the weeping Breen, menacing like the screaming sunshadow. Breen sat in isolation, writing messages that she scattered to the four winds, but the crone intercepted every message and consigned it to the fire.

Then the crone had the permanent contraceptive brew served, unknowingly, to Breen. Though Breen spent every mating season for three years seeking to become pregnant to Ashan, she did not conceive. In the end, resigned to her fate, she took the brew again, not realising it was for the second time, and it killed her.

I shuddered and screamed at the centre of the stone circle. On the bones of the ancestors, I bore witness to the truth.

When it was finished, I lay on my back, staring at the sky.

I knew the performance was imperfect, but I had imbued it with every scrap of emotion in me.

"Stand up, Kapras," somebody said, and it was not Fiyr's voice, which I had dreaded, but instead the voice of a joyspeaker.

I did as I was bidden. The mourners should have bowed their heads and departed after the dance, but the tension was palpable. Nobody moved.

"Have you danced truth on the bones of your ancestors?"

"I have," I said, at the same time as Fiyr shrieked, "She has not!"

The boys who had been with me on top of the cupboard were long banished to the man-packs. The Circle was loyal to Fiyr. There was only Aven to vouch for me; Aven who had taken the brew to Breen while my mother's sense of smell was diminished by sickness; Aven who had smelled something unusual in the drink but had not been able to identify it until she became a woman and was offered the brew herself for the first time.

"We have danced the truth," Aven said, "to my eternal shame. It was Fiyr who gave me the brew to take to Breen, saying that it was to ease her fever. I was only a child at the time."

"Speaker Fiyr," the joyspeaker said with distaste, "though marked a woman, I say that you are a man."

Another joyspeaker stepped reluctantly forward.

"Speaker Fiyr, though marked a woman, I say also that you are a man."

My spirit soared as, one after another, a full hand of five joyspeakers announced that Fiyr was a man.

Yawo, who remained first tumblewatcher, spoke next with grim satisfaction.

"Fiyr is weak of body and slender of form. He is suited to the pelroot planter pack."

"No," Fiyr wheezed. "Be silent, Yawo, you simple-minded stitchbird. You cannot do this. I am no man. I am Speaker. It is the deceiver, Kapras, who is a man. Kapras, who has fooled you all!"

She crossed the stone circle, seizing the replica eagle

spear from Aven. I watched her—no, him—come, feeling triumphantly invulnerable. He could not strike me. If he did, he would only prove himself a man beyond a shadow of a doubt.

Before he could reach me, the falsefinders laid hands on him.

It did not require many hands to restrain him. He was an old man of seventy summers, all his authority stripped away forever.

○─○

My enemies?

My enemies have been women. My enemies have been men. They have been Culwinnans and they have been my own people. Always, always, my enemies have been the enemies of the Tribe, the enemies of our way of life or enemies of the progress we must make to keep ourselves safe from the invader.

Does that seem a contradiction? You recall the things you heard whispered by the man-pack. They wish to take the Thirteen Books for themselves. But did you know that here amongst the women there are those who would have me burn the Thirteen Books? They would have us return to our worship of the Lady, no matter that our numbers can no longer be sustained by hunter-gathering. There are even those who do not believe that there are any lands at all beyond the borders of the Four Nations.

You are the proof?

Well, you are proof and you are not. There are those who would believe you to be a puppet and a falsehood. If I should display you from town to town, pack to pack, there are others who remember the Culwinnan war who would wish you put to death for being an outsider, despite your adoption by the Tribe.

It is true you could be of value in uniting some of those outlying factions, either by your death or by your display as some kind of specimen.

I think your value is greater than that.

I have united people before. That is a skill that I possess. But to maintain the secret of our existence from within the ranks of the invader? I do not have that skill. You are suited to defend us from afar. There is no man-pack stationed beyond our borders, no Mohtian pack hidden amongst the invaders themselves. You will be the first. You may select others to aid you as you see fit.

A name?

You must choose one for yourself.

The keepers? That is a good name for a keeper of secrets.

You may leave me, now, leader of the keeper pack. I will send for you again in the morning.

○─○

At the next new moon, the man-packs came to Windless.

When all the suitable ancestors were chosen for the House of Swelled Bellies, there remained several hundred men behind. The mess collectors were, of course, among them, and Sheppan was among the mess collectors, permanently tainted, now, by the stench. I could not speak to him outside the House, for I was no longer a child to wander at will through the waiting hall. Nor was I a member of the Circle, to call men into my presence for questioning.

The hundreds of left-over men were herded into the House of Sated Hunger, and there I drew Sheppan out of the cushion-strewn copulation common into one of the private rooms. None of the watchful children who skirted the grunting, groaning groups and couples objected, for although Sheppan was my brother, we were not related by blood. Besides, I had only ever copulated with my fellow women before.

"I have no wish to copulate with you," Sheppan said, as was every man's right to say, though I had rarely heard it said, for they were entitled to no second selection.

I shook my head.

"It's Mother," I said. "She died at the full moon."

His still, subservient posture saddened me. I'd half expected him to throw me to the floor and strangle me for allowing our mother to come to harm.

At last, he looked up, smiled and nodded.

"I heard that you danced her life. I heard that is how Fiyr was discovered to be a man and sent to the pelroot planter pack, where he perished in the testing."

I took a deep breath.

"Sheppan, I begged the Circle to retract their judgement of you. I begged them to send you to the thunderbird herders where you belong, but they said that it was too late, that you had already been marked a man by the mess collectors and were beyond their control."

He took my hand and traced a symbol on my palm. It was a moment before I realised it was a bird head with a circle for an eye.

"Do you remember the amulet that you broke, Kapras?"

"Yes."

"I know, now, that I need no amulet to walk in the Lady's favour."

"The Lady?" I frowned. "But that is a children's story."

"It's no children's story. The mess collectors told me the truth. Though I did not have my own mother any more, they led me to The Mother. She watches over us and will gather us to her when we die. Breen is with her, now. Breen saw what you did, Kapras. The Lady saw it, too. She will welcome you, when the time comes."

It was not cold. I shivered.

o–o

Was Fiyr truly a man?

I do not think so. I have often thought on it. It was expedient for the joyspeakers to name her a man, for it saved them the trouble of naming her unfit for office as Speaker. They did not want her to remain in the town of Windless, creating divisions, reminding everyone of her crime, and perhaps it would have been crueller if she had remained.

Weakness is in all of us. Showing weakness did not make Fiyr a man. It is only when dissimilar people form a Circle, with their strengths overlapping, that they can be strong enough to survive.

GIRL OF PREY

TINA STARR

My husband helped people. Nobody had reason to suspect he was evil. Least of all me.

He pinpointed the gene that caused *fibrodysplasia ossificans progressiva*, a rare bone disease. He developed miracle drugs too, one of them to bypass the genetic trigger of excess bone growth that has all but eradicated osteoporosis. Unusual for a scientist, even a genius, to leave a well-funded research group and go independent, but I didn't realize that at the time.

He believed he could cure the world of what ailed it.

I believed in him.

It started when he took a contract job where I worked as a secretary, in one of Wright-Patterson Air Force Base's research buildings. Maddan, an Indian metallographer, quickly attached himself as a sort of a sidekick.

Those two were smarter than an airport hangar full of Ph.Ds. They worked with metal. Calcium's one kind of metal. They researched ways to create stronger ceramics and metal mixes for military use. Of course they didn't share all their discoveries. Certainly not with me.

They had grievances. Maddan's against the Pakistanis who'd shelled his childhood village. My husband's against privileged white men.

A driven man, my husband. Certain of his vision.

I prayed to forget my own day of reckoning: four

white male faces, three laughing and one distorted, a half-circle of horror.

I offered the scientists the child born of that nightmare. Two new, improved daddies for her: my husband and Maddan. For a while.

○─○

When the girl was seven, she jumped from a tall redwood at our cabin in Northern California. Though she fell more than a hundred feet, she didn't break a single bone. Gashed her forehead though. I spanked her before I stitched it. "Don't you ever climb trees again." Someone might see her. A neighbor. A satellite.

Her lower lip trembled but she didn't cry. "I thought I could fly. Daddy said I'm special."

Daddy was her name for my husband. It served. "There are different kinds of special."

"My bones."

"Your bones. The same condition that makes your neck stiffen up, and you can't raise your arms or walk sometimes? It makes your body different from other little girls'."

Her overlong neck let her head dip in a deep nod. Long legs too thin, little wisp-arms dangled down to her knees, slender fingers able to wrap themselves twice around her own neck, as now, a makeshift brace.

She turned toward me with a solemn expression. With only the bird books scattered about, without a TV or magazines or newspapers, Anya had little to compare herself to.

She would grow into our weapon.

So said my husband. He hadn't been wrong yet. Except about Maddan.

Anya extended her odd long legs as a sort of command. My hands automatically began to knead, smooth, massage her joints. How had she climbed so high with such limbs?

"Where's Daddy?"

I had my answer ready. "Working on a cure. When

you're all grown up, you'll take it."

"Why doesn't he visit anymore?"

My hands stopped, tightened. She made a small sound, and I stroked again. "He would if he could, sweetie." Truth. "His partner keeps him awfully busy helping others." Lie.

Maddan monitored their formerly joint endeavor the only way left to an ejected sidekick: He spied and plotted. He still kept our old home under surveillance.

"He wants you to grow up as fast as possible, so he can see you again." Truth again.

My hands tightened. Anya made a frustrated sound, extricating her legs from my harsh ministrations.

○–○

Bruises covered Anya's eyes and nose and cheek, blood oozing. Her lips bloomed lopsided and swollen. Dirt smudged her jeans and her ripped tee shirt. At fourteen, her breasts just tented it.

"Anya. What happened?" One of the bird books slipped from her damp fingers, and I clutched at her. "You've been off the property!"

"Only across the south road. I followed some quail, a momma bird and a line of little ones, into a meadow. There was a group of big kids."

I felt the core of me go cold. Others. Boys? "Did they hurt you? Did they touch you?" Unbidden, the images rose. Four white male faces, three laughing and one distorted.

Anya pulled from my tight grip, glared at me. She rubbed at her arms. "They didn't know what I was. I'm not 'special.' I'm ugly. They laughed."

Teasing? Was that all? Hope warred with fear. "You're not ugly. Everywhere, people are cruel. Especially white people. Anya, did they touch you?" I swallowed a moan, looking at the blood that tipped her long fingers.

"Ugly." Anya touched her face, her too-large eyes, her too-close nose and lips. She walked blood tracks over her too-broad forehead.

"You're still growing. Prejudiced idiots just say things, it means nothing."

"It doesn't mean nothing." Her eyes were cold and dark. "I didn't like it. Their bones broke." I stared, not comprehending, at her slow smile. "They screamed. They ran."

"But they hurt you." Her wounds, self-evident.

"Not as much as I hurt them."

Too soon, too risky, how could she have been so foolish! Dismay and fury swept through me, and I slapped her. Hard. Her body sank to the carpet in a tangle of limbs.

O—O

We had to leave the cabin. The mountain-bright stars overhead and the scent of autumn pine faded to dust and fertilizer and car exhaust.

Her limbs were disguised by baggy clothes, her fingers hidden in pockets. Her unusual face would have drawn stares but for the mask.

My idea, the mask. Lots of kids wore masks around Halloween.

There was even a Halloween party at a pizza chain off the interstate.

Truthfully, I felt guilty for striking her.

Anya stood off to the side and watched the other kids through her mask. She was just a thing. A tool. I felt foolish for my guilt.

I went to take her thin arm, lead her back to our vehicle.

Her body went rigid. She radiated attentiveness as her gaze locked on a little boy, crying and reaching for his toy. Two older boys kept it from his grasping hands.

I heard Anya's voice, puzzled. "He's not ugly. Why do they prey on him? He's not fighting back. Why?"

She slipped from me. I could see the whites of her eyes at the outer edges of the mask holes before she rushed them, plucking the toy from midair. She held it out. When the bully reached for it, her much-longer arm held it far above his head. He jumped for it. Then, perhaps mistaking her for an adult though she was their own age, the boys slunk away. They could have hurt her.

Anya knelt to give the toy to the boy. The two exchanged soft words before I pulled her away. People were beginning to stare. They always did when black kids played with white ones. Anya couldn't know.

"Did the little boy thank you?" We'd been safely on the road for some time. Her silence taunted me.

She still wore her mask. I gripped the steering wheel. Part of me wanted to explain why what she'd done was so wrong. And on which side she should be.

Part of me wanted to hug her, squeeze the evil away. Start anew.

Foolish. Weak. My voice sounded harsh in the small car. "Well, did he thank you, at least?"

She finally broke her silence. "What do you care? You didn't even want me to help him."

"Don't get smart with me, young lady. You have to be careful."

"Yeah, because I'm special," Anya sneered. "Well, you know what? I don't like predators. I care about doing the right thing, instead of just talking about it."

Appalled, I put down my first urge to backhand her. She might just hit back. She was getting stronger. "You don't know what you're talking about."

"Whose fault is that?"

The rest of the trip back east to my husband's alternate shelter, a small rental house, passed in stubborn silence. The unpleasant atmosphere reminded me again of certain hard truths. I hadn't wanted her then. I didn't want to be close to her now. She was a symbol, a weapon. Nothing more.

Her rebellion couldn't continue.

The first night at our destination, while she slept, I carried her lightweight form down to the basement and handcuffed each of her thin wrists to a long, heavy length of chain.

I left her the mask.

She didn't have to wear it, but she did.

For the next three years she wore it.

It hid her face, concealed her expression. I could see her eyeballs move as she tracked me when I entered to feed her or to empty her waste containers.

It wasn't personal, I explained. I couldn't let her hurt herself or others with her disobedience, could I? She was meant for great things. Her father would be so proud of how she'd grown up when he gave her the cure.

Her silence rebuffed.

Anya finished growing, wordless.

In addition to arm muscle gained from lifting those heavy chains, Anya's legs became more shapely. Her slender form filled out beautifully. I tried a few times to look behind the mask at her features, but she always slapped my hands and jumped away.

O–O

"When can I take the cure?"

At her voice, I turned to see she'd taken the mask off.

I dropped her bowl of cereal.

She didn't look like me. Thank God she didn't.

Her paler features had grown into a striking aesthetic balance. Her forehead sloped up and back just enough to set off hair grown long, and braided. Her brows, cheeks, nose, lips, all normal. The whole was even lovely. Her lips widened into a small smile. Her eyes carried a coldness that chilled.

At seventeen, curled sinuously in a ball as if I were a lover come to visit rather than her mother, her adulthood was for the first time evident.

"Anya." I wanted to sit with her. Beg her forgiveness. Set us both free.

"I'm ready now, don't you think? All grown up. All ready for Daddy's cure."

Her voice, so lovely. So resonant with venom.

I cleaned up the granola mess to hide my relief. I'd

almost weakened. My part in this was almost done, and good luck to my husband with his.

o—o

She was willing to ride in the trunk to finally see her daddy. She kept her mask on. I was glad.

Prepared with the windshield sticker to get me through the base's security checkpoint, I felt a prickling of excitement at the familiar sights and smells. I carefully kept to the speed limit driving across Wright-Patterson's vast, yellowing grass fields.

Only one other car had turned off the main route that encircled the base. I slowed further, turned onto an older access road cutting through low-rolling hills dotted with countless prairie-dog holes.

So did the other driver. Then I knew. Seventeen years, and Maddan still vigilant! I cursed him for being as obsessive as my husband.

I made an abrupt right turn, hearing the thump in the trunk as Anya crashed against metal. I hit the gas, made a sharp left turn. Another thump. Anya would be furious.

I whipped across a parking lot, over a curb, and onto a concealed road behind an administrative outpost.

The road had speed bumps.

Thump thump thump.

I shook my head, heading back toward the cluster of research buildings.

When I opened the hatch, Anya leapt out with a screech.

"Behave yourself!" I commanded, backing up hastily. "We're here! Maddan was following us. Back off, damn it, we're here."

Her hands, hooked into talons, sank trembling to her sides. "Maddan?"

"Maddan's a very greedy Indian man." I hurried her inside the old, putty-colored building with its prison-like milky windows.

I rushed her down plain hallways dotted with camouflage-wearing air force lieutenants and captains, too quickly for them to do more than stare in surprise at one middle-aged black woman and her slender, mask-wearing charge. "Maddan ruined everything," I told her. "He's the reason we had to hide. Your daddy had a more important mission than that man's."

"Mission?"

I felt a sudden lightweight drag throwing off my balance. I regretted my words. It was my husband's place to explain. We'd agreed.

She'd dug in her heels, but it only slowed me a little. I simply skidded her along the shiny vinyl floor. "Will you come on?" I hissed. Then, "Don't you want the cure?" She stopped resisting.

His small corner office smelled of mildew. My husband leapt to his feet, knocking his chair over with a clatter. "Were you followed?" He touched Anya, peering underneath her mask, feeling her limbs, measuring the circumference of her skull, lifting her up and setting her back down before examining me. "She's exactly as you described." His welcoming smile seduced me anew, and I basked in his approval. "So special," he observed of her, an endearment. I felt proud... but oddly uncertain. Would it be worth it? I'd sacrificed nearly two decades and my only child.

Where had that thought come from?

I shook my head to clear it. "Maddan," I remembered. "He'll be coming."

He nodded, touched Anya's mask thoughtfully. "A mask. It's ironic. I've another for you, built of a new metal matrix composite."

I could see her outrage in her the way she backed away from both of us. "To hide my face? In case I turned out ugly like this?" As she said it, she ripped off her mask and fixed her cold gaze on his.

When he flinched, only at her abrupt movement, her cruel smile appeared. "That's what I thought. Ugly. Where's the cure, old man?"

Anya thought she was ugly! My mind reeled. I'm ashamed now that part of me calculated how that inform-ation could best be used to manipulate her. Even then I could see our control over her shrinking.

My husband didn't see it yet, I could tell. His increasingly familiar face suddenly looked avaricious, and older than our years apart could account for. The white-ness of his hair seemed a tragedy. I longed to hold him again, to pretend him kindly.

But Maddan threatened. And did I really want all the sacrifice to be for nothing?

I steeled myself. "The research lab," I suggested. "Finish this."

"Everything's here." My husband seemed nearly manic with anticipation as he spun the lock to the free-standing metal cabinet. "Based on the measurements and photographs you've sent, I've customized remarkable equipment."

He spoke to Anya in his lecturing tone. "You'll trust me. It will take time, I realize, but you'll thank me when you see what I've made possible. You are the first. Your modified bone cells, specifically designed to behave as a metal, will enable us to change the world. End injustice. Eradicate racism. Some men and women are redeemable, but others, others like Maddan, are quite simply not. Will-fully ignorant. The world is full of irrational hate. Even secluded as you were, I'm sure you've encountered racism." At her blank look, he explained. "Racism. A belief that humans can be separated into groups based on physical attributes, determining cultural or individual achieve-ment. Being discriminated against because of the color of your skin."

Anya stared at him as if he spoke another language.

"Racism? Prejudice? Lord, you have been sheltered."

Concern chilled me. "She's had little exposure to the world. She's been told only what we'd discussed. About her condition. About the cure." My husband knew that. Why was he rushing her lessons? I'd been accused of doing something wrong. I hadn't done anything wrong. Had I?

"Yes, the cure..."

"Yes, the cure, damn it!"

"Anya!" I scolded.

"First things first." He pulled four packages from the cabinet, three bulky, and one small and thin. "A vest." A matte metal vest worked artfully with curved engravings, balanced on one of his fingers to demonstrate its lightness. "Indestructible. Put it on. Go on," he insisted more sternly when she only looked at him with rebellion in her eyes.

"Good girl. And to replace that child's plastic mask, this half-mask. It's a hawk. Striking! Not only will it hide your features, it's made of the same indestructible metal. Now what?"

"Nothing," she muttered, shoving the mask on with such force she must've hurt her skin.

"Next, a weapon. Your matured bones and their surrounding soft structures give you strength and resilience, but when it comes to punishing the wicked, you'll want to use this lightweight dagger. Here's its sheath. No, it straps onto your leg. There you go. Patience! We're nearly done."

Perhaps in sympathy with Anya's distress and resentment, my anxiety grew. I understood the necessity of it all, but the implementation felt wrong. The whole affair made me uneasy. I again told myself I'd sacrificed too much to let doubts and fears ruin the moment. I made myself remember those four white male faces.

He shook open the largest package. Even knowing what it had to be, I sucked in my breath at the sight.

He attached the wings to the top of the vest garment already belted around her torso. They fell with such smooth-hinged speed that they almost looked liquid: two metal wings hanging long and magnificent. Each the same color of matte metal, the wings displayed a loving attention to detail on each square inch. Every metal feather was a little masterpiece.

Anya seemed a creature from another world as my husband explained the snapping arm movement necessary to lock the wings open. I could see her lips below the small hawk beak of the mask, compressed, controlled. I wondered what she thought. I should have known what she thought. I was her mother.

"We have to go outside to test the wings," my husband said, pride in his voice. "My calculations have them aerodynamically functional based on Anya's weight and strength, even without the aid of wind. We—" He stopped, his skin turning gray. "He's here. Go outside."

I heard him then. Footsteps, running. Maddan.

"Go! Go now!"

I dragged a stubbornly slow Anya. Down one hallway, then another, keeping a corner always between Maddan's gaze and our escape. The three of us weren't as fast as Maddan alone. By the time I punched open one of the double doors to the south parking lot, he'd gained on us enough that I could see the sweat making his bald head shine.

I leaned on the door to make it close faster, then braced my body against it. My husband did too. When Maddan slammed against it, it shoved open only inches, then sank shut again.

Maddan spoke through it. "You will not get away with this." His voice sputtered, choked, unable to express his rage. "I will not let you." The door bowed open again as he shoved his body against it. "You are a thief and a cheat. You, who hates injustice. A cheating nigger."

My husband and I exchanged twin grimaces. "Anya," he called.

"What." She kept a sizable distance from us, but hadn't run away. Her wings swayed with her steps. She still sought the cure.

"It's time. This man—" Maddan rammed the door again, as if on cue. My husband grunted, lowered his voice to a tone of command. "Anya, he'll never stop hunting you. And he'll kill us. You heard him. He's a racist. Use your equipment; kill him. I designed you for this very purpose. No, don't look at your mother."

I made myself nod. I wanted to yell to her: run, fly! Instead I told her, "Anya, this is what it's all been for. This is what we want."

Anya considered us. "No."

"Yes," my husband corrected. "You want the cure, don't you?"

I could see the way she inhaled sharply, as if struck. "Why are you doing this?" she asked, her voice cracking.

The door crashed open, knocking me sprawling. Maddan shoved through, charging Anya. "You! You, do not listen to him. He lies. Do not—"

With a quick sidestep and a little jump that lifted her lightweight body off the ground as if she were one of the birds she'd once studied, Anya was behind the man with a waterfall tinkle of metal feathers. Her dagger rested against his throat.

Maddan cringed. He hyperventilated, tried to pull away from her. "No. Please. They are using you. Can you not see that?"

Anya's voice resonated with anguish when she spoke to my husband. "Then you'll give me the cure?"

"Then you'll have it."

She pinned him with a glittering gaze. "You promise?"

"I promise."

With a keening wail, Anya yanked the blade across Maddan's throat. The finely honed edge cut down to bone, then through it, so that Maddan's head tilted to the side as if he had her old problem of a too-thin neck and couldn't manage to hold up his head. Blood spurted.

She let him crumple to bleed on the sun-warmed pavement.

She panted, her mouth slightly open in a shape of disgust and horror. And with that, I knew her again. I knew what it meant that her fingers interlaced around her own throat, a makeshift and no-longer-needed brace. I felt her horror and her disgust, rose to my feet and would have gone to her to offer a mother's comfort.

She turned to my husband instead. "Give it to me."

"You have it."

Her fingers left her throat, and her head cocked slightly. With the mask it gave her a very birdlike mannerism.

She approached him. "Give it to me. Now. Now. You promised. Haven't I earned it?" Her voice sounded thick with tears.

Remorse coursed through my body, years' worth, weakening my knees until I had to clutch the edge of the building to keep upright.

What had I done? Anya never cried, not even as a small child.

She looked from him to Maddan's body, and back to him, like a hypnotized animal.

I heard a shocked gasp, and saw an intern in the doorway holding a hand over her mouth, and a scientist punching numbers into his cell phone, his gaze fixed on Anya's metallic splendor.

My husband's voice grated my nerves, shattered my spirit. "Anya, my dear girl. You have the cure for what ails the whole world. You already possess it. You are it. Where there's hatred and injustice, where evildoers reign, you'll descend from the sky like God's own avenging angel."

As I watched Anya, witnessed her strength and her dismay, my faith in my husband evaporated.

Hope vanished. The chasm devoured, leaving me hollow. It had been for nothing. I'd suffered for nothing and created nothing but suffering. If I'd had more than an empty shell of self to give Anya, in that moment I would have given it all.

I think I'm the only one who heard the wounded-animal sound that escaped with her breaths.

But she sheathed her blade. She approached him. "You made me. I'm your angel."

He beamed at her, touched her mask. "I'm so proud of you."

Anya killed him with her bare hands. I didn't try to

stop her. The snap of his cervical vertebra made me blink, only.

She just looked at me.

She spread her new wings and ran into Ohio's strong afternoon wind. Her slender, dusky body lifted, the matte metal of her half-mask and chest guard not as vibrant as her gleaming skin, feet together and pointed. Her wings tilted, caught the updraft, thrust her high.

With a bone-chilling scream of defiance she announced her freedom and promised vengeance.

My husband helped people and nobody had reason to suspect he was evil. Least of all me.

But now whenever a cloud crosses the sun, I despair.

CARYATID AND DOG

DOUGLAS J. OGUREK

"On that day you will realize that I am in my Father, and you are in me, and I in you."—John 14:20

The pool is complete, and I remain motionless. For the first time, the sculptor of lizards has lied to me.

The pool reflects the purple and green orbs that move through the Grape Stem building. How blatantly those orbs contrast with the misery beneath me.

Even if they could see over the wall that bars them from the HAV Region, these derelicts, bound by their addictions and their histories, would not care about the Grape Stem building, or the reflecting pool.

Distractedly the lizard sculptor, clutching his dovence slab and terrarium, wanders into the dilapidated square. The dog he calls Girly, her muscles rippling, lumbers after him.

The derelicts stir. Their eyes glisten with disappointment, and the gray of their skin reveals their addictions to the padlock drug.

Girly sits by my sandals. She smells and listens, and watches these defeated men as if they had some significance.

Though they urinate on the folds of my robe, and they vomit on my sandals, I remain. Though they hurl at me the receptacles of the fluids that control them, I remain.

The sculptor sets his slab and terrarium on a concrete platform where technologies once glimmered, and musicians once roared. Girly goes to him. He rubs her belly, and her muscles swell as she stretches and grunts.

Havguards, their lashes dangling severely from their hips, hover above the wall, beyond which a breeze quivers the creeping purple and green reflections.

When construction of the pool began three months ago, the sculptor touched my feet. His lips did not move, but I heard him. "When the pool is complete, you will obtain mobility. You will have one minute to leave this place."

Girly trots around the square. Some of the derelicts pet her, some growl. Some ignore her and talk to themselves. Some scream at her, or throw things at her.

The sculptor looks up at me, squints, and then nods.

Why does he keep returning? Why go through all the effort to give these derelicts such a transient experience?

The derelict with the reptilian tattoo on his neck inhales from his padlock-shaped instrument. He is the grayest of them. Perhaps he would believe in a sentient caryatid.

Two havguards descend from the wall, then land in the plaza. They've come to see his lizards.

Beyond the wall glows the one glass tube of the Grape Stem building that I can see. Lavishly the green and purple orbs waft within it. What is that building's function? Impress, and make money, probably.

If I had motion, I would leave. I would scale that wall. Instead, I remain. For two hundred years, I have remained, bearing this roof, and watching the area below me trans-form from a nucleus of knowledge and technology to a hub in which musicians reached the apex of power and beauty, and then devolve into this den of iniquity.

The sculptor sets up the small canopy around his display, and the derelicts start to gather.

The one with the reptilian tattoo shuffles up to Girly. Her tail resembles the hair of the musicians who once galvanized the square. They played powerfully, slowly, and they played majestically, and mournfully. Guitars, tuned low, churned and entranced. Singers roared with the power of creatures that could not fit beneath this roof.

Now there is no music. The derelict offers Girly something in a bag. She sniffs it. He cuffs her and she yelps. He smiles. Briefly.

Long before these useless men were born, I had a use. Now I do not. He lied to me.

One of the havguards swipes at a fly then looks up at me. "She's too beautiful to be wasted here with these nothings." The other agrees. "They should refurbish her, move her to the HAV Region." There, the green and purple orbs gleam. Here heap the odors of urine and sweat and surrender.

Ten derelicts shuffle and twitch and sway around the sculptor's makeshift tent. The one with the tattoo remains alone, and picks at his gray hands.

Girly has returned to my feet. Her coat shines potently. When the sculptor first granted me sentience two centuries ago, my own dovence shone, and I stood at the center of the Digiagora.

The havguard swipes again. He takes off his lash. "End fly." The weapon lunges out of his hand, pulls back, and then snaps forward. It falls on the concrete. The havguard no longer swipes.

One of the derelicts slurs, "He almost ready."

The havguards join the group. The one has forgotten to retrieve his lash.

The grayest derelict ignores the activity. He screams and lunges at Girly. She patters away, but continues to show interest in him. I wish I could tell her what I've learned after two centuries of observation: that these humans, despite all their ideals, are incapable of a selfless act.

The sculptor removes the canvas. From the shards and the stains and the stagnation, laughter erupts. The havguards laugh, and the derelicts laugh. They nod at one another, and laugh together.

Girly wags her tail, circulates among the observers. Once this square was as vigorous as her body.

This time, he has the lizards posed as bakers on the dovence slab. Since he granted me sentience, he's had them pose as waiters and fishermen, farmers and tech scholars. Even as musicians. Every time he unveils his lizards, his audience laughs.

The grayest derelict approaches the niche with the forgotten lash.

The lizards wear white aprons and floppy hats. One holds a tiny rolling pin. Another holds a wafer-size tray with something that looks like bread. They give the sculptor so little resistance.

How long will I remain here, and bear this roof for those who have elected to squander the gift of mobility?

The group starts to disassemble. Soon they will return to their recesses, where they will sleep and scrounge, and squabble. Scream and sleep.

The derelict with the reptilian tattoo picks up the lash. He brings the weapon to his cheek and watches the sculptor.

The sculptor talks to the havguards, while his lizards remain motionless. I have seen him pet them, and feed them. But shouldn't they want to explore the crevices, frolic in the tufts of vegetation? Climb the wall?

The derelict conceals the lash, stumbles toward the sculptor. The creature on his tattoo flicks a forked tongue, and his skin resembles stone. It is hard to feel anything for stone. He probably is not aware that the pulsing purple and green orbs exist.

When this was The Maiden's Lair, and I radiated at its core, the lizard sculptor promised me the ability to feel and smell. Then the musicians came, and when they played, my skin tingled imperially, and I could smell the strength, belief, and technical prowess that clutched the square.

The grayest derelict mumbles, "End lizard" then releases the lash. The weapon hovers, and the havguard who left it yells, "No."

But the lash does not attack the sculptor's lizards. Instead, it draws back, then slashes. At the derelict's neck. At his reptilian tattoo. He jerks back, brings his hand to his bleeding neck.

Girly charges toward him. The lash draws back again, and she leaps. Her blocky head rises to the derelict's neck. Just before the lash reaches the derelict's neck, Girly bites it.

As Girly descends, the lash jerks beside her and she yelps. She crashes onto the concrete. The lash falls beside her, twitches, and then stops moving.

Girly remains on her side.

The sculptor kneels beside her. "Girly, you saved him. Good good girl."

She breathes quickly, and blood crawls from beneath her.

The derelict responsible—his neck has stopped bleeding—backs into a dark corner.

Girly's breathing slows, and the sculptor strokes her chest. A havguard says, "How the hell?"

Girly begins to make deep grating sounds.

The others gather around the sculptor and his dog. I feel my arm move.

The blood expands, and the grating grows louder, and deeper.

The sculptor strokes her chest. Her eyes are open, and she begins to wheeze. I bend my right knee. The blood reaches the sculptor's feet. Girly inhales deeply, and then, for the last time, exhales.

The sculptor falls back on his hands. "That's my girl. That's my girl."

He puts his arm over his face, and weeps. I twist.

Stumblingly a derelict with brown hands approaches the sculptor, then crouches beside him. The sculptor, surrounded by blood, rubs his face, looks up at me. The pool is complete.

I bend my legs.

The green and purple orbs blaze. The derelict puts his brown hand on the sculptor's back.

I lift my foot from the pedestal. There is a scent. Something sweet, and a bird flits from under the roof. Perhaps for Girly, gray glowed just as vividly as purple and green.

I return my foot to the pedestal.

MAP REF. -4.296° N 239.193° E

ZACHARY JERNIGAN

2117: Bellona Settlement, Mars

"Alice, why do you always stare out the window when we make love?"

My fingertip paused, poised atop Joanna's left nipple. "I do?"

"Yes, you do."

"Hm," I murmured, incurious. My fingertip resumed its idle tracing of her breast. After a moment I answered, "I don't know."

A few minutes passed. Joanna asked another question: "When will you go out again?"

My fingertip had descended to her left shoulder. "Two days—seven?" I shrugged. "No more than two weeks, though."

"Oh, that's right. The lottery's tomorrow, isn't it?"

The fine hair on her forearm stood up as I traced the vein in her bicep.

"That tickles."

"I know."

"This time will make it thirty-seven, right?"

My fingertip made the short hop from her hand to her stomach. I nodded.

"Do you ever get scared?"

"No," I said, meaning it. "I know the territory pretty well."

"I bet."

Softly, my fingertip moved over the fine blond down on her stomach.

Outside, a dust devil kicked a few million particles of Martian sand against the window above Joanna's bed. The room darkened fractionally.

"Is it ever strong enough to knock a person down?" she asked.

"No. The atmosphere's too thin."

"Oh. I guess I knew that."

I smiled. "Then why ask?"

"I'm about to fall asleep, and you're so quiet."

I didn't answer. My fingertip was circling her bellybutton.

"Alice?"

"Hm?"

"Do you have a favorite place?" I felt Joanna's head shift position on the pillow. "It's on Arsia, isn't it?"

I looked out the window, too, at the fractured slope of the dead volcano, its summit lost over the horizon. "Yes. It's on Arsia."

"You've been there more than once?"

My fingertip moved slowly over her hipbone. I shook my head.

"Do you want to go back?"

"Very much," I admitted.

"What is it?"

I tore my gaze from the window, and stared at the tight, bare cleft between Joanna's legs. My fingertip made a short trip: a half circle from hipbone to mons pubis. "A cave."

"A cave? Where are there caves on Mars?"

I resisted the urge to stare out the window again. "On Arsia. Quite a few."

Joanna's head shifted again—a pointless gesture,

lying down. She couldn't see anything but rusty sky. "There are caves inside the mountain? Where?"

It would be useless to point. "On her flanks. Seven of them."

My fingertip delicately slid over her lips. She breathed in softly at the contact, shifted her hips very slightly.

"Mmm. Ah. A real cave you can walk in?"

I pressed very lightly, the merest suggestion of entry. "Are you sure you want to talk about caves, Joanna?"

"No. Ah. No, no... I'm not. Oh, yes—"

Angling her hips forward, she flexed around my finger as I pushed inside. I shifted my body down a little to get better leverage, slipped a second finger in, and began curling and uncurling my fingers against the roof of her vagina. She moaned rhythmically, rocking into my thrusts.

When her breathing shifted suddenly, I pressed the pad of my thumb firmly against her clitoris.

She was quiet. She always was.

I reassumed my position, head propped on my right hand.

Outside, the dust had settled. The room's interior was once again filled with dusk's diffuse light. Joanna's pale skin seemed to glow from inside, the color of Mars' red dust.

"You looked outside again," she said.

"I did?"

"Not as much as usual, but then again, I told you about it. You really don't remember looking outside?"

I didn't. "Sure I do. It's beautiful."

Joanna huffed. "You think so? I know you do. I just don't agree. To me, it's only barren redness everywhere. It makes the Atacama look like an oasis."

I scratched the inside of my thigh. She had a point.

"What about your cave, though, Alice? Was it different?"

"Not really," I answered. "It's just darker, with a steadier temperature."

"You can just walk into it?"

I peered outside, at the southern slopes of Arsia; her huge, cracked flank. The sun wasn't visible, but it cast long shadows across the Daedalla. "No. You have to rappel eighty-two meters to the floor, and from there you can walk a ways underground."

"Wow. You led?"

I nodded.

"Who was with you?"

"McKuen, Foster, and Goula."

"Meatheads," she mumbled. "There was no trouble, though?"

"None."

"What was so hot about this cave?"

I thought of our four lights illuminating the darkness—immense cones of bluish white, searching this way and that, dimly illuminating the tiny suited forms behind; how the dust deposited on the floor only extended ten meters into the cave itself; the oddly ribbed interior; the chatter of the men. "Nothing, really."

"Then why is it your favorite place you've explored?"

"I was the first one there, I guess."

"That's it?"

"Sure. That means a lot to me—I own it, in a way."

I felt her nod again. "That makes sense, I think. Did you get to name it?"

"No. It was discovered and named a long time ago."

At the end of the cave, I'd found a roughly circular opening in the floor, perhaps three meters across. When I shined my light into it, a short, curving passage, maybe two meters long, was illuminated. Beyond that was darkness, and no matter how I angled or focused my beam, nothing more could be illuminated. Using the tightest focus, the light beam had extended nearly three kilometers into the cavity before it was swallowed by the darkness.

"What is its name?"

"Chloë."

"Chloë?" Joanna laughed. "You named my *dildo*

after your cave?"

I smiled but didn't respond, recalling the nearly instinctual way I'd lied to McKuen and the other men, telling them I'd found nothing unusual. I knew it was a foolish thing to do; though we'd been having trouble communicating with Bellona since entering the cave, undoubtedly someone had been watching the feed from our helmet cams.

"That's cute, Alice. Will anyone ever go back?"

I placed my hand on her hip. "I don't see why anyone would."

"Why? Caves aren't common on Mars, are they?"

I shook my head.

"Then why wouldn't anyone go back?" she asked.

"There was nothing there. We took the measurements and got out. Mission accomplished."

I'd checked as soon as we got back to base, curious over the lack of questions regarding the cavity—surely, if someone had seen my footage, I would've been contacted. Amazingly, it hadn't been watched.

I leaned forward and kissed Joanna's right nipple, bit it lightly.

"Oh! Why don't you request to go there again?"

I shook my head, sliding her erect nipple between my teeth.

"Why not?"

I sighed, and lifted my head to meet her eyes. "Why are we talking about this?"

"Because I'm interested."

"You'll still be interested later. Right now, can we talk about something else?" My hand moved slowly along her inner thigh. "Or do something else?"

I remembered watching the footage again, all the way through, perhaps to confirm it had really happened. Then, I erased any evidence of the immense cavity.

Joanna turned to face me, cupping her hand on my right breast. Our lips met briefly. "What would you like to do?"

"Lay on your stomach."

She did. I searched for a moment in the nightstand drawer, and pulled out Chloë. At my touch, it thrummed to life, warming and moistening in my hands, purring almost inaudibly. I stood up and went to the end of the bed.

"Lift up your ass."

Laughing into her pillow, she did as I'd commanded. I crawled up behind her, sliding Chloë along her calves, her thighs. The dildo thrummed faster. I pressed its tip against Joanna's anus briefly, and slid its slick head down her perineum. She moaned.

At the same time, I was pressing Chloë's middle, urging it to bend. I held it firmly for a moment, to lock the position, and slowly inserted its other head into me. Once inside, the shaft ballooned slightly, conforming to my vaginal wall. I started breathing quicker almost immediately, but resisted the urge to tighten around it.

The other end I quickly slid into Joanna, the shaft slipping smoothly into her. She gasped, surprised, and rocked back against the pressure, sending Chloë further into me as well. I gripped Joanna's hips tightly, and began to move with her. Chloë responded to the situation, firming and softening to assist our movements, growing beads and ridges along its shafts, lengthening and contracting to heighten the feeling of penetration.

Joanna moaned softly into the pillow, "Oh, Alice. Fuck. Please, *fuck.*"

I gasped, "Wait. Wait."

I tightened inside for more purchase on Chloë, and thrust harder. In response to our excitement, the dildo formed pseudopods that located and began to palpate our clitorises. I let go of Joanna's hips and arched backwards, pushing Chloë deeper into me. Joanna mirrored the movement, pushing up onto all fours, allowing Chloë to reach a different angle.

Quietly: "Uhn. Alice—oh, there. There!"

I leaned forward, running my hands along Joanna's

spine, kneading the flesh of her hips.

"Come. Come now. With me."

A hiss escaped Joanna's lips. The muscles in her back suddenly tensed, and she rapidly thrust against me. I tightened inside, hugging Chloë. My throat caught, my stomach clenched, trying to prolong the moment of climax. I failed to contain it, and the explosion roared from my lower stomach, expanded into my limbs, into my fingers flexing into Joanna's hips. A low-pitched moan rose from my chest, counterpoint to Joanna's quick panting below me, and then we wound down together, moving slower and slower as the spasms of orgasm faded.

Languidly, we lowered ourselves to the bed, spooning; Chloë still linking us together. The room had become dark around us.

I blew on the nape of Joanna's neck.

"Mm. Thank you." She rose on her elbow to look out the window. "Did you look out the window again?"

I had. The plain was most beautiful at dusk. "No. Yes. Does it matter?"

I couldn't see her exact expression in the dim light.

"No, I guess not. There's no one out there for you."

I nodded. "That's true, Joanna."

For several minutes, both of us were quiet. I thought she'd fallen asleep, but she surprised me by clearing her throat.

"Will you return to Chloë someday?"

"I don't know."

"Are you happy you came here?"

I rubbed her shoulder. "Yes. Very."

"Would you have changed if you'd stayed on Earth?"

"No. For some reason, it wouldn't have made sense there."

"Why?" she asked, twisting her neck further to look down at me in the dark.

"Good question. I don't know. But, it made sense here."

"That's it? If I were to write your autobiography, it'd

go something like this: a man named James went to Mars and became Alice, but she doesn't know why."

I rose on my right elbow, pretended we could see into each other's eyes. "Sounds about right."

"Do you ever miss being a man, or even think of switching back?"

"Sometimes," I lied.

"Really? When?"

I stared outside. The sun had almost set. Arsia seemed to glow along her western flank, as sunlight scattered among the innumerable dust particles thrown up by Mars' winds.

"Only when I'm not with you."

TWO RIVERS

THERESE ARKENBERG

When we met with her several hours before she died, Renal, Red Woman of Maple Path, welcomed us to Two Rivers camp and granted us permission to take photographs of the women at work around it. Her husband Kurim, Huntmaster of Maple Path, had granted our male members similar permission to record the men. Once we explained the principles of photography, the people of Marnnor had taken to it with far fewer concerns about soul-stealing or sympathetic magic than most cultures at a similar stage of development.

It was the one thing that had gone my way in three weeks planetside.

I still hadn't managed to live down the fact that, upon landing, I had made diplomatic overtures to the wrong person. The wrong *type* of person entirely. Though I still held it was an easy mistake to make. The individual in question had worn a loose tunic and leggings, not unusual garments for a Marnnoran woman as far as I could tell; had a small and slender build; and was helping repair one of the bark-roofed houses, a job we'd assumed belonged to the women—with good reason. The homes *were* the responsibility of the women. It was just that they sometimes had help.

Not *male* help, of course.

"It's very odd," Banai told me through the ship's

communications channel. "Not just the obvious—I mean, a biological third sex. Or non-sex, as the case may be. Nothing like it exists anywhere but on the planet of Valdor. Perhaps in reaction to it, these people's notions of gender are... unusual. Not as unheard of as the amen, but rare. Thankfully."

Banai was *oskitush,* a female-bodied gender from Oorai, so sie would know. Gender was hir special focus, so I listened closely.

"Their roles are extremely rigid. Differentiated spheres are not uncommon in the sort of culture they exhibit, but normally there's a sort of escape valve—"

"Third gender," I said. Like oskitush, a chance for females on Oorai to have a purpose beyond the standard of breeding stock and field labor. Or their mustishi counterparts, males who preferred intellectual and artistic pursuits to cutthroat competition, in war or otherwise. Of course, those third options served other purposes as well, from economic to psychosexual or religious, but I knew the "escape valve" was Banai's pet theory, and sie'd produced evidence for it across many cultures on more than a dozen planets.

"But not here. You're born what you are—male-sexed warrior, female-sexed manager, a-sexed... well, aman. If it doesn't suit, too bad."

Especially for amen. Considered a freakish minority, subjected to more taboos than Serrai serfs had rights, they were not the ones you went to for diplomatic greetings. Unless you were very, very new to Marnnor, as I was.

Surine, of course, had *loved* that.

I pushed aside thoughts of my least favorite colleague and asked a passing woman for directions. She told me the fish-drying racks were downstream of the council tent—downstream on the *Path* that was, which meant heading south, while the river flowed north. The Marnnoran mindset was a bit odd when it came to Paths. Perhaps that was a sign of their importance—all the villages connected by one crude road became a political entity, named for trees in some system we hadn't yet explored. The fishing camp of Two Rivers, on the shore of the river that formed a border between Maple and Oak, played host to folk from many other Paths in this season.

A fine photographic opportunity.

The smell of fish hit me like a wall. It wasn't entirely unpleasant, and in moments the rich scent of woodsmoke mixed in, making the air substantially more breathable. At first it looked like A-framed huts, about five meters long by four high, were spread around me; in fact they were racks covered with swaying pink walls of drying fillets. A number of women sat before them, grinding dry fish to powder and mixing it with oil and dried berries. I took a few discrete photos, without even a flash from the camera to give me away.

"Kara," Banai murmured in my earpiece.

"Talk to me." I didn't let my worry show, but hir voice was too neutral.

"Surine is meeting with the leaders of Oak Path."

"Oh. Um." It was either an excellent way to keep peace with both sides of the slowly simmering conflict, which meant I should have gone along, or it was moronic, and I should be preparing for the fallout. "How's it going?"

"So far unremarkable. They've exchanged introductions, but no gifts yet."

Nothing binding, then. Just a polite diplomatic overture. Banai's careful neutrality must be less because sie was concerned about the implications for our mission in Marnnor, and more because I had a reputation for being prickly at the mention of my colleague. An earned one, I'd admit. "I'll keep that in mind."

It was then that I saw it. Skirting the women at work, silent as a particularly inoffensive shadow. Nothing unusual there—amen were forbidden to handle food at any stage of its preparation, except that destined for their own consumption. So that they didn't trespass in the hunting or gathering domains of the other genders, I hypothesized, although of course more data was needed for a complete theory.

That slender, meek being hurrying past the forbidden task struck me as an excellent illustration for whenever the ultimate theory was published. I raised the camera. We'd already agreed that male researchers would study the men and females would get the women, to avoid stepping on any more toes, but I decided there and then that I would do the amen as well. It was incredible none of us had thought to ask about them.

The face-seeking software centered on an expression of such complete anguish that I dropped the camera.

Its weight jerked hard on the strap around my wrist, but I barely noticed. The aman had already passed me, but I turned to follow. It probably was a problem I wasn't equipped to handle. The hell with that. It was a thinking, feeling being, and what it felt now was agony, physical or psychological. I'd be damned, or should be, if I as another thinking, feeling being didn't try to help.

At least Surine wasn't around.

The aman turned down a row of tents, and I followed. It must have noticed me from the corner of its eye, because it turned then, setting its back to a hide wall as if for protection.

"What do you want?"

"Forget about me," I said, holding up my hands—the camera dangled like a particularly tasteless bracelet. "What do *you* need?"

It blinked at me. I wondered if my translation chip was on the fritz, and I wasn't speaking proper Marnnoran.

"You don't look so happy. I just want to help."

The aman sighed, the breath released in a quiver of tension over its entire body. One of its long sleeves was rolled up, caught on the bend of an elbow, and the forearm below was marked an angry red. Five lines, like the grip of fingers. Valdorans as a whole bruised easily, but still, it looked bad.

Amen were unclean. It was forbidden for a Marnnoran of either sex to touch them. Of course, there was no proscribing bullies.

"I'm all right," it said. "...Thank you."

"I'm Kara. What's your name?"

"Rishah."

"Very nice." It was the name of a sort of berry. "And what's your Path?"

"Maple."

"You know, I have a stick of medical gel that's good for bruising. Want some?"

It looked down at its arm and hastily pulled down the sleeve. "It's not important."

"It's not very nice, either."

Rishah smiled in a way that might be a prelude to tears. I took out the gel, and it accepted the stick gingerly, touching only the very tip of the end farthest from me.

"Everything okay?" I asked as it applied the aseptic-smelling gel.

"Yes. It was just... an accident."

I wondered if anyone in Creation's history had ever believed that. "Yeah, crap happens sometimes."

"Thank you." Rishah gave the gel back, and I took it less cautiously, though still without contact. "It's from your *spaceship*, isn't it?" It used the Aragothic word, Mannoran of course not having one.

"Yes. So is this—" I hefted the camera "—and mostly everything, except the sandals and my tunic, which your own Red Woman was generous enough to loan me."

Its expression clouded, though I'd meant it as a compliment. The gift of the soft, russet-stained leather was clearly meant to show geniality, and I'd been flattered.

"I should be going," Rishah said. "I'm supposed to help caulk the fishing boats."

"Would you mind if I took a picture?" I asked without thinking.

It looked at the camera, which I had raised by way of explanation. "You mean..."

"Want to see how it works?"

Rishah nodded.

"All right. Smile."

It was a small, close-lipped smile, shy and surprisingly sweet. It grew wider when I showed Rishah the resulting photo on the display.

"There you are," I said.

It reached out, pressing a fingertip to the screen. The image obediently enlarged.

I said, "I could print a copy on endurance-paper, if you'd like—"

A scream like worlds dying came from my earpiece. I keyed it on, speaking Aragothic. "Banai, what's with the alert?"

"Bad news."

"Surine didn't—"

"No, the meeting with Oak Path went well. But when Yosa went by Maple Path's camp to explain the arrangement, he found—Red Woman Renal's dead, Kara. Head smashed in with one of her husband's clubs. The murderer must have found it close to hand in the lodge. You'd better get back to the ship."

o—o

There was nothing productive to do on board. Rather than join everyone in the galley to speculate on how Marnnorans conducted murder investigations, I went to my room and wrote down my thoughts in my log.

Sex and gender weren't my specialties, or even a particular interest—it would be hard for a photographer to capture the sticky subtleties of it all—but this case was different. A biological third sex—never mind that it was a freakish mutation—offered suggestive answers to all sorts of questions about the original two. Take the fact that, on eighty-six percent of the planets with established gender inequalities, males dominated over females. Where would a third sex fit in? Would they dominate, or be subservient? Or would they lie somewhere in between? Subservient to men or to women or both? Did a phallus secure power, or a womb forfeit it? The best way to tell would be to see where someone who had neither fit in.

Unfortunately, there were no clear conclusions to draw here. Men and women in Marnnor were regarded as equal, strictly so, though their powers and domains were very different—as traders and property owners, women had pervasive economic influence, while men had a monopoly on armed force—and amen were far at the bottom. The freaks. There was no middle ground, no fourth option (almost funny to find myself looking for one). And no escape valve, as Banai had put it, from whatever role your sex had placed you in.

I don't know if I'd rather have discovered that men were natural brutes, or women natural slaves, or if an inversion of the common roles would have comforted me, but I don't think any discovery would have been as disquieting as the lack of choice. We in the Intercultural Exploration Commission knew better than to judge, but any time I encountered rigidity like this, it left me viewing the whole culture as unhealthy.

"*Kara?*" the message box above my door said in Banai's voice.

"Right here."

"*Word came from Maple Path. We've been invited to Renal's funeral. Tomorrow at noon.*"

I pinched the bridge of my nose. "What do we know about funeral customs here?"

"*Not much. We're trying to learn.*"

"Keep me updated." I went back to my keyboard.

Even pronouns, in languages that split such things by gender, could be a problem. Did "She" signify anyone without a phallus, or only those with breasts and a womb? Aragothic, fortunately, had four pronouns: male, female, gender-neutral, and object. The translation chips designed for our Marnnoran mission read the third person pronoun for aman not as *Sie* but *It*.

The choice must have been deliberate. Usually our programs were not so... opinionated. Was that the problem? Surely our software hadn't absorbed the Marnnoran prejudice, the utter contempt that made it forbidden to even touch an aman?

Even Marnnorans, it seemed, didn't hold with that taboo as much as they might claim.

I pushed my note-deck away. What about my own prejudices? The words—*freak, mutant*—came easily enough to my mind. But so did pity. Even as I squirmed, remembering my misplaced first overture on this planet, I knew it had been worse for the poor individual I'd approached.

And then there was Rishah. At that thought, I took up my camera and inserted a new sheet of endurance-paper into its printer slot.

My prejudices pulled in two directions.

○–○

The arrangement Surine's party reached with Oak Path had been simple enough: the parties exchanged small gifts, mostly food items, and reached a mutual understanding of our mission's neutrality. I hoped it was recognized that we attended Renal's funeral as a polite gesture and nothing more, because everyone else there looked prepared for war.

The mourning rituals of many cultures involve self-laceration, shearing of hair, besmearing with ashes. But few feature the grieving widower being escorted by lines of grim-faced men bearing spears and clubs. And the ugly looks cast at Oak Path's representatives had a clear secular meaning.

"Did things seem this bad when you talked to Oak Path yesterday?" I asked Surine in Aragothic.

"No. If anything, they seemed contented." Surine's lips narrowed, for once not because of something a party member had done wrong.

"Do you think..." We exchanged glances. "Tell me if I'm reading too many mysteries," I said, knowing she'd be glad to if that were the case, "but does Oak Path have any particular reason to be... contented with Renal's death?"

"She was the leader-in-peace of Maple Path, not the

War Chief, though she was always more dynamic than her husband." Surine shook her head. "But all Oak would really gain by killing her is the ire of their neighbors."

"And a war."

"Maybe." Her voice almost broke on the word. We had only been planetside a few days and already she'd gotten invested, if only intellectually. And an intellectual investment from her was worth a love affair with anyone else. That was the thing about Surine. She'd all but cut throats to get on this mission. I'd stumbled onto it, picked out by the IEC just to fill an otherwise-empty seat on the ship when somebody more qualified couldn't show. For that she wouldn't forgive me.

Surine had something worth cutting throats over. For that I couldn't forgive her.

So we stood behind the mourners, behaving as respectfully as we knew, all the while observing the proceedings—watching for signs of violence, I admit, and ready to get out at the first hint of it, but also learning, doing our jobs.

Scanning the crowd, I saw that it seemed to be divided along family groups, and hazarded a guess that proximity to the Red Woman's pyre was decided by status. A few rows back, behind the shoulder of a distinguished-looking man, I saw Rishah.

Our eyes met, and I nodded, smiling. Rishah returned my greeting fleetingly. The man shared some of the aman's features—a father? An elder brother? He and Rishah stood close, and some swaying and restless shifting is to be expected over the course of a ceremony as long and tense as Renal's funeral, but I never saw them touch, even accidentally.

When I asked hir idly why nobody had chosen to focus on the amen in their studies, Banai reflected that we didn't know who to ask for permission. I suspected if we did ask, the Marnnorans wouldn't understand why anyone would be interested.

As the smoke of the cremation dispersed, as the

Huntmaster of Maple Path poured the last handful of ash over his bowed head and the gathered crowd began to break up, I dove through it, heading for Rishah. It turned to me, not smiling but looking... if not happy, contented. Or was I imagining that, feeding my ego? But Rishah did let me come close, and there we stood, an island in a river of mourners that parted for us—circling wide around the aman, sometimes brushing me with an elbow.

I pulled the printed photo from my pocket and offered it.

"Thank you." Rishah's fingertips left streaks on the glossy finish. It rubbed at them, only to smear it worse.

"Try using your sleeve," I suggested. "Anyway, now you can see for yourself how lovely your smile is, whenever you want."

It flushed.

"Would you be willing to answer some questions, Rishah?"

"Of course."

It wasn't explicitly considered unethical to exchange bribes for insights. Nor to give gifts. Making friends was positively encouraged. If the skin of my back felt a bit tight as I followed Rishah to the canoe landing, empty on this day of mourning, where we could speak... Well, the Marnnorans themselves already figured I was weird, and if my co-workers didn't like it, they could take it up with someone behind a desk later. But after my disastrous introduction, I didn't have much reputation left to lose.

"Yes, that was my father," Rishah said. It didn't meet my eyes as we spoke, but looked out over the river. "My family is small—Mother died long ago. I have three brothers and sisters, one nimé."

That is, another aman sibling. As I'd expected, the dichotomy was primarily of sexed and unsexed, not between specific genders. Most families didn't seem to have even one amen, and here was a family with multiple; perhaps the V-chromosome ran in families. Although upon reflection that sounded ridiculous, as if daughters or sons ran in families. Yet it was a mutation... I pushed aside such considerations for now—not my area of expertise, by far—and listened to Rishah's soft voice as it continued.

"My father is a fisherman. His eyes are dull, he's never done well with a spear." Rishah's bare toes traced figures in the sand. "Huntmaster Kurim ignores him."

"I'm sorry."

"It's not all bad. I mean, he'd never be called..." Rishah licked its lips.

"To war?" I asked quietly. "How is... I mean, Kurim seems to be more angry than grief-stricken."

"He and his wife weren't close. But Oak Path..."

"I heard Renal was stronger than Kurim."

"She advised him on every treaty, or stepped in herself when she felt he didn't shape them properly. Other Paths learned to hate her." Rishah's voice wavered. "She was... not like a woman."

"In speaking to other Paths? I guess I'm not very womanly, either."

"No, other women go between Paths. But they're like you. Gentle."

"Well, thank you."

Rishah's smile really was something. It brought to life a face with the clean proportions of a handsome young man's, but with a very female softness. If, as some cultures dictate, femininity is vulnerability, Rishah was the most feminine person I'd ever met.

"So your father's a fisherman. What are you, Rishah?"

"I... ?"

"What do you do? What are your talents?"

"I don't have many. I help my father weave nets— sometimes." It spoke in a low voice—was handling the tools used to catch food a little too close to breaking the taboo? "I mend the boats. Sometimes I carry messages in the camp."

"Who for?"

"My father. And others." It chewed its lower lip, then

said, "Sometimes for Red Woman Renal."

"So you knew her well?"

It made the waving-hand gesture that was the Marnnoran shrug. Of course, the strong, ungentle woman had
no reason to grow close to an aman. In any event, Rishah
didn't seem to like talking about Renal, so I asked other
questions—about the boats and the set-up of the camps,
about Rishah's favorite places and its siblings. None of
them were close, even the nimé—they all had separate
duties, except the brother who was also a fisherman, and
he was quiet and aloof like their father.

None of the topics I broached seemed able to make
Rishah smile again. Still, I'd learned some useful things
about Marnnor, as seen through an aman's eyes.

I returned late that day to the clearing south of Two
Rivers where our ship had landed. Surine sat on the
ground outside. She was editing a map of the camp, marking fords across each of the rivers, but the gentle way she
smiled at my approach suggested she'd really been waiting
for me.

"Good afternoon," I said.

"Kara." She folded her hands over the mapscreen.
"You know we're here to research our scattered human relatives in this galaxy, but that doesn't make our mission
humanitarian."

"I'm sorry?"

"I saw you talking with the aman. You have a big
heart, Kara, and I know you don't approve of the way
some things work here—"

I shrugged. First time I'd heard of my big heart, and
from Surine at that. "Don't worry. I'm not trying to spark
a social revolution."

"We're scientists, not saints. Not missionaries,
either."

"I said—" I sighed. "Yes, I do find the gender concepts here—interesting. And I wanted to examine them
more closely. How better than to ask someone?" I rubbed a
bug bite on my arm. "I don't think Rishah even realizes I

disapprove..."

"Your feelings tend to bleed through your expressions." Her lips twisted—still a smile, not a sneer; in fact it seemed almost fond, if less gentle. "I bet it knows."

Not trusting myself not to let something nasty bleed through, I went up the entrance ramp without replying to her.

○-○

Surine called a meeting the next evening.

First I suspected another lecture against civilizing the perceived heathen—as if the IEC training hadn't taught us any cosmopolitan respect—and my mood showed so plainly that Banai looked afraid to sit beside me. But then I saw Surine was as twitchy as I felt.

No lecture then. Something worse.

"The Red Woman of Oak Path sent for me," Surine said. "She told me her husband was in council. As one woman to another—that is, pacifically—she warned me that her people are preparing for war."

"They're attacking Maple Path?" We exchanged glances around the galley. Maybe there was something to the suspicions about Renal's death.

"Or they're preparing to defend themselves. A war council could be in preparation for either, and her husband hadn't consulted her yet." Surine leaned against the wall, crossing her arms and legs. "I propose we leave now. Banai, could you record a vote?"

"Of course." Sie pulled up the ship's log and began an entry.

"So we go?" I said. "For... well, let's face it, skirmishes here shouldn't last more than a few weeks or months. We could wait that out in orbit."

"We could," Surine said, "but there's no knowing when we'll be able to resume study again. The situation is... ugly. A war has never started before in a camp like Two Rivers, shared between Paths. Then, there's rarely been a cold-blooded murder in such a camp, either. This might change the cultural geography." She sounded more interested than horrified. Perhaps she would have liked to stay, too.

But remaining during a cultural watershed almost inevitably meant meddling, and the IEC would not accept that.

"Red Woman Jeral also told me that Maple Path might not be... particularly welcoming should they ever hear of our diplomatic overtures towards Oak. And depending on how things turn out, that might be true the other way around, too."

Well, then. That explained Surine's twitchiness, and all but ensured we couldn't stay.

When Banai asked for the *Yeas,* I raised my hand, reluctantly, along with everyone else.

O—O

Perhaps I only imagined the ugly glances thrown at me in Maple Path's encampment. It wasn't as if I looked like a spy for Oak—just a very nervous visitor. I didn't know where to find Rishah. Not at the boat landing. Not around the fish racks where we had first met—though given the taboos, I had known that was unlikely.

When my search was fruitless everywhere else, I decided I could at least avoid the staring of four hundred Marnnoran eyes by moving along the forest's edge. And only a quarter of an hour later I found Rishah, gathering fallen branches to add to the basket of firewood on its back.

"Hey," I said.

It straightened and smiled at me. "Hey."

"I, um..." I shifted from foot to foot. "We're leaving."

"You..."

"The IEC. Our mission. We're going home. Because of... *Oak Path,*" I said expressively.

"Oh. *Oh,*" Rishah said, shrugging the basket from its back.

Silence except for wind in the trees and the clack of firewood knocking against itself. A hard, ugly sound that made me think of heads being bashed in.

It was just a morbid turn of thought, with the war coming and all.

"So, um..." I found myself drawing closer, as if proximity could make up for the fact that I couldn't think of anything to say. "I thought you should know. We're leaving soon, and I just wanted to take the chance... to say goodbye. I'm sorry."

"Yes. Goodbye..." I caught a flash of pale, anguished expression, and then I couldn't breathe well, because Rishah's arms were locked around my chest. Its face was pressed against my neck, and I felt the wetness of its sobs. Without thinking, I returned the embrace.

"You do," Rishah gasped.

"I do what?"

"Like me. Want me."

"Of course. I like you." I pulled back enough for our eyes to meet. "Didn't you think so?"

"I wasn't sure."

"God, I never meant to send mixed signals." Each breath that filled its lungs forced air out of mine; we were holding each other that closely. Despite the discomfort, I couldn't let go. Rishah must be desperate for an affectionate touch. I'd give whatever I could.

It had pulled back, just a little. A slender hand was in the space between us, hesitating over my chest as if feeling my heartbeat. It traced over my breast and abdomen, raising shivers I couldn't stop, though I tried. Of course it wouldn't understand what that kind of touch meant. And then it slipped father down and rested there, a horrible, delicious pressure, and I was about to explain that what it was doing was improper, taboo even by my culture's standards, when I saw Rishah's face. At first I thought this was meant as a sort of gift, though even then I would have refused it. Because it knew. But it was taking no pleasure from this, not even emotionally. It bit its lower lip so hard it drew blood, dark eyes refusing to meet mine.

I gripped its hands, held them even as I stepped back. Silently damning myself for not stepping back sooner. For not realizing.

"Not like that." My voice was so harsh I hardly recognized it myself. "Not... Rishah, I don't want that from you. I only meant..." Another thought made my grip on those hands tighten until I felt bones grind beneath my fingers. Rishah never protested. "Who asked you to do that?"

"Nobody. I thought you—"

"Because I liked your smile? Because I was friendly? No. That's not... But where did you *learn* that? *Who else* made you—"

Rishah shook its head.

"There was somebody." It wouldn't have learned that on its own. So there had been someone, someone who saw the grace in that slender body, the vulnerability of the sweet smile... perhaps especially that vulnerability. And taboos don't stop bullies; sometimes they even encourage them. Anger burned like bile in my throat. *"Who?"*

A mumbled name, in a voice so thick with fear and shame I hardly understood it. Then, faintly, "...the Red Woman."

"Her." A stranger's lips formed the words; I couldn't control mine enough to make it a question.

"Renal."

I released Rishah's hands. "Good thing the bitch is dead, then."

It took a deep breath. "Yes," it said, deliberately. Perhaps a little proudly.

But then our eyes met, and the pride was drowned in shame.

"Kara, I'm sorry."

"For what?"

"Touching you... and for... her."

"No. Not for either of those things. Don't ever feel sorry—" I remembered when we met—only minutes after Renal's death, it must have been. Those were her fingers bruising Rishah's flesh. And it was Rishah's own arms, strong enough despite its air of appealing vulnerability, that had dealt that monster's death blow.

"But I'm the reason you have to leave!"

"You didn't make Oak and Maple Path hate each other. And that's the real cause of it. There would be war sooner or later. This way, an evil woman's been stopped first."

"The war could have come later. We could have had time..." It stopped, swallowing. But it could meet my eyes now.

"You want us to have more time?"

Rishah nodded.

"So do I."

Those arms surrounded me again, firm and strong. But the touch was innocent, clean. Loving. I held Rishah back and closed my eyes. It deserved more time. We both did. Rishah deserved someone to care for it, and I... Didn't I deserve to care?

I stepped back, taking Rishah's hand. "What would you be willing to give for more time?"

"Anything I had."

"Your family? Your world?"

"Everything."

"Because you will." I spoke around the pounding of my heart. "What I'm trying to do, I'm not sure if it's going to be a reward or a punishment for either of us."

"What is it?"

"I'm getting us more time." As much time as Creation could offer.

○─○

Surine, Banai, and the others in the gallery sat staring at us. I realized Rishah and I still held hands. That had slipped my mind as we told our story. The whole story.

At last Banai spoke, in a low, gentle voice, almost regretfully. "You know we aren't allowed to take anyone on board except employees of the IEC."

So that was all. I nodded. "I've recently felt a need for a secretary."

The corners of Banai's lips curled, digging a rare set

of dimples. Everyone else remained unmoving, faces grave. Except for Surine, who shifted in her seat suddenly. Our eyes met, and I knew she was about to say something that would be absolutely correct, and which would ruin everything.

She gestured to the map on the screen beside her, of the camps of Maple and Oak Path. "Perhaps they should be told they're about to fight a war for the wrong reasons?"

I glanced at Rishah and almost said no. They deserved it, the brutes, the blindly prejudiced primitives who let a monster like Renal rule them, who imprisoned each other in custom, who would probably be disappointed to lose this chance of war.

But Rishah's lips thinned, and the hand gripping mine tightened.

"You should do that, Surine," I said. "You're diplomatic, and you know how to talk to people. You're... very good at it. They'll listen to you. As for me, I'm a scientist, not a saint."

"I meant it," she said softly.

"Meant what?"

"About you having a big heart." Her gaze danced between Rishah and me. "I hadn't thought so, at first. Because you didn't care about the things I did."

"I'm surprised you want to interfere enough to stop a war," I said. Because we were being frank anyway.

The rest of the room had eyes big as holovid consoles, too interested to be embarrassed.

"If peace holds," Surine said, "some of us might appreciate the chance to return to Marnnor."

"Good riddance."

Her smile at me was hardly condescending at all.

o—o

Banai sent a message to Rishah's family. Surine was too preoccupied with preventing a war to carry personal correspondence, and I had no intention of setting foot on Valdor again.

"Do you?" I asked.

"Maybe one day." Rishah sat curled on the single bed. I'd set up a gel mattress on the floor for myself. Now I knelt beside it, putting an arm around the bowed shoulders. I knew it appreciated a comforting touch.

"You'll like Aragoth," I said. "There's something for everyone there. The whole world—all the worlds—at your fingertips, in the corners of your eyes. You'll find somewhere that... fits."

"Have you?"

I shrugged. "Not yet."

"But maybe one day."

"Maybe."

It rested its head on my shoulder, soft hair brushing my chin. Knowing, perhaps, how I appreciated the touch.

"Want to learn how to use the keyboard?" I asked my new secretary.

"And the printer?"

"Sure."

"Is... is my picture still on it? I left the copy you gave me back..." it said slowly, testing the words, "...back in Marnnor."

I grinned. "Let me show you."

THE SKY GOD'S DAUGHTER

Jason Andrew

In the great shimmering spire of Atrahasis, the daughter of the Sky God wept. Clattering servitors composed of golden gears and silver springs dutifully presented purified water and half a pomegranate with the crimson pulpy pungent seeds displayed like a minute temple. Shades of dead priests from a hundred worlds watched over her and dried her tears. Enchanted wooden animals merrily danced around her, desperately trying to elicit a hint of a smile. Nothing could cheer the heart of a daughter worried that her father would die.

She waved them off impatiently and pulled the curtain of rainbow-colored dream-pearls around her wooden canopy bed. She closed her eyes, trying to hear her father. There was great magic contained within her bed. Her father had crafted it from a dead branch of the world tree known as Yggdrasil and it enhanced the bond between them. Always she could hear his songs in her dreams. *He must be very far away for his voice to sound so weak,* she thought.

She peered out her windows by habit now. The night fluctuated. One by one the stars aligned into fighting regiments as her father rallied the heavens for war against Mithras. Brilliant novas and dark stains and crimson nebulae pocked the blanket of night. She knew not how well the war fared, only that the light still shined and that the bull had not yet claimed Atrahasis.

Time did not pass in Atrahasis as it did in the worlds of the sky. She knew not how many cycles had passed since she last heard her father's voice in the waking world; she only knew of the sorrow in his eyes when they parted. Clad only in her nightgown, she ran through the mud and grass and wormed her way through the spectral legions. She fell at his feet and wept. "Father, please don't go."

The god of the skies appeared to her as a handsome man with greying temples. He smiled warmly, beaming with energy as the seven sacred moons of Taris. He wore a high crown with the shape of a shimmering cylinder narrowed at its top and crossed with golden bull horns. The Sky Father was not ashamed to embrace his daughter in the middle of his army. Nor did he whisper to hide his word. "Little Inanna. Nothing would please me more than to ride with you this day. Mithras seeks revenge for the death of his father. If he cannot best Atrahasis, he will seek to end the worlds of the sky and then the ancient lands that came from the void."

"What if you die like Enlil?"

"A sacrifice I am willing to accept, daughter. I slew Ahura-Mazda upon the shores of the Euphrates. I anointed the sand and the clay with his divine blood and used it to build our towers. I molded the first men of the sky worlds from his divinity. We are responsible for those we create."

She struggled not to cry. Her lower lip trembled. "I cannot imagine what we would do without you, Father."

He pointed to a distant fading crimson light in the blanket of night. "There is a very ancient world that circles a dying red star, a land that comes from the Void. They know you as the Shining Dawn That Shatters Storms. And they dream of the time you will lead them across the heavens."

"I'm just a girl."

"They dream of tomorrow, dearest to my heart." He brought her close then kissed her cheeks. She hugged him with the strength to shatter worlds. "If the fates are kind, that will be eons from now. All that live, even the mighty, shall one day pass."

The spotless, white, three-headed elephant steed of the Sky God trumpeted softly. His name was Ardha-Matanga and he was known as the one who knits or binds the clouds. Her father named him King of the Elephants on all of the sky worlds. "Lord Zahrim, we must make haste if we are to arrive at Midgard before the enemy."

The Sky Father released his daughter and then mounted Ardha-Matanga. The three sacred elephant heads blasted their trunks triumphantly. "Daughter, stay within the boundaries of Atrahasis. Learn well your lessons. Attend to your duties. When I return, we shall visit the world of the feathered steeds and eternal fields."

Inanna pondered the last words of her father. She had so many questions. Did those worlds in the sky survive? Were there new universes created and then destroyed in the war? What were the duties of a goddess? The answer came to her after several nights of listless, silent slumber.

She gathered seven of the golden servitors and bid them to follow and tell none of their journey. The first rays of Shamash, the guardian of Atrahasis, arose in the east. They walked out of the towers, through the Sacred Groves of Ecstasy, and past the Fields of Sorrow. The Euphrates marked the border between Atrahasis and the other shadow realms. Removing her sandals, she walked along the cold stones and water until she found a curve in the river that pooled into a small bay.

She sniffed the air and felt the sand upon the ground. Divine blood had been spilled here long ago. The servitors dug at the banks of the river until they found the blessed clay.

She knelt down onto the moist shores of the Euphrates, clawing her hand through the muck, to bring up a floating mass of brown dirt. Inanna sensed the elements with her hand: silicon, magnesium, iron, and potassium. The stuff of life slipped through her fingers. She knew what she would do to honor her father. She would build him a world.

She entered her father's temple for the first time since he'd left and started her work. Her delicate fingers sculpted the mountains, flattened the plains, and dug the valleys. Algae, vines and herbs were scattered upon the new world by the servitors. Inanna stole a small seed from Yggdrasil in her mother's garden to plant in the center of this tiny new world.

The daughter of the Sky God crept into the chamber of the sacred well. The array of the glittering colored glass dome amazed her. Here it was forever night and the stars in the blanket of night were always visible. This place was sacred to her mother. "What are you doing here, daughter?"

"I seek the waters of the sacred well."

A shimmering feminine form appeared. Her mother was known on many of the sky worlds simply as Nox. Born of the formless beginning of all things, the Lady of the Eternal Night had hundreds of forms, all of them tantalizingly more beautiful than the last. "There is great power in these waters. They come from the Void. The time before form, matter, and flesh. Why do you seek these waters?"

Inanna sniffed. Tears would not work on her mother. Neither could she keep her intentions secret. Lady Nox knew all secrets whispered in the cover of darkness. "I want to build a world to honor Father."

"The Sky Father would be touched. You are a very good daughter." The Lady of Eternal Night embraced her daughter. "It is a difficult thing to birth a world. Remember that you are forbidden to leave Atrahasis."

"Can I not visit my new world?"

"Once you have created this world, you may only look upon it from afar. To truly touch it, you must leave our city."

"But, mother, won't I be safe from my own creations?"

"Nothing is safe once it has been given free will." Nox gestured to the stars above them. "And all worlds may have visitors."

Inanna gasped. "Mithras? You think he would invade my new world?"

"If he discovers it, but creation is vast and your world is small. It should be safe for a time. And should its secret be exposed, I will know."

"Thank you, Mother."

The Lady Nox cut a lock of her raven hair with the dagger of Azaroth and presented it to her daughter. "Burn this upon your new world and there will be clouds, mystery, and love."

Inanna then ladled the blessed water from the sacred well of all beginning into a small cup. She carefully protected the water from spilling while she returned to her father's temple. The world had formed nicely during the time she had been away. Algae and herbs had grown and evolved into trees, brush, and even blooming flowers. Water from the sacred well transformed on the new world into a beautiful ocean. Vapors from the burning of Nox's hair did as the Lady of Night had told her. Clouds formed and gentle rain began to fall. Animals gestated in the deep waters of the world and slowly crawled to the surface.

She watched with amazement as her little world started to grow and evolve without her help. And still, the world was not yet complete. Inanna gathered the last of the clay and molded two forms. She made a man that she named Enlil, after her brother, and a woman she named Nin. She took each of them to her lips and then breathed life into them.

Nin and Enlil awoke in a pleasant valley overlooking the ocean. Enlil hunted boars for meat and Nin gathered berries and fruit. Together, they built a small hut. Inanna looked down upon her creation and whispered to them across the void. She taught them language, gifted them with song, and blessed them with the sacred fire. Each night she turned them to the stars and appeared before them as a shining avatar. She whispered stories of the Sky Father, legends of Atrahasis, and of the war against Mithras.

In time, they had a daughter named Ninanna to honor the first mother and Inanna. The daughter of the Sky God realized that her namesake would eventually need a husband. She created a family that built a village on the world that they named Sumer.

Inanna observed the village of Sumer each night and watched her people grow and learn. Nin and Enlil lived to see their great-grandchildren born and play and laugh and love. Inanna felt content and spent less time watching over her little world.

Many cycles passed as the stars waged their war across the cosmos. Inanna still worried for her father, but she took time to play in the sun, knowing that was truly the best way to honor her father. She would venerate his deeds by not surrendering the joys he protected from Mithras.

She felt the sweet whisper of the Lady Nox in her ear. "Daughter, we should look in on your world."

How long had it been since she looked upon the people of Sumer? Inanna dashed to her father's temple. She peered down at her little world and much had changed. The people of Sumer had grown, and the once tiny village had given way to the mighty city of Ur. A shadow had fallen upon her world. The men and women feared the night. "Mother, what has happened?"

Lady Nox appeared to her daughter, shimmering and beautiful as always. "Mithras has found your world. His agents have come to claim it for their lord."

Inanna extended her senses to her new world. A single cycle in Atrahasis was a thousand such cycles to Sumer. Men had spread themselves along the mountains and valleys. They had built roads and ships and art and stories of their own. There was war and love and all of the chaos of life. And yet the shadow of Mithras had tainted Sumer. The star-spawn of Thalatta, known as the Girtab-lilu, nested in the deep caves and hidden places of the world. "What can I do, mother?"

"You must find a champion for your world. As your brother Enlil served for shining Atrahasis."

"What if he dies?" Inanna asked, horrified.

The Lady Nox shimmered out of view, but her words carried upon the wind. "Then you will choose another. And another. It is the call of heroes to die so that others might live and that their blood shall become divine by their sacrifice."

"It isn't fair."

"Little is fair about the demands of the cosmos, child."

"I will go to the new world and fight Mithras," Inanna declared, feeling brave. "He must be weaker there than in the stars."

"It is forbidden by the Sky Father to leave Atrahasis." Lady Nox floated over the new world. "This realm is sealed until Mithras falls. If you choose to leave, you may never be allowed to return."

Defeated, the daughter of the Sky God cried. "I will find a champion, mother."

Inanna shed many tears, but she knew that her mother was wise. She searched Sumer for a hero. There were many warriors protecting their homes, but few that she felt could withstand the hordes of Mithras. She needed someone like her father or her brother. Brave and kind and wise.

Searching the lands, she found a simple man herding cattle along a river that was a reflection of the Euphrates River. His eyes were dark and curious like her father's. The man was very handsome with broad shoulders and a mane of black hair. This man of the sky world had her brother's face. He whistled a song as he led the cattle to drink. It was an old song by the standards of their world.

She appeared to him as a shimmering light. "Sumer needs you, Shepard."

"Lady of the Sacred Dawn?" The man that had only recently been a boy blinked. He had never seen a goddess before and knelt down before her. "I am but a lowly shepherd."

His devotion pleased her. "I will guide you to the world tree. You will eat of its fruit and become a hero to face the dragon with many heads."

"I am not a warrior, Great Lady." He dared to look up through the locks of his black hair. It might have been her imagination, but there was almost a smile upon his lips. "But I will go where you command. It would be wrong to refuse a voice so beautiful."

Inanna blushed. She had been a young girl for many cycles, and had been quite content to stay that way while the stars burned, exploded, and reformed. Her avatar on Sumer shimmered, pleased. "You speak well. What is your name?"

"I am Murduk, Great Lady."

"Follow my voice. It is time."

She led him to the valley named Eden, to the spot where she had planted a seed cycles before. The seedling had sprouted and grown to an impressive towering tree. It swayed angrily as the mortal approached. "Who dares come to this valley?"

Inanna appeared to the world tree. "Peace, seedling of Yggdrasil. I have bidden this mortal to come here to eat of your tree."

The world tree bowed. "Lady Inanna. I remember you from the time before Sumer in fabled Atrahasis. I am called Ashvastha now."

Murduk turned to the form of his goddess. "Is there truly a place called Atrahasis? What is it like, lady?"

"It is a place of joy with shining towers that reach the stars."

"Will I see it one day?" Murduk asked.

The avatar shook her head. "The war against Mithras rages forward. Travel is forbidden until the Eternal Bull is returned to the Void."

"I will fight them until there are none left."

The world tree grumbled. "His followers seek my branches, Lady. They seek my seeds to build their own worlds of lust and hate upon."

"My champion will protect you and this world."

Murduk knelt before his goddess. "I will. I swear it."

Ashvastha dropped a fruit into Murdak's hands. It shimmered with power. He ate of it as bidden and felt his life energies by the godhead. "I feel strong."

Inanna brought Murduk a splinter from Yggdrasil. On Sumer, it was the size of a great spear. Lady Nox gifted her daughter's champion with a thread of her cloak. To Murduk it was a flowing cape that allowed him to float on the winds and hide from prying eyes.

The forces of Girtablilu stalked closer to Eden. The Girtablilu were a fierce enemy. Born from the blood of the Sky People, they were tainted with the dark magics and blessed by their goddess Thalatta, whose hands were colossal claws that could cut a man in sunder with a single snap. Their faces were a maw of teeth and fangs and large yellow hollow eyes.

Murduk fought them bravely with his spear. He dodged their claws, their teeth, and their giant stingers. He slew the Girtablilu in countless wave after wave of death and boiling toxic blood. The power of the fruit kept his arms strong and his legs fast.

In the end, the fearsome Thalatte crawled forth from the deepest place on Sumer. She was a goddess of the ancient sea from which the Void emerged. A child of Mithras, Thalatte had many forms and shapes. She strode upon the world of Sumer as giantess. The mountains and valleys shook from her presence. Many villages were destroyed in her wake.

Murduk did battle with the beast. They raged for many cycles, but in the end, her power was greater. His blood had been charged with the godhead, but Thalatte was a goddess born in the Void. She flung his body upon the ground with a mighty claw.

Inanna cried out. Lady Nox embraced her daughter. "If they claim the seeds, they will create new worlds to generate more fearsome nightmares. They will bring forth the army of Broken Sorrows and the Heart of Acrimony."

Inanna kissed her mother. "I hope that I am one day as brave as father and wise as you."

"If you leave, I will not be able to directly help you."

She tried to be brave like her father and brother. "I know, Mother."

The daughter of the Sky God descended from Atrahasis. She fell to Sumer unnoticed thanks to Nox. She stood before the sea goddess blocking her path to Ashvastha.

The daughter of the beast laughed. "You are a child."

"This is my world and I will defend it."

Inanna fought the beast with shimmering servitors. When the army of Broken Sorrows arose from the dead, she sang until they shattered. When the Pets of Pestilence attempted to kill the world, she froze them with her own life-force and shattered them to a billion pieces.

"Why die to protect this world?" the daughter of Mithras asked.

Inanna reclaimed the spear of Yggdrasil. The gentle words of her father returned to her. "We're responsible for what we create."

She thrust the spear into the heart of the beast and sacred blood blessed the valley of Eden.

o—o

The Sky Father thundered in the clouds above Sumer. Inanna shined through the morning air to greet her father. She was no longer the young girl that he remembered from eons past. Her black hair was long and thick. She had the dangerous curves of her mother and already knew the mysteries that belong to the ancient spirit of women. "Daughter, you have grown!"

Inanna cried and embraced the Sky Father. "Forgive

me for disobeying you, Father. I could not watch my world and my husband die."

"You have married?"

"A good man named Murduk. He fought the daughter of Mithras for this world, but he could not best a goddess."

Zahrim laughed and embraced his daughter. "You protected what you loved. I cannot ask for more than that from a daughter."

"You forgive me?"

"Forgive you? You saved us all! Mithras sent much of his legion to this new world. He could not believe that such a new world could withstand his might. You weakened him enough that my army surrounded him. I slew him in the Crab Cluster at the edge of the multiverse."

"He is dead?"

"The war is over."

"You are not angry with me for marrying one of the sky people?"

The Sky Father laughed. "Daughter, my heart pumped mortal blood when your mother first spied upon me. It was her love that raised me as a god."

Inanna had not imagined that her father had once been mortal. "Truly?"

"You should have seen what she did to my intended before I noticed her. It is still whispered about in a thousand worlds." The old god laughed, slapping his knees. He stopped suddenly and his face turned sour. "Although I am angry over one thing!"

The wrath of the mighty Zahrim was a terror to freeze the heart. "Father?"

"Lady Nox hid your world to protect you from Mithras. It kept the Bull from sending his entire legion against you, but when the war was over I could not find you."

"We did not know, Father."

"And I have not met your husband and Nox has told

me that there are grandchildren. Grandchildren!"

"Father, you tease me still." Inanna patted her womb that carried her first daughter. Then she lifted her son up to the heavens to meet the Sky Father. The old god kissed his grandson upon the forehead and gardens all around Sumer bloomed. "This is Atrayu. He fancies himself a builder. I caught him making a world just this morning."

"My grandson could be nothing less! Our blood flows through his veins. We have that drive to create. And thank the divine that he did! How else could I have found your shining world?"

PRETTY MAIDS
ALL IN A ROW

CAREN GUSSOFF

Margot's garden is a magnificent place. Most of us keep gardens, but my generation doesn't have Margot's touch. I've only been able to grow dumpy, dependable crops for the colony: radishes, potatoes, garlic. To me, Margot's garden is a wonder. She feeds the burned earth with compost like rich dark chocolate; she tills until the calluses on her hands split and bleed. And even then, she squeezes drops of her own blood into the ground. *Life is good for life,* she says.

Plants thrive beneath her hands, rise up to meet her and spill forth seeds. She cuts and divides, roots and pollinates, until every centimeter squirms with life, strains to spread wild, seeds carried by the wind. Margot yanks out stragglers with a savage indifference.

I come and help Margot in her garden. She cuts and divides, roots and pollinates, pointing to each as we name them: hollyhocks, pansies and delphinium; honeysuckle and damask roses; hawthorn, thyme, calendula. I repeat the names faithfully. Then Margot makes up a pitcher of cider, fermented down from the huge apples that drop off her apple tree, and we sit together and we talk.

Margot is number 9. A Gamma.

I help Margot in her garden. We turn the compost,

watching the white maggots and worms tunnel away from the light. We water and rake, sing-song, *Mary, Mary, quite contrary.* We name the plants: rosemary and hidcoate lavender, chocolate mint and giant basil. *How does your garden grow?*

We work in her garden, dirt under our nails, knee deep in it. Margot yanks out weeds with Laodicean disdain, saying, *We have to protect our babies. All our precious babies.* Margot points and says their names: dill, lemon balm, sweet pea, Midge, Maggie, Middy, Beta 3, Delta 5, 12 Epi. She wipes sweat from her brow and says, *This is how our garden grows.* The she smiles and says my name.

I am Meg. Beta 10.

○─○

The late afternoon was still hot and blindingly clear, but a breeze blew in from the beach, carrying pollen puffs, decadent and full as clouds. Margot brought out a pitcher of cider, a plate of blackberries from the back trellis and white disks of zucchini. I opened and closed my mouth but no words would come out, so I pushed food into it and chewed in rhythm, struggled for breath between bites.

Margot was distracted, agitated. She watched the pollen drift around as she picked at her cuticles.

I knew what she was doing. We all do the same thing. I picked at my own cuticles, but for a different reason. I couldn't bear to say it.

Margot peeled back the dead skin from her cuticle, then sucked on the finger. "Those are dandelion pappi," she said, frowning.

A blackberry seed lodged in my back tooth, and I worked it free with my tongue. I swallowed the seed, popped another blackberry in my mouth immediately. I acted normal.

"They're going to sprout everywhere," she continued and shook her head, upset.

"It'll be OK," I said, swallowing. "We can weed them out."

She shook her head. "Once they fruit, they're impossible to control." She watched the fuzzy puffs drift as I shifted nervously in my seat. I was growing, bursting with it. The words pushed up and out, made me feel a little sick. "The bear," I finally said.

"The bear," Margot repeated. "Another bear." She watched the pollen land softly, catching on leaves and disappearing.

"It's not a bear," I continued. I popped another blackberry in my mouth.

Margot didn't seem to notice, didn't change expression. She wiped her finger dry on her uniform leg, staring at the puffs. "It sounds like a bear," she said. "That's how Megan and Maisie described it."

Megan had reported the first sighting. She was clamming the low tide on the southern beach, when she swore she saw something creeping in the short dune brush. Maisie had corroborated it, when she reported seeing a strange figure while she was repairing worn shingles on her backyard shed. Maisie lived close to the beach. She couldn't tell much else, just that it ran away when it saw her, and that it had at least a meter on us, height wise.

Megan is number 28, Gamma. Maisie, also a Gamma, number 19.

"Megan and Maisie've never seen a bear," I continued.

"We've never seen a goat, either," Margot replied. "Or a horse or a whale."

"Or a man," I added.

"Or a man," she agreed. "But that doesn't mean we wouldn't know one when we saw one." She sighed. "Dandelions."

I reached out and forced Margot's face towards me. Her face felt cool. "We can weed them out." With my other hand, I reached into my pocket.

○─○

The Old Lady rarely came down the Hill anymore. Most of us couldn't even remember the last time she came down the Hill, when she walked and lived among us. It was the first time we buried one of us, a late Beta, then the Old Lady locked herself up in the laboratory, away from us, with a few assistants that never leave.

We tell ourselves she stays away because of her critical work. We tell ourselves she can't spare the time. It's vital work she can't pull herself from, building our future. She's the prime mover, the Alpha, orchestrating our very survival, looking down on high. She is our Mother.

We tell ourselves that her staying away is proof-positive of her love. She is proud of us, she loves us, and so we remain devoted. I tell us she is pleased with us, and so we remain—cooking, washing, sitting, talking, waiting. Naming, gardening. We blow kisses up the Hill at her. *Glory to the Mother. We are all one.*

Of course we understand, we tell ourselves. Glory, glory be. All daughters want to please their Mother.

We are liars.

The Old Lady won't come down the Hill because she can't bear to look at us anymore. Generation after generation, she tries to make us different than we are. She doesn't, cannot stop. *This one,* she says, *then the next.* But we're always the same. Beta, Delta, Gamma, Epi, all our faces, just like hers. Every age she's ever been. Everything she could have been, instead of the last woman on earth. All her faces, imperfections magnified: blowing kisses, filled with devotion. She tries again. And again. But still, we remain.

Her face, everywhere. She can't bear to look at herself anymore. We stand in a line, pretty maids all in a row.

O—O

By breakfast, we were all talking of the sighting. After the meal, we stood together, waving our hands excitedly, speculating. We looked at me expectantly, until I volunteered to go up the Hill. I am the last of two Betas, first generation, of her cells. We never think of us as leaders until we have to.

It was a long walk up the Hill. We waved at me as I climbed the road to the laboratory; Mig, Mar, Peg, Pheg walked me half the way. Margot blew me a kiss for the Old Lady.

At the heavy steel door, I shifted my weight from foot to foot as I pressed the intercom. "Mother?" I called.

The intercom crackled.

"It's Meg," I called. "Beta 10."

"Come in, come in," the intercom buzzed. The door bolts retracted like claws. I walked into the cool, decom holding room and the door sealed shut behind me. At the sink, I scrubbed my hands to the elbows, picked out dirt from Margot's garden from beneath my nails. When I was clean, the lab door opened and the Old Lady stood facing me. Margaret. Mother.

She seemed exhausted, dried out, as if cooking us up somehow whittled her down, bit by bit. It's not how it works, but this afternoon she reminded me of the rotten mine shafts that surrounded the colony. She looked as structurally unsound, like she'd splinter and we'd fall right though her.

But Mother embraced me firmly, then pushed back, tucked my bangs behind my ears. "It is good to see you, child," she said, hooking her arm in mine. "Midge, dear, bring us some tea?"

Midge was a Beta too. She was concerned to see me. She pulled her brows down into a straight line.

We make that same expression.

Mother set herself up on a stool at an empty lab table and patted the empty space next to her. "What brings you here, child?"

"I'm not sure you've heard, Mother, but we've spotted a bear."

"Another?" Mother asked. Midge brought us a tea set, poured boiling water over dried chamomile before us, then stood back to let it steep.

Mother didn't answer. She avoided my face, looked deeply into her yellow tea as if something interesting was happening in it.

I knew this gesture; we do the same thing.

But then it was gone, she was composed, she drained her tea to the dregs, and plucked a stray chamomile blossom from between her lips and laid it on the table. "Good child."

I was a good child. I looked down into my untouched tea.

Mother slid off the stool and walked to the tanks that lined the walls. Before I'd realized it, I'd followed Mother and stood above the developing Zetas. They looked like the maggots in Margot's compost. Slick, shiny, pearly white. They jerked a little in their sleep.

"They're beautiful, aren't they?" Mother asked, dreamily. "Perfect."

"Perfect," I repeated.

"More perfect than ever. Rita, Daisy, Greta, Gretchen, Magee, Marg—" Mother said. "All my babies. All my sweet babies."

They wriggled in response.

Mother gazed at them. I was forgotten for the moment. Then with one gesture, she scooped out one Zeta on her finger, held it to the light and frowned,. Then she flicked it over her shoulder onto the floor. It landed with a soft, wet thud.

I must have made a sound because she remembered me then. "There's nothing out there," she said. "Nothing any longer. Nothing but us." She looked from the tank to me, then back to the tank. "Understood?"

Someone squeezed my hand from behind. Midge. I squeezed back and she slipped something into my palm. It was warm and moist. The Zeta.

"Do you know what I am saying?" Mother asked.

I knew. I knew it as well as if it were sung in choir. As well as if I'd said it myself. I slipped the Zeta into my pocket and nodded. Then I clasped the Old Lady's dry hands like a good and dutiful daughter and kissed them in goodbye.

○─○

Down the Hill, a group of us sat on the beach by the

edge of the water, trying to cool off, their uniform legs turned up, shirts unbuttoned, burying their feet in the sand. Margaux, Mamie, Peggy, and Magda, Epi 9, 12, 14, and 22. They waved for me to join them, so I wiped my eyes and nose against my hand, patted my pocket and held myself high as I went to them.

I stood and held my breathing. They smiled and splashed a bit, then dug around in the cool, wet sand and looked across the water. On a day as clear as this, we could just make out the ruined skyline on the distant shore, now a monument in rubble to the nameless, dead city.

One of us finally asked in her most brave and mature voice if we'd seen the bear.

"There's no bear," I said.

The Epis shook their heads and made small noises. They were all slim-hipped, athletic, not long like the Gammas, or round like the Betas.

Epi 9 smoothed her hair into a ponytail with her hands, then let it drop down her back. "No bear?" Then she tossed her hair loose again to indicate that they really would have liked it to be. "Nothing at all?"

The Epis waited for the answer, their eyes wide, mouths dark little holes.

"There's nothing at all." I answered.

"There could be, though," Mamie said. "Right?"

I shook my head, but they ignored me. They started playing again, saying, "If there ever was—" "Coming down from the peninsula—" "Bears—" and then, finally, the Epi 9 spoke loudly. "If there was ever an attack, we'd have to fight. Like this," the Epi 9 said, and punched the air. "Pow."

All the Epis started kicking and punching, laughing, agreeing. "Pow, pow," they said, like danger was a game they couldn't wait to play. I tried to remember being young, being attracted to excitement like insects are drawn to light, but I couldn't. I could feel the Zeta leaking through my pocket. "Now, now," I said loudly. "Let's head on back. It's time we had some lunch."

O—O

I left the Epis at the dining hall, then went back to my house to grab a shovel. I would bury the Zeta. I would bury her somewhere safe. I slung the shovel across my back and set out.

I picked my way south down the shore. Clams spit bubbles up through siphon holes in the wet sand, my lungs filled with the smell of salt and fresh algae, and the shovel bruised my hips. I stopped and turned my pocket inside out, peeled out the Zeta carefully. She'd turned dry, gummy. I rolled her over in my hand and looked at the tiny sprouts of arms, nubs of legs. *Our precious baby,* I thought, and cupped my hand around her.

There was nothing. There was only us. Flies, maggots, worms, clams. Occasionally a scraggly rabbit. I walked, cradling the Zeta until the dunes grew higher, carpeted in bluish beachgrass, crimson sorrel, yellow sand verbena, shaggy thistles. I thought this would be a good place. How proud Margot would be of me for knowing their names. I thought about leading her here to cut specimens. Then I almost fell over the boat.

It was an exotic thing, as out of place on the beach as a space ship. Six meters long, two narrow hulls bound together by tight canvas, a mast twice the length laid behind. The deck, silvery wood, caught the light, fooling the eye.

I dropped the shovel and it stuck in the sand like a flagpole. I sat and I stared. There didn't seem to be anything else to do. My hand sweated around the dead Zeta, but I looked at the boat until the breeze came in, until it ruffled the reeds like footsteps.

I started my run from a crouch. I shoved the Zeta into my pocket as I ran, over the dunes, back to the colony. My legs were heavy, panting so hard I almost choked, the Zeta rattled in my pocket like a stone. But I ran. I ran as hard and as fast as I could towards the colony. I wanted to stop, double over, but I kept running. I didn't know where I was going until I tripped over the roots of the apple tree and landed in a soft bed of fresh compost. It was sticky and wet, slippery. I tried to yell her name, but I could only just lie there.

Then Margot stood over me, gave me her hand. It was warm, a little moist. Then she pulled me up and into her garden.

o—o

Margot took the Zeta between her fingers and held it to the light. Then she looked at me. "Take me there."

As we walked, everything looked unfamiliar, and I wondered if I'd led Margot the wrong way. But when we arrived back at the dunes, I pointed, and Margot drew a little breath.

Then she moved towards it, fearlessly, and ran her hands over the hull. She looked at me, and her face looked strange: smile tight, eyes narrow. "This hasn't been here long." She pointed to where the silver wood turned dark and damp.

I shook my head.

Margot moved away from the boat to the shovel, still lodged in the sand. She rested her hand on the handle. "Well," she said. "It isn't a bear." Margot thought about things, then looked at the sun. "There's a few hours of daylight. We can get another shovel. And an ax."

"Why?" I asked. My voice didn't sound like my voice at all, like our voice. It was too high and too low, too slow and too quick, all at once.

"We need to bury this," she answered, as if that were the most obvious answer in the world. "We need to break this down and bury it all." She pulled the shovel from the sand and laid it on her shoulder. I'd never noticed how long her arms were, how long her legs as she stood with them firm and far apart.

I turned to the boat, busied myself with it, reaching inside the compartment where legs would go, plenty of room for long legs, even longer than Margot's. "There's a compartment here," I said, then pulled out a shoe. It was menacingly large, much larger than would fit our feet. A brown boot. I held it up and out as if it were something beautiful or terribly dangerous. "Look at this."

Margot lowered the shovel, held out a hand, and I tossed it to her. She studied it as I rifled through the rest of the things below deck. The other boot, a pouch of dried fruits and nuts tucked into the toe. A heavy fish hook. A sticky coated scroll. A small book tied with a leather thong and a pen.

Margot passed the boot from hand to hand, then laid it down on the brush. "I'd say the owner's about six feet tall. So—" she looked from the boat to the shoe back to the boat. "There's probably just one."

I sat down on the boat's hull and untied the thong.

"Just one," she said. "One man." Margot shouldered the shovel again. "Come on," she said.

"This is a journal," I said, flipping the pages. I bent over it, trying to make out the strange words.

Margot sat down in the spiky weeds, picked her cuticles and watched me.

"I can't make out what it says," I said. "Do you want to look?"

Margot shook her head. She wiped her fingers on her uniform leg, then dug them in and around the roots, pulling up spikerush and water parsley, gumweed and dwarf pine. She never took her eyes from me. "The dirt here's actually pretty good," she said.

"Margot," I said. "Don't you understand what this means?" My voice sounded even stranger, too excited and too calm.

But she just sat there. "Really good dirt," she said.

I wanted to shake her. Instead I shook the journal. "This isn't a bear. It's a man."

Margot stood up slowly and brushed off her uniform. Then she picked up shovel and held it at the base. "What's the difference?" she asked.

She moved closer to me, and I saw her set up the swing. I wasn't afraid. For those last few seconds, we were all one. We were one person.

○—○

We moved quickly, long legs square, knees bent like we were about to jump. Instead, we swung the shovel like a bat.

The blow connected with the side of our head. Before we fell, we saw double, triple, quadruple my face, smeared across our vision. Every age we've ever been, everything we could have been, adoring, devoted. Glory, glory be.

I didn't see this, but I knew: later, Margot would drag my body up the dunes by the feet, lay it down to bleed in the good dirt. She'd say, "Life is good for life," tear up the map, rip the journal off the leather spine, scatter the pages. She'd fetch an ax, hack the boots and the boat down to pieces. She'd layer everything carefully over me, and on top of the pile, lay the tiny Zeta. "Once they fruit, they're impossible to control."

She'd look over the water towards the ruined skyline with the shovel over her shoulder like a parasol. Then she'd squat in the long brush and wait for the bear. The man. No difference.

The next year, Margot's garden would be even more spectacular. I'd be sorry to miss it: slim-hipped sunflowers with Epi dark eyes; roses dripping with scent; round, ripe muskmelons; peppers, crisp and sweet.

Silver bells and cockle shells, pretty maids, all in a row.

UNATTAINABLE RED

JENNIFER LINNAEA

Lara Zhia looked out her hotel window at the alpine landscape. Flowers grew below—not the huge jungle flowers so popular in indoor decorating, but small delicate flowers growing as if brushed finely over the rocks. Beyond the garden wall Mount Karakys rose like a god of ice and snow. Lara Zhia had never touched ice, or snow, or been cold in any manner, and although her mother had described it as a sort of burning, still in her mind it was a piercing pleasure, like sex.

She reached out one small hand and pressed her palm against the glass.

Lara Zhia was not fit for walking outdoors. She had been born in space and was not really fit to be planetside. Her immune system reacted acutely to every allergen. Her bones were thin and porous. She could totter over to the kitchen, or shuffle across the room to the piano or the vid screen to view the latest Contact information, or to see the travel shows of alien worlds showing wonders beyond wonders. Her husband led one of those shows, and she watched him nightly on the vid, his skin tanned and weathered, his long hair whipped in some wild wind as he grinned into the camera. Next month he would be seen at the top of Mount Karakys. They were filming it now.

Lara Zhia shuffled away from the grand view out the window and sat on the soft green couch. She kneaded her toes in the long, shaggy green carpet, all the while wishing the couch were red and the carpet too. Her husband, Jano, had given her a red flower once. Not a hothouse flower, but a thin-stemmed flower with petals like the red sails of the ship he'd surfed on the solar winds of the gas giant, Nemo. That had been the moment when she'd known Jano was the one she wanted, out of all the other suitors. Like so many of them, he liked to break rules, but, unlike the rest, he liked her to break them with him. Red, he'd told her, was the color of passion. It would be their special color, their secret color, from that day onward.

Lara Zhia wasn't allowed red in her chambers—her doctors said it would agitate her—so she'd hidden the flower in the lining of her suitcase and taken it with her to the stars.

The bell to her chambers chimed a soft note, and Lara Zhia reached for the remote on the coffee table before her. She pushed the intercom button.

"Yes?"

"It's me." Jano!

Lara pushed the button to allow him entry. "But you're supposed to be filming today."

"Yes, well, I... something more important happened, love. I'll be right in."

Lara Zhia listened while her husband came through the lock, while the sanitizer hissed. These were familiar sounds that comforted her. Next would come the silence while he dressed and made himself ready. Then he would open the door.

An off-key note played in the sanitation room. Through the wall she heard the muffled sound of Jano swearing.

"Just a minute," he said through the intercom. "I'm having a spot of bother here."

But Lara Zhia was already off the couch and making her slow way across the living room towards the sanitizer door.

"What's the matter?" she asked. She reached the

door and pressed her palms against it. "Are you sick?" The sanitizer also screened for micro-infestations and parasites.

Jano chuckled. "No," he said, "I'm not sick. I brought you a present, but it seems to be..." There was a thump against the door.

"Jano? Jano?" Lara Zhia called her husband's name, her volume rising, but there was no answer. She banged on the egress key but of course it would not open the door for her. She reached for the remote to call the hotel desk, but it was not in any of her pockets. "Help! Help!" she shouted, shuffling back towards the couch. "Help! Emergency!"

o—o

By the time someone came it was too late. Jano, her husband, was dead. Lara Zhia watched his funeral on an open channel broadcast from the slopes of Mt. Karakys. His support crew said it was the perfect place to bury him —the site of his last grand adventure. They didn't mention the astronomical cost it would have taken the studio to ship his body home.

Lara Zhia listened to the service, her hands opening and closing with the desire to touch Jano's skin. Her view of the casket was blocked by a gaggle of Karok natives. It was the first time Lara had ever seen one. Their wrinkled faces were unreadable, their green clothes blended with the green stems of mountain flowers, and Lara Zhia hated them right away, hated everything green with a raging passion from deep in her breast. Since no one was around to see, she removed the flower from its hiding place and pinned it to the front of her robe. It was still as deeply and richly red as the day he had given it to her.

o—o

Lara Zhia had always had a lot of money, because her family had a lot of money, so at first she thought she didn't really need the trust fund Jano left her, even though it and the life insurance together made her almost the

wealthiest woman on Karok. Then her mother started calling. Her mother, Margarita Zhia, said Lara should come
home to the space station, said the family would take care
of her now that her husband was gone. It was unseemly
for a widow to live alone; it made her look loose and her
family appear irresponsible. Besides, Lara Zhia didn't
belong on a dirtball like a common terrestrial. She was
better than that.

But Lara Zhia didn't want to go home, and when her
mother hinted, not-so-subtly, that perhaps Lara Zhia
would find her family less able to spare money for her now
than they once had, she thought for a long time about
what Jano would have done in her place. Then she sent her
mother a certified letter stating that she would not be
needing her financial support anymore. Ever. And then,
because she didn't know where else to go, she bought a
house on Karok. The native population was eager to
demonstrate their metropolitan diversity, so she was able
to get one without any of the endless bureaucratic
wrangling she and Jano usually had to go through to come
planet-side. The house was large and faced Mt. Karakys. It
was easily sealed up and fitted with an airlock and sanitizer, and it had almost all the comforts she was used to.
The first day in her new home she stood in her living
room and looked out the window at the icy slopes of the
mountain until a cloud bank moved in and covered them.
Then she turned slowly around and looked at her new
space.

It had come already furnished, care of the previous
human occupants, who'd had to leave suddenly on diplomatic business. The walls were a rich, dark orange, hung
with woven tapestries. Creamy white rugs covered the
wooden floor. And all the furniture, armchair and loveseat
and couch, were a beautiful, vibrant red. Lara Zhia did not
feel agitated. She felt loneliness, and grief, and also something else, something she hadn't felt since she'd first left
home with Jano. Lara Zhia felt excited about the future.

o—o

It did not take long for the newness to wear thin. Her family no longer responded to her transmissions. For days, then weeks, no one called, and Lara Zhia sat alone in her new home, staring at the vid screen or out the window. Mt. Karakys never looked the same twice. Sometimes its stark white brilliance made her squint, but other times it took on a rosy or purple blush, and once the setting sun cast an inverted triangle of shadow into the sky above it, like another mountain upended above the first. She and Jano had never stayed in one place for so long. Just hop planetside, film a segment, and off to the next world. Lara Zhia had seen many worlds out her hotel window, but never before had she had such a chance to get a *sense* of one. It made her long for more, like the way she longed for Jano to be alive again, ceaselessly and without hope.

She was halfway through another circular, apology-filled call in attempt to get the proper foodstuffs sent to her house when her husband's theme song came through the speakers.

"Today on *Wild Vistas*," said the show's announcer over dramatic chords, "the most controversial mountain in the known universe—Mt. Karakys."

Lara Zhia dropped the phone. "Considered a god by locals, a site so sacred that offworlders were formerly forbidden from even looking at a facsimile, human beings have never before been granted broadcast rights for this dazzling locale."

Lara Zhia watched in stunned silence. There was Jano, smiling at the cameras and gesturing to some rocks. He wore a thick coat with a fur-lined hood; heavy gloves covered his hands. But it was him. He looked so... real. So happy and perfect and alive. So very much the way she remembered him.

She hadn't gotten to say goodbye.

"Our guide," Jano was saying, gesturing to a wrinkle-faced local swathed in a small mountain of furs, "tells us that this is the site of the first Unification, the first time a Karakyn ever became one with the mountain, the first time—" Here Jano paused for dramatic effect. "—the first time one of them acquired the longevity that today is every Karakyn's birthright."

The camera zoomed in on a pile of rocks at Jano's feet. The broken, gray-colored rubble seemed like nothing much special to Lara Zhia, certainly not the site of something so important. The edit hadn't taken out the sound of the wind wailing.

Jano exchanged a few words with the guide in the native tongue. It always impressed the audience, Jano had told her, made him seem more exotic. Lara had said that he *was* exotic, and Jano had laughed, and kissed her, and that had led to other things.

Lara Zhia cried through the rest of the show, and missed everything else Jano said.

But the next day it was on again. It would be on every day for a week.

"The natives of Karok," the announcer's voice said, "have a peculiar system of beliefs. To them, Mount Karakys is a god. This inhospitable expanse of rock and ice is the benevolent parent who bestows the blessings of life upon them." A shot of Jano trudging through a thick fall of snow, bent nearly double against the wind, showed the audience how "benevolent" the producers thought Mount Karakys was.

"Where else in the galaxy is such reverence given to the harsh realities of the wilderness?" Lara Zhia could think of plenty, but that was the way the show was. Everything always had to be the best, the worst, the longest. The most. "And yet, scientists are baffled by the the longevity of the Karakyns, and their resilience against all manner of illness and disease." The music ramped up to a series of haunting tones over a low rumble of sound. "Perhaps Mount Karakys, this mysterious stone monolith, is more than it seems." The low rumble broke, and cheerful string instruments took up the the melody. "We'll be back after these messages."

Lara Zhia watched the local advertisements, which

were required by inter-planetary law to be inserted into all long-distance broadcasts from the space stations. Some kind of houseplant, but did it freshen the air, or provide protection against intruders? A monorail for the poor. A food that maybe made you taller, or maybe wrinkled your skin. The ads were in Spanish, but with such a thick Karakyn accent she could only understand about one word out of three.

Lara wished Jano were here. He'd tell her what the ads meant, or make up wild, improbable stories about them. Then he'd tell her all about Mount Karakys. Not the way *Wild Vistas* did, with dramatic catch phrases. He'd tell her the whole story.

"Stop it!" she said. The carpets and the tapestries sucked up the words and left her with silence. "Jano is gone. You have to help yourself now." And she *had*. She had helped herself to a new life on a new world in a new, beautiful red living room.

But it was so small. That was what Jano had done for her: he had gone on adventures and come back and told them to her so that it was as if she had gone on them herself. He had made her world big enough to live in.

Lara Zhia reflected on this sadly as she sat half-listening to the announcer describe wildlife and local customs. She had never had to do *anything* herself because Jano did everything in lieu of her. Without him to bring the world to her, she felt like she couldn't breathe. There was not enough air—not enough life in here, that was it. There was no room to *live*.

○–○

Lara Zhia knew how to shop. It was one of the few things she could do, and she had practiced often and with great intensity. The problem she had had in the past was simply this: lack of imagination. Years of her family's constant assurance that she was permanently invalid had convinced her that she, Lara Zhia, could never go on adventures.

But it was a lie. When she found out just how much

so, she cursed her poor mother with every foul word she knew.

The devices were made for people like her, wealthy spaceborn with "planetary adaption deficiency." A sealed body-suit with respirator to protect her from the air. A hydraulic exo-skeleton so she could walk longer distances in gravity. With a shaky voice she told the sales computer she wanted one shipped to her house, and yes she would pay the extra fee for pre-assembly. Then she leaned up against the living room window and watched Mt. Karakys. Before darkness stole it away she had come to a decision.

O—O

Lara Zhia sat before the vid in her best clothes and called the diplomatic corps for offworlders.

"Snow wash," answered the native on the other end in heavily accented Spanish. He was small and wrinkled and she couldn't tell where his eyes were.

"Hello," she said. "I would like to hire a guide to visit... um... make a pilgrimage to Mount Karakys." Jano had called it that—a pilgrimage. A visit to a special place.

"I'm very sorry," said the wrinkled little creature. "Mount Karakys is closed to offworlders."

"But—" she blurted out, before she remembered she was being diplomatic. Lara Zhia knew she was not skilled at being diplomatic, but she had to try. "I am the widow of Jano Savedra. I want to visit his grave." She could visit his grave. Soon she could go anywhere she wanted. The thought made her feel light, as if she were back in space.

"Jano Savedra is a criminal. His grave is now lost to the world."

Lara Zhia plummeted down through the stratosphere. She sat in her couch, gasping for breath. Finally she managed a strangled, "What?"

"He is a criminal. He stole from the Mountain."

Lara Zhia sat frozen in time. A fragment of conversation struggled up through her mind. "I've brought you a present," Jano had said. She had forgotten all about it, had lost it in grief, but could it be that he—

"What did he steal?" she choked out.

"A rock," said the wrinkled man, and when he said it his skin turned a whitish-gray, unhealthy color. "He thought it would grant life, but he brought it low, and it took life instead. The Mountain cursed him for his greed."

"And wh-where is it? Where is it now?"

"Returned."

"Please take me!"

"The Mountain will not see you," said the little man. "It will not see offworlders anymore." He severed the connection and left Lara Zhia sitting in silence.

○─○

Mount Karakys shone white in the sun. A plume of snow blew off its summit. Lara Zhia's new mobility device sat unopened in its crate in the center of the living room.

It was time for *Wild Vistas*. Lara Zhia sat on the couch in her bathrobe, waiting for the first strains of the theme song to soothe her aching heart. Where would Jano be today? The swamps of Montesinos? Under the Frozen Sea of Europa? The clock blinked, six-fifty-nine-fifty-nine, seven-oh-oh-oh-oh. Piano notes—cheerful and hollow like the music her mother favored—flowed out of the speakers. The camera panned in to a sickly blueish woman in a kitchen, bowls of vegetables lined in perfect rows before her. "Welcome to the first episode of *Raw Cuisine Today*," said the woman in a clipped, nasal voice.

Lara Zhia turned off the vid and stared at the dark screen. Then she turned it back on and checked the listings. *Wild Vistas*, Jano's wonderful program, was canceled.

It would not be aired anymore.

"Help, emergency," Lara Zhia whispered. She put her face in her hands and sobbed.

A long time later the light faded from the room. Lara Zhia stretched her sore legs and and stood up. She shuffled to the window. One of Karok's moons had risen, its golden light playing on the soft slopes of the Mountain. Her heart went out, past the wrinkled foothills and the heaped-up Karakyn cities huddled like children around their mother's skirts, over the high alpine meadows.

Opening the crate took her several hours—her weak arms strained against the fastenings. Putting on the suit took several more. The instructions assumed knowledge she did not have, and time and again she shuffled over to the vid to look something up or ask the computers a question. As she fastened on the exoskeleton, the sun rose, staining the rugs red-gold.

Lara Zhia took her first step. She wobbled. She tottered. She stepped again, hesitantly, then again with grace. She sat on the red couch and rose again in two swift, efficient movements.

Lara Zhia walked to the sanitizer door and put her gloved hand on the egress key.

a GIRL, a BIRD, a ROCKeT TO THe moon

a.a. BaLaSKOVITS

No matter how much Wren stomped her feet and flailed her arms and told her parents it was illegal and she'd have them arrested as soon as she found an officer who didn't laugh at her, they grabbed her elbows on the first of every month and dragged her to the red brick building with the floss and toothbrush and braces holding cartoon hands and grinning white sparkling teeth. Her parents refused to believe that the orthodontist was anything other than the short balding man who politely answered all their questions about straight molars and pink gums. They always left the room before he transformed into an eighteen foot high monster. Then he'd get sick thrills when he shoved his hands into the mouths of young kids and yanking on the metal he cruelly wrapped around their teeth. He had great big hairy arms and a voice like an eagle. He smelled like wet, soggy salt.

This is against the law, said Wren, dragging the heels of her black and white shoes. You can't make me go in there again.

Her parents made her go inside and sit in the plastic chairs in the waiting room. They held her arms down as Wren squirmed and tried to bite them.

Wren, said her mother, her smile stretching her lips

thin. Not in public.

Not at all, said her father. He turned pages of a magazine with one hand and rested the other heavily on Wren's shoulder.

A woman in matching blue pants and shirt came out of the monster's lair and called Wren's name. The woman looked at Wren and her face firmed up.

Oh, she said. Hi, again.

You're one of his, said Wren.

Wren decided, if she were to face this monster time and time again, she wouldn't let him see her cry. Even Gizmo, the blackbird with the pink beak who lived on her sill, explained that monsters can't hurt you if they don't know you're afraid of them. He was always saying, Wren, you have to be brave. Be as brave as you can.

So Wren held her head up high and stiffly walked into the small room with the huge chair and the metal tray that held thin torture instruments: pokers and pinchers and slicers and mincers.

The monster man came in with his arms covered in plastic which he had taken to wearing ever since the first couple of times when Wren had drawn blood.

He asked, How have you been, Wren? Teeth okay?

I'll eat your fingers, said Wren.

He jammed his fingers in her mouth and felt all around her teeth and gums. He tightened the tiny screw on her braces. The metal pulled on her teeth and scrunch-ed them together until her entire mouth vibrated in sharp pain. Wren tried to bite his hands but he moved too quick for her, and the woman in blue would pinch her gently on the upper arm whenever Wren caught his pinkie between her incisors.

Her parents never believed her about the monster man, no matter how much she sobbed and said it hurt hurt hurt even long after they had left the lair. This visit was proving to be no different than any of the others, so Wren covered her eyes with her hands the whole way home so that they couldn't see the water.

Her parents were tough to be around sometimes. They always smiled at her, and while Wren liked to smile, she also knew that she didn't like smiling all the time. Sometimes she liked frowning, or laughing, or crying. Often, she wanted to do all of these things at once. But her parents, they only had smiles. Warm smiles, cold smiles, stretched-to-their-ears smiles, and smiles that were so small it was almost like they weren't smiling at all. The only difference between them was that when her father smiled, he always opened his mouth so she could see his tongue and that dangly bit at the back of his throat. But when her mother smiled, she never opened her mouth and, if by chance something inside her made her so happy she couldn't help but show all those teeth and tongue and gums, she'd put her hand over her lips and look at her feet.

Gizmo couldn't smile, what with his beak and all, so when he was happy, he raised his wings above his head, pushed his feathery butt out as far as he could and pooped a white and black turd.

You're gross, Wren always said whenever he was happy, but secretly she was jealous that she couldn't poop every time she was happy, too.

But Gizmo wasn't ever happy when Wren was crying, so when she came home and ran into her room, Gizmo shuffled his feathers into a tight ball, balanced on Wren's thigh and held his smooth, cool beak under her chin. Because she could not fall asleep with her teeth thrumming, Gizmo stayed up with her the whole night.

Wren avoided her parents for as long as she could, which was only until morning when they knocked on her door, and asked her down to breakfast.

Waffles, they said cheerfully. With blueberries. Your favorite.

Wren grudgingly followed them downstairs and sat at their table and ate the creamy-gooey waffles with the sugared blueberries they had made, but she refused to look at them or talk to them, even when she could feel their smiles looking at one another and struggling to stay in place.

Later, Wren was sitting in her room running her hands over Gizmo's soft feathers when she heard her mother say her name. Curious, she crawled on her hands and knees to the edge of the stairs and listened.

Angry, her mother was saying. All the time.

As carefully as she could, Wren tiptoed her way down the stairs. Gizmo spread his wings at the top of the stairs and beckoned her to come back.

You're spying, accused Gizmo. You wouldn't like it if someone did that to you.

Shhhhhhh, said Wren. It's about me.

But Gizmo dropped his beak to his chest and headed back into Wren's room. He stopped at the doorway and said, It'll make you sad, and then I'll be sad with you.

Oh shush, said Wren.

Why must you look for an excuse to break our hearts, said Gizmo, then ruffled his feathers and hopped up onto his sill.

Wren rolled her eyes and turned back to her mother.

Don't know what to do, her mother said and lapsed into silence. Then she said, twenty more visits. She fights us every time.

And then, Doesn't know what's good for her.

Wren ran back into her room and slammed the door, not caring who heard.

Did you hear, Gizmo? she asked. They're going to make me keep going back to that horrible monster!

Well, yes, said Gizmo. That's how braces work. It's to bind your teeth together so they don't fall out. Everyone gets it done these days.

Everyone, grumbled Wren.

Gizmo was right. The next day at school Wren looked closely at the mouths of the kids in her class and everywhere she saw the familiar gleam on their teeth.

They've gotten all of us, thought Wren, and felt a heaviness in her chest for her classmates. She gathered them around her at recess on the hot blacktop and told them she understood their pain, the monthly agony that kept them up in the nights and how parents refused to understand.

Let's go, she told them, to Africa. We can discover the baby of a lion and a giraffe. A Liraffe, or a Girion. We'll be famous and can do whatever we want, then.

But her peers only stared at her dumbly or laughed, then they wandered off and ran around in circles, something they loved to do but which Wren never really saw the point of.

When she told her teachers about Africa, they said animals can't mate like that.

But it's Africa, Wren said. You don't know everything that happens there.

Yes, we do, said her teachers, and handed her several books on the subject.

Wren read each line and grew heavy because it sure seemed like the books did know everything about Africa, and that made that whole continent as boring as her braces.

I've got to get away from here on my own, Wren told Gizmo later that day as they sat on top of the stairs and listened to her parents bang out dinner in the kitchen. She said, I have to go somewhere that's new and nobody knows anything about.

No place like that left, said Gizmo. Everything on Earth is all found out.

Wren pushed her forehead against the railing on top of the stairs and rubbed her cheek where the braces nicked the soft skin. She heard her parents smiling downstairs and felt her stomach bunch up like dirty laundry.

Then I'll have to move, she told Gizmo. I'll move up up up.

She told Gizmo her plan to escape and live on the moon, the one place her smiling parents could not follow and where nobody she knew had braces.

Though he poo-poo'd the idea up and down her room, Gizmo brought her all kinds of thingamabobs he found on his daily flights to help her build a Rocket-To-The-Moon-Rocket. She didn't know where he found these things, but he brought all sorts of stuff and gewgaws and thingys and even managed to find a long, thin doodad with wires coming out of both ends.

She had to ask her father if she could borrow his screwdriver and hammer and wrench.

I'm building a rocket, said Wren, and lowered her eyes to her Mary Janes.

That's wonderful, said her father, beaming. I always wanted to be an astronaut, myself.

The next day he gave her his tools and a stack of books from the library with pictures of long white shuttles with their butts exploding in fire as they zoomed straight up to the lining of the sky. She showed Gizmo the pictures and said she needed parts that looked just like that: white and smooth and able to pierce the atmosphere.

She furiously worked at shaping the things Gizmo gave her into something that looked like it was from the book.

The doohickey was delicate because the thin, copper tubes that made up its long body were super bendy, and the red and green and blue and purple wires that burst out of its head like fireworks gave off little shocks if they touched other metals. It needed to be slowly bent around the whatchamacallit which was so big it was taking up almost all of her bedroom. The whatchamacallit was a block of metal so large that when Gizmo had brought it to her, he had been so impressed with his own birdy strength he shat all over her bedroom in glee. The whatchamacallit held the fuel, and once the Rocket-To-The-Moon-Rocket started firing up, the fuel would roll around and spurt into the doohickey, and that would send all that energy and spurty-power into the Rocket-To-The-Moon-Rocket and take her up up up.

Gizmo was the one who told her the doohickey couldn't be tightened all at once. It was the same excuse her parents gave her when she said that if the braces were tightened really hard just the one time Wren would already have the stupid perfect teeth they wanted her to have. And, she wouldn't have to be in pain at the beginning of every month. Even though they explained that that isn't how teeth worked she knew they were silly. They were in real estate and that had, as far as Wren was concerned, nothing to do with teeth. But Gizmo was a bird and he had no teeth. No teeth meant he was trustworthy.

With her father's wrench and hammer and the screwdriver with the flat head she furiously formed all the contraptions into something that looked like it was from the book. She had to hide it under her bed every morning so that her parents wouldn't find it and spoil her plans.

But her parents were nosy and always liked being in her business. They knocked on her bedroom door and she could hear them smiling at her. Wren, they said, don't you want breakfast? Even astronauts get hungry.

I'm very very busy, Wren said.

Wren, darling, it's time for a shower. We can smell you through the door. You're one little greaseball monkey.

I'm busy!

Wren, darling. You have to go to school.

No, I don't.

You do. It's the law, they said, and she could hear their smiles tremble.

That's silly, said Wren.

Then her parents started to push their way into Wren's room, and even though Wren and Gizmo barricaded themselves against the door and pushed back with all their might, Wren's parents were much stronger. It was her father that overcame Wren and Gizmo's strength, and he pushed the door so hard that Gizmo rolled all the way under the bed, and Wren fell to her stomach.

You can't shut us out, Wren, her father said, wrapping his large arms around her small frame and resting his smile on her shoulder. He added, We are always going to be here for you.

Bah, said Wren.

It took several days for Wren to properly bend the doohickey around the whatchamacallit without breaking it. She sent Gizmo out to look for Elmer's glue but, even though he showed how his wings were falling out from flapping so hard, he couldn't find any. So Wren put him to work making sure the veeblefetzer had enough dirt and water in it (that was the fuel to make the whole thing boom boom boom upwards and away) and that the thingamabobber was able to withstand all kinds of temperature, because that was what would heat up the veeblefetzer and make it all fly.

She snuck downstairs and ran behind potted plants and dived into closets whenever her parents walked into her line of sight. She waited for them to go into another room before she scavenged in cabinets and threw pencils and pens and notebooks and calculators and brooms and the mop and even several coats onto the floor.

Honey, said her mother, making Wren jump. Can I help you find something?

Mother was wearing her I'm-worried-about-you smile, the kind that was all wobbly on one side.

I need Elmer's glue, said Wren.

Why didn't you just ask? Her mother went and got a blue glue stick from a desk drawer in the kitchen and handed it to Wren.

There's no cow on the label.

It's just as good as any other, said her mother.

Cow glue is the best, said Wren.

It's all the same.

Ughhhh, said Wren, and ran back upstairs.

Wren! shouted her mother. You need to clean up the mess you made.

I'm working on a top secret rare assignment! Wren shouted back and locked her door.

Over the next couple of days Wren concentrated on nothing else except getting herself into the air even though she was nervous that when she was up there it might get lonely, because one of the books said there was no sound in space. Still, she didn't want Gizmo to think that she didn't appreciate all the work he had done, and anyway, the Rocket-To-The-Moon-Rocket was rather fun to make.

We need to get it done before the first of the month, said Wren. Else they'll send me back to the monster. She rubbed her jaw and winced.

Wren managed not to get her parents to come into her room (the Rocket-To-The-Moon-Rocket was way too big to hide now) by showering early and being by the door when she had to go to school. Her father bought it right away and smiled and ruffled her hair and said she was growing up, but her mother smiled tightly and narrowed her eyes. When Wren used the bathroom during breaks on the Rocket-To-The-Moon-Rocket she would catch her mother dusting the table in the hallway, the table her mother never dusted, and was very close to Wren's bedroom door.

When it only needed the final finishing touches, Wren and Gizmo smeared generic glue all over the gewgaws and spent the night sitting on them so that they would be firmly fixed in the morning. Then it would be ready for flight.

I made a spot for you, said Wren. She pointed at the perch she'd glued next to the pilot's seat, which was really just a stick Gizmo had brought in by accident one day.

I can't go with you, said Gizmo. I can't breathe all the way up there.

But Gizzy, said Wren. You have to go where I go. We're a team.

But I can't, said Gizmo. You want to go somewhere where no one else can follow.

He turned away from her and jumped on the sill.

Wren didn't know if she wanted to go to the moon all alone, even though she had to escape her aching teeth. Gizmo was the only one she knew who was not like any other of his kind, or her kind, and it was not only the pink beak that made him stand out, or that he could carry way more than he weighed, or even that he once tried to train her to poop when she was happy just like him. She wasn't even sure why she liked him so much, except that he seemed a part of her, if blackbirds with pink beaks could be a part of a little girl.

There was a soft knock at her door. Wren, said her mother's watery smile. I think you slept in. It's time for school.

Uh, said Wren. I'm very sick. Over one hundred and fifty degrees temperature. Cough. I better stay in bed. And you shouldn't come in or you'll get just as sick as I am.

Wren, sighed her mother, I know you hate the orthodontist, but that's no reason to miss school. In a few years you'll thank us for making you go, trust me.

Doubt it, said Wren.

The knob of Wren's bedroom door caught on the lock. Wren, said her mother, you have to let me in.

No, I don't.

Wren's mother called for her husband, and Wren ran to her window to get Gizmo to help her with the door, but Gizmo was gone. Not even a bit of his poop remained on the sill.

Wren felt her braces hurt more than they had ever hurt her before.

Wren! cried her father. Please open the door.

No! said Wren. You can't make me go to school and you can't make me go to the monster! I'm going to the moon!

Wren hopped into her Rocket-To-The-Moon-Rocket and pushed the button that heated up the fuel in the veeblefetzer. She set the straight-o-meter to aim her at the moon and hurried it along because she could hear her father hitting his body against the door.

Wren! they said. Wren, what do you mean?

The gauge-o-meter that told her when everything was filled up and ready to go began to beep and glow, so Wren pushed the button that started the explosion out of the butt and held on to her seat.

Just as the Rocket-To-The-Moon-Rocket began to

lift off the ground, her father broke into her room and stumbled when he saw Wren in her machine. It was the first time Wren saw her parents without their smiles, and she had never realized how grown up they were.

Her parents grabbed onto each side of the Rocket-To-The-Moon-Rocket and held it down. It shook and whined in their grasp, but together they dug their heels into the plush carpet and whitened their knuckles over the wings. They said, Stop, Wren! You haven't done your homework! You haven't eaten dinner! You've got an appointment at the orthodontist!

Wren looked at the straight-o-meter and it said if she didn't get off the ground right-at-this-moment-now she wasn't going to go straight to the moon, so she cried to her parents that they had to let go, or she wouldn't make it.

Her mother openly cried great bit watery tears, and she cried with her mouth open. Wren saw that her mother's teeth were big and gapped. The spaces between the molars and incisors and front two were so large whole pieces or carrot or celery could fit in-between. Her mother had teeth just like Wren's own, except that her mother's weren't covered up with metal and wires. Wren wanted to say just how cool her mother's teeth were, and probably would even be beautiful if she ever showed them in a smile, but her mother saw Wren looking and slapped her hands over her mouth.

Alone, Wren's father couldn't hold down the Rocket-To-The-Moon-Rocket, and it burst out of his hands like a rabbit hops, jittery and with its legs kicking furiously at the air. Wren was pushed to the back of her seat when she rocketed off from her room, breaking into and past the ceiling, and into the great big blue sky. She wanted to turn and say goodbye to her parents but she couldn't turn her head. So she opened her mouth to scream her farewells but the pressure was so great she couldn't form a single sound. The air was so thick and hot that when she pushed her head forward against it she felt the braces on her teeth begin to come undone.

First the small bits of metal bent and twisted against her teeth, but her teeth were slimy from her spit so they screeched and slid off the white part like they were rolling down a slide. Then they formed into a small scratchy ball on her tongue, all that metal torture, and Wren could taste the sour cement-glue. She rolled it to the front of her teeth with her tongue and spit it out, and where it landed against the front of the cockpit there was a small stain of blood. Wren ran her tongue across her teeth and her gums, and though she could feel the bumps of the glue at the edges where the tooth met gum, for the first time in a long time her mouth didn't hurt at all, and she smiled wider than her parents ever did.

She looked down below her and saw that the world was really truly blue and big. She couldn't even see her house, it was all a blur. She strained her eyes hard at the world and thought, maybe, that tiny little speck of pink there was Gizzy flying around looking for parts for something else they would have made, or maybe he was looking for her, or maybe he was saying toodle-hoo.

The pink speck faded into the big blue, and Wren felt, in her stomach, the pressure drop away from all sides of the Rocket-To-The-Moon-Rocket. But when the pressure dropped away so did everything around her. It started as a small vibration, then went into full-out shakes. Outside she could see the gewgaws begin to tear away from one another. She cursed that she had not insisted on the Elmer's Glue, because that cow on the front of the package was reliable. Once the gewgaws fell away the doodads went next, because they were made out of wire and black feathers. Then the whatchamacallit simply dropped out the bottom back to Earth, and then everything else fell away as well except for Wren, who kept on floating and floating towards the moon.

This is better than Africa, supposed Wren, who looked out into space and thought what a grand adventure it was going to be, especially when she discovered all those girions and laraffes that probably lived on the moon.

It was interesting, thought Wren, and new, to not hear a thing at all in space. It was vast and quiet, and she didn't feel anything neither except for a little tinge in her mouth. She stuck her fingers in, cringed, and out came a little bit of blood from where the braces had scratched the side of her tongue.

THE TWELFTH HOUR

Joanna Fay

Siena looked down at the painted feather in her hands. Before she could speak, the message-bearer disappeared. Only the flapping of the summer veil over the cavern's entrance marked her leaving. That, and a slight tinge in the air. Some would call it a taint, but Siena had schooled herself to this moment... and its need.

She stroked a finger along the feather's black filaments, tracing the line of scarlet characters carefully inked to its tip. Some she recognized, others she did not. Curved downstrokes, hooked at the stem, were spell-signs of finding and gathering. A few were subliminal, brought down from the Seeker's trance. A deep crescent in the centre was a gift of protection, in the hope that Siena might return.

The writing was still fresh, painted during the eleventh hour. But now it was the twelfth, and Siena stood and soothed the tremors from her fingers.

Pressing the feather to her forehead, she let the spells seep inward. Their hum ran into her skin, down through her lean frame, licking the curves of her dark, silky wings. The kicks and angles of the characters laced into her own spell-craft, strengthening its fragile patterns. She breathed in, and the energy stored in the characters began to pool in her lungs, charging the air in them with sparks of white light.

She tucked the feather through the back of her

headband for luck, and smoothed the lacings down the sides of her tunic. Black, like her hair and eyes. Black, like the darkness of Deep Corewane. But in that darkness hovered a shining window for one such as her. The tribe knew it. And she heard its siren call building as a dim hum in her blood.

Siena stepped into the cave's opening and drew aside the veil. Tiers of red-brown rock ran down from her high perch into steep ravines clothed in dark green fronds. Clouds hung low over the hills, blotting out the Core's radiance. Despite their ominous colour, they would bring no rain until the Deep had passed... and there would be little for it to fall on, anyway, if Siena didn't succeed.

> *When Deep-dark holds the world in thrall*
> *And Feather-child hears the old blood call*
> *Shimmer-lines open the day's twelfth hour*
> *The Core's fire weaves its liquid flower*
> *Look for one born in the ribbon time*
> *Given the markings, given the sign*

The old rhyme echoed through Siena's mind. At a hundred years old she might still be young in the reckoning of the Feather tribes, but she'd heard the chant from the day of her birthing. She sifted her fingers through a handful of plaits hanging down her front, and glanced at the markings. Even in the dim light, flickers of gold gleamed in her black hair. As a girl, she'd been told the Core had kissed her more than was usual, and had threaded its kisses into flesh, quill, hair and bone.

She'd met only one other marked as she was; but while Siena was a Gatherer, young Faerel was a Dreamer, and knew the signs. Siena scanned the craggy hilltops and cliffs.

Faerel?

She sent out the call, little more than a mental whisper.

Here, Siena.

The response was immediate, with the high-pitched musicality that was Faerel's signature. Siena spread her wings and lifted from the ledge outside her cave. Her pinions caught the sluggish current and took her over a ravine, past chalk-coloured cliffs. The air droned between her feathers, too thick and moist to whistle.

The resonance of Faerel's call pulled her through a narrow canyon, up a sheer rock-face. A slim figure came into view, standing at the top of a cliff, white tunic swelling on a scrap of breeze. Behind her a stake had been driven into the rocks, tied with the blue ribbons of mourning. Of course this would be where Faerel waited, the place where her little brother had fallen. Faerel wasn't much more than a girl herself, but her visions were deferred to, even by old Kalen, who knew the cycles of the Core better than anyone.

Siena's toes touched ground. She sheathed her wings and wrapped her arms around Faerel's shoulders. It was like holding air, but Faerel's eyes were deep, and at close range Siena could see amber swirling in their blackness. Faerel dug in a pocket in her dress and brought out a stone on a thin braid.

"I was instructed to make this for you." Her voice was calm, still half in the dreamworld.

Siena took the stone and pressed it to her lips. Veins of gold ran through it, the colour of the Core's light. She hefted it in her hand, feeling its weight, measuring the complex mesh of spells locked in its facets. The wonder of a child crafting such a thing filled her, but only for a moment. The old blood had spoken in Faerel's dreams since she was a baby; she had arrived understanding her gift to the tribe, and how it would be utilized.

In this you and I are sisters. Faerel's smile was solemn.

Siena nodded and fastened the braid's clasp at the back of her neck. The stone sat snugly between her breasts, casting its own glow. A set of circles, one within another like the ripples in a pond, fired up around a dark hollow in the centre. A spasm of fear caught Siena's belly. The heat safely confined in the stone's spell-lines would be nothing compared to the immolation of the Core, its fire-sprays turned to rivers, wet loops arching out from its heart in this twelfth hour of the Deep.

Could she drown in fluid fire? Even in the old days, her ancestors would not have flown straight into the Core, and they had been as gods...

Siena breathed into her gut until the tremors passed. She must have no doubt or she would surely be consumed. A low grumble sounded above her. The clouds were rolling, suddenly restless. It was almost time.

"Thank you, Faerel cirtha." She used the tribe's formal endearment, ritualizing the farewell.

Faerel pressed her fingers. She looked up at the sky. A gust lifted her hair, spreading black gold over her shoulders. Siena studied the frailty of her body, the bony dips visible through cloth. Like all the tribe, like Siena herself, Faerel was wasting. Slowly, because the spells bound into her hollow bones resisted mortality—and the Nightstars' theft. Spells that fused the Core's light into her cells' tiny triple spiral strands, as they had through generations no one could count any more. But the spells had weakened.

The blue ribbons of the mourning stake lifted and fluttered across Siena's cheek. *Lives stolen,* they whispered to her. She blinked back the moisture rimming her eyes. When the Core contracted, it was the young who perished first, the light dulling from their flesh. Not even the craft of the elders could hold them. Purpose settled harder than the cliffs around her in Siena's mind. She felt fierce, ready to tackle a thousand Nightstars.

A shadow slicked across the cliff-face beside her. Siena jumped and spun around on reflex, but no marauding Nightstar dived towards her. Instead, Kalen's ebony wings flicked back, and he stood perfectly balanced on the ledge's sharp rim.

Be wary, Siena. They will come. His face was severe

and age sat in his eyes, although the only overt sign of his thousand years was a tracery of fine lines at the corners of his mouth and between his brows. *The Nightstars, too, seek the power of the Core's juice.*

Siena couldn't suppress a faint shiver, and nothing escaped Kalen's eyes.

"I'll come with you as far as I can. But it is only you who bears the marks."

"I will be accepted," Siena intoned.

"You will be accepted." Faerel's high voice floated on the wind. "The tribe will be renewed."

Siena glanced down at her sinewy arms. *We shouldn't waste like this at all—we didn't, before the Nightstars came.*

Kalen's head tilted upward. "Come, the window closes."

He sprang into the air, and Siena followed him, adjusting her feathers on a buffeting wall of sky and shredded clouds. Faerel's white dress vanished under roiling grey. Ahead, shadows clumped and shifted, webbing the dull light. Nightstars could be hiding in any one of them, voracious, ready to leap the gap of the other-world, crystallize wings and limbs in mimicry if they so desired.

Your thoughts can draw them, Siena. Keep your mind still. Kalen's silent words rang with authority, bolstered by subtle spells that instilled in Siena's heart a necessary calm.

She pushed her body faster and caught up to him. This time, when shadows flowed around her and left their silver residue on her feathers, Siena focussed on the chink of clear sky just visible between banks of cloud. The thrum in her nerves changed to excitement. This was it! The window. She saw it now, coiled upward in a swaying, wind-tossed tunnel. And at its end, life-giving fire.

Siena sped up the passage. Her instincts flared, and ahead of her Kalen slowed. Shadows furled inward, dragging smoky cloud-tatters with them. The shadows grew wings, spiked and pointed, wings that stretched into vast, curving nets.

Siena!

I see them, Kalen.

As she levelled with him, Kalen gripped her wrist and boosted her into flight so fast that it sucked the air from her nostrils and throat. He shouted a command, and she felt his spell-craft wrap close and propel her onward. At their heels, the air hissed and rattled. White eyes glittered in blackness then dropped away. Kalen glanced back, his mouth thin.

Gods bless, Siena.

He peeled away from her and dropped back through the tunnel that now opened into a pit, a black hole of nothingness. Shadows curled over him as he streaked downward. Some of them grew talons, but Siena couldn't stay to watch the chase, or see whether Kalen outflew his pursuers. Nightstars on the hunt were relentless, but Kalen had tangled with their leaching shadow-arms before and survived.

Siena clung to that thought, then turned all her concentration on the closing gap between the cloud-walls and shot forward.

Siena.

Siena.

Please.

The murmurs of the tribe swept through her like a current, strong enough to propel her on without Kalen. She could feel the twelfth hour stretching, and she must reach the Core before it ended, or the window would be lost for another year.

Siena cirtha.

The voices gathered in her breast, filling it with warmth. She snapped her wingtips down and picked up speed. Even through the dark veil of the Deep, the Core's rays felt hotter against her skin. Shadows groped along the edge of her tunic and tugged at her hair. She muttered a spell of warding and shook them off. Not real. Just the echo of Nightstars, where they had lurked and left their prints.

Faerel's amulet throbbed against her chest. Glancing down, Siena saw the gold veins in the stone pulse into brilliance. The circles engraved in its surface began to glow, calling to the Core.

"Not yet," she gasped.

She felt like a beacon, too bright, radiating through the darkness, summoning—

A stream of black swirled around her, growing claws and barbed skin. Siena let out a curse, swung left and spiralled through the pack. Bones and wing membranes cracked around her, but the Nightstars would simply change their form.

Siena?

Her skin goose-fleshed at the familiar call. Her mother's pale face and black hair shone through the clouds. Against her will, Siena slowed.

Siena darling.

"You're dead, mi'ama." Siena shook her head, trying to dislodge the sticky tendrils of enchantment.

Her mother's fingertips reached out toward her amulet. The braid tightened around Siena's neck, choking her. She shut her eyes. A talon scraped across the stone's front. The sound clattered through Siena's mind, jolting her awake. She wrapped her hand around hot gold veins and circles and lunged backward, not waiting to see the illusion shatter.

She swung into a tighter spiral. She mustn't let the Nightstars slow her again. They could ransack all her mind, every memory, and keep reflecting them until they found the one that would bring her to a halt. A sickening sensation of life being drunk from her arteries started to drag at her pace. She pushed the feeling of weakness aside.

SSiena. SSSiena.SSSiennnnaa.

Voices built in her brain, cajoling, commanding, twisting the power of her name. Siena shut off her mind-link. She would have to do without the comfort of her tribe.

Seconds lengthened. Her heart thumped inside her ribs, each beat distinct, an ocean apart, making it hard to breathe. She scissored her wings through the tiny chink at the top of the tunnel and spilled into blinding heat. Amber flames arched gracefully over her head and plunged back toward the surface of the Core. Here, behind the veils of Deep Corewane, gauzy scarves of fire danced around the planet's heart, weaving a lacework of spells that moulded day and night, summer and winter, the Long Dry and the wet years between.

Siena flew straight into the Core's radiance, beginning her own dance, curving between fiery bands as they lashed and swayed. Time stretched. Her vision jumbled, like a dream—bright arches turned into the summer veil of her cave, into blue mourning ribbons that undulated on the wind. She saw new stakes being erected, Faerel standing very still, following her dive into the fire. Kalen's steady hand on her shoulder. The rattling whine of Night-stars, but they couldn't pursue her into the blaze.

Her skin smarted now where the protective spells of the tribe grew thin. The scarlet characters on the feather in her hair-band must have started to melt. She lifted the stone on its braid between both hands in mute plea. Golden light saturated her breath. Her lungs filled, but the light was like liquor, drowning her.

Time... stopped.

At the end of the twelfth hour, at the far edge of the Deep.

Nothing moved for a second, or a millennium. Siena hung suspended in light, and in her hands an orb of stone burned, flickering. The flickers dripped, raining outside time, unstoppable. The window hung open, adrift, then began to shut. She started to breathe. The Core's light-arms thrust her backward. Sparks landed on her fingers and wrists, blossoming into yellow flowers. The orb's circles opened wide. A torrent of petals poured inside them as Siena hurtled down, drawing in real air, tasting its dust and minerals as if she'd never breathed before.

The skin on her arms was soft amber, and she didn't need to see her eyes to know they were bright, and orange. The Core's spells unfurled around her. No Nightstar could catch her now. Siena laughed. Petals of light dissolved on her tongue. Her body became a riot of glowing colours as she fell. Wind howled past her. Chalky cliffs climbed to embrace her. She didn't know how she would find her feet, but it didn't matter.

Instead, she focussed on the billows of Faerel's white dress and let herself tumble.

Siena!

Such ecstasy in one word.

Siena smiled. Air whistled through feathers. Arms closed around her, breaking her fall. Kalen's scent was there, and others. Core-flowers ran like dew from her fingertips, sparking flesh, eyes, bones. The gift of light swelled out, from cell to mind to subtle spell-web, rippling through the tribe. Laughter wrapped her, the sweetest sound she had ever heard. A finger ran gently over her face. Faerel's soft lips brushed her forehead. Through the hot blur of her vision, Siena saw her tribe sister's cheeks already starting to fill out.

Hands laid her down on the roughness of rock. It felt like ocean, dimpling beneath her body. Siena looked up into the clouds of the Deep as they shredded and rolled away from a diamond of clear daylight. Spells leaked out from under her palms, giving life. She loosened her grip from the stone and closed her eyes. When she opened them again, her world would be changed.

me myself i

aj fitzwater

I met myself that first time across the counter of a coffee shop.

I had been taking long-cuts to work, walking side streets, searching in a desperate attempt to reclaim minutes for myself before the office. I had not seen this coffee shop before. Something new?

I hesitated at the door, low sun glaring off glass. Did I want my first cup that day from an unknown, or did I want my usual corporate comfort?

I wasn't looking for myself just then—I had and gave enough of myself on a daily basis, thank you very much—but I saw something of myself in the fashionably stressed wood, the warm colours, the clean glass, and hint of spotless tables.

Perhaps, in the end, the name struck me. "Lana's." Simple, no bullshit.

My name.

Eyes downcast, I had no need to glance at the menu board. Everyone did a standard, straight up latte. I blurted my order in a too loud voice.

The girl on the counter—no, quick glance, a woman my age—mumbled a greeting. Yeah, I get it, it's too early in the day. Then she said no more. An uncomfortable silence stretched out and I repeated my order, paying close attention to the zip on my wallet.

Then her voice—so similar—coughed out, "Boss, we have another one."

My head snapped up, the shock on my face a muted echo from the counter girl.

She was me. Oh sure, she had bright pink spiky hair. But there we were. The muddy eyes lost in a muddy complexion, too big bottom lip beneath the too small top lip, wide shoulders, and untameable hips.

I began my deep breathing exercises, just as my doctor had instructed I should when my sight started getting hazy like this.

Then another Me came from out the back, wiping wet hands on her apron embroidered with the shop's name. My name.

I recognized the natural unmanageable brown sticks of my hair, a style and colour I refused to sport. Lines around her lips and eyes emphasized a well-used smile. Well, isn't she just the lucky thing.

"Make her the drink," this Boss version of me said, voice all no nonsense. She led me by the elbow to a comfortable chair, the trust intimate. She had done this before.

"You aren't the first, and you certainly won't be the last," the Boss began, no introduction necessary. "This is your place. You found it, it found you. You're safe and welcome here."

My eyes followed her gesture. Yes, I could see my taste in all of this.

"H-how? Wh-why?" I damned myself for my stupid stuttering.

The Boss shrugged. "Those are questions for The Brain. You'll meet her eventually. She's better at explaining what she thinks is the string theory of it all. She's been working on the problem for years. It's almost her life time's work."

Envy warred with suspicion. I narrowed my eyes. "That's a pat answer. You seem very comfortable with all this. Me. Her." My hand described a lazy circle.

She, I, grimaced. "I'm afraid I'm a bit too stupid to

grasp it, really. I simply own this place, and I've watched Us come and go for quite some time. I've gotten used to the not knowing the answers."

Boy, did I recognize that self-effacement.

"So, you're Lana? She's Lana?" I pointed to Pink Hair again, now bringing over the coffee. "This Brain version is a Lana too?"

The Boss dipped her head. "We're all you. Us. Me." She laughed. "Don't worry, you get used to it."

I rubbed my forehead with one hand, eyes squeezed tight, determined that the tears would not come out.

My hand covered my own. "I know, it can be quite a shock. Here, drink your coffee. You'll feel better in a moment."

I sat with myself in a silence that became more comfortable as the minutes went by. Pink Hair watched me from beneath her scruffy fringe, became more recognizable as she made a half-hearted attempt to clean the counter.

"I hope no one else comes in." The Boss stared, unseeing, at the front door. "It can be a little freaky for newbies. Two of Us are more than enough to deal with the first time."

My coffee mug hit the table. "How many of Us are there?" I demanded.

She shrugged. "I've stopped counting. The Brain reckons it could be infinite, based on the infinite choices We've made in Our life." She paused, and corrected herself. "Lives."

A burning, acidic taste of coffee rose up my gullet. Choices? Had I made choices to get here?

"So what do you do? What Lana are you?" Did she read my mind? No. How odd it must be to know the person in front of you almost exactly from the moment they walked in the door.

"I'm an HR manager." I put the pride people told me I should feel into my voice. "For a major retail chain."

"Oh." *I bet you were expecting something else,*

something better, I thought. *Don't worry, you're not the only one.*

"You?" I prompted her before she could ask the usual about husband, house and kids. She gave a wry twist of her lips, recognizing the avoidance tactic.

"Made my way through corporate coffee. Wanted a space for myself. Built this place. They—you all—came." Again, her hand waved in my customary dismissive gesture, a recitation many times done. The clipped words were almost an invitation, a dare, a plea, to come back and find out more.

"Her?" I jerked my head in Pink Hair's direction.

Another habitual expression—my scolding squint. "That's you, you know. Why don't you ask?"

I raised my voice to include the eavesdropping Pink Hair in the conversation. "And you?"

She gave our one-shoulder shrug. I've gotta work on that dismissive and meek thing. "Nothing better to do," she mumbled. "Gotta pay the rent somehow."

She turned almost as pink as her hair, and scuttled away to safety. I raised an eyebrow to The Boss. "It's, she's, complicated. Messy." She waggled her hand to let me know I should *Let It Be.*

"Aren't we all?"

"Some are, shall we say, tidier, than others. You'll get bits out of her eventually."

I grimaced. "Sounds familiar."

The Boss sighed. "Yeah." A world came through in the single sound.

I had to think about it for a minute. I blinked back tears again, scolding and blaming the sun.

"Eventually? You've said that twice now. You think I'll come back here? What's to say I won't have a complete freak out and tell my psychiatrist I've started having hallucinations?"

The admission slipped out so easily. I guess it's easier when you're telling yourself.

Again that shrug. "It's ok if you don't. Some can't

hack it. I don't blame them. Meeting your other possibilities can play with your mind. On the other hand, some of Us love it. It's a vicarious thrill. What if, ya know?"

What if. I had asked that many a time. Over and over.

○─○

I took that away with me, affecting calm as I walked out of the coffee shop.

I did ask The Boss whether I'd find the shop again. I had a panicked moment, at battle with my wariness. I didn't want to lose this perfect thing I'd just found. She replied that if the need existed, I would find it again.

Ego and curiosity won out. I went back the next morning and there the coffee shop stood, waiting.

Pink Hair affected a greeting a little less metallic. Braving eye contact, I noticed her lip-ring. I envied it. I mumbled something about feeling odd paying for the coffee, and the one yesterday I'd forgotten to cash up for, but she gave me the one-shoulder shrug and mumbled something about it "all going back to us anyway." That idea felt good.

The Boss and I spoke to each other in the language of bobbed heads, and then she inclined her head towards a figure sipping coffee in a corner, waiting for and gauging the reaction.

I rewarded her with horror.

This Me had a pram. A Mother.

I drank my latte fast, not caring that it burned my tongue—Pink Hair knew how hot I, we, liked it. My eyes bore holes in the table, my skirt, the back of my hand. I couldn't bring myself to look at The Mum again, but I could feel her curious gaze from across the room. She knew what I knew.

I didn't hate kids. Perhaps better to say I had never felt the maternal pull, fish-needs-a-bicycle, terrible with people (was my job in HR some sort of self-flagellation?)... I could barely look after myself let alone someone else. I had many reasons ready on the edge of my tongue when I made to make proper socialization.

Why did this version of me utterly disregard my, our, logic, and have a child?

I rushed out of the coffee shop, avoidance at a premium. Maybe The Mum was as relieved as I.

For the next few days, I turned aggressive at the mere mention of children. I didn't go back to the coffee shop for a week after that, shaken by the possibility that there could be iterations of me that I didn't want to face.

But I couldn't stay away. Curiosity killed my cat. I sucked up the courage to go back.

And so I met The Rock Star, fabulous in all her glitter and leather glory.

I loved her instantly. She adored my fawning in a bourgeois fashion. I hated her for that, but wanted to suck up every piece of her existence.

I called in sick within minutes of Our eyes meeting across the coffee shop. I had to take my call outside, because cell phones and internet—contrivances of the Outside world—did not work Inside. The Boss shrugged it off by saying the coffee shop existed in some internal little universe mechanic thing. If I wanted to know anything else I needed to ask the wonderful Brain.

When I came back in, I proceeded to buy The Rock Star cappuccino after cappuccino--her favourite, not mine. I urged grander stories out of her purple-stained lips.

The Mum came and went, and with my panic attack over I felt a passing curiosity for the caterwauling sack of my intermingled genes in the pram. With all the choices of procreation available, how could I be sure my offspring would look like this?

The Rock Star demonstrated a more open distaste for the thought of Our procreation. Her juicy grape lips curled up in a sneer, great black-rimmed eyes quickly ushering The Mum out of the shop. I squirmed and avoided the confrontation—a great skill of mine—by fiddling with a napkin.

Later, after breathless discussion of post-show exploits had excited us, I joined The Rock Star in the toilets for a kiss and a feel. Then, she left the store in a languid hurry, one side of her mouth curled in triumph. It left me with a longing I hadn't dared to touch for decades.

I spent the rest of the day at the coffee shop, confused, only slightly aware of the other possibilities around me hoping she would come back. She didn't.

The Boss heaved a sigh to get my attention as she placed an afternoon tea scone in front of me.

"Quit sulking."

I stuck my finger into the whipped cream, and sucked it off, giving her the thousand yard stare. "She was wonderful."

"She's a narcissistic cow." The Boss parked herself across the table, twizzling a napkin through spilt liquid.

"Great, huh?" I grinned. "I wish I had her lack of a mental gate keeper."

The Boss stared at me for a moment. "How many friends do you have?"

I gave the shrug. "A few. Enough. I won't be lonely in my old age, if that's what you mean."

She caught and held my eyes. "She has none. Only acquaintances. She uses people, chews them up, then spits them out."

"Cliché. But touché."

"Ninety-nine percent of Us are better than her." I heard the capitalization.

"That's a bit harsh. What about the other one percent?"

"They think they don't need Us, but they still keep coming back. On the other hand, there are some who come in here wounded, stay for only a little while, then We never see them again. They're the ones who really need Us."

Did I look like one of the walking wounded? And just how did they avoid coming back if I, We, loved this place so much?

"I thought you said I've yet to meet The Brain." My cynical humour—always useful—started to wipe away the childish recalcitrance.

"I'm like a bartender." Shrug. "It's easier to understand when you're talking to Yourself."

I appreciated her considerate words, but still a trace of longing lingered. From that moment on, I knew I could only allow myself to see The Rock Star again in a crowd, the bejewelled, dazzling, tempting dream best left at arm's length.

○─○

Obsession warred with fear of loss. I tried not to go every day. Some weeks were better than others. Some weeks my work so numbed me that I needed the only people who understood. I stopped going to my psychiatrist so much, and she declared--a little too eagerly--my improvement. I decided not to tell her why. My Place belonged to me, and besides, who would believe me?

Eventually I gave way to full-borne curiosity. I wanted to meet so many versions of Me.

Some were so vastly beyond what I imagined I could be. I saw choices I had made, conscious and unconscious. Things I had dreamed of or nightmares I had run from, choices I had dabbled in or passing fancies, decisions that had seemed inconsequential at the time--should I turn left or go right?

Gay, straight, bi and transgender. Married, fickle, celibate, or poly-amorous. I'd had abortions and miscarriages.

I debated atheism with a Priest version of myself, and enlightenment with The Buddhist.

I avoided the Large and Happy, as well as the one with an obvious eating disorder, unsure how to broach either subject.

The stories of loss and courage from the wheelchair-bound, ill, and diseased fascinated me.

A dizzying variety of professions played out before me. From astrophysicist to zoologist, there existed an artist, doctor, athlete, tradesperson, scientist, civil servant, teacher, and home maker of every stripe.

Others were almost unrecognizable. The disgustingly rich, the bankrupt and homeless. The mentally ill almost made sense.

Some of these others didn't even seem like decisions I'd made. Sometimes the only thing We had in common was one parent or the other. Their skin colour or privilege pre-ordained before I exited the womb.

Never were any of them a male.

Fascinating, too, that their concept of the coffee shop occupied another part of the city, country or even another part of the world.

I became enamored of the Romanian Circus Trapeze Artist, made wistful by the Distant English Heiress. I felt emboldened by the ebony-skinned South African Civil Rights Activist, moved to tears by the Chinese Factory Supervisor. I feared for the Middle Eastern Politician, and picked up wonderful cooking tips from the Latina Grocery Owner. Their experiences of growing up were distant echoes of my own childhood.

The One missing, the One we all spoke of in hushed, excited tones, were The Dead. I, we all, figured there must be many versions of them. A group usually headed by The Writer had a grand time discussing morbid possibilities. I dipped in and out of these conversations, depending on the temperature of my outside life. The more pissed off I got with my Lack of Upward Mobility, the more I gravitated towards the morbid.

So much envy, smugness, potential, and wasted time.

○─○

"Thank you for taking the time to debate this with me," The Brain said, holding my gaze over the top of her purple spectacles.

I blushed. We had spent many hours poring over her theories, and The Brain tended to fall into language incomprehensible to me. I felt more intelligent just by virtue of being seen in her presence.

"I must seem so stupid," I acquiesced, flipping a hand.

She scowled. "Don't condescend to me. You, We all, are more intelligent than you give yourself credit for. How else do you think I would have got to be? Our genetics are nearly identical."

My colour deepened. "I'm trying. I do admit, it is fascinating. Maybe I'm too old to start new on something so big."

The Brain sighed and rubbed her eyes. The overwhelming majority of Us had been recalcitrant to attempt any sort of understanding of what she theorized as "The Convergence Of Universes." She found it maddening that so many of us still rejected the beauty of science. Her disappointment a double edge, my experience came from the other side.

As she launched into another lecture, this time attempting to find words more palatable to me, she shuffled the books and papers on the table before us. A lot of them had her, Our, name on them with a flurry of letters after it. I envied the time and energy she had to devote to such a task.

I believed The Brain had the most tangible result of success amongst all of Us. In her world, people, women, flocked to her leadership and ideas. Their welcome and respect, and the pity in her eyes for me, took dark, bitter root in my stomach.

O–O

I want to blame The Boss for not being able to go back again, but no matter. Now I know I made my choices, however unthinking.

Early one quiet morning, we fell into casual conversation. Only The Children's Entertainer and The Crazy Bag Lady were there carrying on an animated chat, well suited.

Our conversation, about expectations, about life, became another unwitting choice among the tenuous threads that connected us all. I thought because we couldn't take an Other with us beyond the door, anything that happened In Here couldn't possibly affect The World Out There. Lazy, stupid, stupid lazy.

I told her that, despairingly enough, I excelled at what I did.

She smiled the half smile, did the half shrug. She dispensed sagacious wisdom. I laughed at the clichés, the likes of which I usually ignored from motivational speakers, conferences, or self-styled mentors.

And as with most of my life, I walked away from confronting thoughts, and let them stew.

Then one day at work, I closed my eyes, thought of the example from The Brain and The Boss, opened my mouth... and things began to happen.

I loved and hated my small real world triumphs. They were Good Enough, but I couldn't exhibit The Brain's fearlessness, or execute The Boss' methodical game plan. I had to go see them for more advice.

Hindsight is beautiful. If I had known I would never again step across the threshold into my safe haven, I would have satisfied some longings. Maybe I would have kissed The Rock Star that one last time. Maybe I would have worked up the courage to hold The Mum's baby. Maybe I would have waited for The Brain for that last conversation, eke out a final piece of understanding. Maybe I would have worked up the gumption to encourage Pink Hair to leave her loser boyfriend.

So many maybes.

This day, I came to the right place, but it was all wrong. The door, now the entrance to a Chinese restaurant, told me what I didn't want to see, what I thought I wasn't ready to come up against.

A tiny Chinese lady with a face like a map of the world found me there, took pity on the devastation newly scribed across my mine, and gently led me inside her restaurant for a cup of tea.

I figured a change from coffee might do me good.

ITEM 317: HORN FRAGMENT W/ILLUS

E. CATHERINE TOBLER

I am a shadow, slipp'd.

Those poor, poor women, sliced apart, carried to God knows where. Me, seemingly whole, though life still taken from my body, warm and crying, never seen by these black eyes. A pale thread of skin across my throat, easily concealed; the rest of me wrapped in black and tucked away, in a place no one would have to look, until I am swallowed by the blessed forgetfulness of time.

○─○

Under the flickering light of the gas lamp struggling to illuminate the apothecary's back room, the horn fragment looked oily, as though one could lay finger to it, and come away with a black stream running down said finger. I did not remove the horn, only looked at it for a long moment before pushing the small, black wood case to the side, where it sat for another week before I eyed its unmarked sides again and drew it close.

A cork-capped glass jar encased the horn fragment, a four-folded slip of paper curling between jar and packing straw. I pulled the paper free and unfolded it, a bull's magnificent head rearing from the page. Gray horns swept upward against the yellowing paper, an address in Greece neatly printed in one corner.

My uncle's voice, when it came, was filled with something I had not heard before. For the first time in my occupancy with him, he sounded genuinely worried. Emotion from him, directed at me, was unusual. "Where did you find that?"

I looked from the illustration to my uncle, frowning at his tone. "It was among the other cases, though unmarked," I began, but said no more, for he tugged the page from my fingers and folded it in half and in half again. He slipped the page under the jar and closed the case's lid before giving me a smile one might give an infant.

"Nothing to worry yourself about." He nodded his graying head toward the other similar cases that lined the counter as if to direct my attention toward them, but my attention didn't waver from my uncle and the case beneath his arm. I watched as he carried it out of the room and down the long, door-lined corridor which led to a narrow, shadowed staircase. I heard his quick steps move upward, toward the living quarters.

Nothing to worry myself about, perhaps, but I couldn't stop *considering* image and artifact, even so. Each time I asked about the horn fragment, my uncle attempted to brush it off, as something random, something that had not been intended for his shop at all, but had been included by clear mistake. He would return it at once. The case wasn't even marked with a number as the others had been. It belonged nowhere, much like me.

When asked again, my uncle hedged, and allowed that horns *did* have certain properties that certain patrons of the shop might find pleasing, but that was not why *he* was in possession of the thing. Certain properties and certain patrons, indeed. His denials only made me believe otherwise, that my uncle, one of London's most respected apothecaries, knew precisely what he was doing with the item, and was ashamed I had discovered it.

Still, the following day, the small wood case sat in

my workspace, as though waiting for me. I lifted the lid and peered inside, finding all as it had been, jar nestled in packing straw with illustration and horn. I looked to the outer room of the shop, seeing my uncle and Missus Baker beyond the dark fall of the velvet curtain in the doorway. Beyond even them, a black-cloaked figure, gloved fingers slipping through the bundled herbs, and a suited gentleman, taking an interest in the tobacco.

"And Stella is here *now?*" Missus Baker murmured. My uncle's head bobbed and Missus Baker exhaled, shaking her own head. "My Oscar is to wed in *three weeks*, Raymond!"

My uncle hushed her and drew her far enough away that I could no longer hear the conversation, but what more did I need to overhear? I drew the curtain closed.

The wooden stool caught me as I sank to sit and I contemplated the thing before me, the small unmarked case. I drew my notebook close and opened it to the ribbon-marked page, adding a line for the box. The box was unnumbered, but I had turned up no item 317 in the lot my uncle had received. Thus, it became *Item 317: horn fragment, w.illus.*

Item 316 was a small vial of dried, Egyptian locusts, resting in a small bundle like brown, papery cigars, and item 318 a bottle of what seemed to be water, but the enclosed documentation assured it was liquefied hail collected from Egypt during a fierce storm. The inclusion of the horn near these Egyptian items seemed to indicate that it, too, originated from that dusty land, but the illustration noted an address in Greece, which made more sense, all things considered.

"Leave it be," my uncle told me over supper that night, setting his knife with undue force upon the table top after cutting a slice of roast. "I was wrong to take the thing from you. I appreciate your willingness to catalogue what we have obtained at all, niece, for surely there are more than nine hundred cases total, and I would not have the time..."

I stopped paying attention to my uncle's spoken words, and watched his eyes instead, how they flitted from knife to roast and back again to knife.

Razor-thin blade drawing under my throat, the heated rush of blood after.

The candle between us illuminated my uncle's dark eyes and made them seem like oil. Restless, that gaze, moving everywhere except to me as he made his denials.

Spill of gaslight down the street and then only dark in the alley—dark, damp, bruised, and screams... no one came.

My head came up sharply as the building around us *groaned.* My uncle fell silent at that, listening to this terrible sound that seemed to rise up through every timber to shake the roof shingles. I imagined I could feel the rumbling through the soles of my shoes.

"Restless spirits, mm?"

My uncle returned to his roast. I pressed my shoes hard to the now-still floor, my hands tight in my skirts. My appetite had fled like... *Dark coattails moving away, heels sharp on stone, bright crimson across my chest and thighs...*

Restless. Every building in this city had a tale of someone being buried in the foundations, to appease the spirits of the land as the city rose from what had once been nothing, and while these buildings did make noise from time to time, I had never imagined it as a spirit until now.

A fresh crack of thunder made me jump in my chair. I came to my feet and tossed my napkin atop my uneaten meal, sliding away from the table. My uncle looked up, eyebrows arched. Surprise on that worn face.

"I think..." I sucked in a breath and resisted the desire to lift a hand to the black lace that covered my throat and the mark of my attack. "I'll do a little more work."

I stepped out of the room to the sound of my uncle's soft laughter; how like him I was even at twenty, he murmured, finding solace in work through the long hours of the night.

I wasn't certain it was solace that my workspace contained, so much as a focus. I lit the lamp and watched its light spread across the collection of boxes. There were too many and, yet, not enough. If cataloging new arrivals at the apothecary were to be my life, how might I make these cases last forever?

My eyes were drawn back to the unmarked box, the one I listed as 317. The box sat close to my left hand, its lid askew. I could not remember leaving it so, and meant only to nudge the lid back into its place, but I found myself lifting the box, looking again at the horn.

What had my uncle been trying to hide?

I traced a finger down the jar and the building seemed to give another low shudder around me. With my finger still pressed to the glass, I looked up, imagining that I saw dust sift down from the ceiling boards, over the tops of the boxes piled before me like faint snow. It was then the gaslight stuttered before going entirely out. My breath caught in my throat and I strained to hear anything in the darkness.

Surely there were footsteps behind me, why didn't I hear them?

There was only a low moan, as if the very building were in pain. And then, another rumble of thunder before a steady thrum of rain on the roof above.

The lid of the case slid easily into place and I stood, gathering the other two boxes already logged. With these held close to my chest, I made my way down the dark and yet familiar hallway, toward the third door on the left, one of many rooms my uncle claimed for storage.

Old dust on brass made the doorknob slippery beneath my fingers, but the door was silent as it moved inward. My first step inside, however, was my last; there was strangely no floor as there should have been and I was falling, small wood boxes flying from my grip as I plummeted downward.

I seemed to fall forever, weightless, which was folly, for all too soon the ground rushed up to meet me. The boxes hit first, wood and glass falling to pieces, then my own hands, striking cold, damp stone and glass. Glass pierced my palms, bright pain, and far above, the sound of a latching door.

A footstep, there must have been, why didn't I hear...

My head snapped toward that distant sound, but there was nothing to see, not even my own injured hand in front of my face, so absolute was the dark. I passed a hand across my face, thinking that perhaps the lace at my throat blinded me, but there was nothing. Even that lace was gone.

"Uncle!" My voice echoed in the space; I somehow had not expected it to, believing this darkness without end. I willed my vision to clear, for my legs to cease their shaking. Neither happened.

I pushed myself up from the damp stone floor and reached out. My injured hands touched the same damp stone on either side, fingers discovering individual stones wedged together with mortar. A man-made thing, then, and narrow enough that I could reach both sides with arms spread. I turned to my left and reached again, but there was no stone, nor any to the right.

I pictured a hallway, but could not make myself move down it. I stood convinced that the floor would vanish if I took a step in either dark direction, and so sank back down into this strange nothingness around me. This little square of stone beneath my shoes, how easy to imagine the rest of the world fallen away, the whole of it dwindled to this small darkness.

"Uncle!"

Again, there came no reply and no echo. Whatever this place was, he could not hear me, or could hear and simply didn't care. How easy for him, if I *did* vanish. I tried to stop myself from shaking, but couldn't, and it was this motion that eventually began to calm me. It was familiar.

My trembling skirts brushed something papery, and I recalled the boxes and reached into the darkness for whatever remained of them. My fingers passed over dried locusts and I felt a chill that seemed darker than even the space around me, bits of broken glass and wood and scattered straw, but not the curled horn. Its loss felt like a knife in my heart.

"Item three sixteen." My whisper sounded impossibly small in the space. I counted out nine locusts and set them to the side. "Item three seventeen... presently unaccounted for. Item three eighteen, likely spilled when the bottle broke." I exhaled, exhaustion starting to curl around my shoulders as though it longed to pull me into a different kind of darkness. "No."

The refusal was not enough, for I slept. I slumped onto the cool, damp stone, one hand covered in blood, still reaching for the dried locusts.

When I woke, it was the curled horn I saw before me. The jar was gone, likely shattered with the others, but the horn fragment lay close to hand, gleaming in—

I blinked, trying to clear my vision. Gleaming. Could a thing gleam without light? I looked up, to a curious warm glow that radiated beyond the rising curve of darkness before me.

"Uncle?"

Had the door opened? Had I only tripped over my skirts as a child might and hit my head? I tried to sit up, but my body protested, bruised from the fall. I frowned at the curve of darkness, amazed I could see anything at all. One's vision might adjust to any circumstance if given time, as would hearing,

but—

A breath that was not my own sounded in the small space. I reached a hand out, meaning to grab the bit of horn and go, get up and run and run and—

The darkness shifted and with it the horn. The curve of black moved and for a moment wholly obliterated the golden light beyond it. *Shadow—no, body.* A different kind of gold made itself known then, one that was rimmed in ink and focused on *me.* Wide eyes, watching.

An immense head lifted and the golden light ran like liquid down twin horns that spiraled from the skull, down wide black shoulders and equally black arms. Gold dipped between and over naked breasts and belly, washing down thighs as the creature rose upon its unshod hoofs with a strange kind of grace. If starlight were gold, this black body was the whole of the sky, stretching to encompass the entire world.

I screamed. Like that night long ago in the alley, I screamed. Instinct made me bolt upright, and heedless of where I was, I sought only to get away. *There must have been a footstep... from this I would have run.* I turned, but quickly realized I was within an enclosed space, one fire providing heat and light, one arched doorway just beyond the creature.

"No locked doors in my house."

The voice startled me into stillness. The voice was as dark as the outlying world around us, as dark as the creature itself, but yet gilded. I curled my shaking hands into my skirts and watched the creature as it—as *she*—stood straight and spread her hands, as if welcoming me to a banquet.

"Many courtyards, many hearths."

Those black hands swept toward the fire, which seemed blinding when compared to what I had known, but my attention moved past the fire, to the doorway. The arch was filled with darkness and I knew not where the corridors might lead. Only knew that I wanted to be there, wanted out and away. And yet... .

My gaze returned to the creature, horrible and fascinating all at once. Tightly curled and glossy black hair covered her scalp and a piece of fabric looped the base of one horn, its color lost to the firelight. Those horns, how like the fragment.

"Three seventeen," I whispered.

"You are injured. Come."

The hands beckoned me forward to the fire, where I noticed a bucket filled with water. Still convinced the floor would evaporate beneath my feet, I moved slowly, eyes on the beast as it turned and curled hands around the bucket's handle. She placed the bucket before me.

That I was dreaming was the simplest explanation, but the cold water against my injured hands felt real enough, each cut screaming pain as I washed the dried blood away.

"Dreaming." I had fallen asleep in my workspace, that was all, and the storm had dragged me down into strange dreams.

"Countless dreams," the creature said.

I looked up at this thing my memory had likely drawn from a half-remembered book. It was less frightening when viewed through a dream's spectacles.

"Asterion?" I asked.

The golden eyes blinked, as if in surprise. The big black head shook once. "Asteria," she said, and offered me a length of clean, old cloth.

I took the fabric, finding it warm from the fire, and wrapped my hands to both warm and dry them. Asteria. The creature had a name and was female. Trapped in darkness—no locked doors, she had said, but did doors matter in a place such as this?

"Such a dream." I closed my hands into loose, aching fists and lowered my head, thinking to only sleep for a moment more. I could no longer hear the storm; perhaps dawn had come and my uncle would soon be laughing at me when he found me slumped over the counter.

When I opened my eyes, however, I found myself in the same stone room, the fire dwindled down to embers. Asteria was gone. This did not relieve me as much as it should have, for I felt more alone than I did even when supping with my uncle. The doorway stood across from me, unguarded.

No locked doors, she had said, and countless dreams. Which dream was this? I did not know as I stood and crossed to the archway. I unwrapped my hands when I arrived there and peered out, dark corridor leading in either direction. I had no idea which branch to take, but then I had no idea where I meant to *go,* either.

I dropped the end of the old fabric in the doorway and stepped into the hall. Letting the fabric fall behind me as I walked, I trailed a hand over the stone wall to my left too, hearing nothing but my own breath as I went. This place was like a womb, dark and unfamiliar, though the farther I walked, the more recognizable it grew. The path I walked curved inward and came to an abrupt end, before seeming to curve back in on itself, and back yet again.

These curving paths seemed endless and the longer I walked them, the more frightened I became. I kept trying to fit this place into the world I knew: the world above, as I came to think of it. My logic didn't work, for this labyrinth seemed old. These stones were not new; they were worn against my hands and beneath my shoes, as though many people had known these corridors for years and years. If this place were so old, then it had always been here, beneath the apothecary, and the apothecary had always been in my family, thus—

It was a train of thought I did not like. I recalled the groans of the building above, the strange scents that often filled the rooms, and wondered if this underground labyrinth—and its monster—were the cause. How long had Asteria been here, and how had she come to this place at all?

The darkness rushed up on me, cold and so black. I shivered and pressed myself against a wall, willing myself to vanish. I could not see, could only navigate with my hands outstretched to either wall. The fabric had long since run out, but I needed no trail to find my way back, for this corridor was not a maze. It seemed to have but one path.

I slept again and on waking, found myself wedged against a warm, black body. My hand was splayed across Asteria's belly; I could feel the rise and fall with each breath. She smelled like warm soil and her skin was smooth like rose petals as I drew my hand back—but here, my fingers discovered a scar marring her ebony flesh.

This closeness should have alarmed me more than it did, but in the dark Asteria's even breathing was a comfort, something to hold on to, proof that I wasn't alone. Which was worse—being alone in the dark or being in the dark with a monster? Whichever, I gravitated toward the monster, curling deeper against her body and closing my eyes to sleep once more.

There seemed to be no time in these dark corridors. When I woke, Asteria threaded her fingers through mine and guided me through the corridor, toward another courtyard of sorts, this one with a pool of water and fire both. Asteria bid me drink, and I did, greedily.

What is this place, I wanted to ask, and how did you come here? But the sight of Asteria in the firelight stole my voice. She was ink given shape, held together by sorrow. I could see that much in her eyes. This place might be home for her now, but it had not always been such. She was not of this damp country, nor maybe even of this time.

"You are also marked," she said. Her hoofs seemed to cause the stone floor to vibrate as she moved, and I imagined this vibration moving upward, through the very timbers of the apothecary far above us. Asteria stepped from the doorway toward the pool of water where she dipped her magnificent head and drank.

"Marked?"

I asked the question, but then I knew, and lifted a hand to cover my bare throat. My cravat was lost, which exposed the thin bright scar against my skin. I drew in an uneasy breath and nodded.

"A man, in an alley." *There must've been a footstep...*

Asteria lifted her head, water gleaming down her chin, and drew her fingers low across her belly. The scar I had felt earlier was plain, very pale against the rest of her.

"A man, on a ship," she said.

She was close enough to touch then, and I found

myself lifting a hand to do just that. My wet fingers felt cool against her dark cheek. She flinched but did not draw away, and I kept my touch slow and gentle, the way one might with a horse. I moved my fingers up to the bit of cloth around her horn.

It was my cravat.

My hand stilled and I looked into those strange gold eyes, wondering. "You're tangled," I said, though the knot in the fabric was quite deliberate.

A small snarl escaped Asteria, but she allowed me to loosen the knot and pull the lace free. Beneath the lace, I saw the deep mark in her horn, a carved number. The number six. Her eyes closed and her ears flicked, the latter just a whisper between us.

I swept my thumb over the marking upon her horn. It felt as old as these stone halls, smooth as if she had tried to worry it away. She turned into my touch, cautious, eyes still closed.

Who marked her wasn't important to me right then. The number, though, made me think of the cases I was meant to catalogue, each item with its own number. A thing labeled and placed in darkness so no one would have to see, unless they came looking for such a terrible thing from the kindly apothecary.

Thoughtful, I slid my fingers upward along the curve of Asteria's horns, finding no place where the fragment may have come from. Another minotaur then, I thought, and wondered if my uncle had requested a sample from such a creature, one who lived far from these city streets. A male perhaps, I allowed myself to imagine, though not meant to keep Asteria company precisely.

"Will you show me your house?" I tied the lace back around her horn, to cover her marking once more.

"It is like no other," Asteria said and she rose, offering me a hand, for I would be blind again when we left the fire's gold glow.

As we walked, I knew not what I meant to do. Every hall was like the one before it, twisting back on itself time and again, until I grew weary of counting. Thirteen, fourteen, Asteria took me past pools of water—one showing me my face like a mirror, others colored gold from tiles, or blue and green from algae; there were pits of crimson fire, and small, soot-smudged temples built to gods who were no longer honored above ground. No doors, no furniture, but when I grew hungry, a small rat, caught and cleaned by Asteria's hands, was cooked to a crisp over one of these fires, so that my stomach might cease its complaints. I grew accustomed to the sound of Asteria's hoof falls beside me as we went, to the left and the right and back again, comforted by the feel of her steady hand in my own.

These winding halls might lead us to Rome, for it felt that we covered this much ground, but the place it did lead us to was special in its own right and, even after all we had seen, just as staggering to me.

This courtyard was different than those we had visited before. Four small bowls of fire were clustered around a damp central slab of stone that was strewn with debris. I squinted as we came into the room, the fire so bright, and peered at what was on the slab: small bones, bits of paper, a coin or two, a cufflink. I couldn't understand the significance of any piece, be they looked at collectively or apart, until I thought of my own work above ground, and the many numbered boxes. But even then I was unsure, for what did Asteria need with a cufflink? A glance at her revealed no answer, so I moved deeper into the room, to the edge of the stone slab, where I saw the hole.

Into the ceiling, a hole had been carved. Large enough for a person to fit inside, the hole reached upward through the stone, and ended in a small metal grate which allowed watery daylight to leak in. I circled the stone slab until I found a rusted set of rungs set into one side of that hole, water trickling down its interior, to drop onto the slab.

It was a way out and the idea made my throat tighten. I looked at Asteria and she bowed her head—she knew, she knew she could leave and she never had. She had kept herself in this dark and cold place, for how long, with a way out right...

"No locked doors in my house," she said, and lifted one long leg, to step onto the stone slab. A bone crunched beneath the step as she gave me a hand up.

Asteria boosted me up toward the rungs, for I could not reach them without her. I clung to them, shaking, and looked down at her, not thinking then of all the things that must keep her here, of all the ways the world had locked the doors for her.

"Come with me," I said and reached a hand down for her, silently begging. Where she would go in such a world, I couldn't say. Nor could she. She shook her head and stepped back, allowing me to climb. I only did so slowly.

At the top of the rung ladder, I looked down, seeing no sign of Asteria below. The stone slab seemed to flicker in the firelight, but all else was still. The grate above me dripped water, and though the metal was rusted and sharp, I took hold of it and pushed it up, which allowed me to climb into a dark alley.

As upon my arrival in Asteria's house, I crouched there, too afraid to move, though this world was more familiar to me. I closed my eyes a moment and then heard the fall of a footstep. My throat tightened in reflex and I ran; ran blindly down this alley and that, until I had to stop and catch my breath and press a hand to the stitch in my side.

Beyond the alley, the world I knew and there, strangely, the entrance to the apothecary. A couple perch-ed upon the steps, laughing softly. Oscar Baker, my heart whispered, once mine but no longer, for how could he claim the wretch this world made of me? I stepped deeper into the alley shadows, and slept there till morning light tried to pry its way between the high stone walls and the mourning doves began to coo to each other.

In the night someone had spread a cloak over me. It smelled of smoke and sweat, but the morning was cold and I drew the fabric around me. The apothecary stood closed, the street quiet yet, so I waited and watched that door. Watched my uncle come and open the drapes, watched him unlock and open the door to test it as he did; watched as he turned the sign to open and dipped his head to a passing merchant.

My shoes made nearly no sound when I eventually crossed the street, the apothecary doorknob cold when I at last took hold of it. How strange to come to this place now, I thought, for Asteria's corridors seemed more familiar. The bell above the door chimed at my entry and I immediately sought my uncle's face amid the room, his head bowed as he listened to a customer describing this ailment or that. I thought he would look up, but he did not.

Even as I crossed the floor, even as my fingers whispered across the bundled herbs, my uncle took no notice of me. Nor did the customer, a sturdy-looking man who gestured to his nose and then his throat. Once, his eyes met mine, his a watery green, and though I know he saw me, I also knew he did not. It was then I understood.

I moved like a ghost through the shop, meaning to reach my workspace when the items in the main counter drew my interest. There, behind the glass display were nine bundled locusts. Another jar that claimed to be liquefied hail from Egypt. I blinked and looked to the last item.

Item 317: horn fragment, w.illus.

It was my own handwriting there upon the slip, a new jar cradling the horn and its illustration. I looked up once, to my uncle and his customer, but they did not see me. They did not see me round the counter and slide open the case, nor reach my hand inward to take the horn and its drawing. They paid me no mind as I left the apothecary and took to the street, the bell chiming once more overhead. I slipped as easily as a shadow between the people who passed in the street, lost in their conversations about the Season, about marriages, and breads, and the tremendous thing the Queen had done last Tuesday. I moved among them, but not with them, and when at last I reached the alley, I did not look back.

Though I had run in a blind panic the night before, my feet seemed to know the way. This turn and then that. A left and then two rights. Past the slumbering drunk, unseen by the thief trying to pick a lock. I let my shoe fall with more weight as I passed and the thief jumped, leaping away. *Surely there must have been a footstep.*

I found the metal grate and knelt beside it, to pry it upward and peer down at the slab of firelit stone. I smiled softly to see the shadowed outline of two curling horns against that stone and then slipped into the narrow passage, pulling the grate into place before I stepped down, rung by rusted rung.

GRAFFITI ON A WALL

JANETT L. GRADY

It started with a battle, a weird war of words between a man and his wife.

"Can we talk?" Karen asked, still in her pajamas, an angry look on her face.

"Not now," Harry answered. "Waste Management has been giving me a hard time for trashing old donuts and stuff. I've got to do something about it." On his way out the door, he kissed his wife on the cheek. "See you tonight," he said. "We'll talk then."

It took Harry an hour to reach his bakery, one of several twentieth-century shops on the mile-long stretches of decks five, six and seven. Constructed on and launched from the Martian Plain, the ship was huge, the size of a small city, too big to be without an elevator every quarter mile or so; it had just two lifts, one at each end of the ship. Walk or run was the name of the game. Aside from his on-board bakery, Harry was a geologist, which meant he had to stay in pretty good shape. Still, Harry didn't like being forced to walk his ass off.

Later, at the end of his liquid lunch, Harry emptied his bottle of beer, snuffed out a cigarette. He slid off the stool. It'd be a long hike back down to his Donut Shop on level five and there'd be no place along the way to empty a bladder, so he headed for the men's room.

"See you later, Mike," he called out to the bartender,

and made his way through the lunch-hour crowd.

The inside of Mike's men's room was scummy, but nothing unexpected, just the usual stink of piss and puke, and the floor littered with paper towels and beer cans. Harry opened his trousers, almost pissing before he had it all the way out. He studied the graffiti on the wall. It was still there:

GREAT ASS-CALL KAREN D3-4321

The 2 and the 1 were smudged but Harry knew. Here we are, he thought, twelve years off Mars, on our way to a dig on Tiatra, and some things never change. Oh, well...

Harry had first noticed it a week before, with a half dozen names listed underneath, and some clown had even scribbled Yamadama in green paint, Yamadama being the first human born on Earth's moon back in 2212. Now there were a dozen more names, and there was no shadow of doubt in Harry's mind that his wife was screwing around. Where there's smoke there's fire, he figured, and besides, Karen had told him how often she played with herself.

"I do it all the time." She had grinned at him. "It feels good and it gives me something to do."

Harry shook off the last few drops, zipped his trousers, then fished through his pockets for a ballpoint pen.

"Might as well," he mumbled to himself, and scratched Harry at the bottom of the list.

Back in his bakery, Harry plunged into his work as he always did, paying bills, checking payables, and reviewing procedures for the disposal of his unsold donuts. Just before quitting time, his pager beeped open. It was his pastry chef, letting him know she was leaving for the day.

"Wait a minute," Harry told her on a sudden impulse. "I'd like to see you for a minute first, Miss Benson."

"Certainly, Mr. Keaton."

His pastry chef, a middle-aged, slightly overweight

Mars-born woman with a hint of youth and hope lingering despairingly on her face, entered his office a moment later.

"Yes, sir?" she said, as she sat in the chair in front of his desk.

"I just want to talk," he told her.

She looked at him with an air of panic. "I don't understand, Mr. Keaton. Is something wrong?"

"I just want to talk," he said. "I don't think I've ever asked for a Martian's advice before. Make your own decisions and act is my motto, but..."

"Oh, yes, sir, and you're doing so well."

"Well, yes, Miss Benson, but now I'm going to ask your advice, as a woman, not as an employee. Do you understand?"

"I think so, sir." She crossed her legs and tugged at the hem of her apron. "I'll try to be helpful," she added.

"Good." He leaned back and laced strong fingers behind his head. "I'm going to be frank, Miss Benson. Do you mind?"

"No, sir. I don't mind."

"Good. Now suppose you were a woman who loved having sex, and, let's say, cheated on your husband. Now, let's suppose your old man found out about it and that he'd do anything to keep you from fooling around. You with me?"

"I'm with you, sir."

"Good. Now, what would this guy have to do to get you to stop fucking around?"

Miss Benson's chin dropped. "Sir!" she gasped. "Please!"

"Relax, Benson. It's just a word."

"But, sir," she said, her Martian, mousy features brightening in a blush.

"But what?" growled Harry. "Look, Benson, it's a word. Fuck, fuck, fuck. There, now get used to it. You know what it means."

"Yes, sir, but there are other words. I mean..."

"Okay, Miss Benson. What would the guy have to do to get you to stop screwing around behind his back?"

She smiled weakly at him, slid back in her seat, the fabric of her white pants shifting over her thighs. Harry glanced at her legs. Not bad, he thought, and winked at her.

"Well, sir," started Miss Benson, a serious expression on her face, "I really wouldn't know about such things, but I suppose the gentleman in question would have to satisfy his wife." She rolled her eyes. "I mean in the bedroom, sir. But if he couldn't, well, sir, then maybe he should try to make her jealous."

"Jealous?"

Harry leaned forward, knotting his fingers together on his desk, bit his lip and thought about it. The germ of an idea popped into his head; he wondered what Karen would do if she found his name on the wall in a ladies room.

"Miss Benson, would you consider doing me a personal favor?"

Miss Benson slowly uncrossed her legs, shifted forward in her chair, and cleared her throat. "I think so, sir." She made a face, narrowed her eyes. "But... Well, sir, if it's not too personal, I will. I'm not..."

"It's not," Harry said sharply, interrupting her. "But it's... Well, it is sort of vulgar, Miss Benson. Relax, though, it's not that I want to take you to bed."

"Why, Mr. Keaton!" exclaimed Miss Benson. "I never..."

"Forget it," said Harry. "Now listen. Karen is screwing around on me. I'm sure of it. And I'm the hypothetical dunce who's trying to stop her. You understand?"

"Why..." Miss Benson looked severe. "...sir, I never would have thought Mrs. Keaton would..."

"She's fucking around!" Harry snapped. "Will you do it?"

"Do what, sir?"

"I want you to write something on a bathroom wall

for me. In a ladies room. Will you do it?"

She just looked at him. It was a look that told Harry she'd do it, and anything else he might ask.

Harry frowned. "Well?"

"Yes, sir, if you think it might help."

"It will, Miss Benson. Now, call Mrs. Keaton and tell her I'll be late for supper. Then we'll go to Mike's, a bar up on deck seven, the Rec-Deck. It's one of those earth-like dumps you might not like, but it's where we all go to check out and relive the ancient lifestyles. We go there to relax once in a while. Okay?"

Harry didn't wait for an answer. He stood up and waved Miss Benson out of the office.

"And bring a sweater, Miss Benson. It's usually cold up there. Not much heat."

"Yes, sir," she replied.

"Oh, and don't forget to bring a pen, Miss Benson, one that'll write on a wall."

She paused, nodded, and then hurried out of his office.

Forty-five minutes later, Harry escorted Miss Benson into Mike's bar and guided her through the crowd to an empty booth. He sat down across from her and offered her a cigarette. Miss Benson shook her head.

"I don't smoke, sir. It's against the law."

"Not here," Harry snarled. "Mike doesn't give a shit about that stupid law. He's going to see the ship's Court Council about it."

The canned music was loud—country, and Harry had to yell at the waitress to get her attention.

"Hey, Peg, we're ready!"

A youngish blond in a short red skirt and a bulging see-through blouse stopped abruptly in front of him, pencil and order pad ready.

"Hello, Harry," she said. "What'll it be?" she asked in a hurried voice.

"Hi, Peg." Harry looked at Miss Benson. "What do you want?" he asked.

Miss Benson shrugged, so Harry ordered two beers and a bowl of popcorn. Peg wiggled away, and Harry's eyes followed the contours of a shapely ass. He wondered why he had asked Benson instead of a sweet young thing with a hot little body just itching for action.

Miss Benson disturbed his thought. "Sir," she said, "I think I've changed my mind. "I really don't like it here. It's too smoky, and I never drink beer." She had a sour look on her face.

"I'll drink the beer," Harry told her. "You just keep an eye on the ladies' room..." he pointed "...and when it's not so crowded, you go in and do me the favor. Okay?"

Miss Benson leaned forward across the table, and whispered, "Sir..." she looked around as if to make sure nobody else could hear what she said "...sir, I don't feel comfortable with all these people and their smoke. Would it be all right if I went in now and just waited until I had a chance?" She grinned at him.

Harry chuckled. "Fine," he said. "If that's what you want. Here, let me have the pen."

She fumbled a Paint-Flow pen from her purse and gave it to him. Harry snapped a napkin from its holder and printed: HARRY KEATON IS A GREAT FUCK. Then he listed a few of his favorite female names. As an afterthought, Harry glanced at Miss Benson. He added Mildred to his list. He pushed it across the table.

Miss Benson's mouth dropped open as she looked at it, eyes wide. Harry shrugged.

"Could be, Mildred." He grinned at her. "You never know."

Before he could say more, Mildred Benson was on her way to the ladies' room. Peg returned and plunked two bottles in front of him.

"Eight bucks," Peg said curtly. "Sorry, but we ran out of popcorn."

Harry gave her a ten. "Keep it," he said, and watched her as she hurried into the crowd. Someday, he promised himself, and took a long pull on one of the bottles. He paused to catch his breath, then emptied it.

A few minutes later, Harry felt anxious. Benson hadn't returned. After all, how long could it take to squirt a little graffiti on a wall? He was lighting a cigarette when Benson finally came back.

"Where in the hell have you been?" he demanded. "Did you do it?"

"Yes, sir," she said, squeezing into her seat. "If Mrs. Keaton sees it, sir, she's certain to be upset."

"She'll see it," smiled Harry. "What took you so long?"

"Sir!" exclaimed Miss Benson, her penciled eyebrows raised. "You wouldn't believe the filth on those walls. I mean..."

"You're right. This is no place for a lady, Miss Benson. You ready?"

Miss Benson had a look on her face that told Harry she was ready to act out the filth on the wall. With him. But Harry whisked her to the nearest elevator, thanked her, and told her to take the next two days off, with pay. Maybe later, he thought, but right now there was something he was in a hurry for Karen to see.

When Harry got home to his quarters on deck three, the sound of splashing water and the melody in Karen's voice promised that she was in a playful mood. Freshly balled, he thought, and settled into his favorite chair with a bottle of beer and a magazine.

Karen pranced in. "Hello, Harry," she said cheerfully. "Work late?"

Harry looked over the top of his magazine. "New client," he told her. "Ship Security, deck four. Hey, you look great!"

"You're kidding." She was barefoot, in a faded robe, and had cold-cream on her face. "I just got out of the shower," she said. "I look like an old hag."

Harry tossed the magazine. "Have you started supper?"

"No. I've been snacking on chicken. What do you

want, leftovers?"

Harry licked his lips. "Your sweet little ass," he said, "but later."

"You've been drinking, love."

"A little. Hey, get dressed. We'll go up to Mike's, have a drink or two and then go have a steak at the Cow Palace. What do you say? We'll have that little talk you mentioned."

Without a word, Karen skipped away, as a child might, and Harry followed her into the bedroom. And, as usual whenever they were going to the Rec-Deck, Harry dressed his wife to suit himself. He zipped her into a velvety red, low-cut dress, and insisted she wear nothing else.

"But Harry..."

"No buts, hon, and no panties."

"You're sick," she giggled, and reached for a comb, brushing it through the long dark hair that fell to her shoulders. "You're weird, Harry. You know that?"

"You like it," he said.

"Wrong," she cooed. "I love it."

It was almost ten o'clock when Harry and Karen strolled into Mike's bar, and the place was packed. There were no empty booths, no vacant tables, and Harry had to do a little shoving to make room for his wife at the bar.

Mike was still there. He was a wiry man, and he looked like a bartender, with a bald head, cheerfully seamed face, and his brilliant red vest that proclaimed he was owner, head bartender and able-bodied bouncer.

"Evening, Harry," he said with his usual smile. "Hello, Karen."

"Good crowd," Harry offered. "What happened to your jukebox?"

"Some jerk cut the wire," Mike growled. "What'll it be?"

Karen ordered bourbon and coke and Harry asked for Plutonion beer. They had three rounds, Harry guzzling beer and Karen sipping her bourbon, before Karen finally announced that she was going to go in and powder her nose.

"Don't wash your fingers," Harry joked, and watched his wife strut sexily through the crowd and into the ladies' room. "Here's hoping," he said to himself.

He wondered how she'd react. He was ready for battle if that's what she wanted. He wouldn't deny screwing around, but he'd demand the truth from her, too.

"What's with you two?" came a serious-sounding voice, and Harry turned back around. It was Mike.

"What's that?" asked Harry, sipping his beer.

"You, goddamn it, and that gorgeous wife of yours. You having trouble?" Mike swept a white towel over the bar. "What in the hell is going on?" he asked.

Harry faked a cough. "What makes you say that?"

"C'mon, buddy. We've been friends a long time. Last week your old lady comes in with that wimpy boss of hers, and today you're in here with a dog."

Harry straightened up. "You mean Daniels?"

"Who?"

"Daniels, that disposal tech from Karen's office."

Mike tossed his towel and braced himself with his hands on the bar.

"Yeah," he said, "I guess that's his name. Wimpy guy, with a big nose, no chin. He was in here last year... at the party we had on New Year's Eve."

"That's Daniels," said Harry, more to himself than to Mike. "When were they in here?"

Mike shook his head. "I don't know," he said. "Last Wednesday, maybe Thursday or Friday." He straightened up, turning his palms up in a gesture of futility. "Hey, look, Harry, I was just trying to be helpful, that's all. Forget it. The guy's a waste wimp."

Mike left to wait on some customers, and Harry did a slow burn. He was suddenly pissed and ready to break Daniels into bits and pieces. He drained his bottle, then emptied Karen's bourbon and coke in one long swallow.

When Karen returned and slid back up onto her stool, Harry glared at her. He had forgotten about the graffiti. He was thinking about smacking his cheating wife right in the mouth, right here and right now. But no. He could never hit the woman he loved. Never, no matter what.

"Guess what?" she blew in his ear.

"What?" he growled at her, forcing himself to remain calm.

"It worked," she whispered.

"What worked?"

Karen squeezed his thigh. "I found it," she said, and slapped at his groin. "Your name on the wall, right out in the open where all the girls can see it."

Harry shrugged. He didn't know what to say. She didn't seem to be upset. She stuck out her tongue, a childish expression on her face.

"I know you put it there," she said, "or had one of your girlfriends do it." She winked at him. "You're jealous," she added,

"Jealous? Jealous of what?"

"You put it there," she said, pursing her lips as if to pout. "Ain't that right, you great fuck?"

Harry didn't know what to say, so he didn't say anything.

Karen was squeezing his thigh, rubbing his groin, poking at his balls and pinching the tip of his dick.

"Come on, love, smile." She giggled. "Hey, how come you're having sex with Mildred? You always said she was a Martian frump."

Harry shoved her hand out from between his legs. "I'm not," he said. "But I'd sure like to know how come you're making it with Daniels."

"Daniels?" She snickered. "You're kidding."

"No, I'm not," he said clearly. "How come?"

"Look, Harry, you've been messing around for years, ever since we hauled ass from Mars..." She paused, looked away, then turned back and went on... "so I had Mr. Daniels do me a favor. I knew you'd find it, and I wanted you to find it, to think about it, love, about how it feels to have someone you love fooling around."

Harry jostled her boob. "I don't believe it," he said. "You mean what's on the wall in the men's room? Daniels? He put it there?"

"Go take another look," she said, "and check out the first five names."

Harry thought for a minute. The only name he remembered was Yamadama.

He swung off the stool, aimed a threatening finger at Karen's chin, then edged his way through the crowd and into the men's room. It was still there:

GREAT ASS-CALL KAREN D3-4321

Harry scratched his head. "Well, I'll be a son-of-a-bitch," he said to himself. "That crazy bitch. I love that woman."

The first five names on the wall were: Hutch, Al, Ray, Roger, and Yamadama.

PLANTLIFE

ERIC BOSSE

Dear Rabbi Cahan,

My name is Monah Feldberger. We met in Chicago twenty-three years ago, during the week of my husband Alvin's funeral. You came to my house and patronized me for fifteen minutes, praising me for what a devoted widow I would be to my husband. Honestly, moments after I met you, I began to hate you. But our conversation soon turned to gardening, and we talked flowers and plants the rest of the afternoon. To this day, you remain the one person I have met who knows more about soil enrichment than I do. So please, Rabbi, bear with me here. I need your advice.

I live alone now, far from Chicago, in a cabin near Green Mountain Falls, Colorado. Yesterday while Oreo, my Chihuahua, and I were on the back patio, the sun passed behind a cloud. A breeze jingled the wind chimes, and one of my tomato plants reached through the air to caress another. Then the second plant caressed the first. Yes, Rabbi, my tomato plants caressed each other—and not as if the breeze had blown them together. Oh no. They gently stroked one another's leaves. Then they bent inward, untied themselves from their stakes, and leaned together in a fluid motion. And they hugged. This nearly gave me an aneurysm.

You know as well as anyone, Rabbi, that plants are

alive. They turn their leaves and flowers to the light. Like us, they grow, they age, and they die. So, with rich soil, plenty of love, and just the right amount of sun, I ask you, why couldn't a few plants start to move a little more freely? And it wasn't just my tomatoes. As they fondled each other's flowers, my larch branches waved in arcs that had nothing to do with wind. The lilac bush pushed against the ground and lifted its roots from the dirt then shuffled across the lawn. My sunflowers danced with the maple saplings poking through the grass. And the grass! The blades of grass themselves milled about the yard like very tall ants.

Little Oreo spun circles of joy, but he did not bark. In fact, he did not so much as step off the porch. Later in the afternoon, I found one of his tiny deposits on the living-room carpet. But I'm getting ahead. After about fifteen minutes of this craziness in the yard, I went inside and checked the TV to see if maybe vegetation had come to life everywhere. I mean, who knows? Though there was nothing on CNN, my houseplants were playing hide-and-seek in the living room. At first they scooted their pots around on the parquet floor, and soon enough they pulled free of the dirt and pattered through the house on their roots.

I went to the kitchen for a sandwich. Thankfully, my bell peppers and cucumbers were not doing anything unmentionable in the crisper drawer. I ate my sandwich at the table and wondered if the plants even knew I was here. As if it could read my mind, my big rubber plant stepped up behind me and wrapped its branches around my shoulders. One leaf patted my head. I froze for fear that the plant would strangle me. But she didn't. In fact, she held me in a gentle, slightly prickly cuddle that lasted several seconds, and I felt a kind of inner warmth I have not known since before my husband Alvin's death. Not that Alvin was a particularly warm human being, Rabbi. Frankly, he was often as cold as a dead fish. Anyhow, when I scooted around in my chair to return the embrace, the rubber plant waddled out the back door.

My place sits at the far end of a dirt road, Rabbi. I get no traffic. The neighbors' places are vacation cottages owned by families from Kansas. So here I was, completely alone with a houseful of sentient, mobile plants. Naturally, I went for the phone. I wasn't sure who to call, so I dialed 9-1-1. The plants grew very still. They cocked their leaves as if to listen. When an operator answered, I mumbled something about a wrong number and hung up. The plants went back to tracking dirt on my carpet and rearranging my furniture. The ridiculous Venus Fly Trap my son sent for my birthday leapt around the room with its traps snapping. The way the Venus clattered up the drapes and shimmied across the curtain rod, that poor moth didn't stand a chance.

Each time I picked up the phone, my plants stopped to listen, so I was careful. I had a mundane conversation with my sister Thelma in Boca Raton, then a humdrum talk with my old nursing buddy Bev. I did not mention the plants to either of them. Celia, my lovely young daughter, picked up the phone once I promised her machine I had not called to nag; but the very instant I mentioned the rubber plant—which had been Celia's back in college, when she did not care for other living things unless they drove sports cars—all the houseplants grew quite still and tense. The rubber plant leaned toward me for a moment and gestured for the other plants to stay calm. I told Celia the plant was fine then changed the subject.

When I hung up, the tension passed. The rubber plant walked down the hall. The other plants seemed harmless again and entirely uninterested in me. My carrots skittered away from the garden when I wanted to cook a soup, but the tomato vines actually delivered their ripest fruits to the kitchen. I took this to mean I could eat the fruit but not the plants. As my soup cooked, I formulated a plan. After dinner I would walk to the car, get behind the wheel, and drive away as fast as I could.

It was dusk when I turned the key in the ignition. I shifted into reverse and looked over my shoulder. Two maple trees stepped behind the car. When I turned to go across the yard, the foxtail pine hopped in front of my car. Rabbi, I doubt you've seen a *Pinus balfouriana* grin, but I can tell you it's almost creepy enough to make an old woman lose control of her bladder. Almost.

I got out of the car, but the trees stood still. As I turned to walk to the road, a coyote began to cry in the woods. The cry was squelched mid-howl. I heard a yelp. Then crunching metal and glass. As I spun around, those trees smashed and folded my car to the size of a suitcase. One perfectly good Saturn, gone. I went to the edge of the yard, but a maple branch kept me from going farther. The plants next door looked normal enough. They did not dance or hop or hug. The world had changed only on my property, it seemed. I stood there for a long time, trying to figure out how I'd gotten into this mess. Was it something in the fertilizer? Was my cabin built with radioactive bricks? The sun fell behind the mountain. I shivered. Because the plants wouldn't let me leave and didn't want to hurt me, I went back inside.

What I found in my living room—well, Rabbi, it was weird. The plants had knocked every remotely religious item—not that I have many—from my walls and shelves. (I admit, I am not active at the local synagogue. Why not? Mostly because arrogant, young Rabbi Faigelman is a fool who compliments every old woman's hair every time he sees us, no matter how bad we look.) Anyhow, my handmade glass mezuzahs were shattered on the living room floor. The plants had swept the shards of colored glass into a swirl of geometric shapes that spiraled out from a green, leafy-looking thing at the center. The effect was a cross between a Tibetan sand mandala and a flowery china plate. Also, the plants had ripped my late husband Alvin's prayer shawl to shreds and hung them from the ceiling like falling snow. The tin Star of David from the wall above the fireplace was now bent into the shape of—of what?—some kind of pagan seed or maybe a nut. Clearly, these were not Jewish plants.

They seemed happy to see me return, though. My rubber plant, which I had nursed from near-death ten years ago, after Celia left it in her hot car for three hours, shuffled over with a glass of fresh-squeezed lemonade. I sat on the sofa and sniffed the lemonade. It smelled fine. I drank it. My spider plant crawled up the wall and tucked itself in the space between the ceiling and the books on my top shelf. The African violets climbed one upon another and switched on the TV for me. Still nothing on CNN about plants, so I clicked over to *Sex and the City.* My eyelids were heavy. I felt drowsy. Only too late did I realize the lemonade had been laced with Valerian and a hint of chamomile.

I dreamt of my husband Alvin. In the dream he had hair. He was buried up to the knees in a large clay pot next to a stream that flowed through the yard. I held a watering can. I wanted to get across the stream to water Alvin, but I saw no bridge. The only way across was to walk on the back of a large snake. I hate snakes. So I waved at Alvin, and he waved at me. I tossed him a fertilizer stick and fell back into the warm embrace of my rubber plant. That is all I remember.

I awoke this morning in my bed. Early sunshine poured through the windows, which was odd because a tall fir tree had always blocked out the light there. The house was silent. I sat up. Nothing moved. Not a plant in sight. Oreo wasn't in my bed. I called, but he did not come. Still dressed in yesterday's clothes, I walked to the living room.

The furniture was gone. My sofa. My end tables. My TV. Everything. Gone. The plants had spread six inches of top soil across the floor. At the far end of the room, where my TV once stood, an altar had been fashioned on a large boulder. Don't ask where the boulder came from, Rabbi, because I couldn't tell you. A golden-green moss was draped over the boulder and gave the room a warm, yellow glow, which was nice. On top of the boulder, the plants had placed the pagan nut or seed icon fashioned from my Star of David.

The plants, and I mean hundreds of them, filled the room and stood perfectly still. They seemed to be worshiping the nut/seed thingamajig. Or maybe they were meditating. I don't know. The smallest plants—violets, carrots, etc.—knelt close to the altar, while the larger plants stayed farther back, in order of height. The room had a palpable, humid energy—very still, very alive. The only plant that moved was the Venus Fly Trap. It crept behind me as I tiptoed to the kitchen. I don't know what it had been eating, but the Venus had grown ten times larger. Now it was the size of an eight-year-old with a healthy appetite.

I went into the kitchen and shut the door. The linoleum floor was still bare, though dirt trails crossed the room here and there. For reasons I could not guess, my gas stove had been disconnected and moved to the center of the room. I opened the refrigerator and took out a carton of milk. As I reached to the cupboard for a glass, some-thing moved in the back yard. Through the window, I saw trees pacing back and forth, guarding the property line like soldiers on patrol. The carton slipped from my hand and milk gurgled into the sink. I picked up the phone. The line was dead.

By now, my little Oreo should have been skittering at my feet, ready for his breakfast. I stepped onto the back deck and called. Oreo did not come. The trees paused a moment in their pacing then kept marching the perimeter. I am a worrier by nature, Rabbi, but this was unnerving. I walked back through the kitchen to search for Oreo among the plants, but the Venus Fly Trap blocked the door to the living room. I hadn't heard the Venus come in. And, unless I am mistaken, it glared at me with the unmistakable arrogance of a predator. Its traps clicked open and shut. They now gaped to the size of a bear's mouth. Yet one of the traps remained closed. Something wiggled inside it. A short, black, fuzzy tail poked out between the trap's teeth.

I lunged for the stove, forgetting it was dis-connec-ted. The Venus chuckled—or it seemed to, Rabbi, but it's difficult to read the body language of plants—as I flipped the burners on high. No flame. I went to my utility drawer, but the matches were gone. The weed killer I kept under the sink had vanished.

That Venus nodded its traps, clickety-clack, and shifted its weight toward me. I clenched my fists. The Venus snorted. I pulled out my big drawer of baking trays. There, under the trays, I found my old butcher knife in a cardboard box the plants had apparently overlooked. I held up the knife and let the blade glimmer in the day-light.

When I turned around the Venus lunged and punched me hard in the belly. I buckled to the floor. My shoulder crashed on the linoleum, but I held onto that knife.

The Venus thrust a trap at my head, but I was ready and hacked at the branch. The trap fell to the floor. Then another lunge and another chop. The Venus's amputated branches flailed, and I kicked it across the room.

I stood up. "Give me the dog," I said, "and I'll let you live."

The topmost of the Venus traps shook from side to side. I came closer. As the plant retreated toward the living room, I swung the knife and, kerchunk, I chopped through that Venus's stem and separated it from its roots.

The Venus toppled and scrambled for the door.

I reached for the stem and caught it just above the first branch. The Venus grasped at the doorknob and opened it a few inches. For one second, while that door gaped on a roomful of plants engaged in a solemn reli-gious ceremony, I thought I was doomed: they would find out I'd attacked one of their own, and they would prob-ably kill me in return.

But a branch from the rubber plant shoved the door shut.

I hacked again at the Venus's stem. Its traps gasped.

What was left of the Venus shuddered, drooled, and went limp in my hand. I pried open the trap that held Oreo. My poor little guy was all sticky and as sad as could be, but he perked up when I poured him a bowl of kibble.

I filleted the Venus's stems, diced its leaves, and removed the teeth from its traps. Then I cut the traps into thin slices, which I marinated in walnut oil and soy sauce. I wrapped the rest in plastic wrap, sealed that in a Tupperware, and stuffed the corpse into my freezer.

When I came out of the kitchen, the nut/seed worship was over. Most of the plants had gone outside. The rubber plant was there still, dusting the altar. As I walked toward her, butcher knife in hand, she froze. A few other plants made a quick move to stop me, but the rubber plant waved them away. She waddled closer, held open a leaf first, then extended a whole branch. I dropped the knife to the floor. Slowly, serenely, the rubber plant opened her branches. I leaned forward. She caressed my cheek. I collapsed into her limbs. What can I say, Rabbi? The strangeness of all this had gotten to me. I wept, and the rubber plant patted my shoulder and ran her leaves through my hair. After a good, long cry I stood up and brushed myself off. The knife was gone. The other plants went about their business. The house felt strangely at peace. I kissed the rubber plant. She lifted my nightgown up, over my head, took my hand, and led me down the hall to the shower.

And that was this morning. I made two more half-hearted attempts to leave the property this afternoon, but the trees would not let me go past the mailbox. Since I sat down at the kitchen table to write this letter, the plants have shown no interest in me at all. I only hope they will permit me to place this in the mailbox. If all goes well, this should reach you by the end of the week. As I said, Rabbi, I need your advice. And here is my question, which pertains to *kashrut* rules about plants. Clearly, land animals that eat other animals are not kosher. But tell me, please, are there grounds to suggest that a carnivorous plant would be non-kosher? Assuming the plant is edible and tastes good, and all the needles have been removed from its traps, may I eat it with a clear conscience?

Thank you for your time, Rabbi Cahan. I anxiously await your reply. Please give my regards to your poor, lovely wife.

Sincerely,
Monah Feldberger

THE ROACH PRINCESS

ERICA LIANNE INGLETT

"So, why are you here?" Princess Cassie picked at her fingernails as she spoke. She had a tired expression, as if she weren't interested in what Richard had to say, but he knew she was.

He stood in the center of the basement that belonged to what was once an upper middle class house in the suburbs. The house had aged to look worn and dirty, but it didn't stop Cassie's underlings from occupying it. The basement was twice as big as the house, with just as many rooms. Richard suspected it was the result of the previous owners trying to survive.

"The Rat King sent me to persuade you to marry him," Richard said firmly. The king hadn't intended to send Richard—that job was generally left to others—but he'd thought that maybe if he sent his best man on the job, Cassie would budge.

She flipped her bright red hair. It almost matched the color of the translucent cockroach shells that covered the floor. He watched the many roaches that still survived squirm at her feet. It made his skin crawl. He'd spent years adapting to the rats in the sewer castle but this was gross. Cassie, however, was gorgeous.

Her nose crinkled as she slammed her fist down on the leather recliner she called a throne. "I'm tired of this! Bernard can't send someone every week just because he feels like it." She stared at the roaches on the hardwood. Her expression was wound tight, as if she were trying to find the right words.

"You tell him," she said, as she continued to gaze absently at the floor. "Tell him if he asks again I'll start shooting his messengers. Literally." She smiled and looked genuinely pleased with her horrible solution.

Richard took three steps forward and the guards grabbed him. Cassie held her hand up with a sigh, signaling them to let Richard go.

"You don't understand," Richard said. "Do you even know how much he loves you? He's told me all about how amazing you are. He told me about the movies he took you to before the disaster hit, and the sapphire ring he gave you the day after you told him you loved him. Does any of that hold water with you?"

Richard stepped forward again as he spoke, ignoring the roaches on top of his shoes. Up close, Cassie looked so child-like. Bernard had told him she'd be well into her early twenties by now, but her eyes told him she might've never grown up.

Richard thought he saw a hint of nostalgia in her husky-blue irises before she said, "You just killed one of my roaches."

He sighed as he saw goo connecting the floor to his foot. Suddenly, he realized that it explained the rest of the goo on the floor.

"I know you remember it. I know you still love him," Richard replied.

He wouldn't allow her to get sidetracked. He stared intently at her, though he caught a few roaches walking along the headboard of the recliner in his peripheral vision.

She ran her tongue across her lips in that familiar way. "Watch the door," she said to the guard. "I'm taking Richard to my room."

The guard grunted as she stood. For the first time, Richard noticed the leather corset she was wearing. He noticed the combat boots and long skirt as well. She flipped her hair some more and stomped into the basement bedroom. As each step echoed in the room, he saw that nobody cared how many roaches she killed.

Cassie's bedroom housed significantly fewer pests, though Richard spied a few stray ones on the walls. She knelt down in the corner of her room, selected a record, and then wound up the recorder to play it. A slow song from the Great Depression crackled to life. Richard kept his distance. He noted the room's cleanliness, despite the infestation.

"You know, these are the only things I love more than my babies," Cassie said as she plucked a roach from the wall and tickled it with one finger. "Records are so timeless. This little box used to be all I had, but my subjects found so many more." She swept her left hand over the room to indicate the records scattered over the bed and floor.

"I know," Richard said bluntly.

"What?"

"Bernard told me about your box. He said you two used to dance in your room."

She scoffed and stood, releasing her "baby" back to the wall. "Will you have this dance?" she asked as she reached out her hand.

Richard took it, hoping he could get through to her eventually. She let him lead. He spun her around the bed and asked, "Why a princess? You have enough power to be Queen Cassiopeia if you want."

She didn't hesitate to answer. "I've always wanted to be a princess. They're pretty and smart and charming. Who wants to be a queen?"

Richard led her to the other side of the bedroom in a familiar motion, seeing what Bernard saw in her, what her loyal subjects saw in her, and why she possessed so much power. Richard couldn't put a finger on it, but she radiated an adamancy that was almost cute.

The dance slowed between them, and as Cassie leaned her head forward, Richard smelled the cherry blossom shampoo that one of her subjects must've scavenged for her.

"Why did the world have to die so soon, Richard?" His shirt muffled her words.

He didn't have a certain answer, but he did respond. "Not many people have connections from before the disaster. You're lucky to have Bernard."

She sighed.

"Why won't you be with him, Cassie?" Richard pulled away to look at her.

She refused to make eye contact, but whispered, "I'm done playing, Bernard. I know this helps you cope, but the world is gone. When you're in your right mind again, sweetheart, I'll marry you," Cassie said as she stroked his shoulder. "But you still need some time, don't you?"

Bernard sighed as he held her gaze. Why did she have to fall out of character to quickly?

She turned to walk out the door, but then stopped and looked back with a sweet smile. "So, I'll see you in a week?"

Bernard nodded.

CHIa GaRDen

JOHN MCCORMACK

There are a few things you need to know before we start. Almost one month before the galaxy went on vacation, we held the wedding reception. For her gift, she received the Apothecary Shoppe, a three-foot high set of shelves holding bottles of baking soda, flour, garlic flakes, an antibiotic, and a skin lotion.

I also got a gag present. Mine was an earthen sculpture of a voluptuous woman's torso. According to the writing on the box, it came with a packet of chia seeds to grow a fertile, green pubic garden around her swollen female plumbing.

My wife's gift produced jokes about her limited domestic skills. Mine was a comment on my limited experience in lovemaking.

About a month later, the Milky Way just got up and sprinted away. In an instant, familiar stars were lost. For the first week, the television featured concerned scientists. One thought that this was further evidence that the Universe was expanding. Another believed that it revealed that the Universe was contracting. Either it was the last stage of the Big Bang, or it was everything being sucked back to its origins.

The TV spoke of a glowing sphere that plunged straight through the earth. The next day Tasmania disappeared. The water off the coast of Norway boiled. Gigantic ice crystals filled the Sahara. There was no oxygen in Peking.

Then we lost electricity. Our lives played out within the geographies available in a day's walking. My child bride was terrified. She turned to me for answers and, when they could not be provided, for strength. My darling wife was fragile. She seldom offered up an opinion for fear she would be thought of as stupid. I was her only acquaintance. My role was to try to console her. "You'll make friends here." "We have each other." "Love conquers all." Our marriage was two people forced upon each other.

I took my chia sculpture from its box. The seeds needed time to soak, to be prepared for germination. The picture on the box promised a lush garden. Outside the window, a fiery rain fell. A large rainbow announced the glow of a warm afternoon. The fields erupted with a jungle of spongy mushrooms. A man hiking down the road offered us some cheese. He said these days he just spent his time walking. My wife opened up the box to the Apothecary Shoppe, making us all cheese mushroom omelets spiced with the garlic flakes.

"Do you think these mushrooms will kill us?" she asked the man.

"Someday," said the man. My bride rubbed his feet with the hand lotion. The man left the next morning.

"I am afraid," she said. "The galaxy is moving. They have timed it at some speed that is too many zeros to have a name yet. Our section of the Universe is going on vacation, or maybe just moving across the room, or going to the can," she said to me. I realized that beneath her awkwardness lived a capable brain that had yet to be challenged. For the first time, I wondered if she might be smarter than me.

My chia seeds had been soaking for three days. I spent the afternoon carefully inserting them within the small holes drilled about the sculpture's private parts.

A man knocked on our door. His hair was long, thick, tied back in an old ribbon, bulging from this constraint like a sheath of wheat. In his hands he held a large box.

"Open this up. You won't believe this," he said. We unwrapped the container. It was filled with sleepy yellow and black creatures.

"Are they lizards?" he asked.

"No, I think more like salamanders," I said.

"They taste like root beer. You know, the kind you used to get in frosty mugs. But watch this."

He pulled a salamander from the box and rubbed it on his arm. The hair on his wrist moved towards the animal, began to dance and then began to grow. Then the man pulled the ribbon from his hair. It too danced all about him. "Just to think, yesterday I was bald," he giggled. My wife helped him with the salamanders, putting them each in mayonnaise jars so that in time they could be eaten.

The next day a woman traded a pink substance she had found on the road for a salamander. The pink goop smelt like a fancy department store cologne. My wife told her to rub the salamander on her head before she ate it.

"A girl's hair is her crown," she said.

My wife and I now shared inside jokes about the events we had in common. She kept busy attending the salamanders and keeping the house clean. Still, she gave off the undercurrent of a prisoner, a solemn, captured bird who had few choices.

In a bedroom lined with jars of curious salaman-ders, we became lovers. The amphibians yawned as they watched sloppy entwined bodies hold controlled biolo-gical experiments. Here was a bedroom filled with a boy, a girl, and entrapped animals, awaiting something better in a speeding galaxy that made every tomorrow different.

Her business practices improved. She traded some of the hand lotion for a metallic substance. This material regrew a leg on a dog, once named "Tripod," now simply called "that dog." She bartered some of this replicating fluid for some blue tonic which cured rashes. My wife gave most of the blue stuff to a man who had fallen into a bee-hive, but no one knew for sure if it helped him out.

A man brought in a goatskin. "It's rainwater." He punctuated his explanation with a drink. He passed the vessel to her.

"What is it going to do to me?" she asked.

"It gives you energy. I haven't slept in eight days and nine nights."

"Aren't you sleepy?"

"No, but I'm running out of things to do."

"Maybe you could help me out," she said, pointing to the growing shelves of labeled items.

He took another toke from his goatskin. "What you need is a sign telling people to come in."

Using the box of the Apothecary Shoppe as a model, he painted a twenty foot sign which told everyone that this life-sized Apothecary Shoppe was open for business. Now every day someone brought in something to trade. She acquired a spotted ooze that tasted like honey and had the property of removing every tooth it touched. My wife kept it in a vinegar bottle until one day she bartered it off to a man with an abscessed tooth.

She told me about the red stuff. We came to call it "the red madness." Even though it looked like cherry gelatin, when she put it on her tongue it tasted like dirt. The walls then shifted and then each of the bottles on her shelves leaped and grew smiling faces. She spent the after-noon grinning as her bottles of inventory put on a floor show. That evening she brought home some of the red gel in an old whiskey bottle. "Try this," she said. "It will calm your nerves."

Gazing at my bald chia pet, I fell into a trance. The brown urn body moved in a seductive rhythm, a green pubic garden grew becoming a dense, vibrant jungle, en-circling swollen sexual territory. I sat mesmerized by the delusion, watching as the bush grew, undulated, and then was sucked back into the pottery, to teasingly re-emerge and grow again. Being without music, I found myself humming, causing my visions to accompany my own cadence. "Honey, come in here, will you? Maybe now that you have had some time to recover from work we might get to spend some time together?"

"Did that red goop calm you down?"

"Yes, dear. Here try some with me. In fact, if you find the guy who has this stuff, get all of it you can."

As we shared our bed, breathlessly watching the animation of our room, she spoke. "People now grow new appendages, cough up old ones as unused organs, change color or just wither away. Every day life changes."

I realized that "child bride" was only a momentary role for her. She was finding her way, learning her own strength.

"Man now has a real space exploration program. We're waving hello to distant stars," she continued.

"Honey, you sound like you are ready for another spoonful of red madness," I said, overwhelmed by her ability to understand this world. Happy only to continue learning about love.

Each day the Apothecary Shoppe was greeted by a line of people who had discovered something to trade. Each had a box that bumped, a bottle that shined, or a bag that kicked. As she talked to each person who displayed their new treasures, she looked at me and whispered, "Soon this will be the only job on earth. Trading things today for things that could be found tomorrow. Science was a lie. Man is a forager."

My role was to be at her side. I was stockboy and inventory clerk to a house alive with new discoveries. My reward was her attention. One day, as I walked down the rows of new-found animals, she turned to me and said, "People will quit going to zoos. Watching the changes in their household pets is far more exotic. Besides, I met a guy yesterday who could fly. Last week a woman whose legs had become shapeless pseudopods she could make into any design."

At night I would feel for her in my bed like a hospitalized soldier checking for lost limbs. I didn't want to think about her presence. I was a reaction. She was a burnt-in habit. She surrendered to lovemaking as if it were a poor choice over conversation.

"Change will eventually kill us off. Mankind, I mean," she said. "This is probably what happened to the dinosaurs, the trilobites, you know. Too much change, then one day they could not find the right things. Most people think this journey is the last of times for the human race. Man began as gatherers and as gatherers we will end."

As we spoke, I continued sweating, filling up her chia garden. "Still, what a journey this will be and what unexpected experiences we will share. New medicines are found falling from the sky. Some people have holes burned into their heads, others blissful ecstasy," she continued. "Science, chemistry, business are over. It's all foraging now," she added.

I asked her to write down some of her insights.

"Writing is over. Everyone's own stories are so fabulous that few are copied down. The wonder of each day always precedes the next, so history is forgotten, boring," she said.

Trying to be helpful, I told her I would write her story so that others could read it.

"You would be the last historian," she said. "In times of change we need collectors, not historians."

I wanted her for myself. I strove at all moments, at all times to cause pain, ambush, and destroy her. The veil of those things which we knew not to say or do was my only playground.

She was the neighborhood leader. Her homes were the survival stores, the community center, the conversational water cooler. I was her insolent assistant. I was a background character, a presence that must be tolerated or ignored. As I talked to a young girl waiting for her parents to complete a trade, my wife shouted at me, "Don't you know that education is over? There is only one truth to learn—all is changing." It was as if my punishment were that she would not even allow me to console a child.

With the demise of the red madness, and the need to taste other harsher colors, my body was older and my heart could no longer bridge the gap. My bedroom was but a moment to linger to hear her slink away. I shuddered to know that my need for her attention was not even noticed. My love for her was consciousness only in my carefulness to not step too deeply in her hallowed, horrific places. She was the voice of our time. "Most believe that mankind will not survive this trip. At least we know why the sabertooths disappeared. They experienced at least part of the journey of a galaxy on holiday."

At my bedside, my chia garden that had struggled to grow turned to brown, bristly nubs. It looked like the bald scalp of a doll where only the holes spoke of lost hair. There was only a stubble where a green fertile jungle should be blossoming. I picked it up and threw it against the wall. Then I looked about the house to find a broom, knowing she would have some irritating comment to make if she saw my weakness.

Textbooks say primordial man was a hunter and a gatherer. Man was nomad, following herds or harvests. My child bride was the Apothecary. The savior of our community. Yet at night, lying in our bed, on a planet speeding through the sky, I still reached out to her. Her response was to give me her unrelenting explanations.

"It seems much of our new environments are eatable, even delicious. The atomic number of the components of a pudding I ate yesterday is probably so far off the periodic chart that I fear what its elements will do to me," she said.

She was full of notions that she felt I needed to know. As she talked, I rubbed her feet with the last of the lotion from the Apothecary Shoppe box.

anceSTORS
ENTHRONED

marissa James

I was not the one to invent the idea, no, but I did perfect the technique. I don't say it to brag but simply because it's true. If I hadn't then someone else would have. The time was right. They were calling us.

From the time I was young, actually just old enough to make the hike myself, my father would take me to see the ancestors. We kept them high in the cliffs; other tribes called it the Palace. So we said our ancestors were Enthroned and made sure that they were.

I could not climb the cliffs at first because my arms and legs weren't long enough to find all the holds. Instead I would help father carry his supplies to the Palace and then watch his ascent. I memorized the positions of all the handholds, all the tricky spots, from down below. And I arched my neck back and back to see where the ancestors perched at the edge of the hewn-out cliff ledge. Some of them opened their mouths in silent greetings and others raised their hands. Some leaned forward in their chairs to see down to where I was. One by one, father would ex-am-ine them. He would pull off vines that had taken root on their clothes or seats and toss them down, check all the ties that held them in their seats to be sure they were still secure. He would polish dirt and lichen off the chairs where the ancestors' names were written so the red paint would show bright again. He'd pull back those who'd been jostled by the wind, so the overhang would shelter them from another year of rain.

And all the time I would stand below and hear him talking to them, talking like they were alive. *Oh, hello Qasiri, and how fine you're looking today. Ah, Grandfather, what a shame the rats have been at you, if only there was a way to prevent them getting up here but we do our best. But Grandmother, didn't you have hair last summer? At this rate there won't be anything left of you in five years.*

It always saddened me to hear him talk like that, just as it saddened me to hear how many he called Grandfather or Grandmother. These ones had been enthroned on the cliff for so long their arm bones were showing through their skin and their names had peeled to the point of illegibility. Not that my father could read; no, he knew the names because his father had known them. And his father before.

Every year when he came back down, after all those hours of loving work, I would tell him how fine they looked now. How much of a change he made. But he would always take the water from me with a sigh and a look of sadness.

"Every year it's more and more dust," he'd say. "Soon there will be Nothing enthroned."

Long ago our people had ceased this practice of enthroning our great ancestors and had instead buried them, like everyone else, in the communal graves. I don't think that even at the time of my father's father's grandfather did they remember how to do it. Once, trudging back to the village I asked him why our people had ever stopped.

He paused and stared up through the canopy of trees. "I don't think anyone remembers that either, Kherlaji."

"Well, why don't they?"

"Because people don't remember what they don't care about. Which makes me wonder if the ancestors should care very much about us anymore."

I thought on that for a very long time. And he did too. I could see it.

O—O

In the time of the ancestors only certain people were enthroned: those who had been leaders, who had made significant contributions. Potishrik was the daughter of one village headman and the wife of the next, Luway, and the couple sat side by side up on the cliff. Qiramn had thwarted an invasion of Faleen raiders by setting the plains on fire so they burned for weeks in a halo around the village. Dulesi had brought the foreign knowledge of reading and writing and keeping books to us. Without him we wouldn't know the names of any of the Enthroned Ancestors; no one would have remembered them for all the generations before my father.

My father's father was a great man. He opened the trade of our village to the nomads and caravans that passed our lands. In exchange for the safety of our village, they would pay us in food or wares that otherwise we could never obtain. Life became a little better for us, though I wasn't old enough to know it then. When he died, my father was very quiet and very still. He was like this for many days before he would allow the burial and by then the whole village stank of corpse. He was thinking, I knew later on, that his father should be on the cliff. He had looked over us in life and why should death take that from him?

After this, father started to visit the cliffs where no one went unless they passed by in hunting and soon he had made himself caretaker of the ancestors. It seemed like a noble task to everyone else whose lives were too busy for it. And every year, when we came back from our pilgrimage to the cliff, they would ask us idly, only half curiously, how the ancestors were faring this year, what they'd had to say this time. And we all laughed and shook our heads, both sides, because we knew the ancestors had nothing left to say to us. No, they hadn't talked for generations.

More like we hadn't listened.

O—O

I had never been up so high in my life so, when I made the ascent for the first time and got to look down at my father, tiny as a barleycorn, I laughed and laughed breathlessly until I could only gasp and then pant from weariness. It was harder to climb that cliff than any amount of tree-scaling would let you think. I patted sweat from my forehead with a skirt end as he followed me up. Beside me the ancestors smiled down on him.

For the first time, I looked at their bulky chairs and bony bodies and wondered how they'd come up here. I could almost imagine them bringing themselves, they were all such forceful and motivated people, and a further chuckle came from my chest at the thought.

When father came up, he was raining sweat from the bald patch of his head and huffing until his face was red. He'd insisted on carrying the supplies because I'd never done it before. Like every time I'd waited for him below, I offered him water when he was safe next to me.

"Good thing you're getting old enough for this, girl," he said between drinks, "because it looks like I'm getting too old."

He showed me the way the ancestors should be cared for, how to dislodge the weeds that had taken root, to brush away the dirt and scrape away the moss. He taught me how to tie the wrists and the dry, withered bodies, and how to know if they were bound in too tight, which would cause them damage. He taught me the way he would use black ink on a brush to brighten up tattoos that they'd had in life but, of course, that would only last until it was fixed up next year. Most of all I learned their faces close up. I said hello to my ancestors, touched them and called their names, all the names I knew. Binyi, who had only one very long bottom tooth but otherwise a full, wrinkled face that looked almost alive. Qasiri had no skin on his fingers anymore. The married couple, Potishrik and Luway, had their hands clasped, bound together with twine even though their bodies were eroding and slowly slipping farther and farther apart. I almost cried when I was close enough to see this cruelty of fate and time.

There were fifteen of them in all, the Ancestors Enthroned, but even so, there were additional bones on that ledge that I hadn't known of before. Skulls and jaws and longbones of those we'd once wanted to remember, but who had been atop the cliff for so long nothing else was left. Now they were just pushed aside so they wouldn't be trod on.

When we had finished the caretaking, we sat together and drank the last of the water and listened to the insects in the forest below. In the distance I could see our village and beyond it the road that led to our closest neighbors. Beyond that, the king's road led to the capital and the trade routes of people who thought themselves big people because they lived in and among big cities. And beyond that, at the end of the only world I would ever know and ever desire to know, were the shapes of blue, ancient mountains. The name we had for them was not what anyone else called them and what would we know, we who lived such small lives outside the realm of these big things.

"It's a beautiful view, isn't it? If they deserve anything from us, it's this."

I pointed at the village. "They watch us every day from here. I never knew it before, that you could see the village from here."

Father sat back. "I only wish I could see this every day of my afterlife. After I die..."

"If they learned how to enthrone the ancestors once in the past then why can't we learn to do it again?"

"Who would, Kherlaji?" He sighed and laughed sadly. "Who would do that?"

O–O

Soon after this, my father grew ill, or rather I discovered he was ill, for he had been hiding it from me. He had the wasting disease and to a strong man like him, it hit hard and took hold deep inside him.

I had to find the secrets of the ancestors because if my father deserved anything in his afterlife, it was to be with them.

I went to the old people of our village and asked what they knew, but Lutikho was almost deaf and toothless, and the few others knew less about the ancestors than I did. When I went to the next village for a wedding, I asked but their people had given up the practice even before we had. The old shaman gave me tantalizing tidbits; honey and smoke and bitumen were used, but she didn't know how. The ancestors of their village, sometimes on certain nights and with certain prayers, would talk to her, and the skin on their faces was supple as ever to allow for speech. I asked her to discover how their bodies had been preserved but she laughed like a fox. The dead didn't give up their secrets, no indeed.

When one of Tamoul's new lambs died, I asked for the body. I took it home and strung it up from the rafters and stared at the body and didn't know what to do first.

I did not have bitumen or honey so my first attempt was sorry indeed. I took out the organs and put the body over the fire to smoke it. Blood and fluids sizzled into the flames. I didn't know how to drain the blood from a body then. I didn't think of taking out the brain or any of a hundred other things that are so obvious now. The body dried out well enough; the skin became leather and the flesh so tough as to be inedible. But flies still swarmed the head and filled the mouth and nose with maggots. The smell of putrefaction filled our small house even while I struggled to salvage my attempt. In the end I took the stiff, dry little body out and buried it away from the village and made notes to myself. Father only got up from his bed a few times a week now. In the stink I'd created he coughed hard enough to bruise his ribs.

I sought out other bodies to improve my technique and no one asked about our garden patch gone to seed, or the way I ventured out little more than father did. And indeed half of my time was taken up with tending him.

Seasons turned and father saved up all his strength for our visit to the ancestors. I saw it. I wanted to tell him not to, not to go. That I would go for him and he could stay home. But I didn't have the courage, and certainly it would be his last chance to look on them. We went early, many weeks early, because of his condition.

He leaned on me and on a walking stick, and I carried all the supplies. We didn't talk, for he was too tired and I was too afraid. He had aged so much in this last year that I no longer recognized him as the same man.

We came to the cliff and I lowered him to sit on a stone so he could catch his breath. I gave him the water but he only sat with his head bowed and held it.

"Father, look. Do you see the cliff? Look up there, do you see it?"

I knelt beside him and rubbed his arm and urged him gently. When he mustered the strength to look up, I could see the haze in his eyes. Weary tears trickled from the heavy, dark shadows that housed them.

"What is it?" he asked, I knew, because he could see it and no longer trusted his eyes.

"It's a chair, father, a wooden throne. It's for you. I brought it for you."

He lowered his head again so the tears crisscrossed themselves, streams feeding into the dry deep seams of his face. "Only dust, Kherlaji, nothing but dust."

I didn't know what he meant then and less do I know it now.

O—O

My father was the first person I prepared for the afterlife and, when I did, I thought he would be the only one. Afterward I'd live the life of any village woman, except that once a year I'd visit him.

That was what I planned, or at least believed, then.

Perhaps it was because I knew him so well that still, to this day, he is the most magnificent example of my handiwork. I think his soul was close to mine when I lit the fire and laid the heated stones over his eyes and packed his body with the dried herbs and drained the fluids from his extremities. It was difficult work but I hardly remember how difficult it was to do alone, perhaps because he guided my hands. The ancestors came down from their thrones to observe, to whisper advice in my ear, to encourage me, or else I wouldn't have had the fortitude required for the many days it took. They stood around me and nodded in approval and touched my father's body, awaited his reawakening as one of them.

What did they say to me? What advice did the ancestors give that helped me better than any book I have ever found? I cannot say. In the weeks that I worked on my father's body I, too, stood in a place between life and death which has no name, or at least no name we can bring back to this place. It is true that the dead keep their secrets; they were merely rented out to me for a time and then taken back. And sometimes I think the ancestors took a little part of me with them as interest. When I visit my father now, I see some quality in him that lacks in my living self.

"Kheyed and Kherlaji? Are you there, Kheyed?"

Men from the village. I rose from tying my father's sandals to his feet and stepped out of the makeshift hut at the foot of the cliff.

"I am here," I said.

"And where's your father, girl? Is he too ill to return home himself? If so, we've come to take him back."

"That's very kind, but he will stay here," I said. I was still partly in the place between life and death and it was clear from their expressions that they could see it.

"You've been gone for days, he cannot stay here in his condition," Tamoul said.

"Days? It has been more than days," I said. "I could not have completed my work in only a few days."

"What work?" the headman asked.

So I explained to them how my father's spirit had left but his body remained. That it would always remain, now, as he had wished it. They had all known of his wish and yet were incredulous at my claim so I pulled back the doorflap to let them go in and see him. They filed in one at a time after the headman, and I could hear the disbelieving voices turn to pure silence. I stood in the door as they looked at the body of my father, his hair wrapped in a blue cloth and chest banded by his blue sash. A blue drape hung over his shoulders. I had placed his twisted copper ring on his finger and he sat with hands folded over his knees and his head forward and down a little. So that when he was seated above, with the rest of the ancestors, he would always be looking down at me.

His eyes and mouth were closed, much like a man who'd dozed off in his favorite chair. The headman reached out and touched his face and exclaimed in surprise that it felt like living flesh. Quietly, reverently, they all touched him, his face, his hands. They made signs and prayers to god. In low voices they debated how to raise him up, chair and all, to the ancestors.

I was weary from all the work so I sat on a stone and watched the men fetch ropes, and two of them scramble up the cliff face, then tie the rope ends to the chair and father's body. I'd wanted to do it myself, yet I was happy to see how they cared, and as I watched them inch the chair up and up, all those men straining to keep it steady so it wouldn't crash into the cliff face, then I realized I couldn't have done it on my own. I was only one girl.

They placed him next in line, closest to the ascension point, then all came down and looked at him there with me. I did not go up to visit him then because I was so tired the men had to carry me home. And also because I knew.

I knew he would be waiting for me for many years to come.

O—O

Word of my father's death and after-death spread

through the village. In groups people went to the cliff, to the ancestors, almost like it was a place of pilgrimage. I watched them through my window, and soon they were not only the people I lived with every day, but people from the next village, and some who had come farther than that, even, I could tell by their headscarves. By the time I was well enough to tend my weedy garden again, to hope to scrape something from it before the growing season was done, the caravan people had returned. The merchants had no interest in the ways of our village but I heard porters and servants inquiring about the living dead man on the Palace cliff. Tamoul and the headman and the others would jerk their chins in my direction and tell the story but no one asked me.

When the men in their camp began discussing a quick trip out to the cliff before sunset, my stomach knotted with heat. I watched them gather to leave then cut through the forest by animal trails. And yet when I reached the spot, I lost my nerve and stayed in the brush. Maybe it was because Tamoul was leading them and I knew, then, that father was safe. He wouldn't permit the foreigners to despoil this place.

They marveled at the sight of him, and those who thought they were clever supposed it was not a real body. A sculpting in clay, perhaps. Some of them wanted to scale the cliff, even partway, so they could see up close if he was real. The light was fading and still Tamoul refused to let them close. The most suspicious ones offered him money to let them go up, and the most skeptical ones scoffed and said this was exactly the point, that the fool villager was trying to make a few coppers off them in just such a way. But he didn't take their money even when they pressed it into his palm and tried to push past him to the base of the cliff. No. He threw it in the dirt and pushed back at them.

"He was the husband of my sister and a good man, not an attraction. Not an attraction," he said.

The caravan men muttered but before they could press the issue, a finely-dressed man parted their ranks.

With a few words he dispersed them back down the dusky path. Then he stepped forward to Tamoul and talked to him evenly so I couldn't hear.

Tamoul turned his face out to the forest where I waited. "Come out, Kherlaji, I know you're there. He wants you."

I had never been stealthy, so I came out and stood close by him and eyed the strange man. His clothes were dark and trimmed with silver, and he had gold rings in his ears and on his fingers, and a jeweled dagger in his sash. He held a torch so that I could see all these things and his costume dazzled me so I almost took no note of his face: a little lighter than mine but not pale, long-nosed and hollow-cheeked, with a trimmed mustache and short beard.

"I know that artists can be temperamental, just as you must know that critics can be overweening, so I must apologize foremost. I came out here alone earlier and yes, I scaled the cliff and met him face to face. Your father, I believe?"

I nodded because I couldn't manage to speak. One half of my tongue was tied in anger, the other half in awe of him. Whoever he was.

"My people practice this art," he said. "Not myself, but we do. But even where I come from the rumors came to us that there was a body out here so perfectly preserved that he seemed to live and breathe. They said it was better even than our most skilled examples, which I found hard to believe, so I came here myself. I tell you I believe it now. I never knew the man in his life but I sat down beside him and spoke to him and I swear I could tell you just what he was like, kind and fair-minded and strong in his principles. He's a better example of humanity even now than many I know."

He waited for me to say something but what could I contribute? He'd spoken a truth that I'd known but hadn't been able to put into words.

"I know your silence means you hate me for trespassing on your sacred ground, but know that I did it with good intentions. Can you forgive me?"

I knew he was trying to make me speak so I stared at my feet and said, very quietly, "Yes."

He leaned over me and held his torch so he could see my face. What was he looking for, the same life he'd seen in my father's face? I stared at the silver ornaments on his belt. "Could you do it again?"

I said yes and he took me back to the camp of the caravan. Tamoul came along and he was unhappy, I could tell; at the same time he didn't have the courage to dismiss the rich man. We entered a tent that was heavy with the smell of incense and cedar, and the man drew a thick carpet back off a large, long box. I knew what to expect before he lifted the lid but the smell of death still made me choke. Tamoul swore and ducked out. He stayed just by the tent flap, though; I could hear him gagging.

The rich man went to the head of the box and took a white cloth away from the sallow, bloated face beneath. The man who lay there had been dead some time. Perhaps a week.

"The keeping of our dead is important to us. The better they are kept, the better they can remember us in the afterlife. He was gravely ill, dying, when I left home." He sat on the edge of the box, and though there were tears in my eyes from the smell, his face was only somber and tired. "My father. I want to be able to remember my father as well as I can remember yours, daughter of Kheyed."

When he said that, I realized what I had done. My father would be remembered not only by our people and our descendants but by the world.

o—o

The world brought its dead to me. Never once did I turn them away, not even the poor or rotted or the few Jamelis brave enough to defy our ancient mutual hatred. Dayeb ka Faleen, the man with his father's corpse, was happy with my handiwork. He paid me well and word spread. People brought their dead from the nearby villages and from the big cities and some only came to ask me what magic, what secret, I knew. I didn't know any magic and my secrets were less than that. Sometimes I would wake to find a corpse laid at my door. These I tended like any others and then had buried in coffins. I made enough money at my work that I could afford to have pity on the nameless dead; at least I would remember a little of who they'd been.

Our village became a place of death instead of life. The young men made more money at building coffins and turning their fields into graveyards and carving intricate markers in the different fashions of different peoples. I saw this through my windows as I stayed so much time inside, busy with the dead. My home became a workshop full of bodies in varying stages of the process of preservation.

And yes, it is true, I became one of them.

I do not know if it was the constant contact with smoke or the many substances, bitumen and wax and honey and natron and pungent herbs and incenses, but my skin became as dark and leathery as the corpses. It did not happen overnight but over many, many decades. Many more than you would believe. Many more than you will live, perhaps. Sometimes I wondered if this was the thing the ancestors had taken from me, the ability of dying, and then I would surrender the question. They kept their secrets. Every year I went to see them and never again would they speak to me as they had at father's death. Even my father only sat forward and held his hands in his lap and awaited me with the benevolent patience of his second life.

I saw to the body of my uncle Tamoul, to the headman of our village. To the headman who succeeded him and the one after him as well. Tamoul's children and others who had been very young when I began. Some who hadn't even been born.

The son of Dayeb ka Faleen brought the body of his father, as he had done so many years before. In a few more decades that man's son brought him; my work had become a tradition of their line, it seemed. The croplands of our village dwindled and the grave fields went on in so many directions, so far that they seemed to stretch to the distant, blue mountains. Though I seemed unable to die, I did age, slowly but certainly. I grew feeble as any village elder. I walked with a stick. I had two girl assistants to assist my work; whatever affected me didn't touch them and they aged like anyone else. I tried to teach them all I knew and yet their results, alone, were never the same as mine. They weren't stupid girls, either. There was only something in my hands that didn't naturally occur in others.

The spreading gravestones made me sad, sadder and sadder with time. These people, who had come from so many places, belonged where they had come from, not in our foreign soil. How could anyone send away the body of a loved one and not want it back? Yes, some of them took our village for a place of pilgrimage—a pilgrimage for the dead, perhaps—but still one must return home. A pilgrimage is not meant to be forever. As this became clearer to me and I grew older, I urged people to take their loved ones home with them. Why should they when there was a cemetery right here waiting to be filled? Many didn't even stay long enough to hear me; they brought their dead, paid the toll, and left them to our arrangements. I could not understand why they would abandon their dead this way and, in the process, abandon a part of themselves.

They wanted the bodies tended and preserved and respected and remembered but did not want to do any of these themselves. I was getting old now, and every new body that came to me, that I drained of blood and bathed in honey and prayed over and perfumed with incense, weighed on my soul as one more person I could never forget. Like the ancestors enthroned above, all these below were my responsibility, too. And the earth under my feet was filling with them like a blister with blood.

○─○

Some of the educated young people tell me I am

over a hundred years old. They reckon it from the time that our village was opened to the caravans. I will tell you, a lot of people can die in a century. Just as many can be forgotten. If you put them in a box and cover it with dirt they are so much easier to forget.

A ladder has been put up on the cliff face, up to where Qasiri and Poteshrik and my father Kheyed sit and wait because now I am too old and stiff to mount the handholds as I once could. I know the exertion of the climb won't kill me and sometimes I wonder if a fall or any dire circumstance at all would be enough.

I am going up the cliff now and it is not for any of the reasons you might believe from reading this account. It is not because I deserve to be enthroned—no, I have no chair. Nor is it because I am done with the dead—rather, I am done with the living.

I have my supplies with me, the same I used to carry for father when I was young, but with them I have one more thing; a leaf that when brewed as tea or smoked in a pipe is meant to leech all the fluid from a body. I will go and sit at the foot of my father after I have tended him and the others. I will drink my tea and smoke my pipe and hope it does what they tell me. And I will look up into his kind, wise face, the same as it has been for so many decades now, and tell him I understand now. It is all dust, all of it, life and death and whatever is in between. Unless there is remembrance, there is only dust.

I have no one to live for but my father and if anyone will remember me after I have gone, it will not be for the right reason. I hope because I understand these things I will be allowed to join the ancestors now. Truly I hope they forget me, all of the living down below, because I never lived for any one of them.

It can't be so bad to be dust.

CERRIDWEN'S BOOK OF DREAMS

CYNTHIA REESER

In my dreams, I wanted to construct an archetype of the Celtic figure Cerridwen, Moon Goddess, Goddess of Dark Prophecy and the Underworld, partly because her name meant the same thing as mine, and partly because I had dreamed her already and wanted to revisit the same shadowy halls and odd angles that haunted my mind during daylight hours, during the times it chose to wander. I wanted to reinvent Cerridwen as the constructor of my dreams. Having always been a vivid dreamer, I wandered the same places over and over, frequenting familiar locales time and again in different situations. But the dream architecture I had built was beginning to wear thin. I could almost see right through it.

My subconscious was an imperfect coder, and did not name the cities I visited, leaving me continually haunted by the glowing clusters of high-rises and arching futuristic roadways I visited in the deep night. I would often lose my train of thought when I was out on assignment, or sitting at my desk writing an article, trying to place the night cities that were so vivid to me. I wondered if I would ever actually see them, have an instant recognition of them, know immediately how to navigate my way through each labyrinthine network of streets. My work had been slipping lately, and I had to get a handle on my ability to focus. I had to find a way to confront the things that interrupted my concentration. After all, I reasoned, if dreams really were the mind's way of sorting through mental aberrations and processing the myriad scraps of nonsensical detail we receive daily, a method of organization, then it would be worth a try. I would have to construct with and rely on Cerridwen, in hopes that she would allow me greater control and knowledge of my mind.

O—O

One night, asleep, I decided to visit the field behind the school where something always went wrong. That night, I walked across the field to an auxiliary building, which was shaped like a capital "I" and consisted merely of a long hall with classrooms on either side. I entered the metal door, whose window was also constructed as a capital letter "I" and was embedded with metal cross-hatching, which was not important as an aesthetic detail, perhaps, but as a fabrication, a construct. I entered through this first bullet-gray door, then opened the first door on my right. A teacher stood next to a podium, as she always did, addressing her class of well-behaved and mostly attentive high school seniors. She waved her arms instructively in the air as her speech alternated between English and German.

Some of the boys were wearing letter jackets, which always struck me as odd, until I saw some of the girls in high ponytails wearing bobby socks and poodle skirts, reminding me what relic of a decade I bore witness to. A few brunettes were dressed smartly in navy blue pleated skirts and had glasses propped on their delicate noses. Was I guilty of somnolent stereotyping? When the teacher handed me a manila envelope, I realized I was a college student, well-regarded; also that I had a furtive mission to accomplish. As soon as I walked through the door, I became aware of the presence of a dangerous, ill-formed man, shadowy, lurking in the hall. I knew I had to quickly leave through the bullet-gray door, and that the building would explode. Something about a bomb. I wanted to reinvent the dream, because it always felt too real to me. I needed to save all the young minds this building contained, but there was some larger force at work here.

That night, the teacher handed me the manila envelope, as always, and this time I called on Cerridwen—just a whisper of a thought. She stepped suddenly from behind the podium, as if she had been waiting there all along, simply unseen. I thought, *come with me*, as if that was all that was needed, and I felt her presence behind me, warm on my back, as I turned to leave. I would not look at the shadowy figure in the hall as I crossed each threshold; I would leave him to Cerridwen.

I exited the classroom door, and then the outer door of the building, and was aware of a struggle that had nothing to do with physical bodies. I would not look, for an unreasonable fear that I would turn into a pillar of salt. The door knob burned hot as it left my hand. I looked out at the field around me: a football had been hefted and hung in midair, a muscled arm flexed solid and static, a referee, unmoving, drew a whistle partway to his lips on the far side of another field off to my right, where a group of students clustered, uniformed, oddly positioned as if in a photograph. All was still. I kept walking. I felt a hot wave move across the field from behind me. I did not turn around. I heard the low beginning of a siren, arcing up in pitch as if it were being cranked in slow motion, an air siren. I felt my legs burn, melt, dissolve, mistaking the warmth for Cerridwen's protection. I was a mannequin in nuclear fallout.

○─○

Another night. This time, a deserted movie theater surrounded by an affluent town. I would search for Cerridwen again. I moved across a freshly paved street, perfectly black with bright yellow stripes. The night was eerie, and all was still, with not a soul in sight. No cats lurked in the bushes, no birds rustled in the branches. There was no noise of traffic, and not a hint of wind. The street was lit with the single, sallow cast of a light on a pole, and a few crumpled pieces of paper blew with a sudden gust, some poor poet's discarded inspiration, across my feet, over my feet, a sign or a silent ruse. I did not pick up the paper, fearing its contents. I walked toward the ticket booth in the front of the theater. It was so palpably devoid of human life that I shuddered. I felt there was something all around me, as if the dark itself were alive and watching.

Cerridwen. I knew without understanding how that it was my duty to enter the theater, and then became aware of myself as an employee of this establishment. I had a job to do. I jangled a ring of keys from my pocket, chose the largest one, entered the building. The room opened up into a large lobby, where dim lights soured the concession area, and a large octagonal hall angled out toward the auditoriums. I heard a couple talking behind me. Where there was no one, suddenly there were a few. And then more. Before I could process this sudden intrusion, people began filing in by the droves. Only a few heartbeats before, the vast dark lobby had been desolate, ominous, and filled with absolute silence. I began fighting the crowd to get to the outer walls; I needed to turn on the lights.

I elbowed my way through the mass. A line formed at the concession stand, and employees suddenly stood bored and half-attentive behind it, the guardians of over-priced popcorn.

Cerridwen. The theater was now flooded with light and sound. I had a task to accomplish, knew there was a certain room I had to unlock and enter, but I could not move through the suffocating mob. I felt her, Cerridwen. She was somewhere here, in this large room. I did not trust the reality of this crowd, the truth of their existence. When I looked up, one of them caught my eye. Cerridwen in a red baseball cap, black ponytail poking out through the back. Her crystal blue eyes betrayed her identity. She glanced at me, nodded, looked across the room, fixed her gaze there. She held the eyes of the shadow-man, who, I realized, must be her rival, must be mine. He was someone who tore at her constructs like flimsy fabric.

I knew I had to reach my destination, find the room I was headed toward. I became more aggressive with the crowd, elbowing them harder. They became like statues of lead, unmoving, leaving only their stale, crunched concessions on the ground beneath their feet. I could not move through or among them; they had me trapped in their solid mass. Again the world had gone still and I was the only one moving in it. I dropped down, crawled through their legs, reached the hall, dared not look around or behind me. I knew that soon, somehow, the fabric of this construct would be torn away.

I reached a door, tried a key. Tried another. Another. None of them worked. I heard a vast rip, and a new light spilled into the room from behind me. I did not look back. A gleam sparked from under the door, the key's sparkle flirting with my eye, just out of reach. I beckoned it a few times in vain with the tip of my pinky. A few false starts, then the key finally skipped forward. Hurriedly, I brought it to meet the door knob. Following the clatter of the metallic jostling of tumblers, the key sprung the door open with a dark gust. A vast, charcoal gray monolith stood beyond the door, seemingly sprouted from the ground. It towered above me, heavy and true.

Cerridwen. I heard the sound of ripping fabric come to a sudden stop. The monolith beamed out a light brighter than the one shining through the jagged hole. I could feel it sealing up the shadow-man's tear, and still I did not turn to look. I feared becoming a pillar of salt. I felt that this monolith was somehow the origin of Cerridwen, that she drew strength from it. And I had conjured her.

O—O

Another night. This time, things were different. I was stuck in my own dream, stuck in my own construct, all the people I had harnessed in it grown too many, too brazen, simultaneously too unhearing. They occupied a city of the future, a city I always visited at night, whose freeways housed looming bridges I swept across in my vehicle from the posh outskirts. Some of the bridges angled up at nearly ninety vertical degrees, which I tackled with my SUV, fearing the height but not the challenge. My reality was organized around a life I would not recognize when I awakened, my thoughts running fast and dis-connected.

I sped down a highway that led directly to the parking lot of a megamarket. Sped past lights of the city, past high rises whose windows twinkled in place of the stars. The baby chirped a protest from the backseat, and my older child bobbed her head, her ears plugged with headphones. I was upset about something, tried to place it, tried to calm some turmoil that broiled within me.

Cerridwen. Her name was a whisper in the air around me.

"Did you say something, honey?" I asked my daughter.

It called again, *Cerridwen.*

I was looking at my daughter in the rearview mirror as I pulled into a parking space, her lips unmoving, her head still bobbing to the music. She had not heard my question.

Then I heard a terrible screaming, a screeching, a squealing of brakes out of control, and looked as a lumbering semi came barreling down the freeway exit ramp leading directly into the megamarket parking lot. The giant truck was a terrifying metal-and-grease beast hurtling out of control.

Cerridwen. I heard the whisper again, urgent this time, close to me. Where was it coming from?

A mother pushed her baby, bundled in the basket of a shopping cart, into the parking lot, not hearing or seeing the semi, heading for her car. An older couple walked past my parked vehicle toward their minivan. I flung open my door.

"Look out!" I screamed. "Look out! Move! Get out

of the way!" I panicked, jumped up and down, as the huge truck flung itself wildly closer, but still no one heard me, no one saw the semi. Was I invisible? What was wrong with everyone? I jumped into my SUV, thankful my daughter was immersed in music, and spun the SUV out of the parking lot, rounding the corner of the building as the truck smashed into the group of cars where I had been parked. I didn't turn to see who the driver was, I didn't turn to see if anyone had been hurt. I didn't want to see what had happened.

I awoke, sun spilling across my duvet, the light somehow eerie and ambient. I was covered in sweat and my heart still pounded. My lips were salty, my hair seemingly a single formidable tangle. How had I failed to so much as recognize Cerridwen's name in last night's dream, when the previous two nights I could summon her at will? I dreaded such a future as the dream architecture of last night suggested, and wondered how I could have been such a slave to my own constructs.

That night, a Friday, I met a few co-workers for drinks after work. My concentration that day had been worse than ever before. I had interviewed several members of the school board for a feature article I was working on, and kept losing my train of thought. I stifled a yawn a few times, hoping no one noticed.

When I came home after several hours of banal chit-chat, I flipped through the channels and fell asleep on the couch to the flickering blue light of the television. I hated falling asleep on the couch, and I hated falling asleep to TV. It always made me feel sloppy, disorganized, as if I had lost control over my life. And that night I dreamed a wicked dream.

I was back in the theater, and Cerridwen was already there. The two of us were in the lobby, but we could not move. I tried to will my body to move, but my feet, my legs, my arms, my torso, even my thoughts were leaden. I looked at Cerridwen, and she looked at me, both of us frozen, locked into one another's eyes.

The fear of turning to salt flooded my heavy chest like ink spilled into water, seized me as if the fear itself had never left me. This loss of control, this lack of movement, this slowing of awareness. This mercy of my body, my being, unprotected as it was, in the midst of the world, as if I were exposed to the whims of the universe itself.

My throat began to tighten, my thoughts turning to sludge. Suddenly the dark figure was hovering between us. *Cerr-* I tried, but the name wouldn't come, frozen heavy on my leaden lips. I felt, if only I could whisper, think, breathe her name, maybe she, my conjured deus ex machina, could save me. She was made to be my rescuer, my interpreter. She was my ultimate construct.

I tried her name again, and now the figure was spreading out his substance, moving his black mass across the room like an icy blanket. His inky darkness spread across us, a chill, a frost that cemented my thoughts in place.

I became firm, blank, elemental. I became permanent.

THE NIGHT BEFORE THE MISSION

MARGARET KARMAZIN

Lisette arrived a few minutes late, stomping her boots before kicking them off. They joined the pile inside the door.

"Somebody was stuck in front of me, holding up traffic," she explained to the two women waiting for her. "Let's hope this is the last snow of the season."

"Well, it's March ninth, so it should be. Probably all melted by tomorrow. They said it's going up to fifty."

"Just so our flights take off all right," said Lisette.

"You all packed?" asked Rona, tall and lanky, her café-au-lait skin smooth as satin and the envy of them all. But no one wanted the scar down the side of her cheek, the constant reminder of what some man had done to her.

"I'm ready," said Lisette, "but I won't be flying 'til the day after tomorrow. I just take a carry on."

Susan, small and freckled, shrugged with impatience. "Come on. The rest are waiting. They're pretty worked up over Trudy's accident and having to replace her."

"Is the new woman here? Nancy brought her, right?"

"She's here," said Susan.

They trooped down a narrow hall past the dining-room-turned-office and kitchen into the added-on family room at the back. The unattached, railroad-style house was in a lower working class neighborhood outside Washington, DC. It was the best Susan could afford, with its orange, pseudo brick siding, rusted porch railing and rotting trim. Close enough to the university and airport by metro, and neighbors not too friendly—things that mattered. They didn't want people stopping by to chat.

Twelve other women were seated haphazardly about the family room, while the TV, tuned to CNN, blared in the background. The women watched in silence.

"What's happened?" said Lisette with urgency. "Anyone make a move?"

Karlyn, a woman in her fifties with long, silver hair, leaned forward. "The President has drawn a line in the sand. Literally. If Syria crosses it, he'll call on Congress to declare war. They're discussing the use of nuclear weapons."

Lisette sighed. "We're working right on the edge."

"I told you we should have done this weeks ago," said Karlyn. "Things would never have gone this far."

"Well, if it works," said Susan. "We don't know that it actually will."

"It'll definitely do something," said Karlyn. She was a bio-chem professor at American University and had, along with her Indian graduate student assistant, Nisha, developed the material. "At this point, anything is better than nothing."

Lisette broke into the conversation. "Nancy, where's your friend?" She glanced around looking for the new face.

"I just don't know," said a small, dark woman in the shadow, apparently ignoring Lisette. She sat on the edge of an old recliner in the corner, obviously edgy. "I mean, we could be destroying everything. Everything in the world."

Rona grunted in disgust. "We've discussed this to smithereens, Miora. We've been over everything we can think of."

"Yeah, but the elephants," Miora half whispered.

"The bull elephants. The alpha male wolves, the dolphins... I-I just—"

"It's a chance we take," said Karlyn firmly. "Stop it."

"NANCY!" said Lisette, clicking her pen. "Where is she?"

Nancy, a plump redhead from Drexel and good friend of Miora's, waved her arm in the air. "Over here. This is Lou." She indicated the lean, middle-aged woman sitting cross-legged on the floor by her feet.

The woman stood up and held out a hand to Lisette. "Lou," she said. Her hair was generously streaked with silver, and her bony face grave.

Lisette gave the hand a quick shake. "You're sure you're willing to take Trudy's place? Her destination was Pakistan."

The woman nodded and returned to her seat on the floor.

"Do you fully understand what you'll be doing?"

"Nancy explained," said Lou.

"Tell me, then, what you understand." Lisette motioned for someone to turn the TV to mute.

Someone did and all eyes turned to the newcomer.

She did not seem nervous, but her eyes were alert. "As I understand it, two of you, that would be Karlyn and Nisha? You ran repeated trials on chimps, rats, mice, rabbits and cats. You also tested on various birds and reptiles. You obtained a ten to fifteen percent drop in effective testosterone in the mammals, ten percent in the birds and twelve in the reptiles. Mating behavior in chimps declined by 2.6 percent, in cats and snakes not at all, rats four percent, mice five. Reproduction continued basically as usual."

"My God," said Karlyn, impressed. "You have a mind like a calculator."

Miora burst in, "Mating was *not* as usual. Not as usual at *all.*"

Susan snapped, "Leave it alone, Miora."

Lisette said, "If Karlyn said that mating continued

relatively normally, then it did, Miora."

Miora shook her head, "But not the strongest, not the strongest."

"What do you mean?" asked Lou.

"I mean," said Miora, "that high testosterone males may no longer fight for access to the females. The females will no longer mate with the fittest, alpha males."

There was a beat of silence, then Rhonda, a heavy black woman on the sofa, picked up the remote and flicked the sound back on. She nodded toward the screen. "Look where the strongest have gotten us, honey. Are you paying attention to the news there?"

"Yeah," snorted Lisette, "alpha males, they really make things better."

The CNN announcer, a perky blonde, said, "Syria has not yet responded. Troops are waiting on the border. Israel is on alert. This morning, President Vladimir Putin has given another warning that he is backing Syria. China put out a cryptic response to the effect that they are considering Russia's statement. Britain and Germany have committed themselves to the US, while France is holding back. Jordan has not given a statement. The President has repeated that he will consider nuclear weapons."

Lisette faced Miora. "Still having reservations?"

Miora did not answer, which infuriated Rona. "Which is better for animal life, Miora? A possible lowering of genetic expectations, or a nuclear winter? Why don't you answer? I don't hear anything coming out of your mouth."

"Fuck you," said Miora.

The women turned away from her and back to Trudy's replacement. Lisette eyed the woman closely and asked, "Do you have any reservations, Lou? If so, say it now and someone else will do Pakistan."

"I don't, but I want to know more about how you got started," Lou said.

Karlyn took over. "Nisha and I were assisting Dr. Weinstein in his examination of a relatively benign virus he named WP-29. I think the '29' was his wife's birthday. What he had in mind was the use of it as a carrier for certain cancer treatments, but of course since then, they've been looking to nanotechnology for that. When Dr. Weinstein started exhibiting signs of dementia eighteen months ago, we kept up the illusion of following his grant procedures. We behaved as if continuing his work, which in effect, we did to some extent. But then Nisha and I quietly took the research into a far different direction." She looked at Nisha.

The younger woman, shy when dealing with social situations, but assertive about her work, spoke up. "We found we could engineer the virus to hook up with testosterone receptors in male chimps, hereby lessening the hormone's effects by ten to fifteen percent. The effects don't seem to get any worse than that; it's a light disease, so to speak." She smiled.

Lou's voice held a hint of anxiety. "What about mutations in the virus? What about testosterone in the female?"

Nisha was unruffled. "Apparently, the presence of estrogen prevents much interference, but in post-menopausal females, it has minimal effect. Well, there'll be less hairs on their chins."

"Hey," said Karlyn, "show some respect. You'll be there someday."

Maybe, everyone thought, but didn't voice it.

"And mutations?" said Lou.

"Of course there were mutations, but in the sixteen months of actual testing, the testosterone drop didn't seem to vary."

"Give us again the behavioral changes in the affected animals," said Rona.

Nisha's dark eyes gleamed. "They stopped fighting. They cooperated, not quite like females, but roughly, like good-natured boys. Viciousness stopped. The mating did not, but the warring did."

"How did the females choose mates if not for the

usual strongest genetics?" asked Lou.

"I suppose," said Nisha, "that they chose who they liked. Is that a bad thing?"

Lou didn't answer, but seemed to relax. She leaned back and selected a corn chip from a nearby bowl.

Nancy spoke up with her usual aggressive tone. "What I still don't get, Nisha, is why you and Karlyn didn't test it, at least a little bit, on humans! I mean, how do we know it even does anything on them?"

"How would we test it?" said Karlyn, with some testiness of her own. "We thought of it, believe me. That prison uprising in Illinois. We'd have liked to go in there, release the stuff and see what happened, but once it's turned loose, there's no going back. The guards or delivery men would have carried the virus to the outside world immediately.

"Don't worry so much about it working on humans," said Nisha. "After we saw what it does to chimps, we engineered it to humans. We're pretty confident it will work."

"Well, one thing we know for sure," said Karlyn, "is that the virus does not turn males gay. That's something you're born with, a matter of brain chemistry or formation."

"I just feel so bad about Trudy," said Miora from her recliner. She always appeared worried, even when nothing was going on.

"Yeah," said Rona, looking at the floor. "What are her chances of coming out of the coma? Does anybody know?"

"She didn't fall into a coma on her own," said Karlyn. "They induced it after releasing the pressure on her brain. They'll wake her up in a day or two. I believe she has a decent chance."

"Damn drunk drivers," said Rona with feeling. "They ought to..."

"I know," said Karlyn, "I know."

"Who wants tuna and who wants turkey?" Susan

asked the room. Hands went up for each offering and Susan took count.

"Where'd you get the hoagies?" asked Joan, the oldest woman among them. She was a retired professor in her late sixties, a botanist and a long time friend of Karlyn's. "Why don't you cut them up into pieces and let people have some of each?"

"Good idea," said Susan as she returned to the kitchen.

"Okay, let's go over this one last time," said Lisette, standing in the middle of the room holding a clipboard. "Mute the TV, okay?"

Someone did.

"Let's start with you, Karlyn. Your flight to London is at 10:15 PM, right? Like everyone else, do a release on the plane. Probably the toilet is best. You're staying at 196 Bishopsgate in the financial district. You should be able to take a walk around as soon as you check in, and do a few releases. Hit Parliament next. The following day, you're off to Belfast. You got all your stuff?"

"Yes," said Karlyn.

"Nisha," said Lisette, moving down the list. You're on an earlier flight to London. It's a long haul to India."

"Yes," nodded Nisha.

"Three hours at Heathrow before your flight to New Delhi. You'll be tired and irritable, but, if you can, do a few releases near government buildings before you crash. You can't do it from a taxi, you'll have to do a lot of walking and don't forget to take water with you, for heaven's sake. Whatever you do, you don't want to pass out from heat exhaustion and risk—"

Nisha laughed. "I was born there, remember? I've been there six times since."

Karlyn interrupted. "How would anyone suspect her anyway? Is there a law in India against carrying a perfume bottle?"

"No," said Lisette, "but—"

"They'd never figure it out. And even if they poured

out what's in the bottle, they'd be doing our work, wouldn't they? Wasting it all in one spot, but give it a few days and it'll be all over."

"I wish we could put the bottles in our carry on," said Rona.

"We have the other," said Karlyn. She was referring to the "vitamin pills."

"You're sure," said Linna from her end of the couch, "they won't suspect that?"

"I doubt it," said Karlyn. "The capsules look like any regular herbal concoction and are sealed professionally into Echinacea and Valerian bottles. If asked, you're taking the Echinacea with you because you always catch something on a plane and suffer for weeks, or you need the Valerian to help you sleep."

"I got mine in my purse," piped up Joan.

Lisette said, "You got your tickets, all your stuff ready, Nisha?"

"Yes," said Nisha. "I'm packed. It bothers me, though, that I'll be over there and can't visit anyone."

"I'm sorry about that," said Lisette, "but we can't have people asking questions. You know your relatives would—"

"I know. Busybodies like you'd never believe."

"Well, then," said Lisette. She fixed the young woman with a severe gaze. "If you deviate in any way from the plan, you put the rest of our lives and the entire mission in danger. If you have any doubts, now is the time..."

"I have no doubts," said Nisha. "I was just expressing."

Susan returned with plates of sandwiches and placed them around the room. She refilled the chip bowls. "Anyone need anything else?" she asked. "Sodas are in the fridge and wine on the counter."

They murmured and nodded while helping themselves to the food.

Next, Lisette went over details with Rona, who was heading to France, and Susan, who was doing Germany.

"Remember, everyone," she said, "If someone presses you for an explanation as to why you're visiting their country, you're a freelance writer working on an article or you've always wanted to see that county and figured you'd better do it before all the trouble starts."

She moved on to Joan, whose destination was China.

"Your situation is the one of the more precarious. Your group is landing in Beijing and going where next?"

Joan rose and handed her a brochure. Lisette leafed through it. "Okay," she said, "I see you'll be in Beijing three nights, then to Xian, Wuxi, Hanzhou and Shanghai. How can you spread the material, do you think? I mean with the group always around."

"The group was the only way to get around," said Joan. "Besides, I've always wanted to go, so this'll kill two birds with one stone."

"Let's hope it doesn't kill anything!" scowled Miora.

They ignored her.

"My question is, though," said Lisette, "how will you shake a capsule out with an audience?"

"I'll figure something out," said Joan. "Go off to the bathroom, whatever."

Lisette nodded. "Your flight's still at 8:30 tomorrow evening?"

"Yes, but if you don't mind, I'd like to leave now and get a good night's sleep. I'm not young like most of you and I know I probably won't get a wink on the plane. If you want me with all my cylinders firing, I'd better be rested."

"Sure," said Lisette. Her expression suddenly turned melancholy and something unidentifiable. "The first one to leave," she said. "Give me a hug."

Joan got up from the couch again with some difficulty and let the younger women embrace her. Then others got up to do the same.

"Good luck, Joan," they said. "Be careful. Call when you get back."

"Yes," said Lisette, "that reminds me. Except for Joan, whose friends think she's just taking the trip she always wanted, call only when you return. Don't make any contact during the mission with family or friends. No emails, nothing. Nisha, what did you tell your brother?"

Nisha gave a small sigh. "I told him I was working on a project with a deadline, that I'd probably be out of commission for a week. We often go a week without checking in."

"I had to tell my roommate I had family issues to deal with," said Terry, a student at American U. "It's spring break, but she'd expected me to go to Florida with her."

"Well, you're lying for a good cause," joked the woman next to her.

Susan got up to walk Joan out, and Lisette returned to her list. "This one, as you all know, is as important as China: Israel. Miora, I'm worried about you after seeing that you still seem to have doubts."

Miora stood up. Though she had olive skin, she looked pale. "I am not interested in backing out. Don't you understand? I just have to go over everything in my mind. I think out loud. You have a problem with that?"

Lisette regarded her with a steely expression. Though Lisette was medium height, slim and blonde, there was something soldierly about her. No one knew her sexuality, no one ever saw her with anyone. She lived alone in a small apartment and never invited anyone over.

"You're going to the most sensitive spot on the globe. If there is even one thousandth of a doubt that you can carry out your part, say it now. Someone will go in your place. It's not a problem now, Miora, but it will be if you insist on going, then wimp out once you're there."

Miora looked sullen. She was beautiful—slender, delicate, ethereal. Her hair was short and shaggy and gleamed in the soft light, myriad colors in its dark depths.

Lisette eyed her coldly. "Don't even think about screwing this up. Think about the future of the world."

"I will not screw up. Though I worry about the

animals, I am firmly committed. You don't have to worry."

"And why wouldn't I worry?" said Lisette. It was as if they were the only two people in the room.

"Because," said Miora, "what we're doing is the lesser of two evils and our only choice."

Lisette stared at her a moment longer. "All right," she said. She paused, then checked her clipboard. "Jerusalem —you'll arrive by ten tomorrow night. Our time. Their time, let's see..." she rifled through her papers, looking for her time table.

"It doesn't matter," said Miora. "I'll start as soon as I can. If it's the middle of the night, I'll go to bed and start the next morning. Doesn't matter."

Lisette stared hard at her. "Miora..."

"Stop it. I'll do my job. That's that."

Lisette sighed and returned to her list. "Nancy. You're Moscow. This is also high priority. You were feeling like you were coming down with the flu a couple of days ago? Are you still sick?"

"No," said Nancy, "I'm fine now. It might have been a touch of food poisoning."

"How's your Russian?"

"Well, duh, it's my second major."

"Sorry," said Lisette. She gave the girl a once-over. "You know, your red hair will stick out like a sore thumb. Maybe you should be the one going to London instead."

"They have redheads in Russia. You want me to put a rinse on it? I can stop by Walmart on the way home and get some Loving Care, tone it down to reddish brown or something. It washes out eventually."

"Would you mind?" said Lisette. "Just better not to stand out, and if there is one thing I can say about you, it's that you definitely stand out."

"I'll get the Loving Care, geesh," said Nancy.

Lisette's expression did not change. "Good. Now, I need not remind you of the importance of remaining below the radar. This is Russia we're talking about. I don't want you to take even one microscopic chance, do you understand me?"

"Of course I understand you," snapped Nancy, obviously not one to be pushed around. "Russia is my subject. My grandparents were from there. Don't talk down to me, please."

"I know you," said Lisette. "You're perky, you're a little reckless, you can be pushy at times. I'm not putting judgments on any of those things. I'm just saying that carrying out our plan in that country is not something you want anyone to notice. Unless you want to spend the rest of your—"

Nancy broke in. "I get it, okay? I'll probably let the stuff loose out a window in the hotel. Besides, I'll get the people on the plane. I'm not interested in not enjoying the rest of my life."

"What time is your flight?"

"You have it right in front of you, don't you?" said Nancy.

"12:45 is what I have."

"That's it then," said Nancy. She leaned back in her chair, making it clear the conversation was over.

"Before we go on, let's check the news," said Lisette, and Nisha picked up the remote to click off "mute".

Four talking heads were discussing the approaching conflict.

"Is that CNN? Go to MSN, let's see what they're saying," suggested Karlyn and Nisha obliged.

A reporter in Pakistan was talking excitedly, his eyes wide with obvious fear.

"Did you expect something different?" said Nancy. "Same shit every channel."

"Try Fox," said Lisette.

"Oh those idiots!" said Nancy. "They're probably creaming themselves, they're so ecstatic the government is about to destroy the planet! God, how anyone with one tenth of a brain—"

"It's important to know what the warmongers are doing," said Lisette.

One of these, a snappy talking, smart-ass type wearing the regulation black suit and red or blue tie to signal his "patriotism," practically squealed, "That's it, friends! Syria has refused to budge! Time to roll in there and show 'em who's boss!"

Lisette crossed the room in two strides, grabbed the remote from Nisha and clicked off the offensive face. "Okay," she said, back to basics.

"I'll handle Washington, of course, then take the train to New York. From there, I'll get an evening flight to Chicago. Next day, on to Los Angeles and, on the way back, Atlanta." She went on to the rest of the list, covering those going to Dubai, South America, Korea, Africa and Indonesia, finishing up with Lou and her instructions for Pakistan.

"Any questions?" she said.

Rona gave a sardonic little laugh. "I just get a little sad thinking about Charlie. You know, what he'll be like after. He's a delicious man, a trustworthy man. What's going to happen to him? Is he going to start highlighting my hair and designing window treatments for the apartment?"

"I told you, that won't happen," said Karlyn firmly.

"I worry a little," said Rhonda, "about my father. I read something the other day about older men with low testosterone being depressed. What if they all get worse?"

"They could give them pills, I guess," said Nancy.

Lisette set down her clipboard. Her eyes, usually steely and impersonal, now flashed. "This is all we can do to save the world. Who knows if we'll even make it out there in time. Pray that Syria holds off for a while, that Israel demands some time, that Washington will listen. If we all perform successfully, in less than a month the virus should have spread over most of the planet. It is extremely contagious, by air, any body fluid; it lives for hours, even days, on surfaces, it lives in water. If Karlyn and Nisha's test animals are an accurate demonstration, men everywhere will lay down their weapons."

"But," said Nancy, tossing her flaming hair from her eyes, "it's old generals and politicians who start the wars."

"But it's young men who fight them," said Lisette. "Without the young men interested, the old ones can do nothing."

She picked up her can of Diet Pepsi. "Well, friends, here's to a successful mission. To all of us, a future on this planet."

The others raised their glasses and cans and solemnly toasted, then rose to gather their things.

Hands

Donna Scott

They never usually looked her in the eye. It was all about the arrangement: the slip and sparkle of the solitaire diamond; the pinch-hold on the stem of a champagne flute; the contrast of alabaster skin against blood-red velvet. These days the "artists" were often little more than computer geeks. They weren't too used to having the objet d'art actually *speak* to them. They would say things like, "Can you just move... a fraction?" and Sophie would have no idea what they wanted her to do. Move a finger? Lift her elbow to get a cleaner shot? What? Mostly they were anxious to get the image they needed then scurry back to their computers to upload, render and airbrush. They would much rather be working with Hands than a hands-model. That was the way things were going—the Hands were taking over.

This photographer was different. His name was Jamie, and he was young, with dull-blond hair in soft spikes and retro black-frame glasses, the sort that people with perfect vision tended to wear to affect a nerdy-intellectual look. He was working with a stylist, Cathy, who wore the cropped hair and quasi-uniform of black shirt and trousers that all stylists wore, and very similar glasses to Jamie. They were both chatty—a good team, Sophie thought.

The product they were selling today was an indulgent rose-scented hand cream. Sophie had never even tried it, nor would she dare to. Work was scarce enough without having to wait for an allergic rash to go down as well.

Cathy was setting up a reverse rose-petal scatter shot —after CGI, the petals would fly through the air before gathering in Sophie's cupped hands. She held a light meter to Sophie's skin. "Oh my, I've never seen such perfect nails. Oh, but they're falsies right?"

"My own," Sophie said. "Trick of Granny's. Eat a cube of jelly every day for strong nails. And drink lots of milk, too."

"Wow," Cathy drawled. "I think I'd need a bit more than that, to be honest. Look at these stubs." She waved her fingers under Sophie's nose. "But yours... they're just like *Hands.*" To that, Sophie responded with silence. "Oh," said Cathy, "I only meant in the sense that they're perfect, you know, flawless. I didn't mean, like, *fake* or anything." She nodded at Jamie and backed away from the shot.

Jamie started firing. "Ignore her, Soph," he spoke between bursts of flash. "Ain't nothing... like... the real thing... Lucky for all of us, though, that some clients can be... more discerning. Know what I mean?"

Sophie gave him a thin smile. Ah, those *discerning* clients. They were the only kind who gave her any work at all of late. The bookings were getting fewer and further between. Time to start thinking of alternatives... not office work. She'd only look stupid and gauche as a new girl. Maybe working with kids would suit her, though... or would it? No, *this* was work. She could get this job, she could get more. Of course she could.

A few more shots and the job was wrapped up. Nice work if you could get it, and Sophie definitely could, she told herself. The photographer checked the files one last time, and Sophie began pulling on her long gloves.

"Hey, before you go," Jamie caught up with her as she reached the studio door, "do we always have to go through your agent to reach you? If we had other work for you?"

"What do you have in mind?"

"Oh, you know. Projects and stuff. We work with artists... real ones, who do installations and the like. They hate paying the ten percent."

"Ten percent?" Sophie arched a brow. "More like twenty."

"What... ? Oh wow. I erm, feel really guilty now. *Twenty* percent? Really?"

"Yes, really." A worm of doubt wriggled in Sophie's head. She'd often wondered herself if that was too much. "It's standard."

"Ah well." Jamie riffled around inside his jeans jacket and produced a black business card with a white fold mark down the centre. "Here. Honestly, we get asked for models all the time. There's loads of work out there. Sorry about the crease."

"Oh, no, it's fine." She smiled and zipped the card away in her purse. A moment passed that would have been long enough to offer a something in return—a bit of small talk, a number, a smile—had Sophie been so inclined.

"Great. Okay, Well, get in touch any time. Whenever you'd like to cut out the middleman..."

"Woman."

"Quite. Well, you've got my email there. And my, er, number..."

○─○

The Hands were waiting for her when she got back to the flat. They'd found a shallow cerulean pot from somewhere—one she'd let some hyacinths die in a few years ago—and had arranged themselves on the telephone table in the hallway, elbows clamped together in the base, palms cupped like tulip petals. They must have done that themselves—Graham wouldn't have thought about putting them in a pot, let alone known where to look for one. They had also chosen an unusual tone for their display: chocolate skin mottled with coral vitiligo. Sophie suppressed a shiver of distaste. She took off her silk scarf and threw it over them. They caught it. Sophie snatched the scarf back.

"Hey, that's Hermès. Off!" Really, they were worse than kids. Or cats, for that matter.

The hum of the fridge in the kitchen resonated through the flat. No TV noise—Graham must still be travelling home from work. Sophie retrieved a chilled bottle of Riesling, picked a glass from the cupboard and carried both through to the sofa in the lounge. Boots were kicked off, and she sat with one heel tucked under her thigh. Her leather blouson landed with a soft flop on the carpet next to her handbag. The gloves stayed on, and Sophie rolled the glass stem between her fingers just as she had done in an ad she had once posed for. Underneath the cotton, her hands felt cool; the gloves allowed her skin to breathe, whilst keeping it smooth and unblemished. Sophie closed her eyes as she sipped her wine; heard the skittering of acrylic across varnished wood; palms slapping ceramic floor tiles. She could hear the things running across the mat, the ring of a glass bowl as they bumped into the side table, then back they went again, racing each other across the room. Sophie didn't have to ask what was up with them. There came the sound of the key in the lock: Graham was home.

"My girls." The Hands were pawing at his legs as he walked through the day room towards Sophie, leaning in to give her a peck on the cheek. "Good day, hun?"

"Yeah, yeah. It was." She eyed Graham as the Hands followed him over to his La-Z-Boy, springing up to the back of the chair to get to his shoulders. They had now transformed to a pale white with candy-pink nails. "You call them *girls*," she said. "They're not *girls*. They're *its*."

"Of course they're girls. They do girl-things, don't they? You think I'd let an 'it' touch me up like this?" The Hands were now giving him a deep shoulder-rub.

"You said *my* girls as well."

"Yeah, I meant you as well. Bloody hell, don't start as soon as I've walked in, just 'cause I've talked to the Hands as well as your face." He chuckled to himself, but Sophie fixed her mouth in a grim line.

"...only they *were* supposed to be a gift for *me*, weren't they?"

"Except you don't bother with them, the poor darlin's. Anyone would think you didn't want 'em. Always Gucci this and Prada that... I try spending a proper bit of dosh on you, and you just turn your nose up."

"No, I don't."

"Yeah, you do. You'd still rather use the dishwasher, when you've got a pair of perfectly good Hands just sitting there."

"Just... feels wrong. You know?"

"No hun, I don't. You eat salmon, what doesn't ask to be eaten, but these Hands here, they'd do anything for you. Wouldn't you, girls?" One hand moved from Graham's shoulder briefly to stroke his chin. Sophie took a big slug of wine, wincing as the alcohol hit her stomach. "Nice, don't I get one?" Graham stuck out his lower lip in a mock pout. Sophie pushed herself off the sofa with an exaggerated sigh and went to fetch him a glass, hearing the electronic fizz of the TV coming to life behind her back as Graham found the remote. She was not sure why she felt so annoyed with him: she could have commanded one of the Hands to fetch him a glass, but she argued that she didn't trust them. She was sure their sensors were slightly out. Besides, she didn't own any cheap glasses.

o–o

He sat in a black leather captain's chair facing the fountains out in the garden. The windows were triple-glazed so he could not hear the splash and gurgle of the droplets striking the marble; he could only sense the resonance of light arcing and waving through the colour-less mediums of water and glass to strike notes against his face, like vibrations from a silent harp. He closed his eyes and focused on the butterfly touch, feeling the ripples burst as the door opened behind his chair, creating that subtle change in the air, which told him the girl had entered, just as instructed, without knocking. No percussion of heels tapped the floor. Good. Her feet had swollen in the shoes she had just kicked off, though. Her feet must be warm— he could smell them, just a slight tang... nylon stockings... or tights. Yes, tights. He could not mistake the heat of her in the room. A presence, nervous and perspiring, wary of him. Pulsing with life. Young.

Her steps ceased. She was still for a second or two, possibly eyeing the back of his head. Then he heard her move across to the instrument, arranging herself on the velveteen pad of the seat. She paused again. Oh, delicious —that last gasp of breath, held sharp before the plunge.

Then, there it was: the sudden break that became a soft, deliberate rhythm; the contrast of low chords with those nostalgic, plummeting notes from higher up the keys; that aching, wrenching sadness that must truly be felt in order to play the piece with any justice, even in the lighter mid-section, which the girl played with deftness before swooping down to sombre depths once more.

The music ended, but he couldn't feel her stir. He glanced back over his shoulder to look at her from the corner of his eye. Her shape was almost slouched; not looking up at him at all. It was as though she were just hanging there, still lost in the feeling, the remembrance of music. He turned his face back to the window before speaking.

"Come and sit with me now."

She walked to his left side, almost on tip-toe, seemingly confused. Ah, of course—no other chairs. The girl hovered, waiting for another instruction, before tentatively lowering herself onto the floor before him to sit Indian-style, looking up at him, a slight furrow on her brow. Sitting there like that, she did not seem seventeen, he thought. Fourteen at a push. What could such a child know of true sorrow?

"So... Miss Delphine Simmons. It seems I am honoured to be in the presence of a true virtuoso. Would you agree?"

The girl glanced down. "I-I wouldn't know, sir. I know my tutor is not of the same mind. She says I'm a *maverick.*"

"How so, a maverick?"

"My technique... I taught myself, you see. And then for a short while I had a teacher—my tutor doesn't rate him. The memory of how to play—how *I* think to play— it's all in my hands. Stuck. I can't unlearn these things."

"Have you tried?"

"I-of course! But I just think Madame Rabelais has tired of me. She says she's not prepared to wait any longer for me to play her way... and now I've lost my place at the Conservatoire." Her voice caught a little as she struggled round the pronunciation with the twang of her East London accent. Oh, little fish... how you must learn to swim in many deep waters.

"Such is the reputation of the Dragon Rabelais! But do not worry, Miss Delphine. Yours would not be the first genius to be dismissed out of hand by that woman. Come here, child." He watched as she stood up. "That's it. Now give me your hands. Don't be nervous now, I'm just an old man. And don't give me that look either—I won't be flattered. I'm a lot older than you might think."

The girl held her hands out to him limply. So trusting! They were as smooth as the face of a doll made from bisque china, and almost as cold, though he could still feel the rapid pulse running down her thumb. Her hands were so slender, he could not help but imagine how easily they might be crushed in the grip of a strong man. "Exquisite, my dear," he said. "What I hold here is so very precious. Do you understand?" The girl nodded. "No, no, I don't think you do... not just yet." He released her. "Miss Delphine, you play Chopin with the dolorous fervour of the man himself. I suspect you are a very morbid sort of child. I pray you never lose that sweet connection... though, I fear that so often goes the way of youth. You need such passion to be able to play... *well.* Therefore, you must know perfection and pain in equal measure.

"I will help you, Miss Delphine. Forget your dreams of the Conservatoire. They would only make a 'jobbing' musician out of you. They would want you to play like an appliance—a washing machine to mangle silk. I will not have that of my new *protégée*."

"Oh. Then, you have accepted me? Thank you, Monsieur. Thank you—"

"Enough! You will listen to me, child. The Dragon Rabelais was indeed a fool to have let you slip through her fingers, but she was right about one thing. Your interpretation is too fluid, your technique lacks vital control. In this house all control is mine, so I will work that abandon out of you. Is that clear?"

"Yes, Monsieur."

"And you will answer me without sulk in your voice. You must give of yourself willingly. That is the price. Is that clear?"

"Yes, Monsieur."

"Good. I think we understand each other. Your mother resides in Walthamstow, does she not?"

"Th-that's right."

"Well, it's certainly too far from here to warrant you going home all the time. You can call her to let her know you are staying indefinitely, and I'll send my man to fetch your things this evening. You can have the Jasper room. Liszt once slept there when he was alive, you know. Since then, he has been known to ghost compositions to the brains and fingers of sensitive girls every now and then. Oh, don't worry, it's usually only girls of very little brain that he picks on." The girl's expression was blank, though she seemed at pains to calm her breathing. He chuckled to himself. "Fear not, child. I, being closer to the dead than you at this juncture, will tell the man to leave you alone. Now, be gone; rest. I will get my man to wake you when it is time to practise."

O–O

Mrs Simmons was sitting upright on the middle cushion of the sofa watching her bit of *Corrie*. The soap magazines were fan-tailed out on the coffee table, the picture of Deirdre wielding an iron uppermost. Mrs Simmons glanced down at the picture. Deirdre. Iron. She looked up at the screen. Deirdre. Iron. Good. Almost kettle time too.

She jumped when she heard the knock on the door. Three knocks. That was good. Only, *Corrie* was still on. She waited, pinching the ends of her fingers. Don't bite your nails. Wait. The music came on with the sponsor's words, and she rushed to the door, willing whoever it was not to knock again. "Is that you, Delphine? Forgot your key again?"

Of course it wasn't Delphine—Mrs Simmons knew how her little girl knocked on a door; not with hard slaps like that, but asking the question gave her time to get her hankie from her pocket so that she could handle the latch without touching the metal. Her mouth was drying out just wondering who it might be. The door opened the full length of the chain and Mrs Simmons peered through the gap. She saw a young man with glasses.

"Yes?" she asked.

"Mrs Simmons?"

"Erm. Yes?"

"Hello, I've come from the estate of Monsieur Leon —I'm his personal assistant. Doubtless you have heard your daughter's good news already. She *has* called you, hasn't she?"

"She'd have a job. I don't have a phone."

"You don't... ? Oh." The man looked bemused. "Oh, well. I imagine it's up to me to tell you then." He paused. "May I come in?"

"No... if you don't mind." Now the man's mouth was opening and closing like a goldfish's. "Sorry, can I help you, only *Corrie* will be back on in a sec?"

"Well... it's just that your daughter has been invited to reside with Monsieur Leon and become his student. I have been sent to collect her things."

"Oh. So she's not coming back?"

"No." The man smiled thinly. "I've come for her things, as I said."

No time for the kettle now. One minute, thirty. Not long, not long. "What things?"

"Anything she might need... clothes, toiletries. Keepsakes?"

"But she can't... she has to come back." However, the man said nothing, merely stood there. *Corrie* would be back on in a minute. "Wait there."

Mrs Simmons closed the door on the fellow. It was suddenly almost like he wasn't there. Perhaps she could pretend, go back to him later? No, she better had not. She rushed into the kitchen and got a plastic bag from the tidy on the wall. Into that went a nightie and toothbrush. She hesitated for a couple of seconds. What keepsake? Something would need to be moved! She settled on a framed photo from the top of the bureau: Delphine's father sitting astride his old Harley, looking like a young Marlon Brando. Behind him, a lass was turning her face away from the camera; not because she was shy, or suffering from her nerves, far from it. No, she was waving a farewell to a crowd on the other side, not visible in this photo, her starched veil sweeping up in a stiff triangle as though whipped by the wind. Just one hand gripping her man about the waist. She didn't care, did she? No, she was off out of it. Fuck you, Frank the Deli, with your wandering hands. Fuck you, bitch sisters. Have the tin bath to yourselves, I'm off. She'd have been grinning like a skull at that point. She remembered: that was just before it had started raining. Their first taste of freedom, and they'd ended up stuck in a caff in the next town, drinking ropey coffee. The next stop after that had been a pub, and there the bike had somehow ended up broken... not starting ever again.

She dropped the photo into the bag, opened the door to the end of its chain again and thrust the carrier into the young man's hand. "Tell her she'll have to come for the rest herself. *Corrie*'s back on now. Sorry." She shut the door again quickly, sealing herself back inside her world.

O─O

Sophie looked over her shoulder as she urged the Hands to climb inside her rucksack. God knows why, she thought. They were hers, she could take them where she liked. Plus Graham wasn't even in the flat to see what she was doing. It just worried her that he might suddenly walk in and object for some reason. What if he took them back, said he was rescinding the gift for non-appreciation? Oh, don't be silly, she told herself. She shrugged on her leather blouson, swilled down the last of her tea, and out she went.

As Sophie walked down to the tube, she could feel the Hands fidgeting, wriggling in the small of her back. They were clicking to each other—she'd never noticed them do that before. Their view of the world must be very limited, she reckoned. Perhaps they felt like sheep do when nearing the slaughterhouse and this was their equivalent of anxious bleating. This journey was certainly out of their routine... not that she liked what *that* had become. She could feel her face reddening at the thought. If Graham thought he could pick and choose when he thought the Hands were girls and when they were gadgets, well, he shouldn't be surprised that the thought of touching him disgusted her.

"Except you can't even do that," he'd grizzled. "The rough side of cotton's all I get. Not exactly intimate."

Where was this leading? She grabbed the pole to hang on, there being no free seats left in the carriage. Had they grown apart, perhaps? Maybe he was sick and tired of paying for everything they did these days, she didn't blame him trying to get his money's worth, but then... oh, bad thought. Bad, *bad* thought!

The man behind her, nose in e-reader, leaned into Sophie's rucksack. She could feel the Hands squirming now, and she gently moved aside to give them more room. Don't worry, girls, she said to herself. Soon be free.

She got out early at Sloane Square, needing the fresh air. She liked to go past the shop fronts and cafés in this part of London, as though the wealth could pass to her simply from staring at things that only the very rich could afford. Too-thin girls stalked past in tottering heels and frilly, belted coats. How had she never noticed before how emaciated they looked? Audrey Hepburn's legacy to a youth who barely knew who the actress was. How many of them were models—*real* models, as Graham would describe them? Ones with bodies and faces and eating disorders.

Sophie pulled her phone from her pocket and waited for the Maps application to catch up. Something-V Terrace, she had to get to... ah yes, that was it. She began walking.

o—o

Jamie had said the client was a sort of collector. He had residences all over the world, was particularly fond of Degas bronzes and grand pianos, and liked beautiful girls to visit him—not for any nefarious reasons. Just for sketches. A good job. But he found hands tricky to master. His place in London was one of those blue plaque jobs— bequeathed to his family by some famous friend back in the Victorian age. She should have recognised the name, apparently, only she had to confess she knew nothing much about anything—not art, nor history, nor music.

The door was answered by a man who looked like some kind of bouncer, a silver hoop earring in one ear. The faint sound of a piano came from somewhere in the house, and she stood in the hallway, taking in the swirly, dark green floral wallpaper, the candle sconces with dangling crystals, the large, ornate mirror, and the smell: something like dust and meat, slightly masked by the sweeter scents of beeswax and incense. This place was old, all right.

Finally, a door opened, and Jamie walked through, smiling. "You made it!" He gestured at the surroundings. "Some place, isn't it? The Leons were never ones for change... anyway, come through. Can I get you anything?"

○–○

Mrs Simmons looked at herself in the hallway mirror. She was buttoning up her raincoat. It might rain when she was outside, mightn't it? The woman who looked back at her seemed some kind of ghost... she could see the girl under the skin; the one who did such mad things as go out into the rain bare-armed, twirling, dancing, singing under the street light with Jack and Maisie, bottle in hand, with the neighbours switching on bedroom lights, shouting through the windows... her father throwing open the front door, dressed in his vest and pyjama bottoms, face of thunder. Jack had run off then as well...

She did up the last button, just as the sun came out and shone through the glass in the door, warming the hallway. So bright. She could always take the coat back off again... but really what choice had she got?

She reached in her pocket again for the letter: *Do not worry about me, Mum. Monsieur Leon has taken care of everything. Clothes, shoes... oh, Mum, they make my Sunday best look like rags. He has made me feel like a princess. We have been out twice now to the Symphonic Hall, and dined in the very best restaurants in London. Soon, he says, he will take me to Paris, but I must practice very hard to earn this. Oh Mum, he tells me he is so very old, but there is a kindness in his eyes and I only want to please him. I have never been so happy...*

○–○

The day was getting weirder and weirder. Work was work, she had told herself, but now that she was actually here, posing with her arms crossed languidly in front of her, under the scrutiny of this man, Sophie realised that "unsettled" had been the level of normality for her emotions pretty much all day. Only now was she becoming aware of it.

"So, Miss Sophie," Monsieur Leon said. "Your hands are your work?"

"Oh yes," she replied. The conversation seemed to be limited to such brief exchanges of small talk. Sophie would wait for the client to speak; he would be concentrating on his sketches. She wondered about him—he was old money; perhaps it had never occurred to him to ask a friend to pose for him? A wife? A daughter? To draw hands that were lined with age; stubby fingers, bitten nails. She had hands that she had striven to preserve in the perfection of youth... that swift passing time. Soon she would have no work at all... perhaps one or two assignments where hands of character were required. *Character!* Commercials needed perfection... but art?

"Miss Sophie... if you don't mind, I am drawing the perfection of all of you, but there is a crease in your brow. It must be removed for me to continue."

Sophie smiled. "If you like, but are you not just sketching my hands?"

Leon placed one of his hands to his armrest and pushed himself out of his chair. He held the pad out to Sophie for her to see. "My eyes are old. I feel I must be closer to you to be able to capture the essence of what your hands are."

"The essence of my hands?" Sophie could not help herself. "They're just hands."

"Just hands, are they?" Leon reached forward and took one of Sophie's hands in his own. Sophie saw that he had long, tapered fingers—piano hands, her Mum would have said, which made sense. He was obviously not the one she could hear playing now, but perhaps he also played?

"My, you have good nails too," Sophie told him. And unlined skin, and a firm grip as well...

"My assistant told me a lot about you, Miss Sophie, and I was very keen to meet you. You are one who seeks to preserve yourself in perfection."

Sophie almost choked. "Excuse me?" She tried to pull her hands back, but Leon tightened his grip.

"I am just trying to pay you a compliment. I have

known many women who have longed to hear such words —the finest of women, old of blood and history. It used to be that one's hands were the measure of nobility. It is hands such as yours that fell limp at the caress of Madame Guillotine. These modern times, even the princesses of Europe in their white gowns bear the marks of the stable and mud-track all over their hands." He nodded up at the ceiling, indicating where the sound of the piano was coming from. "There are some accomplishments that render the hands yet more beautiful, of course." He narrowed his eyes. "My protégée; she is not quite ready, just yet. Perfection awaits her in what she has to achieve.

"But you, Miss Sophie, who does not paint, who does not write, who does not play... your hands can never be more perfect than they are right now. Would you agree?"

Sophie shrugged. "I suppose..."

"Excellent." He pinned both of her hands down with one hand as he reached into his inner jacket pocket. The knife he pulled out was small, with a curved blade no bigger than the line from the pad of Sophie's thumb to the tip of her index finger. Sophie had enough time to see the glint of blood-red stones in the hilt before the blade flashed across the back of each hand. A line of beaded rubies bloomed on her skin before melting together and running down her hands. A scream caught in her throat, emerging as a choked sob.

"Thank you, Miss Sophie. I believe our business is now concluded. I will see you are compensated more than handsomely for any future loss of earnings and trauma that you could possibly lay claim to. My man will see you out now."

"What?" Sophie pushed a tear from her eye, smearing the side of her face with blood.

"Of course. How remiss of me." Leon proffered a handkerchief. Numb, Sophie took it from him: lace edged and monogrammed *CDL*. "It is best that you go now."

It was not Jamie who came to lead her away, but the

broad-shouldered door guy with the earring. It seemed decidedly unwise to resist the request to leave. Only when she found herself blinking in the grey light of London did Sophie realise she had left her rucksack behind.

○─○

Delphine's throat was dry, her stomach a hard, tight ball, but she would not stop until she had got the piece right. It was Rachmaninov, and it was *hard*. But she thought about what Monsieur Leon had said: she would never know perfection until she had mastered this. She never would though, would she? Not while she was thinking about perfection and not the music. It was then she realised she was no longer alone. Monsieur Leon was standing behind her.

"Oh, hello, Monsieur. Is your visitor gone already?"

"Yes. I thought I would come and sit with you a while—see if my little protégée is cooked."

Delphine rolled her eyes. "Oh no, today I am *struggling*. As are you it appears." She gestured towards the silver-topped cane he was leaning against. "Are you in pain?"

"Do not concern yourself with my troubles. Play." Delphine turned back to the piano, but had not played a bar before she messed up. "Do not think of me sitting here," Leon admonished. "Just think of the spirit of the piece you are playing—the soul of it. Tell me your soul, Miss Delphine."

Delphine took a deep breath and began to play once more. The room melted away. She felt the cold, felt herself running, the swell of the ocean. Long darkness, the play of the Northern Lights tripping across the unfamiliar sky... suddenly all was clear.

She came to, hanging over the piano, to the sound of applause. She was exhausted.

"Well done, my little one. You are... there."

"Really?" Delphine could scarcely believe it. "So soon... but this morning I played so badly."

"Nevertheless, I was listening for perfection, and just now I heard it... no, don't touch the keys now. You are most unlikely to repeat your success immediately, and perfection is all I required of you. Indeed..." and a tear rolled down his cheek as he spoke "...it saddens me to think I shall never hear you play so again."

"Monsieur Leon, no. Do not say such things." She rose from her stool and walked over to her tutor.

"It is true, little one. I am so old already. I fear I cannot wait."

"No, Monsieur!" Delphine threw her arms around him. "You are not old to me! In fact, I, I..."

The force of the throw landed the girl on her back. Her head smacked off the floor and her shoulder blades also stung from the impact. Monsieur's grey eyes glowered down at her. Oh, she had crossed the line. "Sorry, Monsieur! Sorry," she pleaded, but he wasn't listening; he had raised the cane above his head and was readying himself to swing it down at her. Delphine held out her hands, frantically gesturing at him to stop.

The cane was poised to swoop down and strike her; the silver head was all she could focus on as it seemed to move in slow motion: hard, solid, blunt. But then it disappeared. Delphine blinked and saw Leon struggling against an invisible force that was pulling the cane from his grip. It was a pair of Hands, one wrestling the cane from Leon's hands while the other pushed and squeezed at Leon's throat. His face was growing a violent shade of red.

"No!" For a split second, Delphine thought to help her tutor. But then, had he not been going to hurt her? Delphine knew only too well what happened when the fists started flying. It only had to happen once and the trap would spring shut. There was only one thing to do. She pushed herself to her feet and ran, out of the room, all the way down the stairs, just as someone started banging on the front door, which the burly security guard had begun to open. Out, out she pushed, past the man, out into the cool London air... straight into the arms of her mother.

○─○

Sophie took time applying her mascara. The hand

that held the brush was decorated with an intricate henna print that framed the feathered scar. She had thought about getting something done on the other one, yet it was like her new friend Treycie said, "You've gotta wear your scars with pride, my gel." She was full of earthy wisdom, that one.

Mascara applied, Sophie decided she'd got enough slap on. Just a drink with the girls from work after all. Forget about pulling in pubs and clubs. Even with the scars and tattoos, it wasn't usually her hands that blokes noticed first anyway. "Gorgeous smile, darlin'!" she'd been told more than once. But she had a brain too, and it was nice that people were starting to notice that as well. She had to agree with Treycie. We are the sum of all our parts, she thought. Now let's go and get a drink.

sanctuary

anna sykora

Jin stretched her arms high and spread her plump fingers, savoring the sunlight on her palms. Closing her eyes, she breathed salt air and listened to the lapping waves. Another morning in her sanctuary. She had everything she needed here—didn't she? A giri bird's cry sounded like "Alone? alone?" Jin sighed—another morning in her small world.

The chime in her armrest tinkled. Popping up a screen, she faced a melon-faced man in a crisp, white uniform.

"Good morning, Jin." Her coordinator smiled tightly.

"Hiya, Shawn."

"I wanted to set a time for your substitute to fly in on Tuesday."

"Who's it going to be this time?"

"Evgenia Rostova. She just got promoted."

Jin scowled. "Frankly, I hate the thought of her serving here. She's not as experienced."

"After you, she's our top-rated EPO. Plus, her neutrality is spotless. Can you say the same, my dear?"

Jin chuckled. "I do feel some sympathy for rebels who want to keep this planet in its natural state."

"You're an EPO. Please, remember your vows."

"Oh, I do... Hey, Shawn, can't Evgeny wait until

Wednesday? I'm running a nutritional experiment on orphans I'd like to finish before I leave."

"OK," he said mildly. "It's easier to book a transport on Wednesday anyway. I'll call you later, to confirm... Jin, you're looking thoughtful today. Aren't you glad to get two weeks off?"

"Not really. You know I love Corona Atoll."

"You need some time off station, Jin—or those little beasts will devour your life."

"Talk to you later, Shawn. I'm late for my rounds."

He pressed his hands together under his chin, and she returned the salute. She popped down the screen and smoothed a fold of white sari trapped between her hip and the airchair's frame. Spinning the chair then, she glided down the path to the clinic, whose low dome looked like a giant egg nestled in the jungle. Nearing the door, she heard scolding and shrieking from within. What had upset her peri-monkeys?

The door stood ajar. An intruder, here—a rebel? Stains like dried blood marred the tile floor. Should she call the Company for back-up? A patrol from the mainland needed an hour. Drawing a stinger, she followed the trail of blood down the hall to Colony 1, where dozens of dwarf peri-monkeys whined and chattered, reaching through the bars of stacked cages.

"Stranger, I know you're here," she called out, and hands grabbed her neck from behind. Pressing the stinger into flesh, Jin fired, and a yelping woman collapsed on the floor, bumping the airchair's frame. Slender and shapely in a camo jumpsuit, her blond hair buzz-cut like a soldier's, she looked haggard, as if she hadn't slept in days.

"Who are you?" Jin aimed the stinger at her combat boots. "Talk, or I'll give you another jolt."

"I'm Connie Murphy, from the Western Archipelago." Her eyes, slightly crescent like a native's, gleamed green as sunlight sifted through a leaf. "We crashed our roamer last night and swam ashore. We broke in here looking for medicine and food."

"This island is a sanctuary, Connie. I'm Jin Tao, resident ecology protection officer. I didn't notice any signal for help."

"We didn't have time to send one when our engine failed." Rubbing her forearm, Connie gazed at the airchair hovering inches above the floor.

"I didn't notice an intruder in the airspace."

"Officer, we used an illegal shield." From behind a stack of cages crept a skinny humanoid dressed like Connie, his skin dark green, hair brown and bushy, the gash on his forehead caked with blood. "My partner and I prospect for DNA. We don't file flight plans with the Company."

"Hush, Michael." Unsteadily Connie rose to her feet: "Officer, he doesn't know what he's saying; he's still in shock."

"Well, whatever you're up to here, his wound looks ugly. Come along to the station house, please, where I keep the humanoid first-aid." They gawked as Jin's chair rose a few inches, pivoting silently. "Let's go," she said impatiently. "We're disturbing an endangered species."

○─○

Working in her sunny living room (which she'd designed, like the airchair, without sharp angles), Jin dabbed Michael's wound with disinfectant and sealed it neatly with stick-on sutures.

"This shouldn't leave any scar."

"Good," he growled. "You wouldn't want to spoil my looks." Jin smiled faintly. With his green skin and crescent eyes, Michael looked like a full-blooded native. If he was a rebel, what did he want in the sanctuary? He and his partner both looked in their twenties, in human years.

Slender Connie stood gazing out the window at the placid sea, the mainland just a shadow line across the Strait of Artemis. "Let's eat lunch," Jin suggested. "You must be very hungry." She set three places at the small, round table and heated up a pot of vita-broth.

Her guests ate greedily, in silence. In the bright light, Connie's skin looked tinged with green.

"That was delicious, thank you." She smiled at Jin, revealing even teeth.

"You're welcome. I don't get much company here."

"Can't we help you clean up?"

"I'm fine, thanks." Gliding along, Jin collected the bowls while Michael studied her every motion. No, her lower body never moved. After loading the clean-up module she turned abruptly and faced her guests: "You know I need to report you to the Interplanetary Trading Company."

"Can't you wait for just a few days?" Michael's eyes narrowed to curved slits.

"You're going to need a flight back out, unless you plan to swim to the mainland." Cocking her head, Jin gazed meaningfully at their heavy boots, and Connie colored. "Do you really think I believe—"

Flashing red, the wall monitor chimed.

"Please move over there—out of sight." Jin pointed her guests to the low sofa. "Don't say a word; don't even cough." Gliding around to face the screen, she tucked a lock of long, black hair back into her bun. When she tapped her armrest the flashes resolved into Shawn's melon face, anxious now, even angry.

"Jin, two rebels who robbed a treasury transport may be headed your way: a young blonde woman and a humanoid male, both of them armed and dangerous."

"Is that so?"

"You'll notify the Company if you see them? You won't let your *sympathy* get in the way?"

"Conservation is more important than politics. You know that."

Shawn stared at her quizzically and said coldly: "Your substitute arrives at noon on Wednesday. Take care, Jin, and work well." He pressed his palms together under his chin. She flicked off the screen and turned to her guests.

"You heard what he said. Now tell me what you really want on Corona Atoll."

After a tense pause, Michael spoke: "So you believe everything the Company tells you?"

"I think for myself, but protect this atoll. It's one of a kind on Aleph A."

"Can't you give us till Wednesday?" Connie begged. "Report us when the other EPO arrives."

"By then we'll be gone," Michael vowed, and Jin looked him coolly up and down.

"We won't interfere here," Connie said quickly. "We know that you EPOs nurture life. Can't we sleep here, though, for just a few hours? We've been through hell, Jin. I'm amazed we're alive."

Jin gazed into her green gem eyes. What difference could a few hours make? "You can use that sofa; it folds out. Now excuse me while I tend to my peri-monkeys." Sitting up stiff and straight as a queen, she glided from the room.

o–o

Hours later, throwing open the door, she saw Connie curled on the sofa. Michael the native had squatted in a corner.

"I'm sorry to wake you," Jin said coldly. "I just found the parachutes you buried near the beach—disrupting the habitat of a rare, squint-eyed squirrel, by the way. You didn't crash at sea like you told me. Somebody dropped you on my doorstep. Why?"

"We should take her hostage." Michael sidled towards her.

Jin whipped out a stinger. "Freeze!"

"We should tell her the truth," said Connie softly as Jin flicked the stinger to a coma setting.

"Wait," Michael urged. "Before you waste us, Company style, and dump our bodies into the sea, let me ask you a question, Jin."

"Shoot."

"Whatever happened to the other two sanctuaries on islands in the Strait of Artemis?"

"The Company closed them last year, on cost

grounds. We moved their most precious species here."

"And you tell me you think for yourself?" He pointed a green finger at her heart. "You're a famous scientist; can't you grasp the sanctuary movement's just a sham? The Company dreamed it up for public relations, while it goes on looting virgin worlds."

Jin—she didn't want to harm him—aimed the stinger at his neck: "It's not my fault the Federated Worlds privatized planetary exploration. It's not my fault the Company has succeeded in settling Aleph A. I really have to report you now."

"Please, wait a minute," Connie pleaded.

"Don't argue with her," he said bitterly. "We can't trust an EPO."

"We have to, Michael; we've got no choice. Jin, you take an oath to protect all life."

"That's right. And I've devoted mine to serving this planet's sanctuaries."

"We rebels want the same as you."

"I'm sorry, dear; I don't believe you. Rebels only crave their freedom of choice. How selfish, how *political.*"

"We didn't land on this atoll to fight with you." Connie's green eyes flashed like heat lightning. "We wanted to secure a data drop with proof of the Company's evil deeds. We can't find our drone. It hasn't transmitted since it crashed."

Michael clutched his hair with both hands. Slowly, Jin lowered the stinger, gazing at her guests with new respect. Settlers say the rebels are obsessed with freedom. She'd never met a rebel in the flesh; they're always on the run, hiding out from the Company's mercenaries.

"So what's so special about your data?"

Connie's lean face glowed with relief: "We've managed to capture some images we hope will mobilize settler opinion. We want an independent planet here, with protection for all life forms."

"But you know I'm not allowed to take sides."

"And that makes you part of the problem," said

Michael with disgust. "It's the Company that funds your sanctuaries, the Company that pays your salary, Jin. How can you possibly be objective?"

"I try to keep an open—"

"Well, the sooner you help us find our data, the sooner you'll be rid of us. You won't have our green blood on your hands."

Scowling, she inspected her stinger and tucked it away in the airchair's arm. "I need to think this over, guys. Give me till tomorrow. That's Tuesday, if you've lost track."

"I hope you can help us." Connie held out her arms, to hug her, but shivering Jin rolled a few inches back. "Somehow I feel you will."

"I can't take sides."

Michael snorted. "Neutrality's an illusion these days."

"Please excuse me, I have to update some data for my substitute." And Jin rushed out of the room.

○─○

That night she dipped her hand into the bubbling tub. Gripping both handrails, she carefully lowered her withered legs, her heavy torso. Closing her eyes, she let her mind drift, lulled by the essence of fresh flowers... Trying to relax, she kept thinking of Connie: her ardent voice, green eyes and lithe, young body.

What if the Company's mercenaries hunted her down and killed her? Just another rebel gone, without a grave to visit or story to tell, simply disappeared, while the settlers kept busy with other business and Jin Tao—top-rated EPO—wrote her seventh study of dwarf peri-monkeys.

She was a scientist; Connie Murphy was not her problem. Michael and Connie seemed so idealistic. Well, they still were young. Had she herself ever felt so strongly about politics?

Though her parents had served the Company as clerks in a mainland refinery, back in her twenties Jin had dreamed of independence for Aleph A... A rich world, with vast resources of minerals, food-fish and DNA, it could manage fine without the Company, if it could win its freedom... *If.*

Politics: the muddle of thwarted wishes, the ongoing war of ignorance and greed. To avoid it she'd taken her vows as an EPO. Gone to fat now and almost forty, she'd grow old and die in some sanctuary. Maybe her heart would stop ticking one night, right in this tub.

Fiddling with her hair to let it down, she bumped the shower head, which clattered to the tiles. "Are you OK?" Connie called out, green eyes gleaming in the doorway's crack. "I thought you fell."

Jin flinched as if waking from a dream. "I'm fine. Just dropped the shower head."

"Please, let me help you." Connie, in a t-shirt and briefs, stepped inside and softly shut the door. "You've done so much for us already; let me help you wash your hair. It's so long and beautiful."

Chuckling, Jin slid deeper, hiding her legs under bubbling foam: "Do you want to spoil me, dear? Oh, go right ahead."

Kneeling Connie picked up the shower head and ran some water over her hand. She moistened the long, black hair that hung like a lustrous curtain down Jin's back:

"Is this too hot for you?"

"No, perfect."

"Is this your shampoo?" She nodded shyly and Connie poured a big pink pearl from the bottle and slowly massaged it into Jin's scalp. "Hair to get lost in," she murmured, "like your jungle here on Corona Atoll." Her damp shirt adhered to her delicate breasts.

"Maybe you should join me?" Reaching up, Jin helped her peel off her shirt. Connie shed her briefs, then stepped into the tub, and gently they soaped and washed each other, Jin's hands lingering on Connie's stubbly scalp, her own heart beating hard, her belly burning with the luscious hunger she'd almost forgotten.

She let Connie touch her twisted legs, which

couldn't feel a thing. Soon the butterfly hands drifted upwards, exploring live hills and thrilling valleys.

Gently Jin caressed the other's breasts with awed fingers, and tongued her rosy nipples for long moments of delight. Her neck arching backwards Connie moaned, "Oh that's good... ."

"I don't get a lot of practice," Jin whispered. "You're such a dream, dear, I don't want to wake."

"Then don't."

O—O

Later Michael pounded on the bedroom door. "Connie?"

"I'm here." She sat up in Jin's bed. "You don't have to break down the door."

"What's the matter?" Jin asked sleepily.

"I intercepted a coded message. The Company's sending a search party here."

"Then I need to hide you." Jin pulled herself to a sitting position. "Don't worry, I can keep you safe."

She met the Company's mercenaries out on the floodlit landing field. Disembarking from a beetle-shaped transporter, the men in bulky body armor surrounded her. The biggest stuck out his black-gloved hand:

"Officer Tao? I'm Commander Ekel from Mainland Garrison 2." When Jin gave his hard hand a squeeze, he grabbed hers as if to arrest her. She peered up at him, trying to hold his gaze of grey steel without flinching. The sides of his face looked mismatched, as if poorly reconstructed by a surgeon: one eye drooped, and his bulbous nose skewed slightly to the right.

Ekel cleared his throat. "We have reason to think two fugitives have taken refuge here: rebels intent on sabotaging Company installations."

"Commander, you must be mistaken."

"We never make mistakes." Dropping her hand, he patted the heavy blaster holstered on his hip. "You shouldn't make one now."

"I know the rules," she said with forced calm. "If you

find a rebel sheltering here, this sanctuary reverts to commercial land."

"You've got beaches the Company likes." His eyes swept the atoll like a searchlight. Dawn already glowed in the west. "We could build high-concentration tourist camps here. What would happen to your peri-monkeys? And your scientific reputation?" Jin gripped her armrests as he bent over her, spewing sour breath in her face: "Officer Tao, don't throw away your career. Now do you have anything more to tell us?"

"No, commander." She felt like a mother bird fluttering before a hunter. "No, I don't."

"You won't mind if we take a look around."

"Please don't harass local species, or step on any flowering plants."

Ekel grunted something under his breath and ordered his soldiers to fan out. Jin tagged after them while they scanned the clinic with wide-angle sensors. "You'll find some peri-monkeys in cages, no heat profiles like yours."

They spent an hour checking the station house and then stamped around the beach. "They could hide anywhere," complained a scarred private, waving his prosthetic claw at the jungle.

"Then why don't you scan this atoll from the air?" Jin suggested calmly. "Check every inch. You won't find any creatures here as dangerous as you." Hissing, the soldiers turned their backs. After conferring, they boarded their craft, which soon launched straight up.

Circled overhead like a bird of prey, it scanned the entire atoll twice before it veered away, heading back to the mainland. Jin waited till the transport dwindled to a speck. Rushing inside, she checked her monitors.

Yes, the Company's goons had gone. She'd saved the lives of two young rebels.

Gliding down to the dock in the lagoon, she tapped a code into a steel column, and the turquoise water started to bubble. Slowly a glass observation sphere rose, dripping from the sea. Reaching dock level, the hatch clicked open, and out crawled Michael, with Connie behind. Standing up, the young woman stretched her arms over her head like a dancer and grinned at Jin.

"They're gone, and I'm glad," Jin confessed. "I hate those killers the Company hires."

"You sound like a rebel," said Michael, surprised.

"When I was a young fool..." She broke off. "Weren't you bored, locked up down there for hours?"

"Not at all," said Connie. "We watched the beautiful fish and the sea-plants. I've never seen such variety."

"That's why this is a sanctuary."

"For now," Michael warned. "While it suits the Company."

"Let's find your data drop," Jin said quickly. "Before you make more trouble for me."

"It must have crashed deep in the jungle. Those mercenaries should have spotted it."

"Bet you my free-living monkeys know exactly where it is."

O─O

Jin piloted her roamer with hand controls, whirring over the jungle at walking speed, everyone gazing down through the floor as clear as a glass-bottomed boat's.

"Over there?" Connie pointed to a broken-off tree, propped on the branches of one still green.

"No, that's from a typhoon last year."

"We'll never find our drone," grumbled Michael.

"Keep an eye out for bands of wild peri-monkeys. They come bouncing out of the canopy."

"I've read they move like the wind," said Connie.

Minutes later Jin spied a flash of gold. "Here's somebody I know." She nudged the roamer lower, feeling her way among the interlacing trees, till they found several chattering creatures clinging to the limbs of a bent gum tree. One tossed a scarlet streamer to another, who bounded away through the tossing branches.

"That's from our drone," cried Michael.

Leaving the roamer on a grassy knoll, they followed the cries of peri-monkeys, and soon discovered the light-weight drone lodged in the gum tree's lowest branches. The monkeys, who had stripped the streamers from its parachute, now wore them like scarves.

"They can be so creative," Jin said proudly. "Too bad I can't write this up... Now let's gather every bit of wreckage we can find." She turned to the noisy peri-monkeys, some hanging from branches by their tails. "Sorry to spoil your fun, kids. Give me your toys back, please." She held out her hands, and one by one they surrendered the streamers and frolicked away. When a silver-backed male hesitated, hiding his behind his back, she tranquillized him lightly with a stinger and pried the streamer from his hand.

"Sometimes they act just like humans, clinging to their precious toys."

"And what about you?" Michael chided. "You've got a good deal here, fronting for the Company."

"Hush," said Connie. "Don't be hard on Jin. She has been risking her life for us."

"I just wish I could do more for Aleph A. This sanctuary is so beautiful."

On the way back, Jin showed them a waterfall plunging down a jagged cliff into the sea. She showed them a grove of trees aflutter with a colony of silver-winged butterflies. She showed them the rose, blue and golden colors of sunset melting together like a dream, and all of these pleasures she'd savored for years seemed the more precious shared.

As the red sun slid into the ocean, seeming for a moment to light it from below, Michael muttered, "Yes, it's beautiful here."

"Please try to understand," said Jin as they headed back to the station house. Connie, walking between them, curled her arms around them both.

○─○

After dinner, Michael lifted the finger-sized data pellet from its frame. "Looks intact. I'd like to view it."

"May I?" Jin asked quietly.

"What's it to you?"

"You've seen my sanctuary. I'd like to see what matters so much to you."

Green fingers closing over the pellet, Michael shook his bushy head.

"No, Jin should see our proof," said Connie. "She should see what the Company's up to, behind the wall of media lies. Come on, Michael—please."

Scowling, he handed the pellet to Jin. "Two rebels died recording this. One was a settler who joined us, a human."

"I respect your sacrifices." Rummaging in a drawer Jin pulled out an old visored headset and a pellet-reader. "This is still working. Hope it's compatible." Adjusting the headset on her head she pressed the pellet into the reader.

The grainy, silent image flickered and resolved into a gigantic, treaded machine grinding through lush jungle. Small creatures fled as it assaulted the towering trees, toppling and dismembering them.... . No, these were the planet's humanoids, scattering and fleeing for their lives.

The clip jumped ahead to a vast, stripped area, barren as an airless moon. One almost limbless tree stood erect, a maimed warrior on the ghostly field of battle. Jin saw hive-like, geometric ruins: the foundations of a native settlement. The mangled body of a child curled beside a shattered cooking pot.

Eyes filling, Jin pulled off the headset: "That's enough. Such devastation violates every treaty the Company signed."

"And it's no exception," Connie declared.

"Don't argue with the EPO," Michael said bitterly. "Minds like hers are part of the problem. Jin may have good intentions, but she has become a Company tool."

"How can you say that? I've devoted my whole life to the sanctuaries!"

"Soothing millions of shareholders scattered across

the galaxy. You EPOs are like old-fashioned gardeners, tending tiny patches of soil—while the Company grinds the rest of us to dust." Michael's dark hands clawed the air.

Green eyes bright, Connie gripped Jin's arm. "You know, you don't have to play this role. You are so gifted and capable. Our rebellion needs your mind, your science. Jin, won't you leave with us tomorrow?"

"And give up my life's work?" she shrilled. "What would my peri-monkeys do without me?"

"Monkeys," Michael scoffed. "I'm sorry for you. You make such a fuss about your perfect atoll, when it's this whole planet we're fighting for."

"You don't understand..."

"Yes, I do. You're content with your reputation, when you could help to save this unique world. Imagine if an EPO joined the rebels! Settlers would listen when you spoke."

"Come on, Michael," Connie said sadly, picking up the pellet. "Let's leave this poor woman alone. That's what she wants. Isn't it, Jin?"

Sitting up straight, Jin cast a glance around the living room, this familiar space in the house she'd designed for work—the work that provided predictable joy.

She felt too old for the rebellion. What would her fellow EPOs say? How could she leave the peri-monkeys?

A fragrant wind wafted through the open window. A giri bird called softly: "Alone, alone."

Connie and Michael would leave tomorrow. These youngsters, who still dreamed of the future. They were already leaving her.

Bending her head, she gripped her armrests till her fingers ached. She felt herself on the edge of a cliff; in a moment she'd plunge over it...

One ghostly tree still stood alone, in the middle of the Company's devastation.

"Wait a minute!" Jin shouted down the hall. "I am—with you."

○–○

How small Corona Atoll looked from 30,000 feet, an emerald pinned to the ocean's cloak. No, a trinket; just window-dressing to distract from the Company's ecocide.

Piloting her roamer due west and out to sea, with Connie humming in the seat beside her, and shaggy Michael grumbling behind, Jin felt wildly excited; she felt her aching heart would burst.

Let Evgenia take care of the peri-monkeys. Let Shawn quibble with the Company to save the atoll. No going back, not ever, now that she had joined the rebels.

A tear dripped down a crease in her cheek, and Connie patted her shoulder. "Don't cry, Jin. We're in this together now."

LIFE AFTER WARTIME

LAURA GIVENS
& NICOLE SPENCER

The left side of the hover transport heaved up under Cassie as though a giant child were trying to flip it over. Cassie Clement was damned if she was going to lose her cargo while in a supposed green zone. She hung onto both joysticks like they were the horns of a charging bull, trying desperately to regain control as the vehicle spasmed again and again, the left side slewing higher each time. "Somebody secure the stabilizers before we turtle."

Zhloh, the mechanic, lunged into the repair shaft with a multi-wrench and a pry-bar, nearly slamming into Lucy, the medic, in his haste. Whatever they had hit was still trying to flip them over, so she took a deep breath and decided to try something they hadn't taught her in transport drivers' training.

"Hang on!" She nosed the hover-transport upwards at a degree that the specs did not recommend and slammed the main thrust hard while cutting the blades full to the right. If she'd tried that at ground level, she would have rolled over, but with a little air under her. She managed a very lovely corkscrew maneuver, just like an old Earth-movie stunt. Pulling an air-born corkscrew on a hover-bike, or even a sled, was stupid if fun. With a seventy-five ton hover hauler—the word *suicidal* came to mind.

"Stabilizers!" she screamed as the metal monster came into upright position again. She hit the down-blow and said a Hail Mary through gritted teeth. They hit the road with a heart-stopping WHUMP and bounced once before spinning to a stop a hundred yards off the road in a thicket of thunderweed.

For a few seconds, Cassie just breathed and tried to slow her heart rate. "Is everyone okay?" she finally managed.

"I'm all right," Fren said tightly from the shotgun seat, her fingers dug into the armrests. "But I think we lost Lucy."

From overhead a huge centipede skittered silently down into the cab. "Lucy survives despite the physics experiment you call driving." The voice came from a grid installed beneath the centipede's eyes. "Lucy also would like to discern health of his fellow travelers." Cassie gave a sigh in relief and raised her hand. The centipede caressed the outstretched fingers and began to crawl over her, looking for signs of injury or shock. Lucencian Lurok didn't have a license to practice medicine on this planet, but one of the reasons Cassie had hired him was his tremendous medical expertise.

"No permanent damage," he proclaimed. "I feared brain damage, as indicated by that bonehead landing maneuver, but found no apparent symptoms." He crawled off Cassie to examine Fren before heading down the repair shaft to see about Zhloh.

Cassie and Fren shared a knowing smile; they knew exactly what was coming next. A few moments later, yelling and banging came from the shaft as Lucy scurried back into the cab, followed by a thrown multi-wrench and a string of curses. "Zhloh also remains in good health. At least his throwing arm and dislike of being examined by me are unchanged." Zhloh had a thing about being touched, especially by long, hairy aliens.

The centipede looked around to find that he was

speaking to no one. Cassie and Fren were already over the side, trying to determine what the hell had happened. "Ah well!" he sighed. Someone had to keep watch, so he snuggled down and raised a feeler as sentinel.

A heavy-haul hover transport looked a lot like a flying saucer. Cargo space was arrayed all around the lower perimeter so that loads could be evenly distributed for stability. Sitting in the middle of the cargo ring were the three main engines, providing thrust and lift through the miles and miles of swamp where roads appeared and disappeared like fleeting mirages. On top of the engine sat the cab, a compact living and control complex with retractable cowls in case of bad weather.

Tightening a loose bolt, Cassie thought she heard a snoring sound coming through an overhead vent. It didn't take much of a detective to realize that Lucy was probably curled up asleep on the driver's seat. When it came to basic mechanical repairs, Cassie knew that the centipede was pretty useless, but he was a great medic and a good driver.

"Boss, number three got jolted loose a bit, but I'm pretty sure she'll make it to Shippa if we don't push it too hard." Zhloh limped to where Cassie was running her seat-of-the-pants diagnostics on the lift exhausts. "Same with the stabilizers, they just don't know what to do with abrupt angle deviations. These three-eighties are just funky that way."

Cassie grinned. The translator chips they all used were a marvel, but where did they dig up words like *funky?* "Well, the fans look workable, and the cargo is intact." She pulled her head out of the cowling to look at Zhloh, noticing the slight limp. "Any idea what happened back there on the road? Dispatch said this route had been swept clean days ago. How do you miss a mine right in the middle of the road?"

"I couldn't find a blast hole," Zhloh replied. "Whatever it was left no traces. The government coverts used something like this on us at Bremmon. Disruptives. That was the official name, but we called them 'chiggers.' They spring up and attach themselves, then send out pulses designed to wreck whatever they're attached to but leave it mostly intact. I saw a heavy artillery piece flip right over once, for no apparent reason. Crushed three good friends." Zhloh had been a rebel guerrilla before signing on as Cassie's chief mechanic.

"Chiggers? Damn! My little stunt must have dislodged it somehow." Cassie blew a piece of thunderweed off her cheek. "We'll report that to Dispatch quick as we hit free skies."

Fren came around the curve to join the discussion. "Don't count on it, Cass. Just before the com went dead a few miles back, the weather report said that a whole front of aerosol flak was settling in over this region. Probably won't let up for a couple of days."

All during the hostilities, the rebels had released vast amounts of aerosol signal jammers into the atmosphere, making satellite imaging, radar, and even wireless communications virtually impossible. It helped to finally turn the tide for guerrilla freedom fighters but was a pain in the neck for everyone else.

Fren came close and whispered in Cassie's ear, "Hey, cheer up! On the bright side, we're all okay and I look very sexy by flak light." Cassie blushed, starting to reply when Zhloh raised a hand for silence. They all heard the rustle of undergrowth and the slight sucking sound of boots in mud.

"Fren, honey, why don't you go topside and prep the engines?" Cassie had caught a glint of mottled sunshine off something metal, maybe a gun barrel. "Whatever these guys are selling, I don't think we can afford it."

Zhloh and Cassie climbed atop the cargo ring as the three strangers approached. She felt helpless with only a wrench as a weapon, but the light arms stashed under the command seat wouldn't help much against the black and red armor that marked the strangers as rebel elite. The rebel elite were supposed to be on their side, but it seemed an awful coincidence that they had appeared from nowhere so quickly after the "accident." Rumors of rogue units were everywhere these days.

"Having trouble, comrades? We'd be happy to take a look." The largest of them smiled and bowed. "Captain Grell of the People's Fourth Elite, at your service." His silvery blue skin was scarred with marks denoting the number of men he'd killed.

"No problems." Cassie worked hard at keeping her smile in place. "One of my team noticed this lovely patch of thunderweed over here. He has this great recipe for thunder pie, so we thought we'd stop and pick a few bushels. We appreciate the offer but we're just fine, thanks loads."

"Ah, then maybe you'd care to exchange recipes with Agla here," Grell gestured towards his companion. "His thunder bread makes even blue beans quite palatable." He raised his weapon and stepped a few paces closer. "I would bet you have many things worth sharing."

Zhloh stepped in front of Cassie. "Comrades, we have nothing you'd be interested in. All we're carrying this run are used medical instruments, some canned food—which we'd be happy to donate part of to the cause—drainage pumps, and insulating fabric. We revere you as heroes of the revolution. Please don't soil your glorious legacy for a prize such as us."

"As it so happens, I could use a good drainage pump to keep Agla's bedroll dry at night," the rebel captain said, waving his weapon at a hatch. "Why don't we take a look and see if you have anything that goes with his armor."

"Crap!" Zhloh looked back at Cassie, who shook her head.

"We need to stall them for another couple of minutes," she whispered, "till Fren gets things back on line. There's no way they can catch us once—"

A war cry broke the tension. Overhead, three more of the elite rebels came arcing out of the sky toward them, jump packs blazing, feet first, weapons brandished. There was barely time to flinch before the first man buckled into an invisible wall a foot over Cassie's head. The other two also met the invisible barrier, all three sliding to the ground in crumpled heaps. Suddenly there were bullets flying everywhere. The aerial threesome had been joined by others charging the vehicle from all sides. None of them got within a foot of the transport, and two of soldiers were thrown down to the ground from the force of their own ricochets. Their leader yelled for them to cease fire.

"A force field?" He pounded his hand into the solid nothing. "Where the hell did you get a working force field?"

Cassie uncurled her arms from over her head and looked around with one eye. "Oh y-yeah," Cassie stammered, "Force field, couple of plasma cannons—we are one badass transport, don't mess with us... Isn't that right, Zhloh?"

Zhloh spit in the rebels' direction, but that, too, hit the invisible barrier, "You aren't worthy to wear those colors! Since when do comrades prey on comrades?"

"Comrades? Bullshit!" the captain screamed. "For ten years I've fought in the name of freedom for all Mazzah against the government thugs and their off-world masters! So what does our glorious newly-elected president do? He declares that we will now open trade negotiations with the alien allies of the deposed regime! He wants us all to become good little farmers and miners to carry on trade with that bunch of imperialist hooligans."

Zhloh knelt and spoke in a softer voice. "The war has been over for three months, Captain. We won. Go home."

Agla, a sergeant by his markings, pushed forward. "Our homes are gone! The war doesn't end for us."

The rebel captain snarled, "We're organizing a counter-revolution to see the principles we fought for finally triumph. Join us, comrade. We can use this vehicle, and you won't have to take any more orders from this off-world bitch." He glared at Cassie, then back at Zhloh.

Zhloh stood and glared back at the rebel. "I trust this off-worlder. The fighting is over, and you're too stupid embrace the victory we have won."

"Look," said Cassie in as reasonable a voice as she could manage. "There's a town that needs these supplies if they're going to have a crop this year. This is your victory right here. These villagers can get what they need and just get on with their lives. They can raise crops, raise families, without fear of being dragged away in the night by faceless government killers. That's why you all fought this war, right? It's time this world got back to some semblance of normalcy."

A cloud came over the captain's face for a moment, and he growled "You'd like that—wouldn't you, bitch? You'd take by treaty what you couldn't get through force."

Cassie got very still. "Look, I've been on this planet for five years, working my ass off for your cause because I believe in it as much as you do, so don't try to hang that off-worlder imperialist crap on me."

"Oh yes!" the captain barked. "Let me kiss your pink toes in gratitude while you reduce proud warriors into lap dogs like that 'man' beside you."

Zhloh shook his head angrily and spit at the captain once more. This time the spittle hit the rebel square on the cheek.

"Oh shit!" Cassie whispered.

"Grab something, we are go!" Fren shouted from the cab above.

"Thank god!" Cassie cried as she and Zhloh grabbed at hatch handles as the lifters shuddered to life, the craft taking off like a bee-stung berl, followed by a hail of bullets.

After a couple of miles, the craft slowed down to a brisk crawl, and the two clambered back up into the cab. Fren sat at the controls, her silver-blue skin an ashen gray. Her tone was flat with terror. "Number three almost came loose," she said mechanically. "We should be okay if we keep it at a reasonable speed, but our sprinting days are over." Cassie leaned over and gave her a big hug.

"We have a force field?" Fren asked.

From the back of the cab came a clicking, nervous sound. Slowly, all of them turned to Lucy, who was curled around a seat, trembling and tapping the metal frame as he did when someone yelled at him or he was in pain.

"It's a personal shield. Where I'm from, everyone who is anyone has one implanted once full growth length is reached."

Cassie gestured for Fren to get them underway again and sat down on a chair near Lucy. "You said personal shield—what you did back there was a lot bigger than any personal shield I've ever heard of."

"My field is bio-impelled, anger and surprise activate it automatically, but I can also access it by an act of will. I just imagined the whole ship as an extension of Lucy, and that it all needed to be protected."

Cassie shook her head quizzically. "Think of a human lifting something very, very heavy," Lucy continued. "Normally the weight might be too much, but you might do it with great effort, in adversity, but not for very long, and you might hurt yourself doing so."

Cassie stood up. "I see... Is there anything else we should know about? Super strength, invisibility—anything like that?"

"Please understand, my people don't speak of such things, they are private, much like the sexual exploits you have with Fren when you think we are all asleep."

Cassie blushed, and Fren cleared her throat.

Zhloh finally broke the awkward silence. "Well, this is good. Comrades getting to know each other better is healthy... It helps us all be better—comrades." He coughed. "Is anyone else hungry? I'm starving!"

Suddenly, Lucy fell off his perch and lay twitching on the floor, secreting green bile from one eye.

Cassie scrambled to his side. "Somebody get his med-kit!" she yelled, but Zhloh already had it open.

After a mad search through the kit, they finally had

to admit that they had no idea what they should do. Fren had stopped the transport and gone searching for a blanket; it was all she could think to do. Eventually the twitching and secreting stopped.

Cassie finally broke the silence. "I can't tell if he's dead or alive, but I vote that he's still alive." She tucked the blanket more soundly around Lucy. "We need to get out from under the flack so we can radio for medical advice. I looked once—he has medical files on how to treat us but nothing about treating him."

Fren wiped tears from her large violet eyes. "That sounds about right. Was he really a famous surgeon on his world, like he always boasted?"

Cassie shrugged her shoulders. "Who knows—and let's not refer to him in the past tense just yet."

Zhloh eased into the driver's seat and started the engines. "We should stay off the road for a while longer just in case our belligerent friends decide to try catching us." He looked over his shoulder and growled softly, "He can't be dead. He owes me money."

o—o

Once night set in, their pace slowed to a crawl. Cassie was all too happy to relinquish the driving to Zhloh. They'd moved Lucy to the below deck sleeping quarters, where Cassie kept one hand gently on his blanket, imagining that she felt a slight tremor every now and then. Who could tell?

Cassie pinched the bridge of her nose, closing her eyes for a moment. Lulled by the quiet hum of the engines and the soft swish of vegetation beneath the transport, she could almost imagine that she was back in Iowa, curled up in the back of her dad's combine. She'd loved that farm, but after her folks had died and she'd been forced out by the bank, she found herself at loose ends and at odds with the world for a couple of years. It was about then that news started breaking on Terra about appalling social conditions on a backwater planet called Mazzah and the popular uprising aimed at removing its oppressive oligarchic regime. Something about the plight of Mazzah's peasants and townspeople really spoke to her, and it wasn't long before she found herself selling everything she owned to make her way to Mazzah and the revolution. What the hell, if it had been good enough for Hemingway...

Cassie glanced over at Fren dozing in the corner. The young Mazzahi's skin was a pale silver in the subdued compartment lighting, a small spot of spit shining from a corner of her lovely mouth. The earth woman couldn't help but raise the corners of her own lips in a smile. When they'd first met, Fren had been hiding in a dumpster, on the lam from rebel troops after they had stormed a government-sponsored cathouse near the capital. The fact that she'd been indentured into service, like so many young Mazzahi females, would not have prevented them from killing her as a collaborator. Cassie risked serious grief herself to smuggle the young fugitive out of the fire zone, hidden in a large duffel bag, to another city where she could make a new start. But it never crossed her mind to do otherwise, or that she'd run into this girl again after hostilities had ceased.

Yet that is exactly what happened. Without resources to return home. and facing sudden peacetime unemployment as an ambulance driver, Cassie began making moves to put together a freelance heavy-haul operation. Much to their mutual astonishment, she found Fren among the first in line to apply as a relief driver, newly-authorized operator's certificate in hand. Taken aback in surprise and admiration, Cassie followed her gut once again and hired the young rookie on the spot.

Fren turned out to be a damned fine driver and a good friend, fiercely loyal to the Earth woman who had saved her. Feelings of trust and affection sprang up between them, quickly blossoming into something much deeper, if a little complicated.

Cassie was glad that their relationship was out in the open. Mazzah had no taboos about off-worlders or partners of the same sex, but the whole silly prohibition on bosses fraternizing with their crews still bothered her. She had such a small crew to begin with.

o–o

Sometime in the middle of the night, Cassie was awakened by the sound of explosions in the distance. Carefully untangling herself from Fren's tree frog embrace, she pulled on pants and a top and went topside.

The transport had stopped, and Zhloh leaned over the railing, watching the distant light show. "It started about five minutes ago. I guess the counter-revolution has begun. That's got to be Shippa, our destination, getting pounded out there."

Cassie pulled her fingers through her hair. "With all the flak cover, that fire has to be local in origin. Want to bet that our pals from this afternoon are the ones playing with firecrackers?"

"I think your money would be safe in such a wager. Anyway, it made no sense to keep heading into their sights, so I stopped." Zhloh plopped back down into the driver's seat.

Cassie tapped her fingernails on the railing. "That insulation we've got below, is that fumar?"

Zhloh's eyes narrowed. "Yeah, great insulation as long as you don't put it under high compression. Should keep the school they're building in Shippa comfortable all year round—if it hasn't been blown up yet."

"You ever work a drainage pump?" She asked lightly.

Zhloh smiled humorlessly. "I'm not in that line of work anymore, and you were an ambulance driver for most of the war."

"I've got my hover bike stowed in compartment C if you feel up to a little flak light ride. I make it about an hour's trip with the two of us and a little baggage."

"What if Fren gets jealous?" He laughed.

Cassie's voice got very quiet. "Those folks out there don't deserve what's happening to them. The war's over. Those 'elite' rebels need to have that explained to them in detail, and we're the only ones with blackboards and chalk."

"Comrade, if I had any idea what you were talking about, I'm sure I would agree completely."

Without another word, they scrambled over the side to prepare for one last charge into the valley of death.

○–○

During her time driving ambulances, Cassie had earned the nickname "Dodge Ball." Many of her passengers threw up at some point during their journey, even ones who had never before been troubled by motion sickness, but she'd never lost an ambulance and almost never a patient. By comparison, this was nothing. She kept low, zipping through trees and rocks that Zhloh could barely see. Most hover bike riders preferred big growling engines that were intimidating from a block away, but Cassie kept her bike tuned to purr like a kitten. It was a little unnerving, whipping through the treacherous countryside almost blind and in near silence. But Zhloh knew that if anyone could pull off this mad charge without getting them killed, it was her. She had blazed into heavy fire in the middle of the battle of Alibin to get him and three of his men out and to a med station, only to rush back in to evacuate more of his comrades still lying wounded in the field. He just wished his stomach believed in her as much as his heart.

Before setting out, they had awakened Fren, leaving her as a guard despite heavy protest. Cassie finally convinced her that someone had to watch over Lucy, and that they had to go on this mission if Lucy were to have any hope of reaching a doctor. When Zhloh instructed her to return to dispatch if they weren't back by morning, she told him flat out to go screw himself. Cassie was very proud of how far this girl, whom she loved so much, had come from cowering in a dumpster.

The rebel camp wasn't hard to find. There was no need to be inconspicuous—they were the only military force left in the entire sector, and they knew that, with the flak cover, the townspeople couldn't call for outside help.

After parking the hover bike some distance away, Cassie and her comrade covered the rest of the distance to the camp's perimeter on hands and knees.

"Mortars," Zhloh whispered as they came up on the edge of the clearing. "And it looks like they are using bam-bams. Makes sense—lots of noise, lots of light, but limited concussion. They want to loot Shippa, not level it."

"So, what's the plan?" Cassie asked.

"Hey! You're the boss!" he whispered back.

"Okay, I just promoted you. Come on, I know you have a plan."

Zhloh mussed her hair and pulled up the bag carrying the doctored drainage pumps. "Okay, we've got three of these things, and there are five mortars—so you need to plant the pumps between the mortars. It probably won't destroy them, but it should mess them up pretty good. If we get lucky, you'll set off all the loose ordnance, and that's all she wrote."

Cassie tried not to smirk at the translation. "So," she asked, "while I plant the pumps, press the five-second timers and run like hell, what will you be doing?" She examined the devices to make sure she knew exactly where to activate each timer.

Zhloh pulled out two small blasters. "Diversion."

Cassie's eyes went wide. "Please tell me there's more to your plan than those things! You couldn't put out your own eyes with those pea shooters."

"Trust me, boss. I am a war hero, after all." Zhloh's eyes narrowed. "Wait for my signal. I don't think you'll miss it." With that, he disappeared into the surrounding foliage.

Five minutes passed, and Cassie became acutely aware of how badly she needed to pee. This always seemed to happen. Then, across the clearing, she heard someone let out a blood curdling scream and saw her comrade blasting full speed toward the clearing on her bike. The Elite rebels scrambled for their weapons and armor.

Bowling through the men who were not engaged

with tending the mortars, Zhloh reached the center of the clearing. Jamming the down thrusters to full, he shot the bike straight up into the air, jumping off at the zenith of its ascent and dropping a match into the open gas tank as he did so. The effect was quite spectacular.

Shit! He blew up my bike! Cassie jumped to her feet and dashed toward the pandemonium that was the rebel camp. Everywhere there were flaming bits of debris and wild gunfire, though, for the moment, none of it was directed at her. She ran past the first mortar and dropped the first device after hitting its timer. Then the second device —so far, so good. The first pump exploded as she sprinted for the area between the last two guns, almost throwing her off her feet. She lurched toward her final drop zone, but no longer unnoticed. Bits of charged plasma whizzed past as she triggered the third device's timer. The second explosion must have gotten the ammunition, as it went off even more spectacularly than the first, throwing her to the ground. Scrambling to her feet, she felt a burning pain in her side but knew that she had to move if she wanted to survive the next three seconds. Then the entire world all around her lit up, and a giant hand sent her flying through the air. She hit the ground with a dull thud, sinking into darkness to the lullaby of automatic weapons fire.

O—O

The sun was coming up as Lucy's eyes fluttered open. Fren smiled and stroked his carapace under the voice-box. It had been a terrifying night. Every breeze had been a skulking assassin, and the noise in the distance just seemed to get louder and louder. Then the noise stopped completely. She'd carried Lucy topside just to have someone to hold onto.

"Hey! Look who decided to wake up!"

Lucy looked around, somewhat confused. "What happened? I feel absolutely awful."

Fren was about to give the centipede a big hug and a kiss when the bushes started to move. Lucy was suddenly alert. "Stay close by, and I will try to extend my shield around both of us."

She was ready to protest but a small hover sled broke through the shrubs driven by a heavily bandaged Zhloh. Behind him was the prone figure of a human woman, badly burned on her right side.

○─○

When Cassie finally came to, it was in a small hospital ward. Asleep, slumped on the chair beside her, was Fren.

"She's been here since we brought you in." Cassie turned painfully to her left toward the voice. Her eyes found Zhloh, with an arm in a sling and bandaged in several places.

"We're alive," she noted.

Her erstwhile comrade laughed and winced at the pain it caused. "After that third pump went off, most of the rebels were pretty banged up. I'd found decent cover behind a rock and kept shooting enough to keep them guessing. If they'd known I was one guy with a couple of pop guns, things might have gone differently." He handed her a glass of water and waited till she'd finished. "Anyway, the commander, captain Grell, and that guy, Agla— remember Agla?—they got into a shouting match about lost causes. Well, to make a long story short, Agla shoots his commander in the head and wants to talk terms. In exchange for safe passage and a sled, I agreed to give them all two days head start to make their way back home."

Cassie nodded her head. "I thought Agla was the guy who had no home to return to."

"I asked him about that, and he said he'd sell his armor—he'd heard there were already collectors. Then he'd look for his nephews and make a new life for himself somehow. It was time."

The door opened, and Lucy crawled in, dragging two medical charts. "Ah! The patient lives. Alas! I have lost another bet." He crawled up the foot of the bed and across Cassie's left leg. "That is how I lost my fortune on my home world, you know, betting against my patients surviving. I am just too great of a healer for my own good, it seems."

Cassie looked on in amazement as the centipede went to Zhloh's bed and proceeded to crawl all over his wounds, checking the dressings. Zhloh made no fuss, but merely shrugged, saying, "I made him promise to wash his feet before he crawled all over me."

To her right a sleepy voice joined in, "Pay up, bug."

Mazzah had survived a long, soul-searing war and now maybe they'd figure out how to survive the peace. Hell, if someone like Agla could leave the war behind, maybe the rest of the planet could make it as well. That was the trick, after all, realizing when you'd won—learning how to live again.

SKY

R.P. STEEVES

Sky woke up and stretched, legs sliding through silk sheets, penis flopping back and forth as the thighs shifted.

Always moving around, that little thing. Never wants to stay still. And don't get me started on the balls.

Sky reached out with an arm, but the other side of the bed was cool. The clock read 15:23.

Crap. I fell asleep. And Terry is gone.

That was not flattering. Afternoon delight was fun, especially with a near stranger, but getting ditched in the afterglow was a kick in the crotch.

And now I have to get home to Ashley. That is not going to be pleasant.

Relations between Sky and Ashley had been strained for a quite a long time. The constant fights, the lack of intimacy, the separate beds. Perhaps all of that had driven Sky into Terry's arms. Perhaps it was just pure unadulterated lust, hormones that needed an outlet. Either way, the bed had been made and Sky had slept in it. And now home was calling.

Sky reached down and dug into those itchy testicles, covered with hair and sweat.

Man, I hate these things.

And Sky bolted up in bed, mind finally clear after the post-coital nap.

Ashley will know. I shall not be able to hide the

guilt. My infidelity will come out and the relationship will be over.

What have I done?

Sky quickly rose from the bed, silk sheets sliding down hair-covered skin and pooling on the floor.

Where is my jumper? My Skyrail pass and Identcard are in there, unless this Terry was some kind of scam artist who picked me up at the strip club, made hard, fast love to me and left me behind, light one wallet and—

But no, it was there. The maroon one-piece outfit, which was as comfortable as it was useful, was draped across the desk chair where it had been discarded in the wake of passion. All of the pockets were perfect for holding tools, wrenches and torches and whatever else a good mechanic needed.

Sky snatched it up and dressed quickly, pausing to look in the full-length mirror on the back of the closet.

I look terrible.

Sure enough, Sky's hair was unkempt, above a haggard face with a blue-black wash of stubble. The jump-suit was ill-fitting, lumpy against a muscular frame and a bit too short in the arms and ankles for such a fashion-conscious city.

I hate this. I hate waking up like this. I hate feeling like this, uncomfortable in my own skin, awkward and ashamed. I cannot live like this. I have to figure something out, and I do not have much time. If I am like this when Ashley gets home, the truth will come out and it will all be over.

Sky sighed and tossed the room. There was not a trace of Terry to be found. Not a key, not a sock, not a note or a stray hair. Typical.

I need to find Terry. We need to make love again. And soon. If we cannot, then I do not know what I am going to do.

Sky breathed deeply and came to a decision.

I shall retrace my steps. I met Terry at Pole Position II. I shall go back there and ask questions. I am not giving up that easily.

And upon exiting, the door slammed resolutely as if to prove a point.

O—O

Sky pushed past the bouncer, ignoring a judging look. Visiting the club twice in one afternoon (especially after leaving arm in arm with one of the dancers just a couple hours earlier) was amusing, apparently. Sky wanted to kick the bouncer in the groin, but the club employee's rippling biceps were reason enough to exercise caution. Besides, there was a mission at stake here, a missing person to find.

Pole Position II was the farthest strip club from the home that Ashley and Sky shared, which made it ideal in some regards. The questionable cleanliness and poor lighting of the place did not contribute to its draw, however. All in all, location trumped ambiance when one was looking for a quick afternoon tryst.

Is that what I was looking for when I came here? Was I merely seeking titillation, or had I fully intended to cheat on Ashley? And why had I fallen asleep after one round of passion? Why had Terry let me? Had the dancer not known about my relationship status? Or was I being used for my body?

The music was pumping, the drinks were flowing and the smoke was wafting as Sky entered the club. A quick glance around the bar area did not reveal the presence of Terry, though Sky wondered if the dancer would be quite as easy to spot now.

I am not even sure I could pick Terry out of a line up, not after what we did.

A mass of people crowded around the bar. Long hair, breasts and narrow waists mingling with broad chests and scruffy faces. Mating rituals thickened the air. Hands touching, eyes locking, whispered comments and hips cocked in welcoming angles. Sky had just completed a similar dance with one of the performers.

On to the stage, then. Maybe Terry will be on soon.

Shaking off a waitperson, Sky stumbled toward the middle of the club, moving with an awkward gait, muscles almost unfamiliar in their strength, settling into a spot between the two stages. To the left, a bevy of breasts shook, pinching bills within their fleshy folds, pointing at salivating customers with erect nipples. To the right, penises swung low, in time with the beat, gyrating in the faces of tittering patrons whose eyes were locked on hairy scrota.

There would have been a time, dozens of years ago, back when society was different, before the Great Evolution, when a place like this would have been viewed as disgusting by many. Now, though, it was merely the kind of place where people met, where they exchanged names and numbers and then, like Terry and Sky had just done, shared quite a bit more.

Now, though, for Sky, it was a place of desperation. Somewhere in here was the answer, the solution to the dilemma at hand. If not Terry, then someone else would have to do.

Okay, calm down. Do not look at your chrono. It does not have to be Terry. It could be anyone. Everyone here wants something; I just need to find someone who wants what I do. And soon. Ashley will be home in a little while and if I am not there when work lets out...

Sky stretched, still uncomfortable in terms of balance and wishing for a larger, looser jumpsuit. Sights and sounds of naked bodies swirled from every direction, and a familiar stirring arose in Sky's crotch.

I am getting an erection. It feels... stiff. Uncomfortable. Worse than the itchy balls. I need to get rid of this now. I do not care who it is, I just need release.

Sky scanned the crowd, hoping to make eye contact with someone in as desperate a plight, someone who needed sex just as much.

I just need someplace to put this penis, some way to achieve release. Who needs it as much as I do?

And then Sky spotted the right person. Across the

way, seated alone at a table, breasts straining mightily against the fabric of a too-small jumper. Long hair unkempt and unwashed, a wave of unhappiness emanated from this fellow lost soul.

Perfect. We both need the same thing, and we're both desperate enough to do whatever it takes.

Sky readied a pick-up line.

I haven't needed one since I met Ashley. Terry was the one who seduced me this morning. What do people say to one another in situations like this?

"You need it and I need it, so let me put my penis in your vagina and we can both end up the way we want to."

Direct and to the point.

And what do you know? It worked.

○─○

There was not enough time to go back to the hotel room. Sky needed to be home when Ashley arrived, so the decision was made to bring the new potential sexual conquest to the home they two lovers shared.

This is going to be awkward, far more awkward than with Terry; that was an explosion of passion and lust. A mistake, obviously, especially in light of my current dilemma.

"So, are we gonna do this, or what?"

Chris, the large-breasted pick-up, shifted uncomfortably, a hand straying down toward moistened crotch. "What? Right now? Can't we, um, talk first or something?"

Sky glanced at the chrono on the wall. Ashley would be home soon. But all the eggs were in Chris' basket now, and this was going to be the last opportunity for sexual contact before it was too late. If this didn't work, Sky was going to have to flee the scene or face a very awkward conversation with Ashley.

"What do you want to talk about?"

Chris chewed a fingernail and glanced around the room, avoiding eye contact. "Umm, it's not like I am comfortable with this. It's all pretty unfamiliar to me." Well-manicured hands moved across firm breasts and along wide hips. Sky's eyes followed those hands closely, a need rising up. Not lust, but something more primal.

"Do you think I am comfortable? There is a reason we found each other. Neither of us is used to our situation, so we need each other. We need the Release. The Change."

Chris nodded absentmindedly. "I just, well, I haven't been in this Situation for very long, you know. I mean, before today, it had been such a long time since I, well, since I had Sex. I'd been so used to my Body the way it was. The form, the balance, the, um, parts... But then I met Terry, and—"

Sky scoffed at that. "Terry seduced you, too, eh? Must have been right before me. Or right after. A Serialist. Never happy to stay in one skin, always looking for contact, yearning for the Change, then aching to Change back. It seems we were both victims today."

A Serialist. I am in a long-term, committed relationship and I succumbed to that succubus. I should be ashamed of myself.

"Can we just get this over with, please?"

Chris looked down, as if considering breasts and vaginas for the first time. "I just, I haven't had this equipment very often, and I, I mean, I want to go back, I want to be..." Eyes popped up, considering Sky, tracing muscles and the bulge of genitalia through tight fabric. "I, I do not know if I can do this..."

Grunting in frustration, Sky moved forward, grabbing Chris with strong arms. "I am desperate. I need this. I have someone... If Ashley comes back and sees me like this, well, my infidelity will be obvious, you know that, right?"

If Ashley even recognizes me in this state. Usually, I do not wear this kind of Form for very long. Ash has such a strong preference, we usually Switched back very quickly. Most Couples are not like that. They are Fluid. They swap Roles and Forms, their physical Bodies do not matter, just what is on the inside. But Ashley, Ashley does not like me like this. Ashley is filled with self-loathing after the

Change, desiring to Change back almost immediately. It is a pathology in this day and age, and maybe a symptom of something more. Maybe it is starting to get to me. I am beginning to put more value on my own physical Form, my Parts, my muscles and Sex organs. Maybe I am the one who needs to Change.

"Go."

"What?"

"Chris, just go. I cannot do this. Take this as an opportunity. Explore your life in this Form, enjoy this Body. And, when you find someone you truly connect with, then you can make love, you can Change back to who you used to be and then, a while later, a few days or minutes even, you can Switch again. That's the beauty of it, you know?"

Chris hesitated, and then, nodding silently, exited the room.

Sky put a hand to comm-plate on the wall. "Call Ashley."

○─○

I told Ashley I was not coming home, that I needed space, and that I needed to feel comfortable in my own skin before we talked again. But I could not leave without one last look.

Sky sat outside in the hovercar, waiting. A taxi pulled up to their home. It was an unusual way for Ashley to travel, but what was even more unusual was the emergence of two figures from the back of the vehicle.

Sky recognized them both immediately.

That is Terry, but in the same form as this morning, not post-coitus. And Ashley, well, Ashley is looking very different.

Sky jumped out of the hovercar and stormed across the street.

"Ashley! What in the name of the Change is going on here?"

Ashley turned, delicate features framed by long, flowing locks. Ample breasts poking out of a too-tight jumper. A conspicuous lack of bulge in the crotch of same.

And Terry, well, Terry was as big and strapping and *masculine* as He had been this morning.

"What did you do, Ashley?"

And Sky stood there, His ire rising, gazing at Ashley as Her face reddened. Between them, the Person they had both slept with, who had Changed them.

And between the Lovers, Ashley and Sky, also hung a thick air of distrust and betrayal, of dissatisfaction with their relationship and their own Bodies and Gender roles. It was a topic they had avoided for far too long, and it had taken one small indiscretion, one moment of weakness and passion with a Stranger, to bring these issues to the forefront. Their Bodies had Changed, but somehow their minds needed to do likewise.

"Ashley, we need to talk."

acknowledgments

A great many thanks are in order to a great many people who helped make *Daughters of Icarus* a real, live book instead of an idea shouted enthusiastically into a telephone as its editor drove down I-90.

To Rose Mambert, Editor-in-Chief at Pink Narcissus Press, without whom I would not be in this mess, "this mess" in context being "a deeply fulfilling job as an editor for a small press that gets important voices to print," and for encouraging me—often by way of threats of violence—to write myself, and to do it often. I owe her a huge debt of gratitude for allowing this project to go forward and for all of her support, enthusiasm and occasional Italian profanity.

To Dr. Neta Crawford of Boston University, whose course on world politics and science fiction provided an exceptional tour of science fiction, particularly several excellent works of feminist science fiction. Not only did the course introduce me to outstanding literature, but it informs my thinking about both politics and about teaching. It was an exhortation to explore politics in any way you can, and I enthusiastically take up the challenge.

To my mother, Becca Brown, for her unwavering support and her lifetime of instruction on how to be a woman, most of which had very little to do with makeup and shoes (where that came from is as much a mystery to me as to you, Mom), and mostly dealt with being a fully realized human being and a good citizen. To my father, Ken, for deciding, "so the first kid's a girl... I'm going to teach her about changing the oil on the car anyway." And to both of them, for showing me what gender parity looks like in a relationship.

To Luciana Musto and Julia Bennett, the two strongest women I know, radically different from each other, both feminists, both powerful, both loyal to the core and fierce as hell, thank you for the support, advice, sleep-away camps and time spent together.

To Erin Bohanan, for believing I am Wonder Woman, for being my beacon in the fog of academic war, and for making me the Robot Lady, I am eternally grateful.

To Ben Goodwin, for his challenges to articulate my feminism, his unending stubbornness, his refusal to let me give up on anything, and his willingness to listen, I owe him a debt I can never repay.

A sincere and heartfelt thank you to all who have challenged me and encouraged me throughout this process... Pete and Sarah, Stacy and Bill, Ben, Billy and Julie, Chris, Will, and Francesca, Chris, Jim, and all the people who bore me up and carried me along.

THE AUTHORS

ELIZABETH ALDRICH is a queer fiction writer. Her work has been published on Autostraddle.com, *Forum,* and other publications. A native Angeleno, she prefers to spend her time in Long Beach and San Francisco, as well as Portland, OR.

JASON ANDREW lives in Seattle, Washington with his wife Lisa. By day, he works as a mild-mannered technical writer. By night, he writes stories of the fantastic and occasionally fights crime. His short story "Moonlight in Scarlet" made Ellen Datlow's Honorable Mention List for Best Horror of 2011. You can read more about Jason at www.jasonbandrew.com.

THERESE ARKENBERG is currently enjoying her last undergraduate semester in Washington, D.C. Her fiction has been published in *Beneath Ceaseless Skies, Daily Science Fiction, The Future Fire,* and *Crossed Genres.* Her science fiction novella, *Aqua Vitae,* has been published by WolfSinger publications, and she has also written a romantic fantasy novel, *Last of the Lesser Kings,* as T.L.K. Arkenberg. She blogs at ThereseArkenberg.blogspot.com.

A. A. BALASKOVITS is a graduate of the MFA program at Bowling Green State University, and a current PhD candidate at the University of Missouri. Her previous and upcoming publications can be found in *Gargoyle, Monkeybicycle, Shimmer, Vestal Review,* and in the *Rapunzel's Daughters* and *WTF?!* anthologies from Pink Narcissus Press. She is currently finishing a collection of fairy tales and working on a novel.

ERIC BOSSE's stories have appeared in *The Sun, Mississippi Review, Zoetrope, The Collagist, Night Train,* and about fifty other magazines and journals. Ravenna Press published his story collection, *Magnificent Mistakes,* in 2011. He teaches writing at the University of Oklahoma and lives in Norman with his wife, kids, and several well-rooted houseplants.

THORAIYA DYER's work has appeared recently in *Apex, Cosmos, Nature,* and *Redstone SF.* Her fantasy story, "Fruit of the Pipal Tree," won the 2011 Aurealis Award in its category. An original collection of her short fiction, *Asymmetry,* will be published in 2012 as part of Twelfth Planet Press' Twelve Planets series. Find out more at www.thoraiyadyer.com.

JOANNA FAY is an awarded and published poet and writer. Her fantasy stories have appeared in two previous Pink Narcissus anthologies, *WTF?!* and *Elf Love. Daughter of Hope* and *Reunion,* the first two novels in her dark epic fantasy sequence *The Siaris Quartet,* have been released by Musa Publishing. Joanna's preferred world is full of winged things, so the theme of *Daughters of Icarus* was an impossible temptation. Joanna lives in the Perth hills, Western Australia, with her teenage son and a magical white rabbit. She writes and works as a therapist by day, and keeps an eye on the sky for low-flying unidentified objects by night. You can find Joanna at joannafay.me.

AJ FITZWATER has been living on shaky ground for the last two years... and that's no metaphor. Having lived in Christchurch, New Zealand for over 15 years, she has found her life and landscape changed in dramatic ways most recently by a series of devastating earthquakes. This new scenery lead to the fundraising anthology *Tales For Canterbury,* to which she contributed "My Dad, The

Tuatara." She is currently dedicated to writing feminist and social justice SFF, and her stories have appeared in *Expanded Horizons, M-Brane SF, Fantastique Unfettered, The Future Fire,* and the Crossed Genres anthologies *Fat Girl in a Strange Land* and *Menial: Skilled Labor in SF.* Her perfect dinner guests would include James Tiptree Jr, Joanna Russ, Freddie Mercury, and Darren Hayes. She blogs at pickledthink.blogspot.com.

HEATHER FOWLER is the author of two collections of magic realism stories, including most recently *People with Holes* published by Pink Narcissus Press. Her third collection comprised of dystopian stories, *This Time While We're Awake,* will include this story and be published in the spring of 2013 by Aqueous Books. Visit her website at www.heatherfowlerwrites.com

LAURA GIVENS is a Denver-based author and artist. Her art has graced the covers of numerous publishers' books and magazines. In 2010 she naively decided she could probably write stories as good as many she had illustrated. She has sold works ranging from zombie stories to space operas. She was co-editor and contributor to *Six-Guns Straight From Hell,* a weird western anthology, and is art director for *Tales of the Talisman* magazine.

JANETT L. GRADY's stories have appeared in magazines, anthologies, and on websites all over the States, and in a few magazines and websites based in Canada, the United Kingdom and Australia.

CAREN GUSSOFF's fiction has been featured in anthologies and magazines such as Serpent's Tail, Seal Press, Hadley Rille, *Fantasy Magazine, Abyss & Apex,* has earned her an Octavia E. Butler scholarship, a Village Voice "Writer on the Verge" nomination, an Elizabeth George award, a Seattle Post-Intelligencer "Geek of the Week," and a Speculative Literature Foundation grant, among other things.

She lives in Seattle, WA with her husband, SF artist Chris Sumption, her cats Molly Bloom and Paul Atreides, and some unnamed dust bunnies. She is everywhere online as "spitkitten."

SUMMER HANFORD was born in Syracuse, New York, in 1975. She grew up on a dairy farm west of the city where she lived until she left to attend college in Washington DC. After obtaining a BS in experimental psychology, she did two years of graduate work in behavioral neurology, followed by two years of doctoral work in the same field. Eventually, Summer realized her true passion was the one that occupied her childhood, writing fantasy and science fiction. She turned away from research and now lives in Michigan where she is a full-time writer.

ERICA LIANNE INGLETT and her husband, David, are from Pensacola, Florida. She spent her childhood as an award-winning baton twirler and majors in Graphic Design at Pensacola State College. She has a soft spot for all animals, loves to travel and favors red lipstick.

When not inhabiting a variety of fantastic worlds, **MARISSA JAMES** lives, works, and attends college in Portland, Oregon. Her interests include archeology, peculiar books, drawing, and her husband, who is quick to remind her of his inimitable, muse-like properties.

ZACHARY JERNIGAN lives in Arizona, where the weather is awesome and the political decisions are horrifying. His fiction has appeared in places such as *Asimov's Science Fiction, Crossed Genres, and Escape Pod.* His short story, "The Succession of Knoorikios Khnum," was shortlisted for a 2010 Spectrum Award. His first novel, *No Return*, comes out from Night Shade Books in the Spring of 2013. He loves it when people become his friend on Facebook (facebook.com/zachary.jernigan) and/or read his blog (zacharyjernigan.blogspot.com).

MARGARET KARMAZIN's credits include 130 stories published in literary and national magazines, including *Rosebud, Chrysalis Reader, North Atlantic Review, Confrontation, Pennsylvania Review* and *Another Realm.* Her stories in *The MacGuffin, Eureka Literary Magazine, Licking River Review* and *Words of Wisdom* were nominated for Pushcart awards. Her story, "The Manly Thing," was nominated for the 2010 Million Writers Award. She has a stories included in *Still Going Strong, Ten Twisted Tales, Pieces of Eight (Autism Acceptance), Zero Gravity, Cover of Darkness and Circling Uranus,* and a novel, *Replacing Fiona,* published by eTreasures Publishing.

AO-HUI LIN spends a lot of her time pondering the nature of motherhood and hopes that when her children are grown they won't wonder why so many of her stories about mothers end in tragedy. Her work has most recently appeared in *Every Day Fiction, Jersey Devil Press Magazine* and *Drabblecast.*

When not writing, JENNIFER LINNAEA studies Japanese, practices Aikido, and works at the local library in her adopted town of Eugene, Oregon. Her fiction has appeared in *Strange Horizons, Daily Science Fiction,* and *Flash Fiction Online.*

JOHN MCCORMACK works as manager/writer for a public radio station. He has recently completed a M.A. degree as a part of his work within a University writing program.

DAVID NORTH-MARTINO's fiction has appeared in *Epitaphs: The Journal of the New England Horror Writers* anthology, the *Extinct Doesn't Mean Forever* anthology, *Dark Recesses Press, Afterburn SF,* and *The Swamp.* He is also hard at work on his first novel. A graduate of the University of Massachusetts, he holds a BLA in English and psychology. When he's not writing, David enjoys studying and teaching martial arts. He lives with his very supportive wife in a small town in Massachusetts.

DOUGLAS J. OGUREK's Christian faith and love of animals inspire his fiction. His work appears in the *British Fantasy Society Journal*, *The Literary Review*, *Morpheus Tales* and several anthologies, including Pink Narcissus Press's *WTF?!* Ogurek is the communications manager of a Chicago-based architecture firm, where he has written over 60 articles about facility planning and design. More at www.douglasjogurek.weebly.com.

CYNTHIA REESER is the Editor-in-Chief and founder of *Prick of the Spindle* and Publisher of Aqueous Books. Her poetry, fiction, reviews, visual art, and articles can be found in a variety of print and online sources. Her books include *Light and Trials of Light* (Finishing Line Press, 2010), a nonfiction book on publishing for children from Atlantic Publishing, which was a finalist in its category in the 2010 Indie Book Awards, and a book on publishing for the Kindle (Atlantic Publishing). Her visual art and a full curriculum vitae can be found at www.cynthiareeser.com.

DONNA SCOTT is an editor and writer, proud to live in Northampton, UK. Sometimes, though, she'll put on her Doc Marten boots and travel elsewhere to perform poetry or comedy. She was the first Bard of Northampton, which is better than being a laureate because you get a cloak and a tankard. She's also Awards Administrator for the British Science Fiction Association, which does not involve special drinking vessels. Donna is a member of Northampton Science Fiction Writers Group and has previously had short fiction published in several magazines and anthologies.

NICOLE SPENCER is a writer and editor in Denver, Colorado. She has a background in several martial arts and is working on becoming a yoga instructor. She paints abstracts and composes poetry, though has shown little of either to the world... yet. This collaboration is her first published work.

TINA STARR lives in an old bungalow in Portland, Oregon, where she likes to write dark fiction and horror stories. A few of these stories have been published in nifty places like Pink Narcissus Press, *Pseudopod, Misfit Magazine,* and *Aoife's Kiss.*

R. P. STEEVES has been writing in just about every format imaginable since he was a child. He's written short stories, newspaper columns, stage plays and even a radio drama. Born and raised in Connecticut, he has a Master's degree in education, and taught middle school for nine years. He enjoys solving puzzles, rollerblading, watching movies and has recently taken up archery. Now he has written his first urban fantasy novel about an adventurous, sarcastic and mysterious woman known only as Misty Johnson, whose mission in life is to uncover the truth that hides in the supernatural underbelly of Washington DC.

ANNA SYKORA has been an attorney in New York and teacher of English in Germany. To date she has placed 122 tales in the small press or on the web, and 267 poems. Writing is her joy... Motto: "eat your rejections like pretzels."

E. CATHERINE TOBLER was born on the other side of the International Dateline, which either gives her an extra day in her life or an extraordinary affinity when it comes to inter-dimensional gateways. Her fiction can be found in *Clarkesworld Magazine, The Mammoth Book of Steampunk,* and *Fantasy Magazine.* She is the senior editor of *Shimmer Magazine* and calls Colorado home.

THE EDITRIX

JOSIE BROWN was an early reader. As she outgrew reading *The Secret Garden* under the covers with a flashlight after her bedtime, she began exploring political theory, eventually arriving at Boston University to let it consume her life. She recognizes the power of good fiction to advance the most important political ideas of humanity, and encourages random acts of science fiction. She lives in Worcester, Massachusetts with her two cats, and loves hockey, shoes and caffeine.

ALSO AVAILABLE FROM PINK NARCISSUS PRESS

AT TIMES I ALMOST DREAM
Modern feminist fairy tales by
Amy E. Yergen

Hailed as "brilliant" by *Publishers Weekly* for her story "Rapunzel's Daughters," Yergen's debut collection pushes the envelope for strong female characters by exploring the very notion of strength. By introducing surrealistically analogous contemporary situations, Yergen's dream-like fiction extends folklore and fairy tales, rendering familiar heroines simultaneously strange and universal. ISBN: 978-0-9829913-5-0

PEOPLE WITH HOLES
Magic realism stories
by Heather Fowler

Hailed as "magic realism at its finest," Fowler's writing reveals the small but essential truths that motivate sex and relationships. Whether in museums of solitude, in airports of dreams, or at the circus, these stories are bound together by transformation, anthropomorphism, and ultimately by love's inevitable consequences. Fowler's unique vision is thought-provoking, with a touch of feminist sensibility, and shot through with quirky and laugh-out-loud humor. ISBN: 978-0-9829913-8-1